MALIBU
BOOKS ON

A Taste of Peace
Devoured by Peace

The entire HEA love story in one volume

J. J. Sorel

Copyright © October 2021 J. J. Sorel

ALL RIGHTS RESERVED

No part of this book may be reproduced or transmitted in any form, including electronic or mechanical, without written permission from the publisher, except in the case of brief quotations embodied in reviews or articles. This is a work of fiction. Names, characters, businesses, events and incidents are pure product of the author's imagination. Any resemblance to actual persons, living or dead, or an actual event is purely coincidental and does not assume any responsibility for author or third-party websites or content therein.

Line Edit – Hidden Gems
Proof – Red Adept Editing.

ALSO BY J. J. SOREL

THORNHILL TRILOGY
Entrance
Enlighten
Enfold

BEAUTIFUL BUT STRANGE SERIES
Flooded
Flirted
Flourished

The Importance of being Wild
The Importance of being Bella
Take My Heart
Dark Descent into Desire
Uncovering Love

"The very essence of romance is uncertainty." **Oscar Wilde**

BOOK ONE

A TASTE OF PEACE

1

MIRANDA

My cell phone pinged with a message to call Britney Gane. She'd interviewed me for a job as an administrative assistant and was the CFO to Peace Holdings, a property development firm, run by billionaire Lachlan Peace.

The position seemed straight-forward enough. I just had to do what she told me. Those hadn't been her exact words, but she seemed pretty bossy. As Harriet, my sister, put it, we don't go to work to have fun. I didn't expect that. But a little cordiality wouldn't have hurt, I thought, recalling Britney's cold, brusque manner.

My five-year-old niece, Ava, tapped me on the arm and then performed a heart-melting dance. I smiled. She always brightened my day, and was one of the nicer aspects to sharing a confined apartment with my messy sister.

I called Britney Gane, and her "Yes" shot into my ear like a missile.

My shoulders tensed. "Um ... this is Miranda Flowers calling. I..."

"Good," she interjected. "Can you start Monday?"

"Oh... of course."

"I'll see you on Monday at eight a.m. sharp. I'll email your contract. If you have any questions, call."

"Okay. Yes. That sounds really good. Thank you."

"Monday, then."

"Yes, I'll be there bright-eyed and bushy-tailed," I said as amiably as possible.

The phone went dead. Gritting my teeth, I told myself to suck it up. Sensitivity and poverty were about as compatible as a bickering couple going through a bitter divorce.

Picking at my chipped nails, I reflected on my new job situated at Lachlan Peace's sprawling estate in Malibu. I imagined strolling through the lush grounds and drooling over fine art. My spirits lifted. I also looked forward to not being on my feet for eight hours straight and coming home exhausted after every shift. I couldn't wait to leave that waitressing job.

Harriet burst through the door, hugging a bag of groceries. "Sorry I'm late."

"It's all good. I didn't need to be anywhere," I said, watching her open the fridge. She removed the orange juice and drank it straight from the carton, one of my sister's bad habits, which also included smoking, drinking too much, and swearing like someone in need of anger management.

"I got the job," I said, propping myself up on a stool at the island of our skinny kitchen.

"Mommy." Ava ran to Harriet, who picked her up and hugged her.

"Watch this!" my niece yelled, leaping and landing in the splits.

"That's lovely, sweetheart." Harriet turned to me. "Oh, I suppose that's good news."

"You suppose?" I frowned. "It's not just good news. It's great. I can get on with my plan now."

"Remind me what that is?" she asked.

"To get enough cash to set up my own art dealership."

"Who's going to look after Ava?"

"What about Mom and Dad? They won't mind."

"Mom's got that part-time teaching job. And she's going to fill Ava's head with all that shit about how we should only speak proper English."

"Some free education, you mean?" I rolled my eyes. "You have no other choice."

"I guess." She headed to the living room, then fell onto the couch and kicked off her shoes. Harriet was only three years older than me, but we were so different, even physically. Although we looked similar if I removed my glasses, Harriet wore contacts and made the most of her assets, preferring to wear tight clothes whenever possible.

As an unabashed chocoholic, not to mention all the emotional eating I'd leaned on during the stress of grad school, I'd ballooned two sizes larger than Harriet. Hiding in baggy clothes, I'd made myself invisible to the opposite sex. Which was fine. A boyfriend wasn't on my to-do list. My career needed to come first.

Instead of partying every night like most people my age, I'd focused on excelling at school, resulting in an art history degree hanging proudly on my wall.

Harriet couldn't believe I was still a virgin, saying things like, "So when are you going to fuck, sis?"

"When I find the right guy," I'd reply.

In truth, I'd been insanely busy juggling my master's in art history, waitressing, and babysitting for my sister, making me too exhausted to even think of the opposite sex.

"What a cliché," she'd scoff. "You're living in la-la land, Andie. The right man could take a lifetime to find. Life's short, and sexual needs are long."

"I think the saying is: life is short, and art is long. Goethe."

"Stop being a bore."

Whenever I got too serious or intellectual, she'd poke her tongue at me and make me laugh.

In any case, I wasn't desperate to hook up with just anyone simply to satisfy a sexual urge, even if it was rare to be a virgin at twenty-three. Because when it came to who not to hook up with, I had a front-row seat to my sister's poor choice in men.

Ava giggled while pointing at the pirouetting pig dressed as a ballerina on TV. Mimicking the dance steps, she was good. I'd suggested dance classes, but Harriet couldn't afford it, and there was no child support either. Aaron, Ava's father and Harriet's college sweetheart, had bailed after finding out she was pregnant.

When Harriet became a single mom at twenty-one while studying for her nursing degree, I promised to help as much as I could, which meant me minding Ava while my sister worked. If the situation had been reversed, she would have done the same for me. Besides, I loved spending time with my niece.

Harry, as everyone called her, worked as a nurse in rehab. Before that, she had a short stint at a drug rehab facility, which had its setbacks. She had this thing for damaged guys who were heavily tattooed, reeked of smoke and alcohol, and looked as though they lived on the streets.

I'd given up judging Harriet and her revolving door of swaggering bad boys. After Aaron broke her heart, she changed virtually overnight and thumbed her nose at my suggestion she get therapy. But despite her flaws, deep down inside my older sister was a good soul.

While she traded sanity for a night of pleasure, I traded mine for a slice of action in the glamorous but cutthroat art scene.

Art had always been a passion for me, ever since I was a child. From the moment my father's anthology of Renaissance art weighed down heavily on my little arms, I was hooked. The problem was that finding a job after graduation had proved more difficult than I'd expected.

I owed big-time on my student loans, and so I had to take what I could get. Every interview I'd gone to had dozens of applicants. Often, the positions were in Silicon Valley, where job titles required you to have a degree in linguistics to decipher.

Art would just have to wait. Or at least, I'd keep looking until something right came along.

"Mommy, can I have ballet lessons?" asked Ava.

Harriet looked at me and sighed. "We'll see, sweetie. The shoes don't come cheap."

"I'll help," I said. "Now that I've got a job, I'll be able to pay for leotards and ballet slippers."

Harriet hugged me. "You're the best." She turned to Ava. "Did you hear that? Auntie Andie's taking you to ballet classes."

"Did I say that?" I asked.

Harriet looked at me and crossed her eyes, making a stupid face. It was something she did whenever she was trying to butter me up, and as always, I laughed.

2

LACHLAN

Britney looked at me as though I'd asked her to swim in a tank full of sharks.

"I'm not sure if there's a Tinder equivalent for what you're asking."

"Well, there should be." I scratched my prickly jaw.

One of the biggest downsides to running a billion-dollar empire were the endless charity balls I was forced to attend, not to mention the many advances that sashayed my way.

That wasn't me bragging but a genuine snapshot of the women who attended these glittering galas. That they sought to marry into wealth didn't come as a surprise. I just wasn't in the market for marriage or even a girlfriend.

Being propositioned with offers to have my dick sucked in a dark corner was not my idea of a fun night. It wasn't that I disliked blow jobs; like any hot-blooded male, I loved them. It was the gossip and expectations that came afterward that I hated, particularly since it was impossible to keep people out of your business. Everyone knew everyone in that scene.

Britney, who loved hanging around wealth in the same way wolves loved roaming among sheep, insisted that we attend. I didn't want to, but I couldn't deny it would be smart to network and make up for lost time.

When it came to talking shop about the money market, I missed out on that gene. But with my father in the hospital, in experimental drug trials for his pancreatic cancer, it was incumbent on me, his remaining son, to run his empire. And due to my older brother's untimely death, I'd developed this burning need to prove that I could cut it.

My dad had always favored Brent, which made perfect sense,

given that they'd matched like a pair of socks.

"Why don't I go as your date?" Britney asked.

I took a deep breath. We had a history that was short, not so sweet, and something I deeply regretted.

Around a year ago while in Aspen at a business convention, after one shot too many, my right-hand woman ended up with her right hand on my dick.

The next day, we laughed it off as a reckless drunken incident. But a hopeful twinkle entered her lingering gaze and had remained.

After a few drinks, my CFO had a tendency to pounce. She had a real Jekyll and Hyde nature. Sober, she was cool, efficient, and sharp. But given a bottle, she'd get all touchy-feely, babbling on and on about what a great couple we'd make.

Had it been a mistake? You bet. But a blow job will do that to a man. It was a poor excuse. But when it came to my dick, it had ruled my brain for far too long. That was why I'd decided to stay away. Not just from Britney but from women in general.

Now that the board of directors had taken flight after some questionable investment scheme had gone belly-up, it was up to me to keep Peace Holdings going.

Britney was crucial for the running of the business. She'd been loyal to my dad for over a decade. While in college, she'd worked by his side, learning all the tricks of running a company that mainly dealt in knocking down buildings and replacing them with cheap but highly sought-after apartments.

Until recently, I'd never taken an interest in the family business. I was the black sheep. The disappointment, as my father would often imply whenever talking about his sons.

My twin passions of surfing and drumming absorbed my time, and assuming that Brent would eventually take the reins of the family business, I just rolled with it.

"The media will have a field day. They'll make us out to be the next power couple," I argued.

She shrugged. "So? All publicity is good publicity."

"If we were in show biz, I suppose. But we're hardly that

interesting."

"Speak for yourself," she said.

I grinned. "You'll be there with me. Just not as my date. You're a part of this company after all." I'd lost count of how often we'd had this conversation. "Anyway, find me a girl. Someone plain and smart."

She took a phone call, giving me a free moment to check the surf report.

"Send her in," she said, ending the call. She looked at me. "That's the new admin assistant. She's starting today."

"Oh, of course. I forgot about that. What's her name?"

"She's here now. I'll introduce you."

Our new employee stepped into the room. Wearing dark-rimmed glasses, she offered me a jittery smile and held out her hand. "Good morning, I'm Miranda Flowers."

Britney acknowledged her with a nod. "This is Lachlan Peace, the head of the company."

"Welcome," I said, taking her cool, slightly shaky hand and gave her my sunniest smile in an attempt to calm the poor girl's nerves.

Britney was hardly the type of person to make someone feel at ease; she was so demanding and such a perfectionist that at times she even made me jumpy. I almost felt sorry for Miranda.

"Well then, I'll leave you to it. Good luck. I'm sure you'll fit right in, and feel free to have a look around the estate," I said.

She looked up at me with a soft smile. "Thank you for this opportunity. I'm really looking forward to working here. It's a beautiful place."

I smiled back and then shifted my attention to Britney. "Come and see me in an hour so we can solve that little problem."

I left them alone, making a mental note to ask Britney to be gentle. We'd already lost three admin assistants in a year. Although Britney blamed it on ineptitude, I knew she was a difficult taskmaster.

I plunked myself down and stared at the expansive view of

the sea. For a moment, I allowed my mind to wander before returning my attention to Benson Gray, an investor who kept making demands about his promised returns. As much as I'd tried, I couldn't find anything about him or the luxury resort he'd sunk his cash into, something he'd referred to as "Bird of Paradise."

When it came to understanding the convoluted pathways my father's projects took, I was way out of my depth. Straight up and down property acquisition and development, I could do in my sleep. But these strange little schemes, which Britney had helped devise, were a labyrinth of complexity.

And now I had this investor virtually stalking me. It was naïve of me to assume that running the family business would be straightforward, especially with my shady father at the driver's seat for over thirty years.

He'd never gotten over Brent's death, and given that I was the creative one in the family, my father was bereft.

For an ex-party animal who played gigs, boozed, and fucked a different girl every night, running Peace Holdings successfully was my only chance to prove that I was no longer that spoiled rich boy whose nights ended at sunrise.

Britney buzzed in over the intercom. "I've come up with something."

"Good. I also need to speak to you about Benson Gray."

"He's been calling again?"

"All morning."

"I'll come now."

I leaned back in my chair, my hands beating on my thighs-turned-drum-pad, practicing paradiddles—a strange little tic known only to drummers. It was a habit I'd formed from the age of five after my first drumming lesson.

I missed having hours of free time for music. There were my neighbors: Sam Chalmer, Orlando Thornhill, and his dad Aidan, who were all talented musicians. Before taking over my dad's empire, we'd often meet up for regular jam sessions and racing. Fast cars were another of my passions.

Britney stepped into my office.

"So tell me all about Benson Gray," I said.

"Don't worry about that. I'll speak to him," she said.

"He mentioned something about calling the cops. I thought it was about the condo developments in San Jose. But he's not listed as an investor on that project."

"It's a little more complicated than that."

I studied her for a moment. "So I gather. He's saying that he sunk ten million into Bird of Paradise. Apparently, there are other investors too. Should I be worried?"

Britney shook her head decisively.

"Then why is he on my fucking back?"

"I'll handle it," she said, lingering. "I thought Miranda, that new hire you met earlier, could accompany you tomorrow night."

I nodded. "That's not a bad idea. She seems like a nice and demure girl. Just my type of date."

Britney's head tilted. "Who are you kidding?"

"I'm not that guy anymore," I said.

"I've noticed," she muttered.

"I heard that," I said. "Tell Miranda she'll be paid for attending. Can you arrange it?"

"Sure. I'll get a stylist on it. I take it you want her to look plain and unphotogenic to keep the cameras away?"

"That's a good plan." I took a deep breath.

"What's wrong?" she asked.

"I visited Dad this morning."

"He was doing fine yesterday," she said.

"Where's Tamara?" I shook my head. "A little wifely support wouldn't hurt."

"She's in Miami. Or I assume she is, according to the credit card statements. A young Latino personal trainer's probably taking up all her time." Britney's cutting comment matched my own views about my father's latest bimbo wife.

"Okay. Leave it to me." She stood at the door. "And about Benson Gray's threats, there's no need to worry about the SEC. I'll make sure the books come up clean."

Had I mentioned the SEC? My neck tensed. The longer I sat behind that imposing mahogany desk, the more I realized that my father didn't share my ethos.

Was it too much to hope a company that I headed be on the straight and narrow?

3

MIRANDA

Britney led me into a guest room, where a dreamy view of the sea and a red wall of art competed for my attention. I turned away from the window as a Monet caught my eye. Recognizing the image of a yellow vase of flowers, I studied it closely. My jaw dropped. The painting was a fake. As a student, I did my senior thesis in undergrad on Monet and had visited Monet's touring shows, where I'd familiarized myself with his brushstrokes.

"Oh right, you studied art history," said Britney.

"Yes," I said, turning toward her.

"I was at Sotheby's when Clarke Peace bid for it."

I kept studying the painting to make sure I wasn't mistaken. "That's kind of weird."

She looked at me. "What do you mean?"

"It's a fake."

"Fake?" She frowned. "Peace Holdings doesn't buy fakes."

"I'm sorry. But this is not an original."

Her piercing scrutiny made me forget about the butterflies in my tummy. I'd never been to a ball before, and when Britney told me I would be my new boss's date, I nearly fell off my chair.

"That's your outfit." She pointed to the bed, where she had placed a gown.

Although I welcomed the shift in focus, I regretted opening my big mouth.

I looked down at the dress. It was awful. Despite not being into fashion, I knew what I liked, and that was one very ugly ball gown. I reminded myself I was being paid a handsome sum to attend, and for that amount of money, I would have worn a clown's costume.

Picking up the voluminous garment, I noticed that it had so much fabric, I wasn't sure how I'd find my body. I grimaced.

"What's the matter?" Britney asked.

I gritted my teeth and said, "Well, it's really horrible. I mean, I'll look like a color-blind idiot wearing it."

"Need I remind you you're being paid over and above what anyone in your position would earn?"

I took a deep breath. She was right. Where was that clown's outfit?

"Okay," I said, clutching the weighty dress to my chest. "I'll try this on."

Britney walked over to the painting. I wanted to wait until she left, but she hung around. I was a little insecure about my body, and my underwear had a few holes. That first paycheck couldn't come soon enough.

"What makes you think this is a fake?" She turned to face me, and her eyes widened slightly.

I stood with my arms crossed to hide my chest, which wasn't easy considering my D-cups. All the late-night bingeing on chocolate, my preferred way of dealing with stress, added more than a few pounds to my figure.

I lifted the brown dress and slipped it over my head. It was so heavy, I stumbled.

"The brushstrokes give it away," I replied. "And the color of the vase isn't the same yellow."

"It could have faded," she said.

"It's too recent for that to have happened. Even exposed to sunlight."

Her frown deepened as she watched me struggle with the zipper. She didn't even offer to help.

Staring into the mirror, I wanted to puke. I wasn't vain like Harriet, but I was human. I hated the idea of being seen in a dress the color of poop brown that looked like a hand-me-down from some eccentric aunt.

Although it nipped at the waist—a small mercy—it bagged

out around the chest, making me look larger than my size ten.

"Perfect," she said, looking at me in the mirror.

The longer I stared at myself, the more I wanted to cry. It looked as though I'd been invited to some bad-taste hipster party where everyone was expected to wear ugly outfits for the irony.

She stared at my face. "Leave your hair up in a bun like that. And perhaps little or no makeup."

"Will that be acceptable?" I asked. "Don't people usually get glammed up at these things?" My spirits sank. I thought I'd at least receive a makeover.

She shrugged. "Lachlan's trying to keep a low profile. He doesn't want the paparazzi all over him. The less glamorous his date, the better."

"What should I tell people when they ask who I'm with?"

"Just smile and remain quiet."

As someone who had made a sport of blending in with the furniture, I was the perfect candidate for playing Ms. Invisible.

But wouldn't wearing the most hideous dress in LA draw attention? As for acting brain-dead, that wouldn't be difficult, I thought. I'd already struggled stringing together a coherent line around my very sexy boss, whose twinkling blue eyes and chiseled features made it difficult to think straight.

***

The following day, Britney let me go home early to prepare for the charity event.

"At least wear some makeup," Harriet said, also appalled by the gown.

"Britney told me to keep it minimal. Something about keeping the paparazzi off Lachlan Peace's back."

"That's kind of strange," she said, looking into the mirror.

"That's what I thought. Why would an attractive woman by his side be any different than a plain one?"

"You're not that plain, Andie. You just don't make the most of what you've got." She paused. "And your new boss is really fucking hot."

I nodded pensively. Lachlan Peace was seriously sexy. I'd only met him for a few minutes, but with that buff body and dazzling smile, he had "Hollywood hunk" etched all over him. Even his woody cologne weakened my knees.

"He used to be a bad boy," she said. "I looked him up on social media. Tattoos, always partying. And a musician."

Now that, I hadn't expected. "Really?"

"He was a drummer before taking over his daddy's empire. Very sexy."

"You've done your research," I said, pulling the fabric taut around my chest.

"That does look better," she said, tilting her head to study me in the mirror.

Before I had a chance to respond, Harriet threaded a needle, and a few stitches later, the bodice fit me tightly.

When she brought the scissors out, I stopped her from making further alterations. "You better not. Britney's set on a certain look."

"A little cleavage wouldn't matter," she said. "You've got a great bod underneath all that fabric."

"You'll get me in trouble. Britney was clear that I look as plain as possible."

"This Britney sounds as though she's got sights on your hot boss."

I'd thought the same thing, having noticed how she switched from cold and officious around me to warm and attentive around Lachlan.

"There is a certain dynamic going on there," I admitted.

Harriet poked at my bun. "Can you at least wear your gorgeous locks down?"

"Britney told me to keep my hair in a bun."

"Bullshit." She started to undo my hair, and I stopped her.

"No. I need this job, and if it means looking dowdy, something I'm good at, I will."

"That's because you don't try. Beauty doesn't just happen. You've got to work hard at it, girl."

"You're right. I haven't got a clue." I smiled tightly.

"You've got me." She raised a perfectly tweezed eyebrow. "What about contacts instead of those?" Harriet pointed at my glasses.

"Not happening. Britney—"

"I hate this woman, and I don't even know her. Here you are, going to an exclusive event that girls like us can only dream of, and you're going like that?"

I sighed. "Let's just be happy I've got a job."

"I suppose." She shook her head.

After I'd applied a little blush, some mascara and lip gloss, I was ready to play my part.

"You look like a librarian who's never seen a dick before," Harriet said.

"Close." We looked at each other and cracked up laughing.

"You're going to have to fuck one day, you know," she said with her hands on her hips.

"So you keep saying." I leaned in and kissed her on the cheek. "I've got to go."

4

LACHLAN

All the usual suspects were there with their much younger wives, who all looked and sounded alike. As with all the charity events I'd attended, my cheeks hurt from keeping a smile plastered on my face.

Miranda followed along, wearing the ugliest dress I'd ever seen. When the guests started whispering and giving her the side-eye, I almost sent her home. I felt sorry for the poor girl. Britney had gone out of her way to make my new employee unattractive. Only, she wasn't. There was an intriguing fire in those pretty brown eyes.

A waiter came by with a tray of champagne, and grabbing two glasses, I passed one over to Miranda. "Here. This will help."

"Thanks."

"Back in a minute." I smiled. "Don't go anywhere." She shook her head. "And ignore all those cats over there. Put them next to a heater, and they'd melt." I cocked my head toward a bunch of young women who'd been making fun of my date from the moment we arrived.

Miranda's giggle made me smile.

I liked her. She was calming. She may have been a little lost for words, but the words that did exit were thoughtful and intelligent. It was a refreshing change from chatting with women who obviously viewed me as a walking bank account.

Crystal chandeliers and gilt-framed mirrors competed with the guests for glitz and gloss in the main ballroom where I spied Britney, chatting with some guests. Her flirtatious smile and flushed cheeks told me she'd been drinking.

I walked over and whispered, "You overdid it a bit with Miranda, don't you think?"

Lines appeared between her brows. "What do you mean?"

"Where did you find that dress? In a dumpster?"

"It's supposed to keep you from getting too much attention," she said.

"That's crap. People can't take their eyes off us. Didn't anyone ever tell you that ugliness is as eye-catching as beauty?"

"You asked for her to look plain," she replied. "It didn't take much. She's already pretty plain."

"Show some respect. She seems like a good person. What I meant was something that wouldn't stand out."

She had nothing to say to that and just smirked while sipping on her champagne.

I left Britney and joined Miranda again, who looked lost at sea.

If only I could go back and redo that Aspen encounter. It had complicated my relationship with Britney, as only sex could. But when it came to women, I needed more than some sexy hard body and a pretty face. I needed someone who could keep me intrigued, which probably explained why I'd dated some seriously messed-up girls in the past, confusing their crazy shit for interesting.

I noticed that Bevan Jones, with that permanent smarmy grin of his, had cornered Miranda. As a hotshot corporate lawyer, he was always poking his nose into people's lives. He'd been my dad's golf partner and close confidante for as long as I could remember.

He turned and looked at me. "Well, if it isn't the prodigal son."

I held up my palms in defense. "That title's getting a bit tired, Bev." I couldn't resist my own little dig, knowing how much he hated his name shortened.

"Where have you been? I've enjoyed chatting with your girl." His eyes sparkled with a hint of malice.

"Miranda's my new admin assistant."

He looked her up and down and returned his attention to

me.

"So, Lachie, will you be bidding tonight? I hear it's mostly modern art." He smirked. "I can't imagine you know your Rothko's from your Bacon's."

My hands clenched into fists. I would have loved to punch that asshole in the nose. Ever since my father fell ill, leaving me to run his business, Bevan Jones had been making snide comments about my lack of experience. Art was no exception.

Miranda's eyes slid over to me, and then with a hint of a grin, she looked at Bevan asked, "You're an authority on art?"

He shrugged slightly. "Sure. I like to buy it."

"And they're auctioning Bacon's and Rothko's tonight?" she asked, sounding surprised.

"Are you kidding?" he said. "They don't normally auction quality at these events. More like landscapes and abstracts by attention-seeking novices."

"Do you like that piece?" She pointed at a minimal abstract on the wall by our side.

"Of course. It's fabulous."

"Is that a Rothko?" she asked.

He looked at me and then at the large canvas. "Funny, I'm the one who normally asks the questions here."

"Well, is it a Rothko?" I asked, enjoying myself at his expense, sensing that Bevan didn't have a clue.

"I'd say it is."

Miranda looked at me, wearing a subtle but triumphant smile. "It's not." She pointed at the canvas. "The blending of color isn't as seamless as Mark Rothko's famous works. Anyone who knows his work knows that's what makes him stand out from the wannabes."

I wanted to laugh in Bevan's face but resisted the urge. We already had enough attention. Miranda had really set him up to look like an ass. Not that he needed much help in that department.

"If you're suggesting it's cheap, then you're very much mistaken and your unsolicited views are insulting to say the least."

"She was only stating a fact, Bev," I said, allowing a smarmy grin to play on my face.

"She'll turn you into a dilettante yet," he said.

Miranda looked at me, her brow furrowing slightly before turning to Bevan. "Mr. Peace doesn't need me for that when he's got acquaintances like you."

Miranda's sharp reply worked nicely. Bevan's face soured.

He turned away without another word, and I laughed.

She touched her mouth. "Oops. Sorry. I better lay off the champagne. I'm not sure where that came from."

"Hey that was gold. And if anyone deserved it, it's Bevan 'Bighead' Jones." I studied her for a moment. Through those lenses, her almond-shaped dark eyes sparkled with intelligent curiosity.

As we moved away, I whispered, "What's a dilettante?"

"An amateur who sees himself as an authority on art."

I punched the air. "Home run. That describes him to a tee."

She returned a sweet smile, and as the trays came our way again, I took another pair of champagne flutes and handed one to her. "Here you go. At least this way, one of us can have some fun."

"You aren't having fun?" she asked.

"These events are all the same. The same dull, superficial conversations. The hand-at-the-side-of-mouth gossip."

"At least it raises money for the needy. That's always good." She pointed at the ceiling. "And the sculptural detail of the dome is mind-blowing. I've never been anywhere like this before."

I nodded slowly as I studied her. My eyes followed hers around the grand ballroom. "You're right. It is a nice room. By the way, I'm sorry Britney didn't have something nicer for you to wear."

Patting the dress, she said, "That's okay. If I get to keep it, it'll come in handy."

"You've got me curious, Ms. Flowers."

"I could use a good potato sack."

I laughed and looked at her. "You're funny. In a good, real way. Thanks."

"There's no need to thank me. I'm the grateful one, since you gave me a job."

I felt a twinge of guilt, considering how Britney treated admin assistants like they were disposable.

"Come on." I gestured. "Let's check out the amateurish art on offer. All proceeds go to charity, and I wouldn't mind adding to my collection."

"To match the fake Monet?" she asked.

I stopped walking. "What do you mean?"

"The still life in the guest room at the estate," she said.

"Twenty years ago, that yellow painting cost my father over a hundred thousand. It's worth a few million now."

"It's a fake," she said.

5

MIRANDA

I might as well have told Lachlan he had to sell a kidney, judging by his shocked expression. Champagne had loosened my tongue, revving up my normally sluggish social skills.

"How do you know?" he finally asked.

"I'm very familiar with Monet and his palette. Any expert eye would tell you that the yellow isn't his, and the brush strokes are all wrong. It's not even a good fake, to be honest."

The frown deepened on his face, as though he was trying to solve a complex riddle.

Wearing a skintight red satin gown, Britney slunk over to join us, just as he was about to speak. She cast Lachlan a seductive smile and ignored me entirely. I couldn't blame her. Lachlan stole the show in that black tux that fit his tall, buff physique like a glove, enough to make anyone's panties melt.

He turned to Britney. "Miranda said that the yellow Monet is a fake. What happened to the original? Is it locked away in a vault somewhere?"

Britney glanced at me, and her glacial glare turned me into an ice sculpture. "That wasn't part of the job description."

I shrank. "I'm sorry. I…"

"She did the right thing. Let's remember who's boss here," he said with a deep, authoritative voice. "I want you to look into it and tell me what happened to the original."

Britney returned a sheepish nod.

He turned toward me and cocked his handsome head. "Coming?"

It wasn't until we'd positioned ourselves on the other side of that grand room that I said, "I hope I haven't done something wrong."

"No. You're a fantastic asset. Brains are a rare commodity these days."

His eyes trapped mine, and although I could have stared at that face all night, I had to look away in order to breathe.

A pretty brunette joined us and whispered something into his ear. Giving them space, I decided to take a look at what was up for auction.

Upon entering the adjacent room, I discovered a space that resembled a museum. Its bold dark-green walls made the gilt-framed art stand out in sharp contrast.

The offerings consisted mainly of abstracts and landscapes and, although well executed, lacked appeal.

"Anything worth buying?" I heard over my shoulder.

I turned, and my boss smiled back at me. "You don't mind if I hang here with you for a minute? Cassandra Castle's been drinking and coming on strong."

"You don't like flirty girls?" I asked.

"It's sexy coming from the right person, which Cassandra is not." He shrugged. "And there's nothing like a bit of mystery." A hint of a smile gracing those shapely lips made my nipples hard, and for the first time, I was thankful for this sack of a gown.

"If you keep showing disinterest, they may get the wrong idea about us," I said.

"They can think whatever they like."

"I keep noticing brows raise every time other guests glance our way."

"Hey, apart from that horrible dress, I'm more than happy to be seen with you. Plus you're an art expert."

"Well maybe not an expert," I said.

"You know more than I do." He smiled. "Would you mind looking over the collection at the estate?"

"I'd love to help where I can. It's my ambition to deal in art."

"That sounds like a noble pursuit," he said, trapping me with one of his lingering stares.

I had to look away because of a sudden dizzy spell, which

wasn't the champagne's doing.

My attention landed on a painting, which served as a welcome distraction. "Oh my. That's beautiful."

Lachlan looked up at the Picassoesque image. "Hmm … it's colorful. I'm not an art expert, but I know what I like." He looked into my eyes again as though we were talking about something other than art. "Well spotted. That's an attractive painting. The longer one looks at it, the more one sees."

"That's the sign of a great work of art."

His burning gaze shifted from the painting to me again, scorching my cheeks.

When he returned his attention to the painting, I was able to breathe again. "Is this worth bidding for?"

I nodded. "It's a George Condo. He's still alive, popular, and very collectible. I'm actually amazed it's here."

"Many people I know donate."

"That's nice to know." My focus shifted to a scribbled work on paper. "Shit," I blurted out and bit my lip. "Sorry for swearing."

"It's all good. I know I've said a lot worse than that." He smiled at me, then his brow creased as he studied the painting closely. "Is that scrawl worth something?"

I had to laugh at his dry tone. "If I'm not mistaken, it's a Basquiat." I peered closely at the signature. "Shit. It is."

"It's pretty out there in that 'my five-year-old could've done that' way."

I giggled. "You have a five-year-old?"

"I don't. But you get my drift."

"I've heard that often enough. It's the sheer audacity of the work that makes it great."

Lachlan studied the art closer and shook his head. "Not really my thing. But who am I to judge? Some of the music I listen to makes people reach for earplugs. They see it as overly intellectual. Even though I find it anything but that."

I looked up at him in surprise. "You're into music like Schoenberg?"

"No. But when I'm needing to let out some steam, I like to listen to cathartic experimental jazz." A question grew on his face. "You've heard of Schoenberg?"

"One of my pals at college dragged me along to a concert once."

He hissed. "That's intense listening there. But it's a fitting analogy to this scribble, which is just as challenging as serialism I guess."

My eyes widened in surprise.

"What?" he asked.

"I can't believe that you've heard of serialism."

He smiled. "I had a wasted youth."

"I wouldn't think one was wasting anything listening to that."

"No… it actually adds brains cells, doesn't it?" A slow smile grew on his face, dragging me along.

I laughed. "That's probably true."

His eyes trapped mine again, and I had to look away. He kept stealing my breath, especially the quirkier he became. Lachlan Peace, it seemed, had many parts to him, which only added to his existing arsenal of charisma.

"So you do think this painting's a worthwhile investment?" He cocked his head toward the Basquiat.

"I'd buy it." I pointed. "And the Condo."

He rubbed his hands together. "Okay. Let's have some fun then and bid on them."

"Have you ever been to an art auction?"

"Nope." His blazing blue eyes impaled me again, and I forgot what we were even talking about. "How about if you do the bidding?"

Bidding for art was as sexy as it got in my little art-obsessed world. "I'd love to. I saw a Condo auctioned last year. That sold for three million."

"And this one's as good?"

"You bet. It's stunning." I studied the large mixed-media canvas depicting a fractured image of a woman in purplish pastel shades.

"It reminds me of Picasso," he said.

"You can definitely see the influence. Especially in his choice of color palette."

Lachlan turned to the Basquiat. "This is kind of frantic."

Bubbling with delight, I wanted to pinch myself. A gorgeous, down-to-earth man without an ounce of ego, believed in me—the plain Jane in the ugliest dress at the ball.

"Dealers love seeing his work come in," I said.

"It's pretty small and looks like a doodle."

"If I had the money, I'd buy it. For the right price, of course," I said, squinting at the pen markings.

"So what would this be worth?"

"Around five hundred thousand, I'd say. I wouldn't pay that, though."

"No… I wouldn't even pay one hundred dollars for it. But you're the expert."

My face ached from smiling.

The bell rang. "We should go in." He turned to look at me. "So, you feel like doing this?"

"You bet." I stopped walking. "What's the budget?"

"Let's play it by ear."

"Okay. Although…" I trailed off and grinned. "We've got Bev to compete against. He's the expert in the room."

Lachlan laughed. "I like you."

I gave him a shy smile in return. *And I like you.*

6

LACHLAN

Britney stood so close her perfume tickled my nasal passages, threatening to make me sneeze.

"You're getting a little touchy-feely with our new girl. I didn't think you went for the plain types."

"You're drunk, Britney." I took a step back. "She's an art expert. It's a good opportunity for me to get a handle on the family collection."

"You know you can leave everything to me, don't you?" She advanced closer again.

"I do, Britney. But that's not how it's going to be from now on. I'm in control."

"Maybe you should just put that sexy body of yours to better use." She raised her eyebrows.

"Don't objectify me."

"You didn't seem to mind in Aspen."

"You're bringing that up again? It's ancient history as far as I'm concerned." I turned away to focus my attention on the auction.

Bevan Jones positioned himself behind me. "Thinking of adding to the collection?"

"Maybe," I said.

"It's all just junk. There. You can have that for free."

"Gee, thanks." I rolled my eyes. "That's big-hearted, coming from such an expert like you."

"Are you making fun of me, Peace? Let me remind you that you were pissing your pants when I was making my first million."

"It's not a pissing contest, Bev. Because if it were, I have a big advantage." Towering over him, I emphasized the word "big."

I turned my back on him and directed my attention to the stage.

When the Condo was auctioned, Miranda won the bid at a million dollars, amid snide little comments from Bevan.

Britney came over to me and whispered, "What the fuck?"

I shrugged. "It's a good investment."

"But you need to run this through me first. I'm in charge of the books."

"I'm the CEO," I said, pushing out my chest.

"We have a cash flow problem," she said.

I frowned. "Last time I looked Peace Holdings was worth two billion."

"In assets. That's not liquid, you know. Or maybe you don't." Her eyebrows lifted.

"Then first thing tomorrow, you're going to lay out the books and explain it in plain fucking English."

Her teeth chewing on her bottom lip made my stomach churn.

On a more positive note, Miranda held her bidding like a seasoned pro, and it came as no surprise that she was the only bidder for the Basquiat.

It went for twenty thousand, which livened things up. Judging by the raised eyebrows, chuckles, and whispers, the guests had finally found their night's entertainment.

Bevan tapped my arm. "Is your new girl on drugs?"

"That's a Basquiat." I spoke with authority, as though I knew the artist personally. And just to prove a point, I brought up the Wikipedia entry for the artist. "Here. Read for yourself."

With a cursory glance at my phone, he said, "It's probably a fake."

"Oh, and you should know. Right?"

"You're nothing like your father, are you? I mean, taking advice from an admin assistant who's wearing a dress that even a hobo wouldn't be seen dead in."

"That was Britney's doing. Now if you'll excuse me, I've got some new art to collect."

I moved away before his patronizing sniggers played havoc with my already surging testosterone levels and ended up in my fists.

Britney said something to Miranda, and judging by the way Miranda's face paled, I sensed Britney wasn't whispering sweet nothings.

I waited for Britney to move away, and then joined Miranda. "You look a little shaken."

"Britney's a bit pissed off because of the Monet."

"I'm glad you told me. I'd like you to report anything that doesn't seem right." I nodded. "Okay?"

Her frown deepened. I felt for her. Her second day on the job, and she'd already been thrown in with the wolves.

"They want to know where the paintings should be delivered," she said.

I thought about the cash flow issues that Britney had mentioned. Growing up in a wealthy family, the thought of running out of cash was not something I'd ever contemplated before. It terrified me.

"What should we do with them?" I asked.

"Depends. Do you want to profit from them? Hold on to them as an investment? Or put them up on the walls to admire?"

I nearly laughed at that latter suggestion. "The Basquiat I probably wouldn't need hanging around."

She chuckled. "That's understandable. He's not everyone's cup of tea. The Condo, however, is pretty. Striking colors."

"What would they sell for?"

"Hmm... probably double what we paid for the Condo, and the Basquiat would fetch at least a few hundred thousand dollars."

I whistled.

She nodded. "For now, I'd suggest placing them in a vault or somewhere dark and dry. And in the coming days, I'll arrange something if you like."

"You're my golden girl, Miranda. Thank you. I'm in the market for a comrade."

Her face brightened. "I'm glad to be of service."

"And by the way, don't worry about Britney. She's just a little controlling. Nothing that a little chaos can't fix."

"You said that as though you enjoy it."

"I don't," I said. "But perfection's overrated. You know?"

She nodded slowly. "That gives me cause for hope."

"You're not a perfectionist?"

"Not unless I'm obsessed by something, and then maybe a little."

"Obsession is a different matter. One has to give that a hundred percent," I said.

"So true."

We looked at each other and smiled. I liked my new comrade. Very much.

***

I sucked back the night air. It was good to be out of that stuffy scene. Miranda had left a few minutes before me, and as I was about to follow her out, Britney bawled me out, slurring her words. That girl just never gave up. I told her she was drunk and to go home, to which she made a face, muttering something about hooking up with a stranger. I shrugged and left her standing alone at the marble-floored entrance.

As I walked to my car, I noticed Miranda waiting at a bus stop. Her arms were crossed tight over her chest. I imagined she was trying to hide that horrible dress since it was a warm night. Peace Holdings deserved a lashing for human rights abuse.

"Hey, let me give you a lift," I said.

A puzzled frown marred her pretty face. "But I'm in Venice, and you're not going in that direction."

"I go there often. I might even drop into the Red House for a jam session tonight."

Her frown deepened. "You have time to be a musician?"

I laughed. "Well, let's put it this way—I don't get much sleep. When I'm not at work, I like to bang things."

"Oh." A tiny smile grew on her face.

"Let me clarify that. I meant objects. Not that I think women are objects or anything." I grinned.

"I got your meaning the first time. And not the X-rated version."

"Good to know. It's only your second day working for Peace Holdings. I'd hate for you to walk away thinking bad things about your boss." He tipped his head and raised his eyebrows.

"Hardly. Thanks for inviting me to participate in the auction. That was an adrenaline hit and a dream come true. For a minute there …" She stopped and chuckled. "I thought Bevan would have a heart attack. I'm sure you saw how red his face went at the mention of the paintings' market value."

"That alone made the auction worth every penny." I smiled. "I think I'm going to like having you around."

"Thank you for your words of encouragement."

I pointed to the side. "I'm parked just over there."

Miranda lifted the hem of her dress with both hands, almost sprinting by my side.

"Sorry. I'll walk a little slower," I said. "Tomorrow, I'll arrange for you to visit a stylist and order some gowns. From now on, you're my date for these things."

She stopped and looked at me. "Oh… Britney won't mind?"

"I call the shots," I said confidently, but doubt crept into my mind as I thought about the tangled web of an accounting system that only Britney and my father understood.

Miranda stumbled all of a sudden, and I held out my hand to help steady her.

"Are you okay?" I asked.

She ended up in my arms somehow, looking all flushed and wearing an apologetic smile.

That moment stood still as I gazed at those pretty eyes. Her floral scent had a subtle but intoxicating effect.

She stepped out of my hold and bent down, lifting her dress. "I just broke a heel."

"That's unfortunate," I said, watching her remove her other

shoe. "I'm just parked there." I pointed to my cream '68 Mustang. "I can carry you if you like."

Shaking her head vigorously, she said, "Oh no. Please. The car's really close. I can manage."

I nodded, and within a few steps, we arrived at the car.

Miranda ran her hand along the hood. "What a gorgeous car."

"Classic cars are one of my weaknesses," I said, not without pride. I loved my car. "I've got a Lincoln and a '59 Chevy parked in the garage. I race them with my neighbors."

"Boys with their toys, am I right?" She smiled.

"You bet. Guilty as charged."

"That's so cool. It's such a stylish car," said Miranda, sliding onto the red leather seat as I held the door open.

"I think so," I said, closing the door for her.

I jumped in and drove off.

"This is very kind of you," she said as we glided off into the night.

"Think nothing of it. I couldn't have you taking a bus in that dress."

She smiled. "A few people looked at me weirdly. I almost felt like telling them I'd escaped from an Amish colony."

"You're just missing the bonnet." I glanced over at her, and we shared a laugh.

We'd been driving for a while and were about to merge onto the freeway when I noticed the same car had been following me from the moment I'd taken off. I pushed down on the gas, and glancing into the rearview mirror, I saw that the car tailing me had sped up. This went on for a while as we drove along the freeway. With each glance into the rearview, my acceleration increased.

"Is something wrong?" asked Miranda as she turned to look at me.

The engine's growl, normally a sound I found sexy, added a note of urgency, which only added to my unease.

"Maybe it's nothing. But I think someone's following me."

She turned to look. "They do seem rather close."

I glanced at the odometer and saw I was pushing eighty miles per hour. One of the advantages of racing at the old track with Sam, my neighbor, was that I knew how to handle my car at high speeds.

The reckless teenager I once was would have been buzzing in this scenario, high on adrenaline. But not now. The only thrill would be in losing the fucker.

"Oh!" Miranda gripped the dash.

"Don't worry. I did a bit of rally driving as a teenager. Misspent youth." I glanced over at her and chuckled, which brought a moment of short-lived relief.

With the SUV on my tail, it became a game of weaving in and out of multiple lanes. My nimble car performed beautifully. If only the adrenaline was the type I normally thrived on.

We took the exit for Venice Boulevard.

Then it got interesting.

The SUV tapped my bumper, and Miranda gasped. I fired up. The prick was not only messing with my car, but more significantly, he was freaking out Miranda.

Gunning it, I surged through a yellow light. Knowing he'd have to stop at the red light, I puffed out a breath of relief. I'd won a small victory.

Wrong. The son of a bitch raced through, narrowly missing the stream of cross traffic.

"Hold on," I urged.

I hooked the car sharply. The wheels squealed as we slid around, and the acrid scent of burning rubber filtered through the window. That was normally a turn-on for me with my need for speed, but at that moment, it was fucking nauseating.

"Should I call the police?" Miranda asked in a high-pitched voice.

I swerved into an alleyway. "No. I've lost my license."

Her head turned sharply. She looked at me as though I'd admitted to having herpes. "You have?"

"It's a long story. Suffice to say, my driver had the night off." This was not the time to tell her that I'd taken the wheel from

Brent when he'd been wasted one night, and my good deed had backfired. Or that I was a gearhead, and that when my unreliable driver called in sick, I jumped at the chance of driving.

I checked the rearview and realized my pursuer was gaining on me as he sent a bin flying through the air.

"Okay. This isn't going to be pretty." I pushed down hard on the gas. Growling like a beast in heat, my car seemed in its element.

"Oh my God." Miranda gripped onto her seat. "Is there someone who hates you?"

"Not that I'm aware of." I did wonder if one of my exes was behind it but kept that to myself.

"I've got an idea," Miranda said as I swerved onto another street, narrowly missing an oncoming vehicle.

"Hit me," I yelled over the cacophony of horns sounding from pissed-off drivers.

"I don't live very far from here. It's just the next street over."

"Okay. Let's head there now. Left or right?"

7

MIRANDA

I could barely think straight, let alone talk. "Turn right."

From the left lane, he cut into the one to our right, barely missing an oncoming car.

I nearly swallowed my tongue.

An ear-piercing horn sounded, and as I turned to look, a middle finger greeted me. Offering an apologetic smile, I was pretty sure "nice car" was not what exited the infuriated driver's lips.

"Quick, take a sharp left there into the parking garage," I said, my heart racing. I peered over my shoulder, which was steadily becoming second nature.

At least we'd appeared to have lost the SUV.

I'd never loved seeing that stinky underground parking garage as much as that moment.

I pointed. "Park there. That's my space." I looked behind again. "I think we've lost him." I wiped my forehead. "Hell."

Lachlan's face had a faint sheen of sweat.

"That was some kick-ass driving." I smiled, trying to make light of the harrowing experience. The last thing he needed was a shrill, hyperventilating passenger blowing into a paper bag, even though that was really what I felt like doing. My heart still pounded in my ears, and I was soaking from cold sweat.

"Thanks," he said, taking a deep breath.

"Do you want to come up and grab some water?"

"I think I need something stronger than water. But yeah, sure. I might have to wait it out for thirty minutes or so. If that's okay." He got out of the car.

"Of course," I said, as he opened my door.

"This was perfect timing. I really mean it. Thanks."

"No problem." I shook my head in disbelief. "I've never been in a car chase before. How terrifying. It looks different on film."

"It's a first for me too. Are you sure you're okay?" He blew a jagged breath. "I'm so sorry you had to experience that."

I could see he was still shaken by his trembling hands as he placed his keys in his pocket.

"I'll live. But yeah, my heart's still racing," I said.

It felt so strange lingering in that dark parking garage with my boss, who, until that night, had been a virtual stranger.

As crazy as it was, I couldn't stop thinking of how hot he looked. It seemed the drama had added to his already considerable masculine appeal.

How could someone like that be interested in me, I thought, especially when I looked like a walking sack of potatoes? Even dressed in something slinky, I could never be a match for someone as handsome as Lachlan Peace.

With his bow tie undone and his shirt half hanging out of those slacks that molded around his strong thighs, Lachlan looked deliciously sexy, as though he'd just fucked someone in an alleyway.

I wondered whether I preferred the slick, tuxedoed hunk or the rugged version that looked like he'd just wrestled a bear.

Both.

"Just to warn you, my place is a little run down," I said.

He spread his large hands wide. "I'm just glad to be here. And that we lost whoever that was."

As we moved to the elevator, I asked, "Have you got a few enemies?"

"Maybe a disgruntled ex or two," he replied. "It doesn't make sense, though. Normally, they just stalk me, turning up randomly and embarrassing the crap out of themselves and me." He shook his head.

"You seem to have a complicated life, if you don't mind me saying."

"Oh yeah. I've got one of those all right," he said with a deep, husky voice that caressed more than just my ears.

The Out of Order sign tacked on the door made me groan inwardly.

We walked up the first flight, dodging fast-food wrappers and the odd scrounging cat along the way. In that shit-ugly dress, I felt like I belonged with them.

"Ouch." I hopped on the spot. I'd stepped on a sharp object as we arrived on the landing.

"Are you okay?" Lachlan asked, looking concerned.

I leaned against the wall and inspected the ball of my bare foot. "I'm fine. I didn't cut it."

He stepped in front of me and patted his back, bending his knees. "Jump on."

"What?" My mouth fell open.

"I'll piggyback you."

I searched his face for a hint of a joke or something, but he looked serious. "But there's two more flights and I'm really heavy."

"Bullshit," he said, smiling so sweetly I couldn't believe this was the same guy who'd just been in a car chase. "I'm not going to take no for an answer."

Resigned to accept his chivalrous offer, I took a deep breath and placed my arms around his shoulders and wrapped my legs around his waist.

He took hold of my thighs covered by the thick fabric and handled my weight effortlessly as I gripped onto his shoulders.

"I hope I'm not weighing you down," I said, my voice wobbling, as we moved up the stairs.

"You're as light as a feather. I train with heavier weights."

I rested my chin on his warm neck, which radiated a seductively intoxicating scent. His body was so powerful, he didn't even struggle.

I even grew to like being carried by him so much, I was disappointed when we arrived at my door.

He lowered me back to the floor. "There you go."

My pulse raced as though it was me who'd done all the work.

I paused at my door. "Sorry. That elevator rarely works."

"No need to apologize. It's a good workout." He smiled.

Despite the return of his boyish charm, my keys still trembled in my hand. I couldn't decide which was worse: that chase where we'd narrowly missed colliding with other cars, my boss holding onto my chubby thighs, or him seeing the tiny apartment I shared with Harry.

When we walked in, Harriet was locking lips with her casual hookup.

I cleared my throat, and he looked up, wiping his lips with the back of his hand.

My sister looked at Lachlan and said, "Oh, you've brought someone home." She combed her fingers through her shoulder-length hair.

"This is Lachlan Peace, my boss. He needs to hang here for a while."

Lachlan said, "Sorry to barge in like this."

"You're welcome. Always," responded Harriet, putting on a soft, welcoming voice. "I'm Harriet, and this is Josh."

Josh jumped up and offered Lachlan his hand.

After giving Lachlan a glass of water, I headed into the bathroom.

Harriet followed me in and said, "What the fuck?"

"It's a long story. We were in a car chase. Screechy tires and all."

Her face lit up. "You're kidding. I bet he handled his car well."

Lachlan with that stick shift in hand came to mind, performing hook turns like a seasoned rally driver. I nodded. "He did. But that was the last thing on my mind."

"He's even sexier in person than in his photos."

"That's probably the testosterone you're smelling," I said.

I washed my hands and headed into my bedroom, dying to free myself from the world's ugliest dress. I unzipped it, and it thudded to the floor.

"What are you putting on?" Harriet asked, kicking the hideous gown into a corner.

I held up my favorite pair of gray sweats. "Comfy loungewear. It's going to feel like silk after being trapped under that scratchy fabric all night."

She rolled her eyes. "Andie, come on. Lachlan Peace is in the living room looking like a sex god, and that's what you're changing into?"

"He's only here because tonight's been really strange. That's all."

She rummaged through my dresser then pulled out leggings and a T-shirt. "Here, put these on. At least show off some curves."

"No fucking way. Are you kidding me? This is me at home. Besides, he's my boss. I'm not going to go all seductress."

"Seductress is a bit of a stretch. A tight shirt without a bra wouldn't hurt, though, would it?" She reached up to my bun, which was so full of styling products and bobby pins, I doubted my hair would ever be the same again. "Why don't you wear your hair down?"

She removed the pins, and my hair tumbled down my back. I rubbed my tender scalp as I glanced in the mirror. "Thanks for the suggestion. This feels so much better already."

We joined the men in the living room. They were watching basketball and seemed to have fallen into the TV.

Lachlan looked up at me and did a double take. His eyes widened. "Wow. Where did all that hair come from?"

"From our Irish granny. She was a redhead," said Harriet.

I fell into the recliner beside the sofa and took a deep breath. What a night.

"You're not having a beer?" he asked.

Shaking my head, I said, "We're all out of expensive champagne." I looked at Harriet and giggled. The most expensive we ever got was ten-dollar prosecco.

"Well then let me arrange a delivery for you." Before I could protest, and with Harriet egging him on with her enthusiastic nod, Lachlan had an app on his phone ready to go. "Moët?" he asked me.

Harriet answered for me. "That would be lovely."

"Hey, look... you don't have to, really," I said.

He tapped away on his phone and then looked up at me and smiled. "Consider it done. Should be here within fifteen minutes."

Fifteen minutes later, a knock came to the door.

When I opened the door, I found the poor delivery guy panting.

He placed a box down on the ground, and Lachlan tipped him with a one-hundred-dollar bill, which put a big grin on the boy's face.

"Wow... there's enough here for a party," Harriet said, laughing.

"I have to work tomorrow." I looked at my boss-turned-party-animal, now sipping on the Corona that Josh had given to him.

"It's only early. A glass or two of champagne shouldn't harm," Lachlan said with that killer smile.

Harriet popped the cork, and we filled our glasses.

She looked at Lachlan. "Are you going to join us?"

"I'll stick to beer. But hey, knock yourself out," he said, looking over at me with that soft, lingering gaze.

Was he seeing me as a woman for the first time? Or was I just reading too much into it?

It was fun kicking back and having a laugh. I'd almost forgotten the car chase but not being carried up the stairs. How could I forget that? My thighs still tingled from where his strong hands had been. I had to keep reminding myself not to crush on my boss.

Lachlan, meanwhile, made himself at home. He stretched his long legs and sat back on the sofa opposite me.

"So what do you do, Josh?" he asked with that velvety voice that traveled down to my core like a form of vocal cunnilingus.

As Harriet's boy babbled on about being a DJ, I just drifted in and out of that twilight zone that only expensive champagne and devilishly handsome men could deliver.

8

LACHLAN

I rubbed my back where the sofa's springs had dug in. As I lifted my stiff body, a little voice roused me out of my haze.

"I'm a ballerina." A small golden angel smiled back at me.

"Hello," I said, combing back my hair with my hands. "And who might you be?"

"I'm Ava. I'm a ballerina." To prove that point, she leapt about and spun, performing for me. Although my head pounded, it was a heartwarming sight nevertheless.

"Aren't you a sweet little dancing fairy," I said, admiring her artful moves when Miranda raced in.

"Ava, don't disturb our guest," she said.

With that waist-length hair, Miranda was a head turner. Her horn-rimmed glasses highlighted her beautiful almond-shaped eyes.

My gaze wandered down her body, and her perfect hourglass figure led me over delectable curves. Suddenly, I had a raging case of morning wood.

Was I looking at the same girl?

"She's adorable," I said, returning my attention to the little girl, who I assumed was Miranda's daughter.

"Be a good girl and eat your breakfast. We have to leave for school soon." She checked the time and gave a little groan then looked up at me apologetically. "I slept in, sorry."

"Hey, don't stress. Do you need a lift?" I asked.

"That would be great. My car's still at the garage being repaired. I've been borrowing my mother's car, but she needed it last night. I was meant to get up early…" She bit into a nail.

"It's all good. We can drop Ava off on the way back to Malibu."

"If it's not a problem, then sure, thanks." She smiled sweetly. "I'm actually ready. Can I make you a coffee?"

I shook my head. "Only water, please."

Miranda left and came back with a large glass of water.

My parched throat had me draining the glass in one gulp.

Fifteen minutes later, we were on the road. I looked into the rearview mirror at Ava sliding all over the red leather on the back seat.

"She's a very excitable child," I said.

Miranda nodded. "Just like her mom."

"I wouldn't exactly describe you in that way." I cast her a sidelong glance. "I haven't seen you leaping about ..." I grinned. "Yet."

She turned sharply. "Ava's not my child."

"Oh." I nodded. "Then why isn't your sister taking care of her? Not that I mind driving her. She's amusing." I glanced at Ava performing the splits and chuckled.

Miranda turned to her niece. "Ava, settle down." She turned back to me. "She's convinced she's a dancer."

"Why not? She's talented," I said, keeping an eye on the busy traffic ahead.

"Harriet's a nurse. She works the graveyard shift at a rehab facility. I take Ava to school in the mornings so Harry can sleep in. I'm not sure where we'd find the time to take her to and from dance classes now that I have a job."

"That must keep you busy."

She sighed. "It sure does. My mom's offered to help, but my sister's worried that she'll turn Ava into a project."

"In what way?"

"Her education. We were homeschooled. My mom has this attitude toward learning that's straight out of the fifties. She's always correcting my grammar, along with everyone else's."

"For what it's worth, I think your grammar is just fine."

"Thanks."

"Thanks for letting me stay last night, by the way."

"I'm sorry if the couch was uncomfortable. But you had one

drink too many."

"Did I insist on driving?" I asked, knowing what a stubborn dick I could be when drunk.

"You did, but we managed to stop you."

I shook my head. "After you went to bed, Josh brought out the bourbon, and with everything that happened last night, I couldn't resist."

"That's understandable." Miranda pointed. "Turn left here. It's that building over there."

After we dropped off Ava, I headed for the boardwalk and parked my car in the first spot I found.

"Where are we going?" asked Miranda

"It's nine thirty. Time for breakfast."

"But I'm supposed to be at work. I'm already late, and Britney will be …"

"Relax. I'm the boss." I pulled out my cell phone, noting that I had a few missed calls from Britney. "I'm just about to call her now."

Miranda's frown remained. "But if she knows we're together here, she'll think …"

"It's none of her business." I dialed Britney.

"There you are," she said.

"What's so urgent?"

"We're being visited by the SEC today."

The throbbing in my temples intensified. "Should I be worried?"

Her long pause answered that.

"I'll be there in an hour. I want you to sit down and explain to me what the fuck is going on. Okay?"

"The new girl's not here. I'm not happy about that."

"She's with me right now. I stayed at her place last night."

Miranda turned to look at me. Her lips parted, and she blinked rapidly.

"I didn't think she'd be your type," Britney said.

I ignored her comment. "We were involved in a car chase. Some creep followed me all the way to Venice. I had to hide."

"Did you call the police?" asked Britney.

"Hell no. My license, remember?"

"You shouldn't be driving, Lachlan. You know that."

"I've got to go. You didn't answer me ... should I be worried?"

"Everything's fine."

I hung up and combed back my hair while my heart pumped a little faster.

The day had gotten worse. Before driving off, I read a message from
the doctor who wished to see me about my father's treatment. He'd tried calling my stepmother, Tamara, but hadn't heard back. That didn't surprise me. She was probably with some cabana boy in Miami.

We opted for an earthy café that had shelves filled with books and plants and sat at a wooden bench by a window with a good view of the beach.

After we ordered, I sat back and reflected on last night's car chase. It couldn't have been Jane, my most recent ex, because as much as she liked throwing plates and objects at me, she wouldn't have gone that far.

"Was Britney okay?" Miranda asked.

"She'll be fine." I pointed at her half-eaten breakfast. "You don't like it?"

"I'm not that hungry."

"Sorry about last night," I said, gulping back my second coffee.

"Don't worry. I'm fine." She wore a faint smile. "Can I ask how your dad's doing?"

"Not too well." I took a deep breath. "I visit him daily. And now the SEC are on their way to audit our accounts."

Her brow furrowed. "That sounds a little scary. But I'm sure things will be fine. Britney strikes me as a perfectionist."

"She's been working alongside my dad for ten years, so she knows about the business in a way I don't."

"Oh?"

"Let's just say my father had a thing for creative accounting."

I shook my head, recalling how he narrowly escaped prison during the 2008 stock market crash. I could still hear those shredding machines going all night.

"Are you worried?" she asked.

"Not sure. We'll find out soon. Expect the unexpected."

"I'm already expecting that." She grinned.

Her big dark eyes shone keenly behind her glasses. Although Miranda struck me as an assertive woman, she possessed a calming nature.

Even with all the shit going down in my life, every time I stared into her pretty eyes, I lost myself. Her hair was pulled back in a ponytail, emphasizing a long neck and high cheekbones.

Taking a deep breath, I reminded myself that I wasn't going to sleep with my new administrative assistant. I needed a comrade more than I needed a lover. I would just have to avoid checking out her perky ass and nice tits that bounced slightly whenever she moved.

When we arrived at the office, I found Britney speaking rapidly on the phone while staring at her screen. She seemed ruffled, and when she looked up and saw me, her voice lowered.

I hovered around, regardless of her obvious desire for privacy.

As soon as she ended the call, I asked, "When are they coming?"

"I'm not sure. They didn't specify. It could be any minute." Her eyes flitted from me to her screen.

"I have to check on Dad. But when I return, I want to know exactly what's got you all freaked out." I added, "And Miranda's a great asset. Treat her nicely."

Her scowl riled me. "I mean it, Britney."

My days of breaking the law were over. I needed a driver, so I called my neighbor, Aidan Thornhill.

"Hey. Lachlan here."

"How's life?" he asked.

"It's been pretty interesting lately. And not in the fun way." I chuckled grimly. "Can you spare one of your drivers? The bigger the better. I need a bodyguard."

"Sure. For how long?"

"I need someone indefinitely. My license is suspended."

"We just went racing a few weeks ago," he said.

"Yeah, I know. I've been a bad boy. But that's changing right now."

"Probably a good plan. You could end up in jail if caught."

Driving without a license was the least of my worries. What if the SEC came after my dad? In his frail state, prison would kill him.

"I'll get in touch with Justin, the head of my security, and tell him to expect your call. I'll text you his number."

"That's great, thanks. You're a lifesaver." I sighed. "How's the family?"

"Good. Always good. Ollie's a bit wild still."

"He's a great guitarist."

"That he is. He takes after his grandfather, in more ways than one."

I chuckled. "You don't sound like a proud father."

"I don't see him until the afternoon. He's up all night, partying hard. Music, girls, booze. Tattoos. Poor Clarissa freaks every time he turns up with a new one."

"He's very talented, though. I love jamming with him. Anyway, let's get together soon."

"I'd like that. Nice hearing from you," he said and hung up.

I thought of Ollie and how we normally caught up almost daily at the beach. I hadn't seen him that week and made a mental note to call.

9

MIRANDA

Britney regarded me as though I was the devil incarnate. "I can see you've made an impression on Lachlan. Let's get one thing straight. He might say he's calling the shots here, but he needs me more than ever, and you're disposable."

The cold look in her eyes sent a shiver through me.

She continued. "For some reason, he thinks you're useful. But I can change all of that in a flash. This best friend act has got to stop." I mumbled an apology, but she spoke over me. "Don't speak. Listen. No more of that girl-next-door shit." Her eyes wandered to my chest and she scowled. "And no fitted tops. Lay off the boss. Now, I need you to get to work." She pulled out some files. "Go through each of these lists and delete anything highlighted. With every document you delete, make sure you clear the recycle bin. Without fail."

Britney's abrasive tone stung. I hadn't been flirting with Lachlan at all.

She placed the large stack of files on my desk. "I need this done yesterday."

"Sure."

"You're going to have to work through your lunch break."

I nodded, sensing something was off about what she'd asked me to do. It was only for Lachlan's sake that I worried. Knowing he'd driven on a suspended license, I did wonder if he was reckless. But I couldn't dislike him, because he struck me as a genuinely nice guy. Especially how he'd protected me against the jeering society girls by staying close and showing no concern about being seen with someone dressed in an ugly dress. Lachlan had treated me kindly and paid attention to every word I uttered. That wasn't what I would have expected from someone as good-looking and wealthy as Lachlan Peace. He'd been so sweet around Ava, and he hadn't looked down on the way my sister and I lived, which was a far cry from the privileged splendor he'd obviously enjoyed all his life.

I'd just started with my first file when my phone buzzed. Seeing it was Lachlan, I took the call.

"Is Britney within hearing distance?" he asked.

"No," I answered. The urgency in his tone had me gripping the phone tight.

"Good. What has she got you doing?"

"I'm deleting files," I said.

"Can you do something for me?"

"Sure."

"Copy everything onto a USB before deleting. And whatever you do, don't let Britney see it."

"All right."

"Good. See you later."

He hung up and my finger trembled as it hovered over the delete button. I found a flash drive and did as Lachlan had asked. When I heard Britney's heels clicking rapidly as she approached the office, I pulled out the USB.

She arrived just as I'd managed to slide it under the files, my palms sweaty.

Two hours later, a couple of men in matching gray suits and buzz cuts walked in. They looked very official and Britney strutted up to them immediately in her tight-fitting pencil skirt.

"You can go to lunch now. Take two hours." It was more an order than anything.

After bathing in the sunshine while taking a pleasant stroll around the vast, flourishing grounds, I returned to my desk.

The two men from earlier passed by me. Their cheap aftershave shot up my nose, leaving a lingering reminder of their unwanted presence.

Britney stood by my desk and watched them leave. After

they were out of sight, she handed me a file. "Here's an inventory of the estate's art collection. I want you to check on current market values."

I nodded.

Shortly after she left me alone, Lachlan strode in and, stopping at my desk, asked, "Did you do it?"

I retrieved the USB from my purse and handed it to him.

"Nice work. Thanks." He looked at the Whistler still life displayed on my screen. "That's one of ours."

"Britney's asked me to check what they're all currently worth."

"Good. That reminds me, I'm taking the Monet to an expert."

I nodded, biting my lip. Britney had returned, hovering in the doorway expectantly.

Lachlan turned to her. "We need to talk."

Watching them head to his office, I released a tight breath.

He returned a few moments later and handed me a credit card. "This is for you. The family stylist should be on a list of contacts you've been emailed. Give her a ring and make an appointment. We have a ball to attend tomorrow night. Assuming you don't already have plans?" A slow, sexy smile grew on his face.

A ball? A new gown? With him? It could be worse.

I shook my head, and looking past him, I sensed Britney would soon plot my murder.

I returned her dark glare with a sweet smile. With Lachlan in charge, my job would be safe for now.

It was 5:00 p.m. when I left work. I called the stylist, and an appointment downtown was arranged for 6:00 p.m.

I thought of Ava. I'd promised to pick her up from my parent's house. I'd never make it in time with the traffic, so I called my mother.

"There you are, stranger," she said.

"Sorry, I've been so busy lately, what with this new job and all."

"Yes, your sister told me."

"I would've called, but it's been really full-on."

"Full-on? Is that the best you can do?"

"Oh, Mom, let's not get into semantics now. I'm really under pressure."

"When are you going to tell us all about your new job?"

"Soon. I promise." I took a breath. "I'm meeting a stylist. My boss has asked me to accompany him to a ball."

I should have expected what would follow. "A ball? Your boss?"

"It's platonic. Really. I promise to tell you all about it when I see you this weekend."

"Mm... I've got a private student coming over at nine. But I can get your father to drop Ava off later. He'll like that. We like having her here. It seems that we only ever see her when you girls need something."

"Life's like that. It's kind of frantic. Even for Harry. She's working the graveyard shift so, you know."

"No, I don't know. I hate that saying."

"Okay. Love you. Bye."

I hung up quickly before she went on one of her rants about the modern day's corruption of language.

10

LACHLAN

The dread of seeing my emaciated father filled me with gloom. I sank into a chair and stared blankly out the window, welcoming the view of the ocean.

What happened to the fun times?

He stirred. "Is that you, Brent?"

"No, Dad, it's me, Lachlan. Brent passed away nine months ago."

"I know when Brent died. I just get your names mixed up sometimes."

Despite his lack of apology, I'd stopped being hurt long ago.

When Brent died, my father fell into a deep depression, followed two months later by his cancer diagnosis.

Sharing the same cavalier attitude to life, they thought themselves invincible. In my brother's case, he believed he could conquer nature, to which the ski slopes in Aspen proved him wrong. And my father's years of heavy drinking and smoking was just as unmerciful.

"How are you doing today?" I asked.

He lifted his frail frame, and I leaned forward to adjust his pillow.

"Close to dying."

"You look a little more rested," I said, hoping to distract him from more of that talk.

"Where's that bimbo wife of mine?" he asked.

"I haven't seen her around for a while."

"You were right about her," he said.

I was right about all of them.

"Hank was here yesterday."

"How's our family attorney doing?"

"He assured me that the prenup's solid. She's not getting a fucking dime."

I nodded slowly. "And Manuel?"

"That's not my fucking child," he snapped. His next words were cut off by a sudden coughing fit.

I touched his shoulder. "Don't get too worked up, please."

Recognizing disapproval in those faded blue eyes, I could tell my father wanted to bark at me but lacked the energy. He'd always hated my creative lifestyle as though it was a disease, accusing me of being my mother's son. While Brent treated each day as though it was his last, I learned to play four rhythms at once. Drumming was not an easy pursuit. My mother, who always encouraged me, was dazzled by my achievements. I didn't do it for her compliments, even though I liked them. I drummed because I loved playing music. I loved jazz. Even though that made me a little different, it didn't justify my father's cold treatment toward me over the years.

"Hank suggested a paternity test."

"How the hell do I do that?" I asked.

"Oh, for Christ's sake, haven't your balls dropped yet? Grab a sample of the kid's fucking hair or something."

"I haven't seen Tammy for weeks." I kept my voice even despite the *fuck you* clawing at my vocal cords. "She's probably in Miami." Switching to another uncomfortable subject, I said, "We had the SEC sniffing about yesterday."

"Britney told me."

"Should I be worried?" I asked.

"She'll take care of it. Any incriminating files have been removed."

"Incriminating?" I studied him, hoping he'd explain.

He ignored my comment. "That child's not mine."

I wanted to ask him about Bird of Paradise, but he could barely keep his eyes open.

He fell back onto his pillow.

I leaned in to cover him with his blanket when he whispered,

"There's four billion in bullion in Geneva." He paused for a gasp of air. "Your mother doesn't get a fucking dime."

Oh, she will. I would see to it. Considering my mother had married a serial cheater, she deserved more than a dime.

"It's all yours and Britney's. Don't let that bitch Tammy get a hint of it."

"Why Britney?" I asked.

He gestured for me to stop asking questions.

I kissed his sunken cheek and left, my heavy tread reflecting my mood.

Why would he leave money to Britney and not my mother, who'd been married to him for fifteen years?

***

I tugged on my cuffs and straightened the satin lapels of my tux. My late grandfather's diamond cuff links sparkled in the dim lighting of the car's cabin. Unlike my father, my paternal grandfather had believed rewards came from honesty and a spotless reputation. I respected him and was a better person for having known him. Without his influence I might have turned out more like Brent.

James pulled up in front of a columned building. Purple and red lights highlighting the sculpted details gave it a magical appeal, especially against the turquoise twilight.

My new driver was about to jump out when I held up my hand and said, "I've got this."

I ran over to Miranda's side to help her out of the limo.

She thanked me and stood on the curb, admiring the architecture of the building where the gala was being held.

I lost my tongue when I first saw her dressed in that hip-hugging pink gown, revealing enough milky cleavage to make my pulse race.

I needed to stop imagining her naked. Miranda was more than just physically beautiful. She had a kind heart and spirit—qualities sorely lacking in my circle.

"Are your eyes okay?" I asked.

She rubbed at her eyes and frowned. "I've never worn contacts before, and they're very irritating."

"You can just wear your glasses if that will make you more comfortable. You look great either way, but glasses really suit you."

"No one's ever told me that before." She gave me a shy smile.

"That's surprising. I think they're cute. Ready?" I held out my arm, and we continued up the stairs to another gala event that looked just like all the others.

After taking over as CEO of Peace Holdings, I'd continued attending these things to raise capital for my own development projects. I'd quickly discovered it was increasingly futile. My dad's old cronies passed on my projects, telling me they were too idealistic and unprofitable. And I had very little in common with the guys my age, who were mostly socially awkward tech guru wannabes from Silicon Valley.

A jazz quartet grooved away on stage, performing the classics. As we sipped on excellent champagne, I centered my attention on the drummer, an elderly Black man, who could have taught me a thing or two about syncopation.

Standing close by, Britney acknowledged me with a grin. As her eyes shifted from me to Miranda, her smile faded. Miranda was the belle of the ball. No one came close in the beauty stakes —not even Britney in her tight blue number with a plunging neckline. Judging by her scowl, she knew it too.

I wanted to wait until she'd had a few drinks before asking her for more details on Bird of Paradise. She'd sidestepped my earlier questions like a crab on a full moon and scuttled off when I got distracted by a call relating to the car chase.

I'd learned who was responsible for turning a dull night into anything but. It had been a disgruntled investor named Tony Varela. He wanted his dough. "Ten million plus interest," he'd growled, sounding like a Scorsese character.

"Instead of ramming my car and frightening the shit out of my passenger, you could have just called," I said.

"Where's the fun in that?" he asked with a sinister chuckle.

He threatened to send someone to have a "friendly" chat

with me if I didn't pay up within twenty-four hours.

This time, I was prepared. I had an ex-Special Forces fighter as my driver. And with Miranda close I needed to protect her.

I wondered why Peace Holdings had dealings with such a shady character, considering that my father was a serious snob and preferred to rub shoulders with high society. Even though, when it came to the opposite sex, he had a thing for wild women, my mother was the only exception. With Tamara, he'd really outdone himself. Before marrying my father, my stepmother had worked as a stripper and escort.

I tapped my foot to the beat of the music and felt Miranda's shoulder close by my arm. I was tempted to take her hand in mine. But I didn't want to abuse my position as her boss, even if she was my date for the evening.

All the regular power brokers were present. This time, Miranda stood out for all the right reasons as people's eyes lingered on her.

I stopped a passing waiter and grabbed refills. As I handed one to Miranda, her hand shook.

"Are you nervous?"

"Kind of." She gave a wan smile. "Everyone's looking at me."

"That's because you're the most beautiful woman in this room."

Her red lips parted, and I fell into those dark almond-shaped eyes which had become so addictive, I found it hard to leave.

Just as I reminded myself she was my employee, I noticed a guy to the side had his phone angled at us. I puffed out a breath. Paparazzi were the least of my problems. For all I cared, the tabloids could describe me as a coke-sniffing cyborg who'd knocked up a one-eyed Martian.

I had too many other issues on my plate, namely that USB stick of deleted files.

Bevan Jones sauntered over and said, "You're getting around, I see."

"Attending these things is part of my duty as CEO of Peace Holdings," I said.

"You're not really one of us, though, are you?" He glanced over at Miranda, who was fixated on a painting. It was adorable. "Well, hello. Haven't we scrubbed up well." He looked at me with his head cocked. "Is this the same girl?"

Miranda looked at him and said, "Yes, they let me out again."

I laughed at her droll tone. I liked a person who stood up to assholes.

He turned away from her and looked at me. "Word has it you're being audited."

I wore the blankest expression I could muster. "And?"

"Well ... some of Clarke's little schemes have that smell about them."

"Because you're in on them?" I asked.

"I've kept my distance from those particular ones."

I was dying to know what he meant but chose to feign indifference instead.

That there was more than one shady scheme I needed to worry about settled in my stomach like a rock. "Excuse me."

I turned to Miranda. "Come with me." She seemed a little distant. "Are you okay?"

She nodded. "I'm good. I just don't like that guy."

"That makes two of us," I said. "Let me show you something."

11

MIRANDA

The luxurious and impressive portraits lining the walls made me sigh. They were similar to works by Thomas Gainsborough, a painter whose work I'd loved when I was younger. "This room's gorgeous," I said, running my fingers along a red velvet sofa.

"I thought you'd like it," he said, nodding at the walls.

Living up to his reputation as the hottest billionaire in town, Lachlan switched from boyish to devilishly handsome within a blink. With those ocean-blue eyes, he offered so many shades of gorgeous, I kept forgetting to breathe around him.

I kept touching my pink silk gown, which hugged my hips and flounced to my feet.

"I'm sorry if Britney's giving you a hard time," Lachlan said.

"You don't have to apologize. It's nothing I can't handle." He didn't need to know that Britney looked like she'd burn me at the stake after seeing me in my low-cut ball gown.

I'd tried to select something more modest, but the stylist refused. "Why would you want to hide that body?" she asked. "You've got the perfect hourglass figure. I wish more of my clients had your curves. I have just the perfect dress for you. It'll really emphasize your tiny waist."

That left me speechless. Did I really have a perfect hourglass figure?

"I've got a few issues to deal with at the moment, so I hope you'll understand if I seem a little distracted," Lachlan said.

"Of course." I smiled.

"By the way, how's Ava? Have you found a dance class yet?"

That took me by surprise. For someone with so much on his

plate, Lachlan still remembered to ask about my niece.

"Not yet," I said.

"My mother has her own dance school where she teaches. Ava's welcome to take all the classes she wants there."

"You'd do that?"

"Why not? I could see she loves dancing."

"I'd really appreciate that, Lachlan. Ava will be so thrilled. But it seems like you've got your hands full right now. I don't want to add to that."

He shook his head. "It gives me an excuse to drop in on my mother."

"Is she a ballet teacher?" I asked.

"She teaches Spanish dance." He stuck his arms up in a dramatic pose, making me laugh.

"That looks really authentic. Did she teach you some moves?"

"She tried. But I was more into drumming."

"Dance and music are related," I said.

"Absolutely." He sighed.

I felt his frustration. "You miss playing?"

"Yep. Ever since my older brother, Brent, passed away and my father became ill the pressure's been on me to carry the family business." He shrugged. "If only it was as simple as acquiring land and developing."

I was about to bring up the deleted files when a couple of young men burst into the room with cigars hanging out of their mouths. They stopped dead in their tracks and looked at Lachlan, then at me. Lachlan placed his hand at the small of my back.

"Let's go into the ballroom," he said, keeping his palm right where it was. The heat of his hand sent tingles through my body.

"Sure." I floated along as though in a dream.

"You're making quite an impression this evening," said Lachlan.

"I don't know why."

"You look stunning."

I blushed. "Thanks. It's nice not feeling invisible."

"Trust me, you could never be invisible." His gaze lingered.

Warmth swept through me. Shame he was my boss. I felt a powerful crush coming on.

"I'll be right back," he said with a sparkling smile.

After he was out of sight, Britney joined me. "Didn't I tell you to stay away from Lachlan?"

"I'm here at his request," I said as calmly as possible.

She thrust her finger in my face, and I was almost tempted to bite it.

"Listen to me," she said with a sneer. "I've got enough dirt on this family to send Lachlan to prison. I want you to resign."

Her breath reeked of booze and made my stomach turn. "Excuse me?"

"Why do you think the SEC was at the office yesterday? Clarke Peace didn't become a billionaire because he always played by the rules. I think you'll agree that Lachlan's not going to let his father die in prison. If you don't quit, I'll make sure Lachlan takes the fall." She arched an eyebrow. "And thanks to me, we managed to avoid detection."

I opened my mouth, and she lifted a finger. "I'm not finished. Lachlan Peace is mine. I know exactly what you're doing, and he'd never go for someone like you."

My cheeks burned as my hands clenched at my sides. "I'm not doing anything, Britney. Besides, he's not interested in me like that. Lachlan's just a nice person."

"Nice? The only thing nice about him is his big cock. I'm sure you'll feel it later if you dance with him. Enjoy tonight. Tomorrow, you'd better hand in your resignation."

I finally found my voice. "What's stopping me from telling the authorities about you?"

She leaned in close, her gray eyes piercingly malevolent. "You don't want to mess with me. It's your word against mine. And no one's going to believe a nobody like you." She smirked. "Your digital prints are all over the system now. You were the only one who accessed those files I told you to delete." She looked over my shoulder and I turned to see Lachlan heading toward us.

"Sorry, Miranda, but I'll just be a few more minutes." He looked at Britney. "We need to talk. Now." Without waiting for a reply, he turned and walked out of the ballroom.

Britney pushed past me, knocking into my shoulder in an obvious act of intimidation.

Tears burned behind my eyes. All I'd wanted was a job so I could start paying down my student loans. I hadn't asked for any of this. If I hadn't just been drawn into some corporate conspiracy, I would have told her to go fuck herself.

12

LACHLAN

"What's Bird of Paradise?"

"A plant with pretty flowers," Britney said.

"Stop playing games. An investor named Tony Varela's been threatening me. He says we owe him ten million plus interest."

"I'll talk to him," she said.

"Why don't you tell me what Bird of Paradise is instead?"

She grabbed my dick. "Only if you let me suck you off."

I shoved her hand away. "Cut that shit out, Britney. Why my dad hired you is beyond me."

"You may not like what you hear. In any case"—she trailed a hand down my chest—"you weren't too disgusted in Aspen. You couldn't stop fucking me then."

"I'm not that guy anymore."

She pouted. "I liked him better. He was fun."

"Stop fucking with me. Tell me everything."

"The quick and dirty version?" She placed emphasis on *dirty*.

I rolled my eyes. "Any version. Just tell me what's going on." A nearby couple turned toward us as my voice raised.

I led Britany away from the guests.

"Clarke overstretched himself. He bought US and foreign bonds to use as security. His bank covered the losses. Everything's mortgaged, including the estate."

"When were you two going to tell me about this?"

"We were hoping things would turn around. But then Clarke got sick and the bank's restless."

"What was Bird of Paradise supposed to be?"

"A luxury resort. Think adult Disneyland on a Caribbean island."

I frowned. "An adult Disneyland?"

"For those who want complete freedom to fuck whoever they want."

My father was sicker in heart and soul than the cancer eating away at his body. "Why would he want to build something like that?"

"You don't know your father."

She got that right. "How much are we talking about here?"

"About a billion," she said.

I thought about the four billion in Geneva.

Britney read my mind. "I know about the bullion in Geneva. I set it up."

"Did you fuck my dad?"

She shrugged. "We had our fun here and there."

"Here and there?" I could barely look at her.

"Oh, don't look like that. Considering Clarke's appetite for pussy, it shouldn't come as a shock."

"Watch your mouth. That's my dad you're talking about."

"Why you've gone all pale." She chuckled. "My stepfather fucked me when I was thirteen. I enjoyed every inch of his big dick taking my virginity. He couldn't get enough of me after that." She giggled, and it made the hair on the back of my neck stand up. My soul had been polluted.

"That explains a lot." I took a breath. Should I feel sorry? Was she a victim of abuse? "Perhaps you should see someone about that."

Her face scrunched. "Are you kidding me? I don't need a shrink. I wanted my stepfather to fuck me so I could get back at my mom. I hated her."

"You're sick, Britney. I want you out of my life. Take this as your official resignation."

She grabbed my arm. "You can't let me go, Lachie."

I brushed her off. "It's Lachlan to you."

"Ew …I can almost smell the testosterone. Sexy." She leaned in close and lowered her voice. "I've fucked a lot of men in my life. And your dick's the biggest and the hungriest."

"Don't talk like that to me. You're my biggest fucking regret."

"Stop acting like my pussy isn't the best you've ever had." She added in a soft voice, "Geneva's for us."

My hands clenched into fists. "There is no *us*, Britney." I looked at her with hate in my eyes. "I want you out."

She smiled. "Don't you get it? If you try to get rid of me, I'll give all the dirt I have on Peace Holdings to the authorities."

"I'm innocent. Records will show I only took over the company nine months ago."

She giggled again, and it sounded like nails on a chalkboard. "You'd let your own father die in prison?" She raised an eyebrow. "It's a bold choice. I'm impressed."

"They'd go soft on him because he's ill. I'm this close to reporting the company to the authorities myself."

"They wouldn't give a shit about his health. Clarke would go to prison."

I puffed out an agitated breath. I was cornered. Snitch on my father and I'd burn in my own hell of guilt.

And why was I being so loyal to a man whose morals were as rotten as the cancer eating away at him? The answer was simple. Peace Holdings had been set up by my grandfather. I couldn't bring the family name into disrepute. And the thought of my dad in prison or, at the very least, having to sit through trials, along with the media assault, turned me inside out. That was why I couldn't go to the authorities. But Britney didn't need to know that.

I changed the subject. "What happens when the investors find out the truth?"

"They knew the risk. The ones who are bitching and moaning came in during the last two years."

I thought about that. "This is a Ponzi scheme."

"So? They're more common than you think. The trick is to dress them up. We did that. They were investing in a project. If Clarke hadn't gotten sick, everything would be going well. Like it or not, you need me."

I pushed past her. I'd had enough of her and my father's shit for one night.

With a chest tangled in knots, I reentered the ballroom and discovered Miranda chatting with one of my dad's buddies.

Harvey Goldman stood close, whispering in her ear.

He turned and greeted me. "Good evening, Lachlan."

I nodded. "I see you've met Miranda."

"I have. She was telling me about the artwork she acquired for you at the auction."

I glanced at Miranda and we exchanged smiles.

"I'm looking to invest in something new. What have you got?" he asked with one eye on Miranda.

I suspected he was showing off. But I needed some capital for a large waterfront development, and Harvey could bankroll the entire project by himself. He'd made his fortune investing in the biggest Hollywood blockbusters.

After what I'd just learned, we needed to get some legitimate projects moving along. The two developments in San Jose I'd been overseeing were squeaky-clean. However, the lack of cash flow meant they'd be in limbo if I didn't figure something out quick.

"Let's get dinner next week. There's a project in Florida I think you'll like," I said.

"I have a few buddies in Florida. That would give me a good excuse to visit." He chuckled and winked at Miranda.

"I'll be in touch," I responded while taking Miranda by the hand. "I need a quick chat with my girl."

13

MIRANDA

His girl? Lachlan's hand wrapped around mine. My body heated from the contact, and I gazed up at him with a smile that evaporated when I saw the dark look in his eyes. I frowned. Had something happened when he'd left to speak with Britney? I hoped she hadn't convinced him to fire me.

We hovered about, watching couples swirling around the dance floor.

"You've become a popular girl," Lachlan said as he released my hand, leaving a smoldering sensation behind.

"I clean up well, I suppose," I joked, trying to lighten the mood. His intensity had me on edge.

"You look sensational. Did Harvey ask you out?"

I was taken aback, but I told him the truth. "He did."

"Don't feel obligated to go out with him."

"I don't."

He stared deeply into my eyes, revving up my pulse.

"Why are you looking at me like that?" I asked.

"It's strange," he said. "We've only known each other for a few days but you seem so familiar to me. I like talking to you."

I nodded. "Same here."

He ran his hands through his hair. "Things are a mess right now. I'm tempted to fire Britney and hire you in her place."

My heart did a cartwheel. "Sounds like things aren't working out with her."

If Britney left, I could keep my job. Plus, I'd be free to keep attending these charity events with Lachlan without her glaring daggers at me the entire night.

"Trouble is"—he exhaled—"I can't. She's got me over a fucking barrel." He rubbed his neck.

My cartwheel came crashing down.

"This shitstorm must be awful for you. You get a job, and then next thing you know, you're dealing with a car chase, a bitchy manager, the SEC, and a boss dying to visit a secluded island with his admin assistant." A slow grin grew on his face.

Mm... when can we go?

He held my gaze. I was sure I looked like a creature trapped in headlights at night.

He tilted his head. "How about a dance?"

"I don't know how to waltz."

"I'll take it nice and slow." He stared into my eyes again as though he was talking about something more than just dancing.

I gulped as he took my hand and led me out onto the dance floor.

My hand trembled slightly as I placed it on his shoulder. I wanted to wipe my searing palm from where he'd held my hand, but he wrapped his large hand around it.

As his chest touched my shoulder, his scent drifted through my pores, and I couldn't feel my feet. Either he'd lifted me when we moved, or I'd just left my body.

"Relax. I won't eat you." He smiled.

"I wouldn't have thought I was your flavor," I said, wanting to hit myself over the head after speaking the words. Was that the best I could do?

"I like many flavors," he said in a deep drawl that reverberated through my rib cage.

I looked up and was met by a slow, sexy smile. Was he flirting with me?

"Many flavors suggests you're into the whole spectrum of offerings. Not that there's anything wrong with that," I said.

"I'm not gay, Miranda."

I had to laugh. "I wouldn't judge you if you were."

"I'm also not bi. I'm pretty vanilla."

"Vanilla's a classic flavor, I guess."

"Is vanilla your flavor?" he asked.

"I'm a fan of Neapolitan. Why choose just one when you can have three flavors?" I looked up at him. "We are talking about ice cream?"

"What else?" He raised an eyebrow.

We glided along as though in a dream. His fingers laced in mine.

He held me close to his chest, and I breathed in his scent—a blend of the sea and pine cologne.

The chanteuse on stage sang "Close to You," which was apt considering how our bodies melded together as one. We were suddenly alone, the guests now a blur of color like an expressionist painting.

"You're very graceful," he whispered in my ear, setting a spark that traveled to my nipples.

"That's thanks to you. It's almost effortless."

His strong body pressed against mine, and I felt something big and hard throbbing against my leg, making my pulse race.

The song ended, and much to my disappointment, the band took a break.

Lachlan removed his hands, leaving behind a smoldering sensation all over my body.

His eyes held mine again, and once more, I forgot to breathe. "Thanks. I enjoyed that."

"So did I," I said with an embarrassingly thin voice.

He peered over my shoulders. "I'll be back in a minute. Don't go anywhere."

As Lachlan strode away to speak to a male guest, I noticed the guests checking me out again. For someone who'd spent her life unnoticed, this newfound attention startled me.

Lachlan returned, along with his dark mood from earlier.

"Are you okay?" I asked.

"I want to leave. Is that okay with you?"

I shrugged. "Sure."

"I'll have Justin pull the car around."

Britney teetered over and joined us, ignoring me and looking at Lachlan.

I gritted my teeth and focused on the carved dome ceiling.

"You look like you're about to leave," she said.

"Jason Stents just asked me about Bird of Paradise," Lachlan said. "He wants to know where his ten million is. He said you promised to transfer the funds last week."

"I can take care of Jason. He likes to party. I'll take him to dinner, get him some coke, and make a night of it." She ran her tongue over her lips suggestively.

Lachlan shook his head and turned away.

She grabbed him by the arm. "Remember, you need me." Her eyes slid over to me, casting me an icy look.

He shrugged out of her grasp, and taking me by the hand, he led me outside.

I took a deep breath of the warm night air. It was only ten o'clock and the thought of going home dampened my mood as we walked toward our waiting black SUV, where Justin leaned against the side.

"I noticed you hired a driver," I said.

"I thought it was time I stopped taking risks. Especially after that little adventure the other night." He turned and looked at me. "Justin is pulling double duty as my bodyguard."

"I hope you're not in any real danger."

He paused and stared at me for what seemed like a lifetime, stealing my breath again. "Life's pretty messy at the moment. It's nothing I can't handle, though."

I nodded. I wasn't sure what I'd gotten myself into with this job, but Lachlan seemed capable enough, if a little stressed out.

Justin opened the door for me. I thanked him and slid in while Lachlan followed, moving up close.

I caught a hint of Lachlan's scent again and drew him in deeply, imagining that was how hot sex smelled.

"It's early." He glanced down at his Mickey Mouse watch, which amused me. It wasn't exactly the watch of a billionaire. That was why I liked him. He was down-to-earth. Unlike the cocky people I'd met at the ball.

"Want to grab a drink somewhere? Or…"

"Or?" I asked.

"I've got a penthouse downtown. We could go there and play board games." His sculptured lips curled up at one end.

"I'd agree, but it wouldn't be fair to you," I said.

He cocked his head at me. "How so?"

"When it comes to Scrabble, I'm a beast."

He laughed. "Okay, no board games, then."

"I didn't realize you had a place downtown too."

"It's my oasis in the middle of the city. I crashed there a lot up to a year ago, before becoming the CEO." He stared out the window and said almost to himself, "I wouldn't mind returning to those days."

"Why's that?"

He exhaled audibly. "There are a few problems."

"I'm sorry to hear that."

"Nothing I can't handle." He looked at me and smiled. "So should we grab a drink or head back to my place? Actually, I just realized there is something you could do for me."

"That being?"

"My grandfather collected modern art and left it all to me when he passed. There's a dozen Jackson Pollocks, among others. I'd love to know what you think they're worth. I need to free up some cash."

My jaw dropped at the mention of the famous artist. "You haven't had them valued for insurance?"

"Eight years ago."

"I'd love to see them. A dozen Jackson Pollocks, if they're his standard size, could be worth up to a billion dollars."

He whistled. "Fuck." He cocked his head adorably. "Sorry to swear."

"You've met my sister. Don't apologize." His gaze trapped mine again.

"I can't wait to see them," I said.

He touched my hand and looked at me. Those seductive blue eyes registered straight to my nipples. "Thanks for doing this.

Let me know if I'm not paying you enough for your time."

"I've had a great time tonight. The money is just a nice bonus. For a minute there, I thought you'd drop me off at home. That would've been disappointing after all the trouble I went through to look like this." I gestured to the silk fabric of my gown.

"You do look beautiful. But I thought you looked pretty good the other night too." He smiled.

"In my potato sack? Or my leggings?"

"All of it. It's not your clothing that makes you nice to look at." He pointed to my eyes.

It was time to get used to contact lenses, I thought. My eyes were my best feature.

"Ready to see some Pollocks?" He tilted his head.

"I thought you'd never ask." I smiled.

14

LACHLAN

I hated the thought of letting my grandfather's paintings go, but they were my only way of securing Malibu. My childhood home was more important to me.

I expected one day in the distant future I'd have children of my own who would run wildly through the garden or play in the tree house that my grandfather had built. I had too many fond memories of that house. And now, thanks to my grandfather's love of modern art, I'd found a way to keep it.

Miranda studied the large, vibrant canvases I'd lived with for nine years.

She looked from one painting to another. "These are extraordinary."

"My grandfather had a thing for art."

"He chose well. They're worth a fortune."

"How much would you say?" I asked.

"You're sitting on about a billion dollars here, I think. Give or take."

My jaw dropped. "You're kidding me."

She frowned. "Wouldn't you miss them?"

"I will. But there are family debts to clear. I've also got some personal projects on the horizon."

"Sounds like a good plan." She smiled sweetly, drawing my attention to her beautiful rosebud lips. "You won't have any problems selling these. The market's always on the lookout for quality modern art."

"I've got more in the other room," I said.

"More Pollocks?" she asked.

"No. Contemporary art," I said, leading her into the dining

area.

She gasped, shaking her head as though I'd shown her something incredibly rare. "Oh. My. God. Willem de Kooning. You've got de Kooning?"

Miranda moved with little moans of delight from one frame to another.

"I've got a large one in the bedroom. As well as a few others," I added.

"Lead the way," she said.

We entered my bedroom, and Miranda made a beeline for an orange- and-green image of a seated woman.

"Magnificent." She sighed. "I've only seen this in textbooks. And you have the original. Here."

Her enthusiasm was contagious, which made me smile, albeit sadly. I felt a pang of regret at the thought of selling it.

"Can you help me sell these? Discreetly, of course. You'll receive commission."

"You've got documents of provenance?" she asked.

"Sure do."

"Leave it to me. I'll get on it tomorrow…" She trailed off and looked worried. "There is a problem."

"How so?" I asked.

Having her in my bedroom suddenly felt intimate. The old me would have had her naked and screaming my name by now.

I led Miranda out to the living room so I could concentrate on money matters.

I poured us champagne and passed her a glass. "What kind of problem?"

"Britney asked me to resign."

I shook my head. "What a nerve. I'm the boss. Britney doesn't get a say."

"I shouldn't even be telling you. She threatened me. Threatened you too."

"That doesn't surprise me," I replied.

"She's pretty intimidating. She also strikes me as someone who follows through on things."

"Yeah. That's her. Vindictive, nasty, and fucking efficient." A thought struck me suddenly. "What about if you work here instead of the estate?"

"Really?" Her eyes widened slightly. "It's closer to home. And art is my passion."

"Good. Then it's settled. This is your new workplace." I paused. "On one condition."

Her brow knitted.

As I fell into her gorgeous dark eyes, I forgot what I was going to say.

As Miranda looked at me expectantly, I was reminded of how she'd pressed against my body when we danced earlier.

"I'm waiting," she said with a challenging grin.

I sat down on the leather sofa and patted the cushion beside me.

As she sunk down next to me, the delicate scent of her floral perfume steered me onto another path.

"Tell me about your love life," I said.

Miranda looked as though I'd asked her to kiss a skunk.

"That's your one condition?" she asked. "I tell you about my love life?"

I chuckled. She had a feisty side. I liked that about her.

"No. The job's yours. Even if you were a vampire, I'd still want you working for me."

She giggled. "I'm not a fan of blood. You're pretty safe there."

"That's a shame. I'm fond of having my neck bitten."

Miranda gave me a puzzled look. "Is this how you treat all your employees?"

"Nope. But the more I get to know you, the more attracted I become."

"I'm attracted to you too." Her voice quivered as she stared down at her clasped hands. "But I think we should keep things professional."

As someone who didn't mind breaking rules for the sake of pleasure, I was disappointed, but I also wanted to respect Miranda's wishes.

"I understand. I can still ask about your love life, though, can't I?" I couldn't resist.

"There's nothing to tell." She crossed her legs and angled her body away from me.

I knew I'd crossed the line, but I persisted anyway. I was dying to know more about Miranda. "I'm sure you've broken plenty of hearts."

She shook her head. "I've lived a very dull life."

When she turned toward me, I didn't just step over the line, I leapt over it. Before another thought entered my head, I took Miranda into my arms, and my mouth landed on hers.

Her soft lips parted, and my tongue traced the fullness of her lips before entering deeply. She tasted sweet, like ripe fruit.

As my fingers slid down her arm, her soft skin held me captive while I devoured her. Blood charged straight to my dick.

I was reaching for the zipper on her gown when she pulled away and looked at me. "Do I have to sleep with you for this job?"

That was like dropping a block of ice onto my head.

I moved away from her. "Hell no."

My father's womanizing ways entered my thoughts. I wasn't going to be like him, despite Miranda inflaming my libido.

"I'm just attracted to you," I said. "I feel like we know each other well. Hell, I've even crashed on your sofa."

Miranda smiled at that recollection.

She sipped on her drink and looked up at me. Her moist lips parted slightly. "I've never been with a man before."

I nodded. "I understand. Only boys. That makes sense for someone so young. You're only twenty-three."

"That's not what I meant. I'm a virgin." She stared down at her feet.

I nearly dropped my drink.

At her age?

"Oh," was all I could say. She was obviously saving herself for marriage. I respected that. I'd never met a girl like Miranda before. All the girls I'd hung out with were free and easy, just like me.

    I had to take a step back. I wasn't ready for marriage, no matter how attracted I was to Miranda.

15

MIRANDA

I rose from the couch. That kiss still tingled on my lips, and my body burned. If I hadn't moved away, I would have let him take things further. I desperately wanted to give in to my desire, but I had a list of reasons why hooking up with Lachlan would be a bad idea.

I was curious about all the objects on display in his apartment and moved to examine them in detail. If anything, it would help put some distance between me and Lachlan so I could think straight. I stroked a bronze statuette of Mercury, reminiscent of the works of Rodin. Next to that was a doll of a flamenco dancer wearing a ruffled dress. The room was more eclectic than I expected for an ultramodern luxury penthouse.

"You've got so many interesting things in here."

"That was a gift from my mother. She's from Spain," he said, watching me play with the doll's braid.

"It's cute." I turned my attention to the floor-to-ceiling window on one wall. "And the view's spectacular." A telescope on the balcony caught my eye. "Are you into astronomy?"

"Not in the technical sense. But I love gazing up at the moon. Some nights I can even see the moons of Jupiter. Want to take a look with me?"

He slid open the door, and we stepped out onto the balcony. The warm evening air felt so nice, it prickled my skin.

Lachlan fiddled with the telescope and looked into it.

"Come take a look at Jupiter. It's the purplish sparkling star."

It took me a moment, but when I found it, I said, "That's amazing."

"Isn't it? I always get a thrill from seeing it." He became a boy all of a sudden.

He stepped away from the telescope. "The galaxy fills me with wonder."

"How so?" I asked.

"Well for one, the universe gives us vital clues about who we are and how we got here." He pointed to the starlit sky. "Whenever I look up at all those glittering stars and planets, I forget about myself. I like that." He paused for a moment. "It also reminds me just how tiny we are within the scheme of things. Like the stars. Even though stars are their own worlds. As we, as individuals, are our own world."

"You mean the microcosm being a reflection of the macrocosm?" I asked, recalling a similar conversation with my dad.

"Exactly," he said.

A magnetic pull drew me into his turquoise-blue gaze.

I wanted to remove my pretty ball gown and dance with him naked.

"That's deep," I said, snapping out of my dream.

"I have my moments." His eyes softened as he held me captive. He looked different all of a sudden but still dashingly handsome with that perfectly messed up light-brown hair and chiseled features.

Within a blink, his eyes darkened, and that raw need I'd seen earlier returned. His searing attention moved from my eyes to my lips and down to my spiked nipples.

I sighed internally and had to turn around and head back inside.

"So do you think you'll be able to work from here?" he asked, following me back in.

"Oh. yes." I paused to think. "Would I get in your way?"

"I'm not here that often. Most of the time, I'm in Malibu. I love to surf." His half smile dimpled his cheeks, and I had the sudden urge to kiss him and continue where we'd left off earlier.

That kiss had melted my brain. If he were to touch me again, I'd turn into a puddle.

I thought about money, about art. Anything but Lachlan's lips close to mine. I even worried steam might billow from my ears.

"You can stay here. No commuting," he said with a grin.

My eyebrows shot up. "That would be awesome. Are you sure I wouldn't be crowding you?"

What if you bring home a girl? A knot twisted at the thought of that.

"Nope. I'm only in the city for these boring charity events, which I might have to put a pause to."

That was disappointing. I liked dressing up. "What do I say to Britney? Should I go in tomorrow and resign officially?"

"No. This is between us, and it's none of Britney's business."

"Okay." I grabbed my purse. "I should probably be getting home. I have a lot to sort out before the morning."

He walked to the kitchen at the other side of the huge open-concept space. Standing at the island, he lifted the bottle of champagne. "Stay for one more drink."

He refilled my empty glass.

It was hard to say no. I could see he liked the company.

I also liked spending time with him.

Lachlan joined me on the leather sofa. His lips curled up at one end. "I hope you can forgive me for that earlier kiss. I couldn't resist."

I shook my head. "It was nice."

Again, our eyes locked.

Job. Money.

"Let me get through this process in one piece."

He chuckled. "What do you think I'll do to you?"

"Break my heart." That just shot out, surprising me.

He studied me as though trying to solve a complex puzzle. "I'm seriously attracted to you." He played with a silver ring on one of his long fingers. "I'm just not looking for a relationship at the moment. If you weren't a virgin, I'd be all over you by now."

"What makes you think I would've let you?" I asked.

"Can't blame a guy for trying." His grin faded. "I do take no for an answer."

"I can't imagine any women turning you down," I replied.

"Different strokes for different folks, right? Not everybody loves vanilla." His voice deepened on the last part and made my pulse quicken.

He tilted his head. "Are you saving yourself for marriage? I'm just curious."

I took a deep breath. "I'm not saving myself. It's just that men have never really noticed me." I shrugged. "Grad school was challenging, so I was more focused on finishing my degree instead of hooking up. I know I could stand to lose a few pounds too."

"You're perfect, Miranda. And you had the attention of all the men at the ball tonight." He arched an eyebrow. "I'm sure guys have always noticed you. You just didn't see it." He took a sip of his drink. "I wish I'd been more like you in college. Most young guys are only interested in one thing."

"And you're speaking from experience?"

He exhaled. "Guilty as charged." I searched for his usual playfulness but was met with a frown. "The more I think about it, hooking up with a different girl every weekend in college didn't really make me any happier."

I coughed.

"Too much information?" he asked.

I shook my head. "No. I like honesty. Plenty of people have that same experience in college."

"I guess." He sniffed. "I'm not too proud of it."

"And now?" I asked.

"Some things happened in my life and I decided I didn't want to be that guy anymore …" He looked me in the eye. "I don't miss it. I've been looking for more of this."

As his hand landed on mine, I swallowed tightly. "This?"

"Talking to someone smart and real." He paused for my response, but I was speechless.

"You're the total package, Miranda, beauty and brains. I love how passionate you are when you talk about art, even if I don't know much about it. When all of this is done, will you have dinner with me?"

"I will gladly have dinner with you, Lachlan."

And I hope you'll have me for dessert afterward.

16

LACHLAN

I made sure the fridge was stocked for Miranda's stay. Her comfort was important to me. I would pay off my father's debts then hopefully fuck Miranda.

Although she deserved more than a hookup, I wasn't ready for a relationship. That was why God invented the hand.

Sobering thoughts of my stepmother entered my head. I wondered about Manuel. If he wasn't my dad's, whose child was he? My father and Tamara's eyes were blue while Manuel's were dark. My chest deflated at the prospect of a paternity test.

Security buzzed through the intercom, saying Miranda was here to see me. "Send her up."

After last night, I couldn't get thoughts of her gorgeous body out of my head. The way her auburn hair cascaded over her shoulders and the feel of her voluptuous body pressed against mine as we'd danced drove me wild. Then there was our kiss.

I had to jerk off, and I came harder than usual. Miranda had raised my bar. Literally. Her intelligence, grace, and beauty made for an irresistible mix.

When the elevator doors opened, I said, "Good morning."

"Good morning," she replied.

I handed her a key card. "Sometime today, go down to security. They'll get you set up."

She nodded. "Sure."

I noticed she only carried a handbag and laptop. "Not planning on staying? My offer still stands."

"I thought I'd get down to work and see how things go first." She seemed a little flustered. "Is something wrong?"

"Britney called me first thing this morning. Said she had a

change of heart and wanted me to come in."

"What did you say?"

She took a deep breath. "I lied and told her I couldn't work there anymore."

I nodded.

"She told me that I'd be blacklisted."

"Don't worry. I'll write you a glowing recommendation letter after this is done. Anyway, I've got other plans. I like the art world, and you're talented."

Miranda studied me for a moment. Her puzzled expression turned into a grin. "But it's not your world. I was finger painting and flicking through my dad's art books while you slurped back cornflakes with a silver spoon."

I shook my head. "That's bullshit."

"Oh?" She grinned.

"I hate cornflakes. And I don't slurp."

She chuckled. "Jokes aside, I'm grateful for any kind of employment until I can find something in my field. Thanks again for this."

"You're really helping me out. If I can help you in return, all the better," I said. My motives for helping her might not have been completely selfless, but I did want to see her succeed.

I held her gaze. Miranda was just as beautiful in broad daylight.

I rubbed my hands together. "Help yourself to anything in the kitchen."

She smiled. "I already ate breakfast, but coffee sounds good."

"I've got one of those fancy-schmancy Italian espresso machines."

"That's cool. I was a barista for a while. I should manage."

"Good. I'm heading out now. Make yourself at home, and call me if you need anything."

"I'll take photos of the paintings first and compile a portfolio. Where are the documents of provenance you said you had?"

"Follow me."

We entered my study, which housed my muted drum kit and

a desk in disarray.

Miranda's look of surprise made me smile. "I normally practice at the estate. I have a large soundproof room there."

She ran a hand along the rim of the snare drum.

"You're welcome to play any time."

She laughed. "I should be able to control that urge."

Pulling out a folder, I handed it to her. "Hopefully, everything's there. I've never actually looked inside it."

Our hands touched as she took the folder, causing a spark up my forearm.

"I'll leave you to it. Remember to visit security later."

"Will do. And thank you."

I was about to leave when I removed a credit card from my wallet and handed it to her. "Use this if you need anything."

She nodded.

It was hard to leave. I'd fallen captive to those expressive dark eyes again. I blamed my inappropriate behavior last night on champagne, but in the sobering light of day, I'd fallen into the same drugged stupor. She was soft. Strong. Real. And seriously curvy.

"See you later." I saluted her and left.

After visiting my father, I returned to Malibu. He'd slept for most of the time, leaving my questions about Britney and Geneva unanswered.

When I walked through the terrace into the living room, I found my half brother playing with plastic blocks.

Sherry, Manuel's nanny, smiled as I tickled his belly. He was sweet and cute, especially the way his large brown eyes danced with exuberance. There was a familiar glint in his gaze. My dad must have had it all wrong, I thought, ruffling the five-year-old's hair.

Heading into the kitchen, I spotted Tamara painting her nails.

"You're here," I said.

"Why wouldn't I be?" she asked with a Southern twang.

"You haven't visited Dad for two months. I figured you'd

moved to Miami for good."

Her lips curled up. "You wish."

I wasn't about to contradict her.

"This is my home." Manuel ran up to her, eager to show her the impressive-looking monster he'd built. True to form, she ignored him.

Whenever I could, I'd play with Manuel and take him to the beach or for a spin in my car to buy ice cream. Sherry was a great asset too. The last thing I wanted was for Manuel to suffer because of parents who didn't give a shit.

My dislike for Tamara extended beyond her being my stepmother.

She rose from the sofa and sashayed off, wearing a skin-tight outfit that left nothing to the imagination. Addicted to cosmetic procedures, she looked ridiculous. As if her fake tits weren't big enough, now she had a giant ass to match.

After grabbing some juice from the fridge, I headed off to deal with Britney.

My father's former office was at the front of the house. It was a large sunny room boasting pre-war architectural embellishments, lined with shelves of books that had belonged to my grandfather. The only book my dad had ever held was a ledger.

I entered the adjacent office and found Britney glancing at her screen.

She looked me up and down. "The new girl's gone."

"Can't say I blame her. You weren't exactly nice."

Her eyes narrowed. "Did you have something to do with it?"

"It's got nothing to do with you."

"I'll make sure she never works in this town again."

"Don't flatter yourself. You're not that fucking important."

"I am to you. Remember that," she said.

"Where are we at with Bird of Paradise?"

"The SEC have gone quiet for now," she said.

"For now?"

"I have some incriminating files. As protection."

I braced my palms on her desk and leaned forward. "What do

you want, Britney?"

"You." She rose and stood next to me.

"That's never going to happen."

"Good luck getting the money in Geneva without me."

I blew out a breath and stalked out.

Why did my father trust Britney so much? He may have been many things, but he wasn't stupid.

I walked back to the kitchen and found Tamara talking softly and giggling on her phone. When she noticed me, she quickly ended her call, gulping down a shot of vodka.

"It's a bit early for that."

"My grandmother's Russian. She's over eighty, and she always starts her day with a shot. I'm just following tradition."

I recalled how she'd drank while breast-feeding. After I called her out on it, she slurred that she'd stopped, bouncing her tits. "Got to look after my girls."

I turned away. She'd been in my life six years too long. Her being there, in the house that my great-grandparents had built, made me sick.

I heard Manuel scream and looked at Tamara. "Shouldn't you go to him?"

"It's Sherry's job to deal with him."

I rolled my eyes and ran out to the courtyard to see what had happened.

Manuel was on a chair while Sherry stuck a bandage on his knee.

"He tripped," she said, looking up at me. "Nothing's broken, thankfully." She smiled. Sherry had a serene nature that always amazed me, and Manuel adored her.

I studied his little face, which had calmed. "How are you, little buddy?"

"It's sore," he said.

I made a silly face, and a cute smile touched his lips. The smile was oddly familiar, and as I studied his dark features, my mother's side of the family came to mind.

"He'll be all right," said Sherry, helping him up.

"Nothing a nice banana split can't fix," I said.

At that suggestion, Manuel brightened immediately.

I went inside and passed Tamara, who'd been watching from the French doors. "I see you stopped his whining. You've got the magic touch. Maybe I should fire Sherry and hire you instead." Her piercing giggle grated.

She came and stood close, eye fucking me. If Manuel hadn't been within earshot, I would have told her to fuck off. Instead, I rolled my eyes and walked back outside.

Manuel, Sherry, and I headed out to get ice cream, with Sherry driving. Wearing a big smile, Manuel seemed to have forgotten about his fall.

I planned to make sure he had a happy childhood. Maybe another visit to Disneyland. We'd already visited it when he was four. Brent had tagged along, and jumped on all the rides. Manuel had a ball. He opened up around us, especially Brent, which didn't surprise me, since my brother had never really grown up.

When Brent passed, Manuel took it badly. He became even more distant than usual, going off his food for a few days. I would take him to the beach and for rides in the car, which eventually helped him come out of his shell.

17

MIRANDA

I'd lost track of time. Standing and stretching, I gave a start when I checked the time and saw hours had passed. I was just finishing up when my phone lit up with Lachlan's name. "Hey," I said.

"How's my favorite art expert doing?"

His compliment made me smile. "Great. I've completed an inventory of the Pollocks. I think we should start there."

"Sounds good."

"Tomorrow I'm meeting with a prominent dealer to see if he has any clients who'd be interested in your collection."

"Great, keep me posted. How are you enjoying your new office?"

"It's stunning here," I said, looking out at the blue sky. "I've never been so high up before."

"Are you staying there tonight?" he asked.

"After I stop by Harry's and pack some things, yes. Are you sure I won't be crowding you?"

"I'm mainly in Malibu. I'll give you a heads-up if I plan to crash there."

"It's your place," I said.

"I need you to be comfortable. I might pop in later, though."

I hesitated for a moment. "Okay. Sure." What else could I say? *No. Stay away. I can't think while you're around.* "I better get moving, then. I have some packing to do."

"Bye for now."

"Bye." I hung up and took a deep breath. Even on the phone, his smoky voice played havoc with my hormones.

Elevated by sexual attraction and high-end art, I sprinted to my old Honda. Like a hobo among Hollywood A-listers, the car was so out of place parked next to sleek luxury models. Even the security guard had given me a dubious glance when I'd first arrived.

My car wasn't the only thing looking tired and worn out. My outfit reminded me I needed some new clothes, if only to look the part when visiting dealers.

In the art scene, the only people who got around in worn clothes were either artists or eccentric collectors. I couldn't afford designer clothing, but I needed to make an effort. I chewed on my bottom lip. My credit card was maxed out.

I wondered if Lachlan would mind me asking for an advance.

When I arrived home, I found Harriet slouched on the sofa, looking exhausted. She was on call all week, and I hadn't seen her for a few days.

"Where's Ava?" I asked.

"She's with Mom and Dad. I don't know what to do without you here to help out." She let out a loud sigh.

"It was always going to be a temporary arrangement, Harry. I need to work."

"But to move out?"

"It's not permanent, just while I'm working on getting Lachlan's collection sold. I'm sure Dad won't mind taking Ava to school in the mornings," I said. "She'll be in dance classes soon, and I'm sure he won't mind helping out there too."

"How am I supposed to afford that?" she asked.

"It's on the house. Lachlan's mother owns a dance studio, so it was his suggestion," I replied. "I'll see you later. I have an important meeting tomorrow and I need to get some new clothes."

"That's generous of him."

"He's actually really nice. And he liked Ava."

"You're going shopping now?"

I nodded. "I hope so. I've got to speak to my new boss first." I cringed at the thought of asking for an advance.

I sent a text to Lachlan.

The phone pinged immediately.

Harriet watched with interest. "Mm… he's keen."

I shrugged, despite entertaining a warm fuzzy feeling.

The text read: *Use that card I gave you earlier. It's for any business expense you deem necessary. Catch you later tonight.*

"So?" asked Harriet.

"I'm shopping. Want to come along? I can show you where I'm staying."

She sprang up. "That sounds like fun. Let me just change first." She pulled at her scrubs with a grimace.

"No rush. I'll pack a few things in the meantime."

Half an hour later, Harriet had changed, and I'd managed to toss essentials into a duffle bag.

We headed to a nearby shopping mall. I hadn't shopped for clothes in ages. Most of my wardrobe came from thrift stores or consignment shops.

After an hour of shopping without buying anything, Harriet was visibly frustrated. To placate her, I suggested she pick out some outfits for me. Unsurprisingly, she opted for short skirts and fitted blouses. I met her at the fitting rooms, carrying two pencil skirts.

Harry rolled her eyes. "Still living your best librarian life, I see."

I laughed. She was probably right. But I needed to look professional for now.

A green shirt I selected gained her approval, and I grabbed a pink one too.

I leaned in for a cardigan, and Harriet said, "Are you fucking kidding? You're not visiting Grandma."

She was right. With her help, I settled on a sleek black blazer.

We were on our way back to the car when Harriet stopped and entered a lingerie store.

"Why are we stopping here?" I asked.

"You need something sexy in case your boss undresses you." She arched an eyebrow.

That little pleasant throb in my clit started again at the mention of Lachlan.

She picked up a red lacy bra complete with matching thong and dangled them before me. "This is nice."

"I don't think that qualifies as a business expense," I protested.

"You'll be ready to slay in your meeting tomorrow if you're confident, sis. Feeling sexy is all part of it."

I looked at the price tag and my jaw dropped. "Holy shit. That's more than my student loan payment each month."

"Buy it. If Lachlan's into you, you need sexy underwear."

It was hard to resist that logic. I ended up buying two silk camisoles, plus the bra and panty set.

"I hope he doesn't get pissed off if he sees I spent three hundred bucks on lingerie," I said as we headed to the parking garage.

"I think he'll be turned on by it." Harriet's wicked grin made me roll my eyes.

"Business expenses, really?" I said, shaking my head.

"He's into you, so I think that counts."

I shook my head. "I'm not going there, Harry. In addition to him being my boss, he's too good-looking. He'll break my heart."

"You have to fuck sometime, Andie. Why not go for Lachlan instead of some one-minute man."

"One-minute man?" I asked.

"Someone who blows his load before you get off."

I sighed. "That's definitely not Lachlan. He's virility incarnate."

She giggled. "I'm not sure what that means, but it sounds hot."

"It means that I felt his hard-on against my thigh when we danced at that last charity event."

She opened the door to the car. "Really? You danced?"

I nodded. "We waltzed. I tried, anyway. I wasn't very good at it."

"Fuck a waltz. I'd have given him a lap-dance then bent down in front of him without panties," said Harriet.

I laughed. "You're sick, Harry."

"Was he big?"

"It felt huge," I said, flushing from the memory. I'd already had to replace my vibrator's batteries twice since then. Thinking about taking his thick cock in my hand before placing it in my mouth had become my top fantasy.

"Anyway, I need this job, so I have to remain focused," I said, leaving the mall and merging into traffic.

"Has he kissed you?" she asked.

A smile grew at the memory of his sensual, warm lips turning my night into magic.

She squealed. "You're shitting me," she said. "Oh. My. God. When were you going to tell me?"

"I haven't seen you all week."

"Why the fuck didn't you pounce on him?"

"Hello. He's my boss."

"So what?" She rolled her eyes.

We sang along to Taylor Swift as we headed to the luxurious penthouse that would serve as my temporary home.

As I drove into the parking garage for the complex, Harriet whistled. "This is really impressive. Is a company car another perk of this new job? Your car's pretty busted. Imagine if clients see you in it."

I let out a sigh. "One thing at a time. I'll Uber it. It'll be easier."

We climbed out of the car, and I grabbed my duffle bag.

Carrying my shopping bags, Harriet virtually skipped along. "This is amazing. I'm proud of you, sis."

"It's way more than anything I could have expected." I scanned my key card, and the private elevator opened. Harriet looked suitably impressed.

When the elevator delivered us straight into the penthouse, Harriet jumped out, shook her head in disbelief, and walked straight over to the balcony.

"Woo-hoo! We're at the top of the world. This is so high up." She peered down. "Shit. It's making me dizzy."

I left her there and headed for my new bedroom.

Harriet followed me in and sniffed the air. "I can almost smell sex in the air."

I chuckled. "You've got sex on the brain." I hung my new purchases in the closet then started to unpack. "Let me put all this away, and then we'll watch a movie or something."

"Are you kidding? This is my night off. We're going out."

"I can't. I've got an early meeting tomorrow."

She spread her hands wide and tilted her head. "Let's grab dinner and a drink."

I thought about it and agreed. It had been a big day. A big week. I could use a stiff drink and a meal somewhere relaxing.

18

LACHLAN

A rush of wind charged through every sinew in my body as a powerful force propelled me along. I shifted my weight carefully, bending my knees slightly. This wave had my name on it.

Swallowed by the watery tunnel, adrenaline pumped through me. As a deafening roar enveloped me, it was either conquer or be conquered. There was little room for error in that merciless sea, prepared to devour its victims.

The thrill was well worth the risk.

I exited the perfect tube, yelling with glee.

Salty spray hit my face, and the wave carried me back to shore.

It didn't get much better than that.

We'd been catching waves for over an hour and I would have loved to have kept surfing, but I needed to get some work done.

Reveling in the endorphin rush, I unzipped my wetsuit to my waist, indulging in the sun's warmth as I combed through my hair.

Orlando Thornhill untied his ankle strap. "That last wave was fucking awesome. Rode it all the way," he said, wiping his face with his towel.

"It's been pumping the past few days. I just haven't had time to get here lately. I was way overdue for some surfing."

"Good old vitamin sea." He chuckled. "So when are we jamming again?"

"Wish we could go right now. I've just got so much happening."

"How's your dad doing?"

"About the same. Thanks for asking," I said, wiping down my

board.

"There's a jam tonight at the Red House."

"Are you playing?" I asked.

"Sure am. Dad's coming as well."

"Awesome. I haven't heard Aidan play for a while. He just gets better each time," I said.

He smiled. "Miles should be there too."

"He's got some pretty cool chops for a kid."

"Kid? He's nineteen," said Orlando with a laugh. "I promised Juni and Sam I'd make sure he doesn't go near alcohol."

I laughed. "Oh, so now you're his babysitter?"

"If only they knew." He chuckled.

Orlando's tanned face screamed bad boy. "Are you still playing with that jazz fusion band?"

He nodded. "Round Midnight."

"That's a great name. You'll make Thelonious Monk proud."

"Hope so." He smiled. "I'm really into Wes Montgomery and John McLaughlin at the moment."

"Great guitarists. Very different in style."

"I like variety." He shrugged. "My grandfather also exposed me to Hendrix and Jeff Beck."

"You're in good hands there," I said.

"You should be in a band, Lachie. You're the hottest drummer in town. We could use a drummer like you."

"Who's been saying that?"

"My dad. And anyone that's ever jammed with you, including some dude named Eddie. He said he was one of your old band members? He played a set with us at the Red House last time. Great sax player. He's turned up to a few rehearsals as well. His chick caused a few issues, though."

"Was that Jane?" I asked.

"Maybe? I didn't catch her name," he said. "She's got a few tattoos on her arms. Her hair's purple. And she's got a pierced tongue."

"Yeah, that's Jane. I used to date her. She doesn't handle her liquor that well."

"Some girl started talking to Eddie, and Jane lost it. She threw her drink all over Eddie and pulled the other chick's hair. It was insane."

I shook my head. Yep, that was definitely Jane. She'd stalked me after I told her it wasn't working out. It had been a while since I'd seen her, and maybe her relationship with Eddie was the reason why.

"I'll try to pop in tonight. I like the kit there."

He nodded. "I'll tell Dad. He'll like that."

I picked up my board. "Later then."

With my board tucked under my arm, I climbed the steps to the estate. Miranda came to mind again. I couldn't stop thinking about that kiss and how she felt in my arms. But she was a virgin, and that came with a lot of responsibility.

I was so lost in my thoughts, I nearly bumped into Tamara in the hallway. Her sheer blouse revealed a skimpy bikini underneath. "The pool boy's been here again?"

"No." Her eyes started at my face and traveled down to my naked torso. "Why would you ask that?"

I moved past her. "Got to wash the salt off."

"Do you want me to join you?" she asked.

I ignored her. Even if she hadn't been my father's wife, I still wouldn't have fucked Tamara. There was something so twisted in that botoxed face of hers.

"I won't tell if you don't," she said with a high-pitched giggle, following me down the hallway. I turned again, ready to tell her to fuck off when she placed her hand in her bikini bottom and played with herself.

"Cut that shit out, Tammy. You're married. To my father."

"That's never stopped me before. And Brent didn't seem to mind."

"What?"

"Your brother loved having my mouth around his cock." She raised a brow and sauntered off.

Brent had been fucking Tamara? Or was it just a blow job? And how did that make it any better?

I followed her. "Did you fuck Brent?"

"Wouldn't you like to know?" She reached out to stroke my chest. "I saw you getting your nice big dick sucked one night. It really turned me on. I'm all wet now." She ran her tongue over her lips.

"You're fucking sick." I walked off. That was the second time that day Jane had come up in conversation. How stupid of me for letting her blow me by the pool, thinking nobody would notice.

My family were all sick, except for my mother. She was so obsessed with her career she'd never really cared about the women my father screwed practically in front of her.

I jumped into the shower in the downstairs bathroom, sighing with pleasure as hot water cascaded over me, washing off salt, sand, and Tammy's filthy words.

I stroked my dick and shut my eyes as I fantasized having Miranda naked and hot, straddling me.

Just as I was about to blow, I sensed a presence.

Tamara joined me in the shower, dropped to her knees and grabbed my cock. "You're hung like a fucking horse. And so hard…"

Before I could say anything, she'd wrapped her lips around me.

"Fuck off," I said, pulling away from her. Her teeth scraped along my dick, but I was too shocked to feel anything.

"Oh, come on. A little blow job won't hurt."

"Get the hell out of here," I snapped.

I gently pushed her away. But then she lost her balance and stumbled back, and a sickening crack echoed off the tiled floor.

I looked down, and the water had turned red. Turning off the faucets, I yelled, "Fuck!"

Britney came running into the bathroom.

"What happened?" she asked.

Although only a few seconds had passed, it felt like ages. Everything seemed to be moving in slow motion.

"What are you doing here?" I asked, regretting that I'd opted for the ground floor shower, which happened to be close to the office.

Britney stared down at Tamara then looked at me. "Is she dead?"

I knelt down and ran my finger along her neck, feeling for a pulse. I let out a loud sigh of relief.

"She's alive." I looked up at Britney. "Quick, call nine-one-one."

She didn't move, and her eyes wandered down my body. Forgetting I was naked, I grabbed a towel and wrapped it around my waist.

"Were you about to fuck her?" she asked, following me while I hunted for my phone.

"No fucking way. She came in while I was showering."

My heart raced like mad as I looked for my cell.

In contrast, Britney remained coolheaded. When I couldn't find my phone, she passed me hers. "You were showering together before you planned to fuck her?"

"She entered uninvited," I snapped, shaking my head as it dawned on me just how bad it looked.

I got through to the 911 operator and explained that Tamara had slipped in the shower.

After I hung up, I followed Britney back into the bathroom. "I should just tell the paramedics exactly what happened."

"They'll never believe you. Just make it look like she was showering alone and she had an accident."

I thought about this for a moment. The last thing I needed was for the scandal-hungry media to get involved. It would only throw up all kinds of questions. And Tamara would probably point the finger at me. How could I prove otherwise?

"Okay," I said, rubbing my neck.

The sight of blood, along with having to lie, made me want to puke.

Britney pointed at Tamara's heels. "Who takes a shower wearing those?"

I noticed blood on my feet and wiped them down with a T-shirt I had lying about.

Britney, meanwhile, bent down and removed Tamara's shoes. "You better get dressed," she said, as though we were about to go on a picnic. I sensed she was getting off on the drama.

After I threw on jeans and a T-shirt, I returned to the ugly scene that had turned my day upside down.

Fuck. Fuck. Fuck.

Britney stood by watching with her arms crossed.

"Go wait for the ambulance," I said.

She nodded and left.

As I bent down to check on Tamara, she stirred and moaned.

"Are you okay?" I asked.

"Oh …" She groaned, touching her scalp.

"Don't move," I said. "An ambulance is on its way." I grabbed a bathrobe for her.

"You did this," she croaked.

"You know that's not true," I said, watching her trying to stand up. "Maybe you should wait until the paramedics check you out."

"I'm fine," she said, wobbling as she tried to stand.

I took her arm to steady her. "You're not. You're bleeding"

"Why did you remove my shoes?" she asked.

Acid dripped down my throat just as Britney returned to tell us that the ambulance had arrived.

19

MIRANDA

I sank into the white leather sofa in the reception area and waited for my meeting with prominent LA art dealer, Florian Storm. Apart from a huge abstract painting on the wall, there wasn't much to look at in that gleaming white space.

My eyes settled on the mirrored conversation of cylindrical and rectangular buildings in reflection with each other. The sliver of blue sky here and there softened an otherwise hard-edged skyline. Blurring my eyes, I turned it into a work of art. A strange habit I'd developed as a child.

I snapped out of my daydream when a man wearing red-rimmed glasses approached me. Dressed in red slacks and a shirt with a print of an expressionist portrait, he wore his love of art literally on his sleeve.

"Florian Storm."

I rose and shook the hand he offered me. "Miranda Flowers."

"Pleased to meet you."

I followed him into his office, where, resembling an art gallery, the space was a refreshing departure from the stark minimalism of the rest of the building.

He pointed to a seat. "Please."

I sat down in front of his antique desk.

"This is the most exciting collection we've seen for some time." He spoke with an English accent. "I'll have no problems selling these. There's an overwhelming interest in Pollock. When hasn't there been?" He chuckled. "I have a Russian client who's obsessed."

"I see. Will you also go public with this sale?" I asked.

"I would prefer to sell everything in one go to a single collector. The fact it's a well-matched collection helps. Mid-twentieth-century American art is highly sought after amongst serious collectors."

"That doesn't surprise me," I said. "It seems to take forty to fifty years for art to gather its admirers."

He nodded slowly. "Where do you hail from? We haven't dealt with you before. I can't recall seeing you around the scene."

"I only just completed my masters in art history last year, so I'm new to the scene. My advisor was James O'Donnell."

"Jamie's great, isn't he?"

"Oh, you know each other?" I asked.

"This is a small scene."

"Of course. Silly me."

"You're not silly. You, dear girl, are very enterprising. I'm impressed with how you've compiled this catalogue." His infectious smile warmed my face. All my hard work was starting to pay off.

"Thank you. That's very kind of you," I said.

"No need to thank me. Tell me, are you freelancing at the moment?"

I took a deep breath. "I'm working for Peace Holdings. After this sale goes through, I'm not sure what's next."

"I might have something for you here," he said. "Your notes are learned and immaculately detailed. I could use someone like you working for me."

I sat up tall. "Thank you. It was a labor of love."

He studied me for a moment and nodded. "You'd be a great asset. There's nothing like someone fresh to invigorate the scene."

"That sounds really exciting and something I'd love."

"What are we looking at pricewise for the collection?"

His sudden shift in subject was jarring. I'd been inwardly dancing a conga line at the prospect of working for such an illustrious art dealer.

"Our commission is ten percent," he added.

"We'd like to see how the market responds and go from there," I said.

He studied me closely. "Of course, that commission could be reviewed."

He waited for a response, but I remained quiet.

Was he offering me a job in return for selling the art through him?

"May I ask if you've approached other dealers?" he asked.

"You were my first choice. Stormy Galleries has a great reputation when it comes to modern art," I said. "That said, it's my intention to get the best price for my client."

Client? My boss? My crush? I smiled nonchalantly. *Client* had a nice ring to it.

"Naturally." He smiled. "When can we arrange a viewing?"

"Whenever you like," I said.

"Excellent." He stood and lingered. "Perhaps we can discuss the position I have in mind for you over lunch?"

"I'd like that," I said.

He walked me to the reception area. "Thank you for coming to us first. I think we can work well together and deliver some fabulous results." He shook my hand. "I'll be in touch soon."

"Sounds great. Thank you again," I said, smiling brightly.

I walked out of the pristine lobby with my shoulders pulled back and feeling like the world was mine to play with.

I couldn't stop thinking about Florian Storm's offer. To work for such a highly regarded dealer would truly launch my career.

The only downside was that I'd miss working for Lachlan.

On the other hand, if I was no longer an employee of Peace Holdings, there was nothing stopping me from hooking up with him.

My heart raced at that prospect.

I took a deep breath and headed back to the penthouse.

***

I woke suddenly after hearing someone moving about in the penthouse. Sitting up, I grabbed my cell and discovered it was

2:00 a.m.

It must have been Lachlan, I thought, rubbing my face and yawning. Who else could it have been? Considering the CIA-style security, I couldn't imagine an intruder.

Lachlan had seemed so remote when I'd called him earlier to tell him how my meeting went. With a rushed tone, he'd said we'd talk later. Accustomed to his amiable manner, his brusque manner had me pressing pause on that Hollywood romance rolling away in my head.

I must have had rocks in my head to think Lachlan Peace could become my happily ever after.

He probably just wanted a quick fuck, and after he heard *virgin,* he ran for the hills.

"Ouch!" echoed from the kitchen.

I jumped out of bed and ran out to see what had happened.

Lachlan rubbed his elbow while wincing. He looked up and jumped at my sudden appearance.

It was cooler in the kitchen than the bedroom. Shivering, I wasn't wearing much, since I fell asleep in a short T-shirt and panties.

He stared at me for what seemed a long time. His eyes left my face and trailed down my half naked state, making my nipples, with a mind of their own, spike my palms.

"I'm a little over the limit," he slurred, combing back a stray strand. "I'm heading to bed."

"Give me a minute to grab some stuff from the bedroom."

Wearing fitted jeans and a long-sleeve blue polo that accented those ridiculously blue eyes and clung to his big shoulders and biceps, Lachlan made my heart skip a few beats.

"No need," he said, after taking a tour of my body with that smoldering gaze. "I'll just crash on the sofa."

"But it's your bed. I don't mind crashing on the sofa."

As I clutched my arms, waiting for a response, he kept staring at me. The air between us seemed to spark. Or was that my steamy breath?

"Go back to bed, Miranda. Sorry to wake you." He leaned

against the counter.

I went back to the bedroom, wondering if he'd remember this in the morning.

As I lay there, I felt wide-awake knowing he was in the other room. Part of me wanted him to join me in bed, pick up where we left off the other night. He wouldn't have to say or do much for that to happen. Or at least have his hands all over me.

I shook my head. I needed to keep this strictly professional. And then there was his earlier aloof manner. But his eyes burned when he noticed me semi-naked. Maybe he had a split personality.

The memory of him openly eye fucking me made my core ache. I opened my thighs wide and stroked my clit, imagining his big dick in my mouth. It didn't take long for fireworks, of the combustive, earth-shattering kind to explode between my legs.

20

LACHLAN

My back was stiff after sleeping on the couch. Last night was a blur. I ran into a few friends I hadn't seen in a while and ended up having one shot too many. After the bartender cut me off, I'd headed back to my apartment.

Was it an excuse to be around Miranda? I rubbed my pounding head. The truth wasn't as sexy. I couldn't face the shitshow back at the estate. Crashing here was me avoiding reality, not because of some subconscious desire to fuck Miranda. Although seeing her beautiful ass peeking out and braless in that tiny T-shirt soon changed that.

I headed into the kitchen for some water. My furry tongue threatened biological warfare. Maybe I'd have some aspirin too.

Still wearing very little, Miranda made coffee. That curvy butt looked so fucking squeezable, and the thought of rubbing myself against it immediately made my morning wood spring to action.

Her tits bounced as she moved around, and it was just plain fucking difficult to think straight around her.

"You're as quiet as a mouse. I didn't know you were in here," I said, realizing that apart from my boxer briefs, I was naked.

Grabbing a carton of juice from the fridge, I hid behind the door, hoping that the cool air would convince my dick to chill out.

"I'll get out of your way," she said.

She turned away, and copping an eyeful of her curvy ass, I felt steam oozing out of my pores.

Not having had sex for over six months hurt.

"You're not in my way," I said at last. The blood had drained away from my brain and had headed down south. "I'm going to hop in the shower."

I entered the bathroom and spotted a pair of panties on the floor. After a second or two, I picked them up. As I went to deposit them on the seat, I dangled the little red thong.

I stepped under the showerhead and jerked off. I blew so hard, I had to bite my lip from yelling out.

As I dried off and got dressed, the events from yesterday popped into my head, and a sinking feeling emerged.

Britney had reported that Tamara was fine and had been released. There was no bleeding in the brain or mental impairment. I hated my stepmother but not enough to wish her harm.

After I left the apartment, I decided to visit my mother at her studio. It had been some time since catching up, and I needed to be around my one good family member.

The sounds of a guitar strumming and foot-stomping grew louder the closer I got to the converted warehouse, which was now a dance school. Each show my mother produced had received raving reviews.

Warming to the rhythms I'd grown up listening to, I had fond memories of my dance-obsessed mom practicing at home. She loved to tell people I'd kicked along with her stomping rhythms when she'd been pregnant with me.

Standing with her back to the mirror, she banged her foot and clapped in time with the guitarist, who was also her boyfriend. Juan was only seven years older than me. After I raised an eyebrow at the age difference between them, she'd reminded me that my father was with a woman half his age, and no one batted an eye at that.

I couldn't argue there.

Juan was a skilled and accomplished guitarist, and I'd grown to like him. I appreciated his devotion and support for my mother.

She looked over at me and smiled.

I watched on as her students' footwork built up to a crescendo. It was such a fiery art form and a complex one at that. They whipped their heads around, performing a frenzied turn, finishing on the beat with their arms up.

"Olé!" yelled my mother.

The class applauded, and she bowed her head in gratitude.

My mother came over and hugged me. "*Hola, guapo.*"

"Hey, Mom. Sorry it's been a while."

"We're all busy, *cariño.*"

"Another tour?" I asked.

She nodded. "*Sud* America."

"The same show?" I asked.

"No. A brand-new ballet. That was a rehearsal."

"It looks great."

"We're running a season here. You'll come to the opening next month, I hope?" She wiped her face with a towel.

"I got the flyer. I'll be there. I'll bring Miranda."

"Miranda?" She smiled. "When did you get a new girl?"

"She's not my girl. She's working on my art collection."

My mother looked at me for a moment. "You like her. I can see that."

"You can?"

"I'm your mother. Is she nice?"

"She's lovely, smart, and driven. A hard worker."

"Pretty?" she asked.

I nodded. "Very pretty. Long red hair. Dark beautiful eyes."

She tapped my hand. "Good. It's about time. All those other girls were trash."

I laughed. "That's a bit extreme, Mom. But I've changed."

"You have, *hijo mio.*" She stroked my cheek lovingly. "*Venga.* Let's get a coffee. Give me a minute to change."

I headed over to Juan, who was bent over his guitar, strumming with his ear close to the strings. He was equally obsessed in his chosen artform as my mother, which inspired admiration and a tinge of envy in me.

I needed to be that drummer again.

"Hey, Juan."

"Hey, man." He placed his guitar down, rose, and hugged me. "Long time no see."

"That sounded great."

"Yeah. I've been composing like crazy for this show. It's got a little bit of Paco de Lucia and John McLaughlin." He grinned.

I nodded approvingly.

"I've also transposed a Chick Corea piece. Belen's come up with some killer choreography."

"I'm sure she has." I felt a rippling of pride for my mother. "Can't wait. I'm looking forward to the show."

My mother had changed into jeans and a T-shirt printed with the logo of her latest show. She carried an extra shirt and handed it to me. "Here, this is the biggest size."

She patted my biceps. "Have you been lifting weights again?"

"Sometimes. I've set up some equipment at home."

She looked over at Juan who'd returned to his guitar. Smiling, she said, "He would sleep with that guitar if he could."

"I've never seen him without it. Even at gatherings, he's always got it in his arms."

"That's why I love him." She tapped her head. "Discipline and commitment are sexy."

"Sure are," I said, thinking of Miranda.

We settled down at the little café around the corner. After placing our orders, I said, "Can you let me know the schedule for the children's ballet classes?"

Her dark eyes widened. "Is there something you're not telling me?"

I laughed at her husky Spanish accent, which always added a little color to her words. "No. You're not going to be a grandmother."

"Ah…" She nodded. "You had me worried."

"It's for Miranda's niece Ava. She's five and loves dancing."

"This Miranda again."

"I like her," I said, staring down at my hands. I more than liked her. I was fucking obsessed.

"It's about time. You're a good man. And very *guapo*. All that shit you hung out with before." She shook her head. "Tattoos, piercings, *dios mio*."

"You haven't gotten more tattoos?" she asked.

"Nope. Just the upper arms plus the one on my chest."

"The Scorpio symbol, I like. It's our sign. You and me. We're alike." She cast me a warm smile. "Tell me, are you playing in a band?"

I sighed heavily.

"What's wrong?" she asked, touching my hand.

The waiter arrived with our coffee and cakes. I nodded at him then returned my attention to my mother. "There's a lot of shit happening back home."

"How's your father?"

"He's not well. I don't think he'll last the year."

She sipped her coffee. "He's a bad man, but I'm still sorry for him. It's not a nice way to go."

"Something happened yesterday." I rubbed my tense neck.

She held my hand. "Tell me."

I told her all about the Tamara incident, leaving out the cock-grabbing bit. Strange how I still felt like a boy around my mother.

"She's bad. Rotten. A *puta*." She nearly spat that last word. "Your father always went for those types of women."

I shook my head. "Why did you stay with him?"

"Because I had two sons to bring up." She sighed.

I sipped my coffee. "Now that she's out of the hospital, I'm wondering if she'll retaliate. What lies she'll tell."

She nodded pensively. "Have you got anyone who can vouch for you?"

"Britney."

She rolled her eyes. "She's poison, that one."

I leaned forward. "What do you know about her?"

"Your father met her when he was with me." She paused then added, "He's a bad man."

"So you keep saying." I looked at her. "I need to know everything. I might be the CEO, but Britney knows more about the company than I do. I don't understand why Dad's given her so much power."

She bit her lip, nodding. "That doesn't surprise me." Setting her cup down, my mother took a deep breath. "We were at a party in Beverly Hills. There was this young girl. A waitress. Your father took a liking to her. She was very young, and she kept playing up to him by bending over in front of him. It was disgusting. We had a big fight that night."

"How young?" I asked.

"Fifteen." Her eyebrows lifted. "Later on, after I confronted him, he insisted she'd told him she was eighteen."

"So what happened?"

She took out a cigarette and lit it. I refrained from lecturing her about how she needed to quit.

"I found them together." She puffed out smoke.

"At the party?"

Shaking her head, she replied, "No. At home. They were in bed together. A week after he met her."

I frowned. "Where was I?"

"At school. It was daytime. And that wasn't the only time." She wore a dark expression. "That's why I left. I could tolerate him cheating with women my age. But such a young girl." She shook her head. "She was a piece of work. Flirty and playing up to him. All the time. I found her swimming topless in the pool around your brother. At least they were of a similar age."

"Brent too?"

"I think so. It was disgusting. I wanted to tell her parents. Her stepfather didn't care. Her mother was worse than her."

"But Dad gave her a job."

"That's right. He put her through college too."

I nodded pensively. I thought of Britney and her drunken admission to enjoying sex with her stepfather.

Thirty minutes later, I left my mother with a head full of ugly stories.

21

MIRANDA

Florian arrived on time, and with Lachlan lost in his own world, my earlier confidence crashed.

The art dealer took my hand and kissed me on the cheek.

I glanced at Lachlan, and a little muscle above his eyebrow moved.

"Florian Storm, this is Lachlan Peace."

Florian shook his hand and nodded. "Thank you for inviting me into your home."

Lachlan said nothing, only gave Florian a hint of a smile, as though it was a struggle for that gorgeous mouth of his to move.

In green slacks and a retro striped shirt, Florian wore his eccentric chic with ease.

I'd decided on the black pencil skirt and pink shirt I'd bought at the mall. Harriet said it made me look slimmer and professional. With the help of some new clothes, contact lenses, and a smidgen of confidence, I truly felt like a woman about to conquer the art world.

"Can I offer you a coffee or a drink?" I asked.

"A drink might be nice," he said.

I looked at Lachlan.

"I've got beer, wine, and bourbon," he said.

"Bourbon," Florian said.

Lachlan headed to the kitchen, looking morose. Considering this was a business meeting, some charm, normally Lachlan's middle name, would have helped.

He returned and handed Florian a crystal tumbler.

"Thanks." He took a swig of the amber liquid then returned

his attention to me. He pointed to a quirky splotch of mismatched colors on one of the canvases. "Look at that."

I smiled. "It's magnificent, isn't it? The sheer audacity of Pollock's work never fails to impress. Timeless, like all great art."

I showed Florian the other works, and after thirty minutes of discussing the brash idiosyncrasies of modern art, I escorted him to the garage, leaving Lachlan brooding on the balcony.

"They're sublime. Better than I'd hoped. I already have four buyers interested. We could go public, but the commission will rise."

I nodded. "Let me discuss it with Lachlan. He's insisting on confidentiality."

"Of course." He lingered. "How about breakfast tomorrow? We can go over some of the offers, and talk more about you joining us."

I nodded. "Sounds great."

"I'll be in touch." He kissed me on both cheeks and left.

When I returned to the penthouse, Lachlan was standing by the window, gazing out at the skyline.

"That went well," I said.

He turned and looked at me with such intensity that my nails dug into my palms.

As his thumb stroked his bottom lip, desire shivered through me, recalling how those lips had tasted.

I missed seeing that boyish grin on his handsome face.

"Why are you being like this?" I blurted out.

"I'm not being like anything. There's something about him that I don't like."

He poured some bourbon into a glass. "Do you want one?"

I nodded. "I think I need one."

As he passed me a tumbler, our fingers touched, and a tingling sensation slid through me.

Lachlan knocked back the bourbon and wiped his lips with the back of his hand. I averted my eyes because the dark intensity in his turquoise gaze threatened to overwhelm me. Whenever we made eye contact, I found myself lost in a wilderness of burning lust, and the air seemed to crackle between us.

"Do you still want to sell?" I asked. "I can find another dealer. We don't have to go with Florian."

"No. I need this handled discreetly, and he's got the contacts."

"Is it because you're being forced to sell your grandfather's collection that you're being so …?" I wanted to say *rude* but hesitated.

He stared straight at me. "What am I being, Miranda?"

Tears spiked the back of my eyes. I'd never experienced this kind of angst before. His dark mood intimidated and aroused me at the same time. I could barely look at him.

"Maybe I should leave you alone," I said.

"No." He touched my arm.

Our eyes locked for what seemed like ages.

"What do you want from me?" I asked.

"I want you." He ran his hands down his handsome face.

"Is that why you're being unpleasant?" My heart raced like mad.

He combed his hands through his hair and exhaled. "There's a lot of shit going down in my life at the moment. You're the only good person I know apart from my mother and a few buddies … and then there's Manuel …" He rubbed his face again.

"Who's Manuel?"

"He's my half brother. He's five, and his mother's the worst. She completely neglects him. I wish I could do more for him. He's a great kid."

"That's understandable. I have that same connection with Ava. Although Harriet's a little wild at times, she's actually a good mom."

"Maybe sometime Manuel and Ava can have a playdate or something like that." His voice softened, and I wanted to hold him. It was concern for his young brother that helped explain his earlier dark mood.

"I worry about Manuel," he continued. "He's shy and doesn't make friends that easily."

"Have you thought of hiring a nanny?"

"He has one. Sherry's great. She takes care of him twenty-four seven."

"I'm sure things will be fine."

He nodded.

"Florian's influential. He could get your career off the ground."

The sudden shift in topic was abrupt, but at least Lachlan had opened up to me. "It's important for me to get a foot in the door for sure."

He studied me for a moment. "Would you fuck to get ahead?"

My eyebrows crashed. Was he joking?

There was no hint of his playful smile. He was deadly serious as his eyes drilled into mine.

"Excuse me?" Fire bit my belly. "I can't believe you'd even ask me that." I grabbed my purse.

He followed me. "Don't go. I was out of line." He took my hand.

"Something's gotten to you, Lachlan, I can see that. But you shouldn't take it out on me." I clutched the strap of my bag so tightly that it dug into my palm.

He stroked my hand and stood so close his warm breath touched my cheek. "You're even more beautiful when fired up."

"Why would you ask me that?" I asked, doing my utmost to ignore the tingling sensation from his touch.

"I'm sorry. Please accept my apology." He exhaled. "I guess I can't believe that I've finally met someone who's real. Who's good. And isn't into me for what I can give them."

His eyes penetrated deeply, and I just couldn't move, as though gripped by a spell.

My bag tumbled to the ground as I sent my principles packing.

Our lips met, and the sparks turned into a blaze as his soft, warm mouth explored mine slowly.

He pulled me in close, our bodies pressing together. His tongue parted my lips and danced with my tongue in a wild swirl.

I melted in his arms and surrendered.

22

LACHLAN

All it took was a whiff of rose from her lustrous hair and my mouth exploring her pillowy, sensuous lips for the ground to virtually sway beneath me.

Locked in each other's arms, we stumbled onto the sofa, and tongues tangled passionately.

Her lips parted with a gasp as I licked and sucked her long neck. I ran my hands over her full tits, and when her nipples spiked my palm, I virtually ripped her bra off. Her naked tits tumbled into my hands, and my heart thumped against my chest.

I unzipped my pants to release my straining cock.

While sucking on her rosy nipples, I undid the zip to her skirt and helped her wiggle out of it.

My fingers traveled down her curvy silk thighs to her pussy. Through the damp, lacy fabric, I felt her heat and wetness. I hooked my finger inside her panties and slid a finger between her slick folds. She was so tight and wet. My dick grew steel hard.

Removing her thong, I lifted her leg, placed it over my shoulder and lowered my face to her pussy.

I buried my face between her soft thighs and held her curvy ass. My tongue settled on her swollen clit, sucking and teasing her bud. Intoxicated by her flavor, I lapped at her swollen clit. Teasing and nibbling her bud, I wanted her to come and scream with pleasure.

Miranda writhed in my grasp, and as she drenched my tongue with cum, she cried out.

I wiped my mouth on her thigh and fingered her. Her pussy

sucked on my finger tightly, while my throbbing dick grew wet, pleading to be inside.

"Oh my God, you're so beautiful," I said, removing my drenched my finger. "I'm dying to fuck you."

Her cheeks were flushed, and her dark eyes dilated. She looked drugged. I sure was.

I took a breath. "I don't want you to do anything you aren't comfortable with."

She gazed up at me. "I want you to, Lachlan."

I kissed her moist lips. "Are you sure you want me to be your first?"

"Yes." Her hot breath touched my cheek.

"You know I'm not looking for a relationship right now," I said.

She nodded. "I still want you to."

I stroked her cheek tenderly, and our eyes met. I read sincerity and something deeper, as though she knew me better than I knew myself.

While falling into her dark eyes, I removed my clothes.

Her eyes widened. My dick was so hard it felt like it would erupt any minute.

"I'll take it slow." I stroked her cheek and kissed her tenderly.

"Let's do this in bed," I said, helping her up and leading her to the bedroom.

I opened my drawer to get a condom, only to find I'd run out. "Damn."

"What's the matter?" she asked.

"I haven't got any condoms."

"I'm on the pill," she said.

I studied her and nodded slowly when, in the same drawer, a recent blood test stared back at me. Removing the document, I passed it to her.

"What's this?" she asked.

"A blood test that shows I'm clean."

"Oh." She took the document, barely looked at it, and passed it back to me.

We lay down and held each other as I indulged in the feel of her warm curves. I ran my tongue over her lips while my fingers glided over her smooth skin.

My heart thumped against my chest as I placed the head of my dick between her folds.

I entered her slowly, one inch at a time.

"You're a goddess." I sighed.

My dick hit a wall of resistance, and she flinched.

I paused and looked at her. Her beautiful eyes shone up at me.

"Don't stop," she murmured.

"Are you sure?"

"Yes."

I withdrew and re-entered her gently, careful not to move too fast. I let out a groan as her tight pussy clung to my cock.

We found a fluid rhythm, and as her pussy opened up, my thrusts grew deeper and faster. The intense friction stole my breath.

Clenching my jaw, I fondled her swollen breasts, sucking on her nipples, while I entered her deeper and deeper.

"My God, I could easily become addicted to you," I said, struggling to speak.

The fit was so snug, it threatened to take me somewhere I'd never been before.

As she lay beneath me, writhing, our eyes locked. Her heavy-lidded stare did things to me that I didn't understand.

As I remained transfixed on her eyes, my hips moved to and fro, grinding against her pelvis.

We found a nice pace. I couldn't have slammed if I wanted to because it would have been all over. Miranda was beyond arousing.

I kissed her neck as we moved together in perfect rhythm.

"How is this? Are you okay?" I asked, my breath mingling with my words.

"Uh-huh." Her breath touched my cheek.

23

MIRANDA

As he thrust in and out, Lachlan's groan reverberated against my ribcage.

I gripped his firm ass, feeling all of him inside of me. I hadn't seen a dick before. But hell, he was excruciatingly big.

Lachlan eyes remained on mine. He seemed vulnerable, as though he was letting me into his own private space.

I winced as a sharp pain shuddered through me. He paused, and I encouraged him to continue by arching my back and lifting my pelvis to meet his thrusts.

Pain soon melted away into burning pleasure. My muscles relaxed, and heat flooded my core.

"I need you to come," he whispered into my ear.

As his thrusts increased in strength and speed, little spasms grew and grew, and then colors exploded before my eyes. My core spasmed uncontrollably, and I dug my nails into Lachlan's firm biceps.

I fell apart at the seams and yelled, "Oh my God."

"Fuck," yelled Lachlan, his head tipped back. His jaw clenched. As his body trembled in my arms, his dick pulsated inside of me.

While he held me tight, I felt his heart pounding against my chest. We remained like that for a long time, with me nuzzling into his burning neck, drawing in his male scent.

He lifted himself up and stared me in the eyes. "That was insane. In the most perfect sense." A gentle smile graced his lips as his finger traced along my face. "I've never experienced anything like that before. Ever."

Ever?

How startling. A man like Lachlan would have had more women that I'd had breakfasts.

As I stared into his shining gaze, there was something raw in the way his eyes trapped mine. A wordless conversation that only my soul understood.

When Lachlan rose, I checked him out. Long, lean legs, a tight ass perfect for grasping onto, and abs befitting a god.

I released a silent sigh as he walked around naked, comfortable in his own skin, and as my slightly sore pussy tingled with desire, all I could think of was him fucking me again.

But he did seem distracted as he moved about.

"What are you looking for?" I asked.

"My sanity," he said.

I grinned. "When did you last see it?"

He laughed then approached the bed and took me into his arms. "Sometime before you got naked."

He stroked my arm. "You take my breath away."

"You're not so bad yourself," I said, feeling flirty.

He sat there and just kept looking at me.

"What?" I asked.

"Sorry, am I staring?" he asked.

"You are. But I like staring at you too," I admitted.

He smiled sweetly, cupped my chin, and kissed me tenderly before standing up.

Stretching his long muscular arms, he asked, "Would you like to eat something?"

"I am hungry," I said

"What would you like?" he asked, sitting on the side of the bed and stroking my arm with a feathery touch.

I could barely think as shivery pleasure from his fingers puckered my skin. "Whatever. I'm not picky."

"A woman after my own heart," he said with a chuckle. "Pizza? Thai? Do you like Japanese? I know an amazing sushi place."

"Pizza sounds great," I said. "I could use a hit of carbs."

"Done. Don't go anywhere," he said.

"It's kind of chilly." I crossed my arms. "I'd like to get dressed."

He came to the bed and took me into his arms. "I'll keep you warm." Passing me a robe, he added, "Here, put this on. That was only the entrée. I need these tits and sexy little pussy naked."

"You're kind of dirty, aren't you?" I said, feeling a throb of heat as he palmed my nipples.

"Is it too much?" he asked with a searching gaze.

I shook my head. "I like knowing I turn you on."

"You turned me on from the moment you bent over in front of me."

"When was that?" I asked.

"Your first day in the office, when I caught sight of your perfect ass."

"It's hard to miss, I suppose." I grinned.

"You're body's stunning. A womanly shape." He released a breath. "I'm getting hard just thinking about it." His hands traveled over my body, making my skin tingle.

"To hell with food," he said, gently pushing me down onto the bed.

***

I desperately needed some caffeine after a sleepless night of being fucked to a point of rawness. Lachlan, I'd quickly discovered, was insatiable. Although I was sore, it was a nice pain. The type one feels after a hard workout. Only this was a squillion times more pleasurable.

Thoughts of our passionate lovemaking followed me along as I rushed to meet Florian Storm for breakfast.

My phone went off as I stepped into the bustling café. It was Harriet. Despite dying to talk to her about my new sex life, I tapped a quick text then headed over to Florian, who was sitting in a corner, scrolling over his phone.

"Sorry I'm late I got caught up in something," I said.

"It's fine. You're only five minutes late," he said.

I took a deep breath. Reality had crashed my sex fest with

Lachlan. Before I left, Lachlan took a call from Britney. The mention of police had come up, and he went from being touchy-feely to dark and remote.

I'd been in too much of a hurry to ask questions, even though that worried look in his eyes when I kissed him good-bye filled me with concerned curiosity.

Florian signaled our waiter, who came over promptly. "What can I get you?"

I ordered coffee and a croissant.

"I'll have the same," Florian said.

Our waiter nodded and left.

Florian leaned forward and said, "Good news. My Russian contact wants the entire Pollock collection."

I nodded. "That sounds easy."

"It is. How does eight hundred million for the dozen sound?"

I thought about that for a moment. "Is that net?"

"Yes, after commission."

I mused over his offer. I'd been hoping for more, but ultimately it was up to Lachlan.

"The market's not so great at the moment," he added. "Plus, it would be easier logistically, since the paintings will be packaged in one lot."

"That makes sense," I replied. "Let me run this by Lachlan, and I'll get back to you."

When the waiter returned with our orders, I couldn't drink my coffee fast enough. I was exhausted. All night long, Lachlan's hands, mouth, dick, and tongue had done things to me that still had my nerve endings buzzing.

"I also have this for you." He opened his briefcase and handed me a contract. "I'd like to offer you a position. Have a read of it and let me know what you think."

"I don't have to consider it. I would love to work for you," I said. It was perfect timing. Now that Lachlan and I had slept together, I could no longer work for him. I would expedite the sale of his grandfather's collection, and that would be it. Nice and tidy.

I felt a sudden pang of sadness, though. Despite being at that apartment for only a few days, I would miss it.

"Can you start on Monday?" he asked.

"I don't see why not. I'll go over this offer with Lachlan and get back to you by tomorrow morning."

"That would be super. Let's talk about the role I have in mind for you."

I took a sip of coffee and nodded.

"I'd like you to go on the hunt for New York art. Preferably from the sixties to the nineties."

"I recently stumbled on a George Condo and a Basquiat. I bid for them at a charity gala."

He studied me. "You've got the Midas touch."

"It was mostly luck." I smiled.

"What are you up to tonight?" he asked.

"I haven't made any plans." I thought of Lachlan, and how I'd hovered about hoping he'd suggest something. He kissed me passionately, but I left with the taste of him on my lips and lots of questions.

"There's an exhibition of new works by someone fresh and exciting. I'd love for you to come check it out. He's a bit wild but very interesting. Self-taught."

I nodded. "Sure. I'd love to."

"Great. I'll send you the details."

I finished my coffee and stood. "I better get moving. I'll discuss the Pollock deal with Lachlan and let you know what he says."

"Lovely." He smiled brightly. "I look forward to seeing you at the exhibit later."

I made it to my car when my phone buzzed.

I took a deep, steadying breath.

"Hey." Lachlan's deep voice entered my ear and rode down to my panties.

"How did the meeting go?"

"I'm going to be working for him. He's asked me to start on Monday." There was a long pause. "Are you there?"

"What if I set you up with your own gallery?" he asked.

I bit my lip. "You seem to have a lot on your plate right now. I appreciate the offer, but I need to be independent when it comes to my career."

"I respect that, I do." He paused. "But there's something off about that guy."

"I know you're not a fan. But I could learn a lot from him."

"I'm sure you'll go far."

"Thanks for believing in me," I said.

Another pause followed as I tried to collect my thoughts again. The romantic in me wanted to keep working for Lachlan and seeing where things went on a personal level. But the more practical part of me knew that in order to further my career, I needed to go it alone.

I snapped out of the personal and into professional mode. "Florian's got an offer on the Pollocks."

"Good. I'm about to visit my dad. I should be done around lunchtime. We can meet at the apartment at one o'clock so you can fill me in."

"That works," I said.

"See you then, gorgeous."

I hung up and stared in space. It took a moment to come back down to earth. Even talking to him on the phone made my heart race.

24

LACHLAN

My father stared blankly at me.

I'd assumed he wasn't going to respond when he said, "She looked older."

I refrained from rolling my eyes. At least he'd admitted the truth, as repulsive as it was for him to have slept with Britney when she was only fifteen.

"Britney's got me over a barrel," I said.

"You could do worse. Marry the woman."

My face scrunched in disbelief. "Are you kidding? I have zero desire to marry Britney. It's fucking sick you'd even suggest that."

The thought of sleeping with someone my father had fucked seemed wrong on so many levels. Then it hit me. I'd slept with Britney too. Now I really wished it had never happened.

I'd changed since Aspen. I wasn't looking for marriage, but I wasn't looking for drunken hookups either. Especially not since meeting Miranda.

"Britney's smart and will make you a lot of money," he said.

"The last time we spoke, you mentioned four billion in Geneva. That's all the money I need."

"That was her clever doing, you realize. If you marry her, it will be all yours."

"No amount of money would be worth it." I changed tactics. "What about Manuel?" I asked. "He's your son too."

"You're the only son I have left. More's the pity," he said with a scowl.

My hands clenched into fists at my sides, and I took a deep breath. "The SEC's still digging around."

He shrugged.

"With your condition, they'll come after me instead."

No apology. Nothing. My father didn't do remorse.

The emaciated man staring at me barely resembled the man I knew to be my father. In the past, he would have just bulldozed his way through everything, including the SEC.

"So this Ponzi scheme, Dad ..."

"Don't call it that," he said. "It was the real deal. Bird of Paradise was going to happen if this fucking disease hadn't eaten into me."

"Where's the land? The business plan? The architect's designs?"

"Britney will dig us out of this. She's brilliant like that. You need her. Marry the woman."

I took a deep breath. Miranda entered my thoughts. Beautiful, pure Miranda. Clever. Sexy. Exactly the kind of woman I wanted by my side.

"Get rid of that bitch Tamara," he said.

I frowned. "What are you saying?"

"She's rotten. I don't want her getting one red cent of the Peace wealth. Britney deserves it. She's been loyal to me through everything."

"Why didn't you marry her?" I asked.

"I wanted to," he said, his mouth turning up at one end. "But your mother threatened to report me to the cops."

Why hadn't I seen it happening? Living in such a large mansion meant that dirty secrets had many doors to hide behind.

"Tammy fell over in my shower and cracked her head. She entered uninvited. When she grabbed my ..." I had to pause there. I felt like a teenager getting the dreaded sex talk from his dad.

"Let me guess. She tried to fuck you?" he said.

I nodded.

"And now she's claiming that you attacked her?"

I nodded again.

"Then you've got to do what I told you earlier. Get the bitch knocked off."

I shook my head. Openly discussing murder was a lot, even for him. As a welcome distraction, a nurse entered just as his disturbing suggestion turned me into ice.

After she administered his morphine, he drifted off.

For a moment or two, I remained there, studying him. He looked so peaceful, completely unaffected by the shitshow he'd created for me and Manuel.

I trudged out of the hospital. With my eyes glued to my feet, I contemplated crawling under a rock.

I called Britney.

"I'm leaving the hospital now. Did you get those figures together like I asked?"

"Yes. I think you'll like what I have to show you. Bird of Paradise looks like a very desirable investment."

"Count me out."

She sniffed at my dry response. "Tamara's bitching and moaning," she added. "She wants her credit card limit raised."

"I'll be there in half an hour."

25

MIRANDA

Harriet shook her head, smiling. "You're finally a woman. Yay."

Remaining cool, even though I was anything but, I shrugged while staring down at the fruits of my latest shopping spree on top of my bed.

"That's going to look super sexy," she said, staring down at the floral peasant blouse and tulip-shaped skirt I'd bought for the exhibition that evening.

My faint smile faded. I hadn't heard from Lachlan. Had the SEC paid them another visit? Was that why he'd gone pale while speaking to Britney?

He'd promised to call. And most annoyingly, that was all I could think about. I should have been focusing on the vague contract Florian gave me, which didn't really say much, and more worryingly, there was no mention of money.

Harriet stood at the window. "I'm going to miss this place."

"That makes two of us." I sighed.

Lachlan had said it was fine for me to remain at his penthouse, but I'd declined now that we'd slept together. Some small part of me would have loved to stay, but I needed my independence.

Harriet studied me. "What's wrong?"

"Lachlan was supposed to call."

She handed me the glass of wine. "Don't worry. He's probably really busy."

Recalling how preoccupied he'd been earlier, I nodded. "I'm actually concerned about him, to be honest."

"Why? He seems like someone who can look after himself."

I nodded distractedly. "He's also got a driver who's a body

guard."

"Let's just get ready for tonight," she said. "Are you sure you don't mind me tagging along?"

"Of course not."

"Thanks, Andie. I need to unwind. And it's my weekend off. I want to party. I might have to check out Tinder later."

I shook my head. "That's so random."

"That's the idea," she said, combing her hair in the full-length mirror. The same mirror I used to ogle Lachlan when he was getting dressed this morning.

"You might meet a nice guy at the exhibition," I said, pulling my blouse higher up my shoulders.

"I doubt it. It's not really my scene." She cocked her head then came to stand by me and adjusted my top so more of my cleavage showed. I rolled my eyes and pulled it back up.

"That's the problem, Harry, you need to start thinking long term."

"Yawn. I'm only twenty-six."

"Then why do you cry when it doesn't work out with your guys?"

"I haven't done that in months. I haven't even checked on Josh's Instagram to see who he's been fucking this week."

"I've been too busy to check Lachlan's Instagram," I said, brushing my lashes with mascara. "I don't even do social media, unless it's related to art and business."

"Lucky for you, I'm already following him." Harriet tapped her phone and scrolled. "Hmm."

"Well?" I asked.

"There's not much," she said evasively.

"Show me," I said.

"Nothing worthwhile, Andie. Let's go."

I grabbed her phone and saw a photo of Lachlan holding his surfboard. The image would have made a great advertisement for male health products.

I felt a shiver of desire, seeing him in that wet suit unzipped below the navel, teasingly showing his happy trail. His wet hair and rippling torso brought back memories of having my hands braced against the shower door as he entered me from behind. A surge of heat traveled down between my legs.

I continued scrolling to an image of him at his drum kit. Tattoos wrapped around his biceps, emphasizing their delicious bulge. He gripped his drumsticks and looked as though he was about to fuck.

I continued down his feed, and wished I hadn't because I found an image of a beautiful girl in a tiny bikini with her pouty lips on his cheek.

I scrolled from one image to another that caught my eye. Shots were lined up at a bar, and Lachlan wore a cheeky smirk. There were girls everywhere. One even straddled him.

My face pinched as jealousy twisted a knot in my stomach.

I passed the phone back. "Well. That says a lot."

"According to the dates, those were taken forever ago. So what if he used to be a party animal?"

I took a deep breath. "You're right. I'm being immature. He fucked me, and now I'm acting like we're together."

"I can't blame you. He's pretty hot. But don't jump to conclusions. He's a thirty-year-old man. People change."

Harriet had made a good point. After all, Lachlan had admitted to being a bad boy and having regrets.

"Thanks, Harry," I said, finishing my drink.

"For what?" she asked, looking in the mirror and applying fresh lip gloss.

"For being the voice of reason for a change."

She giggled. "Enjoy it while it lasts."

After we'd finished getting ready, we left for the exhibition.

In order to drink, we'd opted for an Uber, and just as we jumped in, my phone pinged with a text from Lachlan.

Sorry I didn't call earlier. I've been super busy all day. Can you text me the address of the exhibition?

I replied, *No worries. I'll text it over right now.*

I sent him the info, and a moment later, Lachlan said, *I'm on my way. Looking forward to seeing you.*

My finger hovered over the screen. I wasn't sure how to reply. Was an "X" for a kiss too lame?

Harriet poked my arm. "Are you rewriting the fucking constitution?"

I laughed. "No. But how should I reply?"

"Just tell him you can't wait to feel him inside of you again."

"I can't, what if he's in a meeting or something?" I quickly tapped out *See you soon* and added a smiley emoji.

"What did you write?" asked Harriet.

"A smiley emoji," I said.

"Ugh, you should've sent him a picture of your tits," she said.

I giggled.

Hearing from Lachlan had put a smile on my face, despite lingering questions about that conversation I overheard him having with Britney.

26

LACHLAN

Britney played the femme fatale, flirting with the SEC officials. Considering we needed all the help we could get, I abstained from rolling my eyes.

My interview with them had gone okay. I kept my cool despite images of rotting forever in prison popping into my head. In the end, Britney showed them the Bird of Paradise plans. She also managed to prove somehow that the investors' money had gone straight to the project. I had to hand it to her creative accounting. Hopefully, it would clear the company of any wrongdoing.

After they left, I went straight to the liquor cabinet and grabbed the vodka. I poured two shots, knowing Britney would want one.

"I'm about to sell some of my private art collection to pay everyone off."

"There's Geneva," she said, gulping down her shot.

"There's that little issue of my father being alive," I said. "As much as I hate this shit I'm having to deal with because of him, I still want him to recover."

"He won't." She looked at me blankly.

"I also want you out," I said.

"You need me. I've got a lot of dirt on this family."

"If it's about my father fucking you when you were fifteen, I already know."

"Oh, there's more than that." Her grin made my skin crawl.

I grabbed the bottle from her hand and poured myself another shot.

"I can testify either for or against you when it comes to your step mommy."

I rubbed my neck then shook my head. "I'm going out."

"Remember, tomorrow we're heading to the Grenadines to see how Bird of Paradise is coming along."

"Why bother?" I asked.

"The SEC need to see it's a bona fide project that stalled due to a lack of capital, not that it's some scam."

"Which is what it was," I said.

"Your father had his heart set on that resort."

"I'm sure he did." My eyes landed on the fake Monet. I pointed at the frame. "What happened to the original?"

"I sold it. Your father asked me to," she replied.

"But why cover it up with a fake?" I asked. "It was his painting to do as he wished."

She shrugged. "He liked it hanging there."

"Any others?"

She shook her head. "No. It's too bad the new girl didn't stick around longer. I needed her to evaluate the entire collection."

"She's working for me now. Thanks to her, we'll keep those asshats off our backs. You should be grateful."

She sniffed. "You've always had a thing for chubby chicks with big tits, haven't you? Have you slept with her yet?"

"That's none of your fucking business. And she's not fucking chubby. Show some respect."

"Make sure you don't miss our flight tomorrow morning."

I took a deep breath. "You can't do this without me?"

"They still prefer to deal with men in those regions."

It pissed me off, but I couldn't argue with that. I had to get the SEC off my back. At least until I paid everyone off, and then the project could just stall. There was no way I wanted to be attached to some debauched paradise for perverts.

"What time's the flight?" I asked.

"Eleven," she said.

My shoulders slumped. I'd planned a weekend of unbridled lust with Miranda. For a minute, I even imagined asking her along. I would have loved seeing Miranda in a skimpy bikini and having nice, long walks along the beach. It was too late to work out the travel logistics, and Britney was guaranteed to give Miranda a ton of shit the entire trip. I'd make it up to her by taking her out when I got back. By then the paintings would be sold, and she'd let me do all kinds of dirty things to her.

***

After a surf, I had a quick bash on the drums and then headed out to meet Miranda at the gallery. It would have to be quick because I was playing a set with Round Midnight at the Red House later. I planned to ask her along. Not so much to expose her to my music but to ravage her afterward.

I jumped into the black Mercedes waiting for me.

"Nice car," I said, touching the wooden dash and console.

Justin, my new driver and bodyguard, turned to me and said, "Yeah, I like it. It's part of a new fleet."

I looked down at my phone. "Looks like I'm headed to the Arts District."

He tapped the address into the console and got on the road.

I loved twilight, especially seeing the deep teal ocean swallowing the sun. When I was a kid, I used to imagine the sun going for a swim. Back then, the sea had filled my imagination with all kinds of adventures. Like being a pirate, or being shipwrecked on an island with lots of buried treasure and mermaids.

"How's the bass playing going?" I asked.

"Good. That's when I can find the time," he said.

"I hear you. I hardly get the time to play. I'm having a bash tonight, though. At the Red House."

"Oh, for real?" he said.

"Yep."

"I might come in and watch for a bit. Is Orlando going to be there too?"

"Sure is."

"Nice. I love jazz," he said, merging onto the freeway.

"Same. I just wish I had more time to practice."

"You were killing it last time I heard you," he said.

"Thanks. I could always be better," I said.

"You sound frustrated," he said.

I scratched my prickly jaw. "Maybe a little. Life and music haven't really been lining up lately."

He chuckled. "Without music, life's kind of meaningless."

"I've met a new girl recently. She's taking a lot of my focus."

"That'll do it. That's one of the many advantages to being married."

I turned to look at him. "Not that I'm planning to get married any time soon, but it's nice to know there's at least one advantage to it. Miranda's pretty amazing."

"You sound like you've got it bad for her."

"Maybe." I looked out the window at the blur of trees as we sped along the highway. "You don't miss the thrill of a new woman?"

"That shit got old real quick after I turned thirty. Before I married, I had my fair share." He laughed. "When I was in my twenties, I got around enough."

I nodded. I knew that bachelor life all too well.

"I love my wife. I got lucky there. But there are other thrills, like my two girls. Melitta just won a music scholarship." His deep voice thickened with pride.

"Oh man, how great. You must be one proud dad." I stared down at my hands. "To be honest, fatherhood scares the shit out of me."

"I was like that. But I got over that the minute I held my little girl in my arms for the first time."

I studied the giant man who could hold his own against a gang of bikers.

"I've heard that before," I said, wondering how my father had felt when he held me as a baby. He'd been stingy with affection. Even Brent had gotten only the occasional bear hug. My mother made up for it, constantly hugging and kissing me. It was embarrassing at times, but I loved her for it.

"What's going on in the Arts District tonight?" he asked.

"I'm only going to see Miranda, the new girl I mentioned."

"She's an artist?"

"Miranda's more into the business of selling art," I said. "But she's got a creative spirit. She's been working for me. I hadn't planned on it, but we hooked up last night."

"Oh really? I hear workplace hookups are really in right now."

I laughed. "Something tells me they've been in for a long time."

He took the exit for the Arts District. "This chick sounds like she's got you sprung."

I took a deep breath. "Lust will do that."

"Can't have love without lust, man."

I'd never been in love, but I couldn't stop thinking of how Miranda tasted. How she'd felt with me buried deep inside. And she was smart and beautiful. My perfect woman in many ways.

There was no doubt I'd been hijacked by lust.

He pulled up to the curb. "This is it here," he said.

The gallery occupied a double shop front, and through the windows, I saw a big crowd of people chatting and laughing.

"I won't be too long," I said.

"Sure thing. Have fun. And hey, I'm pretty sure she's into you too. You're a sought-after billionaire."

I smirked. "Was that trending too?"

"I read an article while waiting at the doctor's the other day. You were with some girl wearing an ugly brown dress."

"Remind me to explain the context to you sometime." I shook my head. I hoped Miranda would never see that. I'd never allowed the media to upset me before. But knowing an image was floating around of Miranda in that dress irritated me.

I stepped out the car and stood on the sidewalk.

The first thing I saw on entering the gallery was a large screen displaying a woman wearing plastic bottles strapped to her chest. She squeezed the bottles and squirted white paint all over a black sheet. On a second screen, a man dressed in a diaper stepped into a bucket of paint then stomped around on a large canvas. Works of their messy cathartic labor hung for sale nearby.

Looking around, I spotted Miranda and her sister surrounded by a group of males and ambled over to join them.

"Sorry to make you wait," I whispered. "Looks like you've got a bunch of admirers."

She chuckled. "That's more Harriet than me. She attracts them."

Seeing Miranda's shoulders naked made my mouth water at the thought of trailing her silky skin with kisses. I loved her hair loose, as an image of her red locks coiled around my hand came to mind.

"You shouldn't sell yourself short, Miranda."

She gave me a shy smile as her large dark eyes locked with mine.

I took her soft hand.

Miranda looked at me, and her eyes widened slightly.

Was it too soon for a public display of affection?

It was a big gesture. Especially for me. I wasn't normally a hand-holding type of guy.

I looked around the room. The collectors were easy enough to spot with their designer outfits while the artists and eccentrics brought color to the scene.

Florian Storm sauntered over and nodded a greeting. "My Russian client is ecstatic about the Pollocks."

"He's good to go?" I asked.

"Yes. It's small change for him."

I squeezed Miranda's hand gently, and she glanced up at me with a faint smile.

"Miranda," he said. "There's someone here I'd like you to meet." He nodded at me before leaving us to join his group.

Miranda looked at me apologetically. "I'll be back in a minute."

"Take all the time you need. I understand the importance of networking," I said.

"I've already been here for an hour doing just that."

"You're not enjoying yourself?" I asked.

She shrugged. "The art isn't exactly doing it for me."

I looked up at the walls. "Me either. Does this stuff sell?"

Miranda nodded. "These abstract minimal pieces are highly sought after. They hang well in ultra-modern spaces and are often chosen more for decoration than for any emotional reason. In the case of collectors, it's more to do with the artist's name or if they're a rising star."

"You're my rising star," I said, leaning in to kiss her smooth, warm cheek.

She smiled sweetly, and as her floral sent wafted through me, I had the urge to take her away to an intimate corner.

I stroked her palm. "You look stunning, by the way."

"Thanks." Her cheeks flushed pink. "I better go meet that artist."

"Knock them dead."

After I grabbed a beer, I took a tour of the art, moving from one work to another. One piece made me wonder if the artist had run out of paint. None of the pieces grabbed me.

Noticing Harriet talking to a much older man, who stood pretty close, I headed over to join her. The look in her eyes was practically asking me to save her from the man wearing an ugly floral jacket.

"Can you excuse us for a moment?" Harriet asked him.

He looked at me then back to her. "Is this your boyfriend?"

"Just a friend," I said, standing between them.

We headed to the opposite corner.

Harriet rolled her eyes. "Thanks for saving me. What a boring creep."

I smiled. "This place is full of them."

"You're not kidding. I'm two seconds away from leaving."

"I've got a gig to go to," I said.

"Who's the band?"

"It's a jam at the Red House in Venice."

"Sounds like fun. It's close to home too."

"You're all invited. I need to head out soon, though. I'll see if

Miranda's ready to leave. If she wants to stay, maybe you can talk her into coming to the gig later. My driver can get you there, when you're both ready."

"That works for me," Harriet said.

"I'll go and check on Miranda. She looks pretty engrossed in conversation."

"He's not her type," said Harriet.

"Am I that obvious?" I asked.

"You keep looking over at her." She grinned. "She's done nothing but talk about you."

I smiled. "See you at the Red House later?"

"Definitely," she said. "I'm dying to get out of here, and that's way more my scene."

"I'll go touch base with Miranda," I said.

27

MIRANDA

In what was commonly known in those circles as art speak, words spilled effortlessly from Patrick Hold's mouth. I'd heard it all before. Nevertheless, I gave him my undivided attention and nodded so often anyone could have thought I had a neurological disorder.

My attention soon shifted to the man who'd stolen my virginity and my mind. And my heart.

Wearing Levi's and a Beatles T-shirt, Lachlan was effortlessly sexy. He definitely had the attention of the women and some men judging by how everyone's heads turned toward him.

I was ready to leave, but I felt obligated to remain by Florian's side, working the room with him. But my brain dissolved into a puddle as I watched Lachlan. Instead of discussing the latest trends in brazen minimalism, all I could think of was placing my hand underneath that faded T-shirt and sliding my fingers over those hard pecs, all the way down his delicious manly body.

Lachlan came over to join me. His presence still managed to make me dizzy, even after I'd let him virtually dangle me upside down to fuck me.

"Lachlan, this is Patrick," I said, finally finding my voice. "His work is here on show tonight." I pointed to a canvas with just four dots painted on it, which I didn't like. In fact, all of Patrick's work failed to appeal to me. But the market had its own strange way of judging art. I'd learned to accept that personal tastes didn't matter when it came to art.

Patrick gave Lachlan a quick nod without so much as a smile.

By the way Patrick's eyes roamed all over my body, his interest in me was less about art and more about me as a woman. For a moment there, I even fantasized pouring my drink over his head. But I sucked it up. I'd make a name for myself first before making a spectacle of myself.

Lachlan took my hand and led me a few feet away. "I have to go. I've got a gig to get to. I'd really love it if you came. Harriet's leaving with me now."

I frowned. "Harry's going with you?"

"She asked if she could. I would love for you to come, though."

I was about to answer when a slow smirk grew on his lips. "I mean I'd love you to accompany me." He leaned in, and his warm breath on my ear made my nipples harden. "I'd also love you to come." His raised eyebrow made me laugh.

That was all I needed to make up my mind.

Gesturing for Lachlan to wait, I headed over to Florian, who'd just joined Patrick.

"I have to go," I said. Without waiting for his response, I turned to Patrick. "It's been lovely meeting you."

Even though you haven't heard a word I've said, you mediocre excuse for an artist.

Florian looked surprised.

I hastily added, "I'll see you on Monday. I'm really looking forward to it."

Lachlan, who had joined us, looked at Florian and said, "Miranda will arrange the final details for the Jackson Pollock sale."

At the mention of the famous artist, Patrick's head nearly swung off his neck as he turned to Lachlan then me.

We walked off hand in hand. My feet didn't touch the floor. Or so it seemed.

When Justin stepped out and opened our doors, Harriet, bubbling with glee, painted on a flirty smile, and jumped into the front seat. That suited me because it left me alone in the back with Lachlan and his roaming hands.

As the car glided along smoothly, so did Lachlan's fingers up my blouse. He rubbed my nipples through my bra.

He held me in his arms and kissed me passionately. His hungry tongue parted my lips roughly, igniting a fire in my core.

He broke our kiss to look into my eyes. "You've been driving me crazy all night." He ran a finger along my collarbone. "This blouse is very flattering. You had that artist eye fucking you." He kissed my neck. "I hated his art."

"That makes two of us." I studied him closely. "Were you jealous?"

"I'm not the jealous type, but if you were to ask me if I wanted to stand on his toes, I'd reply in the affirmative."

"So is that a yes?" I asked.

"Maybe. I don't know, Miranda. This is new to me," he said, rubbing his jaw, something he did when challenged.

"As it is for me. But I wouldn't like girls hitting on you."

He stroked my cheek. "Even if they did, I'm a one-woman guy. I've only got eyes for you."

I had to look away. His luminescent gaze, loaded with lust, made my brain melt. "That's nice."

What I really meant to say was: "I'm scared as hell that I'll wake from this heavenly dream and find my heart shattered in pieces." My overactive imagination, always a tad dramatic, had a nasty way of spoiling the party. Call it insecurity, but Lachlan lusting after me had that ordinary girl within scratching her head.

As the car sped along, oncoming traffic blurred past us, and I surrendered to that heartwarming sense of belonging. I felt so cozy in Lachlan's arms as he stroked my hair tenderly. Although I loved him hot and bothered, his tenderness made my heart burst into an aria.

His hand slid up my thigh and dipped into my panties. "I'm so fucking hot for you. It's insane." He released a staggered breath. "I can't stop thinking about you, Miranda. I'm always hard."

I stared down at his big bulge, and my breath hitched.

His finger tickled my clit, and the soft leather seat nearly swallowed my heavily aroused body.

"I need to devour you and make you come before we arrive."

His teasing fingers made it hard to think. Thank God we were behind a sheet of dark glass.

He parted my legs roughly as though desperate to get to me.

I nearly swallowed my tongue, stifling a groan as he licked my sensitive bud.

Lachlan ravaged me within an inch of sanity, eating away at my pussy as though I was a mouth-watering treat, until the pleasure became so unbearable, a head-exploding release gushed through me.

My head dropped back with my tongue virtually hanging out of my mouth.

After I made my way back to reality, I saw that Lachlan had popped my panties in his pocket. "What are you doing with those?"

"Some inspiration to help me play better."

"Play better?"

"The drums." He smiled, looking pleased with himself as though my thong was a prized possession.

Was that what boyfriends did? Take their girlfriend's worn panties? Was Lachlan my boyfriend?

Tasting of me, his lips touched mine for one last devouring kiss just as we arrived at our destination.

Breaking out of his arms, I asked, "Are we here?" I quickly readjusted my skirt and blouse.

"We are." He combed back his hair. "Are you ready for some fun?"

"What, more fun?" I grinned.

"Oh, there's always plenty of that. Why else be alive?" He smirked, and his cheeks dimpled, making me want to slap him for being so hot.

He opened his door and raced over to let me out. Lachlan was a natural at playing the gentleman. And I loved it.

When it came to career, I planned to be anyone's equal—man, woman or nonbinary. But when it came to Lachlan opening doors, my inner hot-blooded romantic purred.

Justin opened the door for Harriet, and she stepped onto the sidewalk with her chin in the air, playing a princess. "Thanks." She smiled sweetly and then turned to me. "Now what have you been up to?"

I bit my lip. "Nothing."

"Don't bullshit," she said. "Look at those glowing cheeks." She linked her arm in mine. "This is fun. And a chauffeur too."

Lachlan said something to Justin and then came and took my hand.

As we passed a long line, Harriet said, "This looks popular."

"It's got a reputation," said Lachlan.

"There are lots of women," I said, noticing beautiful, young women with lots of exposed flesh.

"I think I'm going to be the oldest here," said Harriet, staring at the crowd.

"They're here for Ollie," said Lachlan, greeting the security, who nodded and let us pass through.

"Who's Ollie?" I asked.

"Orlando Thornhill. He's a young guitarist who's destined to become famous, if he gets his shit together."

"I look forward to seeing him," Harriet said.

"I'll introduce you. He's a great guy." He looked at Harriet. "He's a bit wild."

"Then we'll get on well." She giggled.

28

LACHLAN

This time, I had the good sense to knock. The last time I walked into that band room, I'd interrupted a girl going down on Ollie.

"Enter if you're good-looking," a voice from inside bellowed.

I looked at Miranda and cocked my head. "You better go in, then."

She laughed and shook her head in that modest way of hers.

We trundled in and found Orlando strumming his guitar.

"Hey, good to see you made it," he said, looking from me to Miranda, and then lingering on Harriet.

"This is Miranda and her sister Harriet," I said, pointing to my guests. "And this is Orlando."

"My friends call me Ollie," he said. "Nice to meet you." He smiled at Miranda and then locked eyes with Harriet, who returned a flirtatious smile. Placing his guitar on a stand, he added, "We're on in half an hour. Do you want a spliff?"

I shook my head. "No. I've given up."

He popped the joint in his mouth. "Promise not to tell my folks?"

I saluted. "Scout's honor."

His mother had recently quizzed me on whether I'd seen Ollie smoking pot. I hated lying, especially to Clarissa and Aidan, who I considered great people. I just said that I'd never seen him doing it in front of me. Which was true.

He looked at Miranda and Harriet. "Would you like to partake?"

When Miranda passed on his offer, I wasn't surprised. I couldn't imagine her popping anything too harmful into her mouth. Only my cock, which wasn't that harmful. Well…

maybe a little. When starved of pussy.

Dirty thoughts of her luscious lips wrapped around my dick sent a rush of blood between my legs. The steamy session in the car hadn't helped matters either.

"I wouldn't mind a puff," said Harriet.

"Follow me," said Ollie.

When they left the room, Miranda rolled her eyes. "My sister's a bit of a nympho, I'm afraid."

"And Ollie's the male equivalent. They should get on well." I smiled.

"How old is he?"

"Twenty going on forty. He's an old soul." I chuckled. "A good guy. A great surfer… and a gentleman on the waves." In response to Miranda's puzzled frown, I added, "A good way to judge a person is by how they behave on the surf."

"There's surfing etiquette?"

I nodded. "Believe it or not, it can be cut-throat out there. I've seen my share of punch-ups on the beach from dudes cutting in on each other's waves. Ollie might be a pleasure junkie, but he's a top guy."

"Harriet's twenty-six," she said.

"So?" I shrugged. "Age doesn't matter. In fact, a lot of young guys find older women sexy."

"Do you?" she asked.

"I'm not that young." I grinned. "I need to warm up a little. Do you want to wait here for Harriet, so that you're not out there alone? You might get eaten alive."

"By who? There are mainly women."

"I saw guys checking you out." I held her close. "And why wouldn't they? You're the most beautiful woman here."

"I think that's a stretch. But hey, thanks. You say the nicest things."

I ran my hand up her leg and caressed her naked ass.

That did it. Warming up could wait.

I locked the door, licked my lips, and crooked my finger. Patting my thigh, I said, "Come and sit on my lap."

Miranda lowered herself onto me. "I hope I'm not too heavy."

"Light as a feather." I untied her blouse, unclasped her bra, and teased her nipples with my tongue.

"This might be quick and hard." I raised her skirt.

Her slick, hot pussy sucked up my finger approvingly. I almost growled from anticipation. "You take my breath away."

I unzipped my pants and pulled out my throbbing dick. Lifting her by the hips, I guided her on top of me.

I hissed at how tight she was. "My God, Miranda, you're going to ruin me."

I watched in the mirror. Her tits danced in my face as I ate at her nipples. It was hard and fast. Frenzied thrusts that sent currents of pleasure through me. Friction of the kind to turn a man into a blubbering mess.

Miranda dug her nails into my arms and moaned as her pussy convulsed around my shaft.

I knew that any minute we'd be interrupted, which only heightened my arousal as my cock became a piston.

A cataclysmic rush swept through me. Stars exploded before me, and a tight groan shot from my lips as I erupted violently inside her.

Seconds later, a knock came at the door.

Miranda immediately jumped off and pulled a face. We were like teenagers getting caught in the act. Only we were hot-blooded adults.

As she buttoned up her blouse, I ambled to the door. Noticing her bra on the ground, I cocked my head toward it before releasing the lock.

Orlando and Harriet looked at us. They might as well have winked.

Noticing Miranda's crooked blouse, I pointed at it. She bit her lip, and I smiled.

"Now what have you two been up to?" asked Harriet.

"Just warming up." I stretched my arms.

"You've been gone for a while," said Miranda, looking at her sister.

Orlando looked at Harriet and smiled. Something told me that it wasn't just a spliff they'd been sucking on.

"We better get out there," I said to Orlando.

Miranda followed me out to the side of the stage. I stroked her pretty face and, cupping her chin, kissed her soft lips.

"I'll catch you after the set. I hope you enjoy it." I gazed into her pretty eyes and added, "I'm going to drum like a savage on steroids knowing that you're not wearing a bra and panties."

She rolled her eyes and shook her head.

Yep. I had it bad, all right.

29

MIRANDA

After we managed to find a table with a decent view of the band, I finally got a good look at the visually stimulating venue. Suiting the jazz atmosphere, instruments and black-and-white photos of musicians fought for space on the red walls.

Lachlan sat behind his drumkit in front of lush red velvet drapes. His inked biceps flexed as he brushed over different parts of his kit, creating a texture of rhythm. With his lips parted and eyes half-closed, Lachlan looked like he did when we fucked.

"Oh my God," Harriet said, fanning her face. "Orlando."

I had to agree, with that cocky strut, he was a natural rock star. Away from the stage, however, he seemed very down-to-earth, lacking the type of vanity that some good-looking people possessed. And all the girls in the audience loved him. The more he pranced about, the louder they screamed.

"You didn't, did you?" I asked.

"Do what?"

"He couldn't stop looking at you, Harry," I said.

Harriet's smile widened. "We only did some disgusting flirting."

"Disgusting?" I asked.

"Everything had a sexual connotation. You know, sexy banter. I nearly orgasmed watching him suck on a spliff."

I wondered if rampant sex drive was genetic, considering that in the space of a few weeks I'd gone from zero to greedy.

"He's only twenty, Harry," I said.

She shrugged. "So? I don't care. I don't want to marry the guy."

I just want to fuck him."

I opened my hands. "But aren't you scared you might get hurt? I've seen how teary you get when it doesn't work out."

"Yeah… sure…" She shrugged. "But hey, he's too young for me to think of as a potential boyfriend. He's just into fun, and as long as I remind myself of that, why not? I mean, look at him."

Tall, dark, and handsome, Orlando definitely exuded a certain Dionysian allure as the cry of his guitar joined an oozy saxophone solo, inciting rapturous applause. He pushed his pelvis against his instrument suggestively, acting like the consummate guitarist, while his fingers moved rapidly over the strings.

I returned my attention to Lachlan, who epitomized a Viking god, up there behind that large drumkit. His artful strokes resonated all the way down to my pelvis.

The band's sophisticated and mesmerizing tunes conjured up images of the New York art scene in the sixties and seventies, and although the rhythms were complex, I couldn't stop swaying as though in a trance.

When the set came to an end, the girls pounced. Lachlan and Orlando had women lining up to speak to them.

"Oh well, I'm probably punching above my weight," admitted Harriet, pointing to the huddle of girls. "But he did kiss me." She brimmed with pride like she'd won a prize.

"I thought so," I said. "Your cheeks had that glow about them."

"He rubbed himself against me too. He was so fucking hard and really big."

"What? He showed you his penis?"

Harriet laughed. "No. But I felt it against my leg."

I went to respond when I observed Lachlan being cornered by an older woman who'd wrapped her arms around his neck and went to kiss him. Even though he extricated himself from her clutches and shook his head, she persisted and followed him down the corridor as he came toward me. She kept talking to him despite his obvious disinterest.

He looked over at me and cocked his head, gesturing for me to follow him.

Orlando, meanwhile, ignoring the girls chasing him along, glanced over at Harriet and gestured toward the band room.

"I think he's inviting you back, Harry," I said.

"Do you think? But did you see all those girls? Hell, they're gorgeous."

"And so are you. You're real, Harry."

"About that." She bit her lip. "I want to get my boobs done."

"Huh? But you're a C-cup, you crazy girl. And men like real tits," I said, thinking about Lachlan's insatiable fondness for fondling mine.

"How would you know? You only just started fucking," she said.

"Well..." I opened my hands. "Lachlan mentioned something about men preferring real breasts."

She pointed to a pair of women whose very large breasts defied gravity. "I want a pair like those."

I pulled a face. "My boobs don't look like that, and without a bra, they swing around."

"You're not kidding. They're moving all over the place. Where's your bra, sis?" Harry asked. "When you were swaying earlier to the music, I noticed them jiggling about. Lachlan noticed."

"You saw him?" I asked, my face heating.

"Yeah. I did. He's into you. And he's really hot and rich. Lucky you."

I studied her, looking for a hint of envy but instead only caught a supportive smile.

She clutched my hand. "Come on. Let's go and claim them before some of those babes shimmy their perfect bodies into the band room."

"Harry, you're really beautiful. And real. That's why guys go for you."

"Thanks, sis. But I still want bigger tits."

I puffed out a frustrated breath. "You're crazy. You don't want to become one of those girls."

"No. I don't. But I can still have big boobs and be me," she replied.

Picturing our mom's horrified reaction, I reassured myself that Harriet would never be able to afford it.

"Do what you want, Harry. But it's a waste of money. And you've got great breasts. I wish mine were like yours," I said, burning at the thought of Lachlan's lips drenching my nipples.

"Come on, let's go to the band room," I said.

"Woo-hoo, sis, look at us. Groupies," Harriet squealed.

That title, although a joke, sat uncomfortably with me. It reminded me of all the girls that Lachlan attracted performing that sexy musician role. Although he could have had a job cleaning sewerage pipes and women would still circle him.

As expected, hordes of females barricaded the door, waiting for Orlando to grace them with his presence.

Harriet brazenly walked through amid grumblings and squawks. I even heard the word "slut." Harriet obviously didn't hear. Otherwise, it may have gotten ugly.

We hurried through the door and shut it quickly.

"Lock it," said Orlando, lounging back with an unlit cigarette dangling from his lips, twisting off the top from a beer bottle.

"Sorry about that. It's crazy out there. Blame it on him," Lachlan said, pointing at his guitarist.

Orlando shrugged it off with a chuckle. I could see that Lachlan was like an older brother.

"That was amazing. I haven't heard that kind of music live before. Where can we buy it?" I asked.

"There's a ton of brilliant seventies jazz fusion out there," said Lachlan. "We're not playing originals."

"But still. It's so hypnotic," I said.

"Did you like it, Harriet?" asked Orlando.

"You bet. It was super cool. You've got a truckload of fans out there." She pointed to the door. "I thought a few were about to pull my hair out."

"Oh, that only happens around Lachlan and his ex. Jane's been known to pull hair."

"Don't worry." Lachlan turned to me. "I told her that I'll call the cops if she comes close."

I waited for a grin that never arrived. "Oh. Really? She's trouble?"

"Uh-huh. She's nuts." He opened out his arm for me.

Lachlan squeezed me gently against his hot, inviting body. When his masculine scent swept through me, I forgot all about his potentially psycho ex.

"You really liked the music?" he asked.

"I loved it."

He leaned in and whispered, "You're not wearing a bra, and I'm seriously fucking hard."

I moved away and studied him. "Is that all you think about all the time?"

He touched my hand. "No. Only every seven seconds."

I had to laugh at how crazy that sounded. "Oh well. I'm glad you like my boobs."

"I like more than your boobs. I like you. All over. Including your brain. You're smart. That's what drew me to you in the first place. Hell, I even liked you in that ugly brown dress."

My eyebrows flew up. "Really? Shit. That was my ugly phase."

"You've never had an ugly phase I bet."

Just as an image of me at college, overweight and pimply, intruded my thoughts, a woman entered the room, and Lachlan's body tensed.

Her eyes trapped him, and I became invisible.

30

LACHLAN

Holy shit. Linda. I should've known inviting Miranda to my regular hangout would spell trouble. Although I'd never taken any girl to the Red House before, I wanted her there.

Linda stood so close that the liquor on her breath made me want to puke.

"You haven't been returning my calls," she said.

Had Miranda not been within earshot, I would have said, "Last time I saw you, I threatened to call the cops." Instead, I said, "I've been busy."

Her eyes narrowed.

We only hooked up twice. The first time, Linda crawled under a table and sucked me off at some dark, smoky joint that I'd stumbled into one night. That was back in my bad days. But I had no excuse for the more recent experience, when I hooked her knee under my arm, after she pleaded with me to fuck her.

"I think you should leave." I rose and led Linda to the door. "The guards can call you a cab and wait with you."

"No," she snapped, yanking her arm away.

I rolled my eyes and joined Miranda. "I'm just going to walk her outside before she causes a scene," I whispered.

"She's already doing that," she replied, looking over my shoulder.

Linda stood close again, breathing down my neck. "So this is your new girl." She turned to Miranda and said, "Watch him… he'll use you, like he did me. All that fucking Mr. Charming shit. He virtually ripped my panties off and fucked me on the street. And now he doesn't want anything to do with me."

"That's bullshit, Linda, and you know it," I said. "You have to go, or else I'll call security."

The next minute, she started to cry. Taking her gently by the arm, I led Linda out of the room, catching a sympathetic look from Orlando.

When we stepped outside, Linda fell into my arms. "I'm crazy about you, Lachie." She grabbed my crotch and started to rub it. "Your big dick has done things to me that I've never experienced before in a man. I just want you to fuck me. Real dirty like. The dirtier the better. I know you like it that way. You told me so last time."

"I'm not that guy anymore."

When she erupted into sobs, I placed my arm around her. A bad idea because within a breath, she clawed at my chest and my zipper.

I pushed away from her. "No."

"What's wrong with me? Is it because I'm older? Young men chase me all the time."

"It's not because of your age." I paused to choose my words carefully. "It was just that once. A casual fuck. You even referred to it as that. I'm sorry if you read more into it. There was never going to be more."

Tears streamed down her face. "I had an abortion. You know that?"

I frowned. "But I used protection. And you also insisted you were on the pill."

She stared down at her feet. "Well, I got pregnant, and I aborted because"—she pointed into my face— "you wouldn't return my calls. Mr. High-and-Fucking-Mighty."

"Now look, Linda, I'm sorry you had to experience that. If I had known..." I searched for the right words. What would I have done?

Hell.

Tears poured down her cheeks. "You're going to pay for this. How dare you lead me on, make me pregnant, and then toss me away like a common whore." Her voice rang through the air like rocks pelting down on me.

Although we were in a quiet alleyway that backed the venue, there were smokers present, watching on.

Sensing a presence, I turned and discovered Miranda frowning. She'd obviously heard Linda's accusations.

I opened my palms. "Hey, Miranda, no. Please let me explain."

"I don't feel well. I'm heading off," she said in quiet and controlled voice. Unlike Linda, Miranda maintained a dignified manner.

I followed her down the alleyway and left Linda, ranting and raving, behind.

"Let me explain," I said, sprinting by Miranda's side.

She stopped. "This is a bad idea. Please let me go." She jerked back her hand.

"Don't do this," I said.

"I'll do what I like." Her eyes filled with fire before turning cold.

"That's right. Run away from him. He's no good. He'll fuck you and leave you," yelled Linda.

Now that pissed me off. I turned sharply to Linda. "When did this so-called abortion happen?"

"A month ago."

"But we got together at least six or seven months ago," I said, trying to figure out exactly when it was. I recalled returning from Hawaii. When was that? I had to check.

"Well..." She stared down at her feet.

I could see she was disturbed. "Look, I can't do anything about that. But if you like, I can pay for a counselor."

She looked up at me as though I'd asked her to confess her sins to a priest. "I don't need a fucking counselor."

I puffed. "I'm just trying to help. Is there anything else I can do?"

"Yes. Fuck me again." She bit her lip and started to cry again.

I shook my head. "I'm not that guy anymore, Linda. I'm sorry for giving you the wrong impression. I..." What more could I say?

"Oh, Lachie... you need to be with someone like me. We're

compatible. We're both Scorpios. We love it dark and dirty."

I removed her hand from mine. "It's not going to happen. You're an attractive woman. I'm sure you'll find someone."

I walked away, and much to my relief, she remained silent.

When I turned, I saw Harriet standing close by. "I guess you heard all of that?"

She nodded. "She seems off her face. I came out looking for Miranda. I didn't mean to listen."

"I've got nothing to hide. It's how it is. I was away in Hawaii. And it couldn't have been me."

"You were nice to her. You offered to pay for counseling."

I grabbed my cell phone and called Miranda. Of course, she didn't pick up. Where was she? I should have run after her.

"I need you to call your sister and explain to her that Linda was nothing to me, and that I was in Hawaii. So I couldn't've gotten her pregnant."

"She was pretty upset." She raised a brow. "She's not very experienced when it comes to these situations."

"These situations?" I repeated under my breath. "I'm sure you get the whole casual hookup thing."

She studied me for a moment. I hoped she hadn't taken that the wrong way.

"I do. But Andie's really different." She pulled a mock smile. "She's never been with a guy. And then you come along, sweep her off her feet, and install her into that sexy penthouse, and now I don't even recognize her. But hey"—she pulled out her phone—"I'll call her. Just wait there." She tapped on her phone.

I puffed a breath. Frustration punched my gut at the thought of Miranda thinking I'd gotten Linda pregnant and then abandoned her.

I thought of the condom and the fact that Linda was forty. While Harriet called her sister, I opened up some pictures I'd taken of sunsets in Hawaii and looked at the dates. My chest finally untangled. It was eight months ago. Linda was bullshitting.

It was still a fucked-up situation that I could've done without.

"Andie, talk to him," Harriet urged. "Lachlan's seriously worried about you." There was a pause. "He's thirty. People fuck. And to be honest, she struck me as being a little unhinged. And seriously drunk."

After a moment, Harriet passed me her phone. I took it and nodded.

"Hey," I said.

"Hey."

"I'm sorry. I really am. How much of that did you hear?"

"I heard enough to know that I shouldn't continue seeing you," she said.

"It was twice. We hooked up twice."

"While you were seeing me?"

"No way," I said, almost laughing at that notion, considering I had nothing left for anyone else. "I've just worked it out. It was around eight months ago. So I couldn't have made her pregnant. Don't you see? She's bullshitting."

"Have you fucked other women while you've been with me?" she asked, sniffling.

"Are you kidding me?" I breathed.

"Lachlan, I really need some space. Please leave me alone." She hung up.

I passed the phone back to Harriet. "Thanks."

"Give her a few days."

31

MIRANDA

Moans and groans penetrated through the wall. A sad reminder that I was in my saggy, old bed and not stretching out like some sated feline on Lachlan's firm king-size mattress.

Reality had crashed my party, and I'd come down with a thumping emotional hangover.

When I heard those ugly words firing from that drunken woman, I charged back to his apartment, chucked all my stuff into my suitcase, and cabbed it back to my former life, crying all the way.

I lifted my sad, sorry body, and seeing that it was seven in the morning, rather than sleeping off my heavy head and heart, I rose. Mainly because I couldn't bear Harriet and her operatic fucking any longer. They'd been at it all night.

Ava was at our mom's, and being Saturday, I'd booked her into her first ballet class. I didn't have the heart to renege on my promise, since she'd spoken of little else. And as promised, Lachlan had arranged a generous annual subscription, which included flamenco. His generosity made it hard for me to hate him. Why couldn't he be bad? Instead, I pined for him.

I hadn't even had a chance to buy Ava's ballet slippers as promised.

After showering and crying again, I headed into the kitchen, grumbling at the mess of beer bottles and smelly half-eaten pizza left-overs.

I made myself a coffee, stepped over clothes strewn on the ground, and plonked myself on the sofa. A guitar case with a bra dripping over it told me that Orlando must have stayed over, which didn't come as a surprise.

Thirty minutes later, feeling semi-human, I stumbled out of the apartment, descended the stairs, and was reminded of how shitty my life looked before Lachlan had swept me off into a fairy tale. Even the emaciated cats with their noses in empty cartons stared up at me. Instead of pleading for more food, their eyes reflected pity. Was I that transparent that even stray cats could read my misery?

Half an hour later, I walked through my parents' door.

Ava skipped up to me and wrapped her little arms around my thighs, which helped lift my sagging spirit.

My mother strode out of the kitchen, carrying a cup of tea and a copy of *The Magic Faraway Tree* under her arm.

"There you are." Her eyes narrowed. "You look awful."

"Thanks, Mom," I said.

Sitting in his favorite armchair, my dad looked up from his newspaper and smiled warmly. "Don't listen to her. You look lovely as always."

I went over and kissed him on the cheek. "Thanks, Dad."

His soft, kind eyes radiated so much support and love, a lump formed in my throat.

Ava leaped and sang, "I'm going to ballerina classes."

"Do you think that's a good idea? She'd get more from going to book readings and playgroups devoted to intellectual development," my mother said.

I glanced over at my dad and rolled my eyes, to which he responded with a "Oh well, you know your mother" look.

He was gentle and forgiving, the counter-opposite of my mother. Harriet said that was why they'd lasted. The romantic in me liked to think it was also love and attraction. For a man in his late forties, my father was still very handsome. My mother adored him, as he did her.

Theirs was an insta-love story. My dad met my mother at college, they became sweethearts, and married within a couple of months. My mother side-stepped that question of why they'd hurried into it. But when doing the math, Harriet was born six months later. My mom was twenty-two at the time.

My father was the demonstrative one whereas my mother, suffering the kind of anxiety that came from being a perfectionist, kept her feelings locked away. But every now and then, I'd notice that eagle-like stare fade away into a smile.

"Ava already knows how to read," I countered. "Which is advanced for a five-year-old. In any case, dance and music are known to develop neural pathways. The more we have, the brainier we are."

I found myself wondering whether orgasms destroyed synapses, considering how air-headed I'd become since Lachlan pressed his buff body against mine.

"At least you got the brains in the family. You take after me," she said, looking impressed by my neurological justification for sending Ava to dance classes.

"I think I'm more like Dad," I said, giving my dad a subtle wink. "He's the brains in the family. He's the one with a PhD."

He laughed. "I don't know about that. Your mother always beats me at Scrabble."

A flicker of a smile touched my mother's mouth as she handed me the dog-eared book that I'd adored as a child. The smell of it alone flooded me with memories of when I was young and carefree and had no idea what an orgasm was or what falling hard for a hot guy felt like.

I wanted the old me back. That girl who couldn't understand why my sister always cried over boys.

"Harriet has forgotten we exist," my mother complained. "You're not much better."

"Oh, Mom, life's kind of hectic. Promise I'll make more of an effort."

"I'd like you to think about taking Ava to that school where they accelerate reading and writing skills."

"It's not my decision to make. I'm the aunt."

"You might as well be her mother." I couldn't argue with that. Harriet relied too heavily on my parents and me. But as I stared at my high-spirited niece with those big blue eyes, my mood lifted. I loved her as if she were my own.

"We have to go and buy some slippers before class," I said.

"They're very expensive. And her feet are growing all the time."

"True. But she can't go to ballet without them," I argued.

I went and grabbed Ava's overnight bag and then hugged my parents before heading off.

Just as we were leaving, my phone vibrated. My pulse raced but came to a crashing halt when Lachlan's name didn't appear.

Why hadn't he at least called and tried to explain? Some begging or that line "I can't live without you" would have been nice.

Do guys even say that?

I looked at the screen and read: *"It was hot. You're hot."* Ollie.

Biting into my cheek, I realized that I had somehow ended up with my sister's phone.

I called my number, and it went to voicemail, which I was informed was not taking messages. The last time my voicemail did that was due to an overload. And the sudden thought that Lachlan may have left some messages sent a bolt of energy through me.

With Ava skipping along, I virtually sprinted to my car.

Just my luck, the traffic was thick. There was no way I'd find the time to shop for shoes and stop by at the apartment. But I needed my phone.

I suddenly recalled seeing a box of used dance shoes the day I'd visited the dance school. That came as a relief, given that my heart was stubbornly determined to get that phone.

Having resolved the issue of dance shoes, I exited the freeway and headed back home.

When we arrived at the apartment, Ava said, "What about my shoes?"

"I've run out of time, sweetie."

Her mouth turned down.

"Promise I'll get them for you. Come on. Let's hurry. I just left something behind."

When we entered the apartment, Harriet was still asleep. I

knocked first and then opened the door slightly to take a peek. Seeing her asleep alone, I entered.

Ava followed me in and jumped on the bed, waking her mother.

Harriet yawned. "Mommy's had a big night and needs to sleep." She rubbed her head.

Noticing hickeys, I pointed at her neck, and Harriet lifted the sheet to cover herself.

"We've somehow ended up with each other's phones," I said, setting her phone down. I turned to Ava. "Give me a minute, and then we'll leave for classes. Okay? Go and get that little tutu from your room. The rainbow one you like."

At the mention of her favorite garment, Ava bounded off.

"She can't wear that, she'll look like a hippy's kid," said Harriet.

"That's all she's got, and real tutus cost a fortune."

Harriet's frown melted into a bright smile. "Oh my God."

"Boy toy?"

She nodded. "Boy toy is a sex god. I mean, he's only twenty, but hell, he's got the moves. The body. And the stamina…"

"I noticed," I replied dryly.

"Oh… did we keep you awake?" Her brow puckered. "Why were you here? I thought you would've been with your own sex god."

"He didn't tell you?" I asked, wondering what had taken place after I ran away.

"He had to leave suddenly." She stared at me for a moment. "He obviously didn't know she was pregnant. Is that why you moved out? For that?"

I couldn't believe how forgiving she was. "I don't know what to think. She made such a scene about him ignoring her calls."

"She was smashed, Andie."

As Ava came fluttering back in, I rose. "You look very nice."

"Come here, darling." Harriet kissed Ava. "Now you show them what a great little ballerina you really are."

"Catch you in a few hours," I said.

After enrolling Ava, I found a pair of shoes that fit and then left the studio to check my phone.

Lachlan had left twenty messages.

32

LACHLAN

I'd spent the whole damn night hugging a bottle and not Miranda. It all came flashing past me like a movie edited on crack. It was late morning when I surfaced, and rubbing my eyes, I went in search of my cell phone. A vague recollection of throwing it against the wall in a rage suddenly struck me, and my body slumped.

As a sad testament to pathetic rage, the shattered device lay by the coffee table. I picked it up and removed the SIM card. Luckily, I had some older ones lying about. Although I soon discovered that bleary-eyed hangovers and SIM card insertion didn't mix well.

I finally got it to work and called Miranda.

"Hey," she said.

"You answered," I said.

"I thought I better after all those messages."

"You listened to them?"

"I did," she said.

"I bet I rambled like some drunken idiot."

"You were actually very complimentary," she said.

I took a breath. "What are you doing now? Can we meet for a quick coffee?"

"Quick?" she asked.

"I have to go on a trip. I'll be away for the week. I did mention that, didn't I?"

"Yes, with Britney."

"Are we okay?" I asked.

"We? There's a we?"

"There is for me," I said. Her surprise was matched by my

own. Was I asking her to be my one and only? Was that my dick talking or my heart?

"I'm not sure what to think, Lachlan. It's been a whirlwind, this thing between us, and maybe it's moving too fast."

"So what? I like you. A lot."

"You do?"

"I thought that would have been obvious by now," I said.

"You can't take your hands off me, I suppose."

"Hey, it's more than your beautiful body. I like being around you. I like talking to you. You're clever and calming."

"Calming?" she asked.

"Miranda, why don't you come over for a coffee and chat while I pack?" There was a long pause. "Are you there?"

"I guess I can."

"Good. I'll see you soon?"

"See you then," she said and ended the call.

In spite of Miranda's cool tone, I felt a sense of relief. At least I could explain how I couldn't have gotten Linda pregnant.

My phone buzzed. It was Britney.

"I'm just making sure you remembered. You've become pretty distracted since you started dating our ex-admin assistant."

"I'll be there." I ended the call abruptly.

Two coffees later, I'd managed to gather my belongings for the trip, and just as I zipped up my luggage, the intercom buzzed.

I picked up the phone and said, "Hey, good-looking. You've still got your pass, I trust."

"I have. I just didn't want to barge in."

"Barging isn't really your style. I'd expect a glide," I returned.

Her giggle brought a smile to my face.

I waited by the private elevator for her.

When the doors opened, Miranda stepped out and I took her into my arms, where she remained rigid.

"Can I get you a coffee?" I asked.

She nodded. "I just took Ava to ballet, and we passed your

mother's very loud but captivating class in action."

I chuckled. "Loud and captivating sums it up well."

"Ava was so spellbound, I had to drag her away."

"Sign her up. My mother loves teaching kids. I bought her an annual pass, which means she can try as many classes as she likes."

"That's so kind of you. Thank you. She really loved it. And her ballet teacher was impressed."

"Good. A dancer in the family. That should keep things real."

Miranda pulled a face. "Real? There's a hungry dancer on every corner."

"Sure, but talent has a way of standing out," I said.

I headed for the kitchen and turned on my espresso machine, watching steamy water gush out. Although it had taken me a while, I'd finally mastered that noisy machine.

"A cappuccino?" I asked.

"Sure. Do you want me to make it?"

"Nope. I've got it down to a fine art."

With the concentration of a rookie barista, I made Miranda a cup of coffee and then followed her into the living room.

"Speaking of talent," said Miranda, walking over to the window. "You've got more than your fair share."

"Thanks. I'm glad you liked our kind of music."

"You seem very committed. Is it something you'd like to do full-time?" she asked.

"Sure. But I'd also like to turn Peace Holdings into a successful company that focuses on socially beneficial projects."

"That sounds like a noble ambition." Her cool response wasn't lost on me.

As my eyes met hers, I searched for a smile, but she remained cool.

When Miranda returned her attention to the cloudless blue sky, I joined her on the balcony.

"Tell me, do you prefer me as a CEO, or a musician?"

Miranda turned and studied me for a moment. "I like both. Although, if I were your girlfriend, I'd find it difficult. All the women at the Red House were virtually throwing themselves at you."

I took her hand. "I thought you *were* my girlfriend."

A line grew between her brows. "But we've only been seeing each other for a month or so."

"I want you to be my girlfriend." I held her soft hand and played with her fingers. "As for the women at the Red House, I've been there, done that. I got that out of my system."

"And Linda?"

I puffed. "That was just a couple of regrettable times, after which she stalked me and became obsessed. I'm sorry you had to hear that. And you do believe me when I say it wasn't me who got her pregnant?" I grabbed my phone to find the Hawaii images. "Oh shit... I trashed my phone. I had images of Hawaii. I'd just returned from there when..." I couldn't bring myself to utter those ugly words.

"Harriet told me what happened. I believe you." She knitted her fingers. "You're about to spend a week with Britney. I don't know if I've got the constitution for this manic lifestyle of yours."

"Neither have I." I pulled a tight smile. "In any case, you've heard the worst."

"Have I?" She held my eyes.

"I've got nothing to hide," I said.

Miranda followed me back to the sofa.

I turned to look at her. "Are you're still angry with me?"

She sipped on her coffee. "No. I get that you've got a past. I just need to know you a little better."

I stroked her cheek. "Feel free to ask questions."

"It's not that. Time reveals the person."

I took her into my arms. "Then why don't we just go with the flow?"

33

MIRANDA

We had been going with the flow before rapids swept us onto some rocks.

I'd resolved to tell Lachlan we needed to slow things down. Maybe keep it to weekends. The thought of not seeing him was too painful. And stupid on my part. He hadn't really done anything wrong. I knew he once partied hard. So what? Harriet was right—people had a right to make mistakes as long as they changed.

According to her, it was normal for new lovers to be insatiable. But I hated how attached to Lachlan I'd become.

I also had a career to think of.

But as I fell into those shimmering blue eyes, I just couldn't run away.

He pulled me into his strong body almost roughly. Our bodies crushed together, and an agonizing need swept through me as his tongue traced my lips.

It was a slow, drugging kiss. My body surrendered into his arms, and he pressed against me, making me ache for his touch.

A buzzer sounded, interrupting that steamy moment. Painful though it was unravelling from his arms, it was timely too. I had to remain strong. And as much as I would miss him, at least this trip would give me some space.

Lachlan sighed. "It can't be that time, surely?" He glanced down at his watch. "Damn. I have to go."

He walked to the intercom. "Give me ten minutes." He combed back his hair. "Stay here," he said, touching my arm as I adjusted my blouse.

Boy how much I wanted to say "yes" but instead, I remained silent.

He rubbed his jaw. "After all, you're helping me, which means the world to me. With everything that's happening around the family business, I don't know who to trust anymore."

"I hope you're not in any danger," I said, noticing his tensed brow.

"You do believe it's my dad's handy work, don't you? I hope you don't think I'm some kind of white-collar criminal."

"I don't ..." I thought about the car chase and added, "Although driving without a license suggests an element of recklessness."

"I've got a driver now. See, I told you, I've finally grown up." His smile quickly faded. "Losing my license was not because of me being irresponsible, though. I took the wheel from my drunk brother. I drove us home one night after a function. I'd had a few drinks. I was far from drunk. Anyway, the cops pulled us over and I took the rap. And this trip's about clearing my father's name to avoid me having to go to prison."

My eyebrows sprung up. "But you're not responsible for his actions."

"Yes, I know. But he's a very frail man. I wouldn't be able to live with myself if he went to prison." He smiled grimly.

His willingness to sacrifice his own freedom and reputation demonstrated just how decent he really was, despite the bone-chilling thought of him languishing in a dirty prison cell.

He stroked my cheek. "I have to go."

His lips touched mine, and then he withdrew.

I watched as he raced around collecting his bits and pieces, throwing them into a leather satchel along with his laptop. He leaned in and kissed me again. Something he kept doing. My body liked that little obsession.

"Ride the elevator with me. That way I can hold you," he said, smiling sweetly.

After he pressed the button, Lachlan's fingers crept under my blouse, fondling my breasts and then groping my ass while he groaned and ate at my mouth.

Talk about hot and steamy. By the time we stepped out onto the lobby, I needed another shower.

"I'll call you."

I looked at him for a moment, even though I'd let him touch me, which had distracted me from what I really needed to say.

"Lachlan. This is moving too fast for me."

He stopped and looked at me as though trying to understand a complex puzzle. His frown deepened. "You want to stop seeing me?"

I shifted my weight as I fought with my heart. "No... but maybe while you're away, it will give me time to reflect."

"You decided this between the elevator and the street?" he asked.

"I actually decided it before I arrived. I've grown too attached and I've got my career to think about."

He squinted in the sun. He took my hand. "I'll miss you while I'm gone."

My voice cracked. Tears welled in my eyes. Oh no. I was stronger than that. "Let's just take it a little slower. That's all."

"If that's what you want." Our eyes locked for what seemed like ages.

I stood on the busy sidewalk. Everything became a blur again. Had I just suggested to that beautiful man that I needed space?

I needed my head examined.

Lachlan jumped into the passenger seat of his limousine. Watching on, I waved him good-bye, and he cast me a lingering gaze that wasn't so much sultry but serious and questioning.

***

"You're fucking crazy," said Harriet as she watched me unpack my suitcase. "You're giving up a penthouse apartment and a sexy, attentive guy, who also happens to be a really nice person. I mean, I saw his concern for that wacko Linda. I can't think of many guys who would've discussed her well-being and offered to pay for a fucking counselor."

I stopped hanging my clothes and turned to her. "He offered to do that?"

"Uh-huh. She was bawling her eyes out, and he looked genuinely concerned. He sat with her and let her have her say. I've been with enough guys to know what's bullshit. And that was real." She nodded. "So what's your problem?"

"It's just moving so fast. I'm wondering if it's only lust, and that he'll soon tire of me when I'm in deeper. That would break me."

"Fear only helps if you're being chased by a bear."

I looked at my sister, and my mouth curled for the first time since saying good-bye to Lachlan.

"It's always lust in the beginning," she continued. "And then you get to know each other, and if it's meant to work it just does. You're only twenty-three."

"That's the point. He wants me to be his girlfriend."

Her eyes widened. "Holy fuck. Lucky you."

I shook my head. "I guess…I mean… I haven't broken up with him. I just asked for some space."

"Right. And how does that feel?"

"I'm missing him like hell. And he only left yesterday. We've been together almost nonstop for over four weeks now." My throat tightened. "All I do is think about him."

"So now that you've created this space, how's your focus?"

I bit my lip to stem another flow of tears. "It's worse. I can't concentrate at all."

"Well there you go. Has he called?"

I shook my head and bit into a miserably short nail.

"You've got to suck it up." She stared at her face in the mirror. "So what if he eventually breaks your heart."

"Thanks for the vote of confidence." I sniffed. "In any case, I just asked for some space while he was gone. I'm not breaking up with him."

"Space is a euphemism for breaking up, Andie."

"Do you think that's what he would've thought?" I asked. The fact he hadn't texted had left a bitter taste. And recalling how precarious his life was, if any time he needed support, it was now.

"Maybe. Look, Andie, a man like Lachlan can have whomever he wants."

"That's my point. I don't want to be one of many."

She rolled her eyes. "You're not. He wouldn't have asked you to be his girlfriend." She shook her head in disbelief. "I'll have to train some emotional toughness into you."

"You can't talk. One night with Ollie, and you've been acting like a lovesick teenager."

Harriet opened her hands. "We had a deep connection. I've been with enough guys to know the difference. And sure, I'm still a bit bummed by it. But that's how it is. You can't control those deep feelings. And unlike you and your tight-assed reaction to sexual chemistry, I know when it feels right. There was something between us that just clicked. The air crackled when we stood close."

I patted my hair in the mirror. "I best be off. I've got my new job starting today."

"That's something to look forward to." She smiled and then hugged me. "Don't worry. Just call him. Tell him you thought about it, and that you've had all the space you need."

Nodding slowly, I decided to wait and see.

After Lachlan drove off, I received an intriguing text from Florian, advising that I'd be working at a new location.

I stared down blankly at my clothes, unsure of whether to stick to plain and professional or individual and expressive. I settled for a green fitted skirt and a cream silk shirt that I'd bought in a moment of extravagance. It was novel for me to have some extra cash, and having done without for so long, I couldn't resist.

I arrived at the Arts District and found a car space right away, much to my surprise. Taking careful steps, I crept over a cracked pavement in an alleyway with gaping holes big enough to swallow me whole.

Standing before a loud graffiti-splattered door yelling rage, I turned the rusty knob, and after I managed to open the door, I discovered a derelict, run-down space. And not in that fashionably distressed way either. More abandoned and creepy. My expectation of working in a sleek, ultra-modern office with eye-catching art was suddenly dashed.

As I gulped back bitter disappointment, an outline of a body came to view behind a glass door. I knocked, and Florian opened the door, moving out of the way for me to enter.

The ramshackle room looked out onto an empty parking lot. It was as though I'd stepped into some dystopian world where humans were a rare sight.

"Bright and early. Good," he said, staring me up and down.

"When I noticed it wasn't the same address as your office, I wanted to give myself time to find it," I said.

"I've only just procured this space. This will be your little kingdom."

"Oh?" That sounded interesting. I liked the idea of being autonomous. That little bright moment dimmed, however, when a large insect-infested spiderweb caught my eye.

"It needs painting and cleaning, of course." He stepped over a box and I followed him back out into the large open space that probably once housed a large workforce.

"This area"—he stretched his arm—"will make a great exhibiting space." Florian gestured for me to follow him.

We headed down a dark corridor, where I took small, tentative steps to avoid stumbling over junk. When we arrived at an unlit staircase, I waited while Florian switched on the light in the basement. As I descended the rickety steps, I promised myself if I made it out alive, I'd wear sensible shoes and coveralls next time.

"This is ideal for storage." He pointed.

Claustrophobia threatened to steal my breath away. There were no windows, and my overactive morbid imagination suddenly pictured skeletons slumped in some dark corner. I even conjured up a scene from a British detective show where some psycho collected body parts for dinner.

Florian studied me and said, "Are you okay? You seem a bit squeamish."

"No. It's fine. I've just got a ton of questions, that's all."

A ton? More like a million.

I tried to hide my disappointment, even though my heart sank to an all-time low. Talk about a huge crash, especially after working at Lachlan's opulent estate.

I thought about the Pollocks, which Lachlan had asked after. I told him I'd look into it as soon as the right time came up, given that the paintings had been removed from their frames and were now stored in Florian's vaults. That was after he'd signed the contract that I'd drafted using Lachlan's attorney.

Florian's eyes roamed up and down my body. "You're a bit over dressed."

I nodded. "I wasn't sure what to expect. I thought I might have to meet with clients or…"

He wore a patronizing grin. "All in good time. I'd like you to focus on new talent and source tomorrow's million-dollar sale."

I thought about my passion for art history and the dream of one day handling works by the great masters at auctions. Or rummaging through family estates and finding a lost masterpiece in some dusty loft. Reality had suddenly turned that ambition into a fanciful dream.

As we returned to the front room, Florian said, "I like that you're driven." He wore a buttery smile. "Your first task is to have the foyer painted and ready for running as many shows as you can. This will make a great gallery space, I believe."

I sucked back a breath and studied the mess before me, imagining myself becoming more a janitor-slash-caretaker.

"I've also procured a couple of art students. They can help with heavy lifting and the renovations."

I nodded pensively. There was no mention of a budget, and the wage we'd agreed on was meager in comparison to what I'd earned working for Peace Holdings. Nevertheless, it was a foot in the door.

There was so much to gestate, I left those questions alone for now. Taking a deep breath, I looked around me. With hard work and steady focus, I could make it work, I told myself. And the natural light was excellent.

34

LACHLAN

It was surfers' heaven. A slow swell formed a perfect tube as two lone surfers rode back to the shore. What a rare sight. Great waves like that back home enticed hundreds into the water.

I stood at the balcony of the hotel, wishing that was me riding that sparkling turquoise wave.

Britney stepped out and joined me.

Since learning of her relationship with my sleazy father, I found it difficult to stare her in the eyes, regardless of whether my father, with that smooth tongue of his, had groomed her or not.

"They want more money." She rolled her eyes. "Typical fucking natives."

"Hey. We'll have none of that." I hated racism. As a jazz musician, most of my heroes were of African American descent, and I played with some great dudes, who I thought of as my creative brothers.

She clicked her tongue and stood before me with her hands on her hips. "Why aren't you bad like Brent?"

"I'm the black sheep of the family. Only this black sheep is the honest one."

"Well then, you're not going to like the bullshit story we're about to cook up."

"I never expected to. But I value my freedom more. Had Dad been well, I wouldn't be here. I'd let him take the rap. He should. He's been totally fucking dishonest." I pointed in her face. "And you're his fucking accomplice."

"Are we going to do this again?" she asked, unbuttoning her

shirt.

"You've got your own room."

"It's nothing you haven't seen before, and we're in a hurry. I haven't even got time for a shower. So, can I change my top without making you blush?" She smirked.

I rolled my eyes and returned my attention to the ocean.

"I'm decent now. You can look."

"Decent? You're dressed, you mean?" I pulled an ironic smirk.

Britney stuck her middle finger up.

"I'll meet you at the desk," I said.

As I waited at reception, I pressed on Miranda's pretty face, and my finger hovered over it for a moment. But respecting her need to take things slowly, I didn't text. That left a strange sensation. I liked speaking to her.

I studied her intelligent, sexy eyes and those lips, which had my cock lengthening. Maybe a quick text, something brief. But respecting her need for space, I decided not to.

My head was so filled with beautiful Miranda that when the receptionist arrived, it took me a moment to remember why I was there.

"Good afternoon. Do you know where I can rent a surfboard?"

She disappeared under the counter and returned with a leaflet. "Here, you'll find everything you need."

Just as I took the brochure and thanked her, Britney arrived and joined me.

"I don't think we'll have much time for sight-seeing."

"That's not what I had in mind." I tapped on an image of a surfboard.

"You've got a one-track mind," she commented.

"Where surfing and music's involved, I have," I said, leaving out women, despite them featuring at the top of my list of personal pleasures.

I tilted my head. "Let's see how Bird of Paradise is shaping up, shall we?"

The driver took the scenic route, indulging me with a spectacular vista of an endless inky sea as we snaked around the coastline.

"Are you sure this is the correct way?" Britney asked from the back seat.

I turned and looked at the driver and smiled apologetically. "Yes, madam."

Ten minutes later, having ascended to the peak of the island, we arrived at the site.

I looked at the driver. "Can you wait for us? We shouldn't be too long."

When we stepped out of the car, I saw a couple of men smoking cigarettes by the bare plot of land with no construction to speak of. One of the men was shirtless and built like a personal trainer.

Britney smoothed her hair and wiggled her ass as she walked over to them.

Holding out my hand, I introduced myself.

The older of the two nodded. "I'm Hector, and this is Rick." He pointed to the shirtless man.

"So..." I looked around the leveled ground. "Shouldn't the foundations be down, at least?"

"Yes, well... we've had trouble finding the men. Most of them are working as waiters. The tips and the girls are worth it." He chuckled.

I turned to Britney. "I thought we had a sizeable budget?"

Her uncertain nod contradicted that surmise.

Turning to Hector, I asked, "Do you mind if I talk to my colleague in private?"

"No, man, of course. We're here enjoying the view and discussing how we can get this up quickly and efficiently for you."

Britney followed me to the other side of the land—a jewel, situated at the highest point of the island, boasting unhindered views of the sea and a tropical forest. Not one reminder of civilization in sight, making it an ideal locale for a sleazy resort.

"What did you promise them?"

"I sent you the figures," she said. "I promised them a million."

"That should be enough for materials and labor, surely. I mean things come cheaply in these parts, don't they?"

Her face remained blank.

I thought of the Pollocks and how that business had yet to be concluded. I'd managed, through some cash I had sitting in an account, to quiet Varela. But not for long.

"Why do I get this feeling you're not telling me the whole story?"

"The check didn't clear," she said.

"What, the tiny sum of one mil?"

"It was *once* a tiny sum." Her mouth drew a tight line.

My heart sank. I took a deep breath, imagining myself showering in prison among burly desperados.

"Then we need to raise some cash," I said.

"What about your girlfriend and that spectacular sale of yours?"

"We're working on it." I exhaled a tight breath, thinking of Florian, and how he'd told me that the buyer had some cash flow issues at the eleventh hour.

"And where's the art?"

I rubbed my prickly jaw. "In the vaults at the dealer's."

Her eyebrows flung up so quickly, I felt a bead of sweat drip between my tightened shoulder blades.

"Is your insurance up to date?" she asked.

I shifted my weight. "Well…"

"Fuck, Lachlan."

I took a deep breath. "I'm not worried. Florian Storm's a reputable dealer who's been in the game for over twenty years. We've got a contract."

Her frown deepened. Britney was many things but not a fool, which was how I felt for not getting my shit together.

"I've got an idea," she said. "I set it up before I left. All I need is the go-ahead from you." I went to respond when she added, "After that nosey girl of yours opened up a can of worms by discovering the fake Monet, I stalled."

"Stalled at what?" I asked.

"Someone's interested in buying the Degas for half of its ten-million-dollar value."

I went to protest when she lifted her finger. "No questions asked. He'll send the cash straight over."

"What do you mean by no questions asked?"

"There's no provenance."

I combed back my hair roughly. "It's stolen property?"

She shrugged. "Can't say. I've been offered five million for it, though. I wanted to see what these guys had delivered first."

"How much was that?"

"You're looking at fifty thousand dollars' worth here."

I studied the flattened land. "Sell it." I rubbed my prickly jaw. "I loved that piece. Here I was thinking that one day it would belong to my children."

She frowned. "Children? One day? My, you've changed. I'll be seeing you with a pipe and a book soon."

"No need for fucking sarcasm. Although that book looks likely if I land in fucking prison, thanks to you and my father's dirty little tricks."

"Five million will get this done."

"I didn't have to be here for this." I kicked a stone away. "It could take weeks to have something to show here."

Britney eyed Rick, who was stretching his muscular arms. "I'm not in any hurry. I could stay here and oversee it."

"I'm sure you could," I replied dryly.

"Aren't you meant to be into surfing?"

"Yeah … but I can't stay here for weeks. There's Dad for one, and…"

"Miranda?" She cocked her head.

"Let's go back and talk money with these guys. Ring your guy, get that painting sold. No provenance?"

"One of your dad's buddies who needed some quick cash."

I shook my head. "Tell me, was he selling drugs to teenagers too?"

"Your father wouldn't have stooped that low," she said.

Britney's respect for my father maybe explained why they were so close. For a man addicted to power and accolades, my father sure as hell needed someone rooting for him. He'd lost my respect after trophy wife number two.

35

MIRANDA

Once I'd gotten over my disappointment, I could see that there was potential to make that space work. And I liked the idea of being my own boss. I would just have to budget.

Stepping over old newspapers, empty wrappers, and squashed soda cans, I decided to have a go at clearing the office. I changed into an old shirt and jeans, which I had in my car from the time I'd helped my dad paint the attic at home, and rolled in a bin that I'd dragged in from the alleyway.

After an hour of bending and lifting, I wiped the sweat away from my brow and perched myself against the window for a breather. At least it beat going to the gym.

I took solace from a truck making a delivery to a warehouse on the other side of the parking lot. At least, I wasn't completely alone in that industrial wasteland.

My phone vibrated, and seeing that it was Lachlan calling, my heart skipped a beat.

"Hey," I responded with a breezy tone, hiding my true feelings.

Knowing that Lachlan was with Britney made me jumpy. I had no right to feel that way. But as Harriet had put it, jealousy was love's psycho twin.

Was I in love?

"So how's it going?"

"You really don't want to know." He exhaled a breath.

"You sound stressed," I said.

"I am a little. There's a serious amount of bullshit going on in my life. Hey, I've tried calling Florian, but he's not returning my calls."

"Oh really? I've started this new job, as you know."

"How is it?"

"Not what I expected. I'll fill you in later. You sound a little rushed."

"I am. I wish it were otherwise. Any mention of when that transaction is going ahead? Is he there now? Perhaps you can pass me over to him."

Although Lachlan's request to speak to Florian was perfectly reasonable, a pang of disappointment still bubbled away.

Was that why he'd called?

"He's not here. I'm actually at a warehouse in the deserted end of the Arts District."

"Oh really? Is that good for you?"

"Mm… not sure."

"Can he be trusted?"

Good question.

"I think so," I said with a hint of hesitation.

"I shouldn't have placed those canvases in those vaults. Can you get him to call me urgently?"

My heart froze. "Sure."

"I have to go."

"Sure," I said, as my shoulders slumped.

"Are you okay?" he asked.

"I'm all right," I lied.

"Good, and…"

"I'll remind him," I interjected.

"I was just about to say I miss you."

My heart leapt.

"Are you there?" he asked.

"I am."

"Was that too much? I know we're supposed to be buddies. But hey … I can miss you still, can't I?"

"I miss you too," I said, my voice cracking.

"Can we do dinner or something when I get back? If I promise not to ravage you."

Oh God, I wanted that.

"That sounds nice. Dinner. I mean…" My brain had dissolved. Why did that clit-stroking drawl affect me so?

"You sound sexy," he said.

"Do I? I'm just talking like me."

"That's why you sound sexy."

I heard a woman's voice in the background.

"I'll be there in a minute," he said away from the phone. "Sorry. That was Britney."

"Thanks for the call. And I'll talk to Florian."

"Nice hearing your sweet voice."

"And yours too," I said, my smile stretching from ear to ear.

After that, I managed to clear all the rubbish from the office. Lachlan's velvet voice had certainly put a charge through me.

Florian finally took my call and reassured me that he was all ready to go. He expected to close the deal within a couple days max.

I sent Lachlan a text to that effect.

I stared up at the stained walls where a vintage Playboy calendar hung crookedly. Standing on a rickety chair, I removed it, and flicked through the yellowed pages. The only difference between then and now, I noticed, was that the models' breasts weren't as large as today's nude models.

As I continued to browse through the calendar, I thought about sex. Everything seemed to remind me of fucking, even that once innocent act of licking an ice cream cone.

A girl with red hair looked at me as though she was about to orgasm. Heavy-lidded and pursed lips, she reminded me of how I felt when Lachlan's big dick took me over the edge. A hot ache of desire throbbed through me. Lachlan's hungry fondling and that hard dick that rarely went down had me reaching into my damp panties when a loud bang at the door roused me from my erotic daydream.

I tossed the calendar in the bin and headed out to the front. After I managed to open the heavy door, two young men, unmistakably art students, smiled back at me.

"You must be Ethan and Clint," I said, stepping out of the way for them to enter.

Streaks of sunlight beamed in as they inspected the big open space, which despite highlighting dust and grime, I read as a positive omen.

"This has a lot of potential," said Clint with a feminine voice. "At least it's not dark and dingy like a lot of warehouses around here."

The more serious of the two, Ethan, nodded slowly as he studied the walls and then me.

His gaze lingered. Mm… he was attractive too.

I took a deep breath. This was going to be interesting.

I showed them the other spaces, including the dark basement.

"It's spooky in here," said Clint.

"Ideal for storing canvases, though," said Ethan, matter-of-factly.

They were yin and yang, and I did wonder if they were a couple. But when Ethan's penetrating eyes met mine, I dispelled that possibility.

"So, out of curiosity," I asked as they followed me back out, "what exactly did Florian offer you?"

"He's offered us the space for exhibiting commission free. He raved on about an impressive clientele, and we jumped at it. He's very well- connected and worth a few weeks of labor."

"Has he mentioned a budget?"

They looked at each other and shook their heads.

"Okay. I'll have a word with him about that. We're going to need paint."

"Sure are. And the floorboards need repairing. But other than that, there's not a lot to do. It's got great potential," Ethan said, who had already taken charge of the project.

Clint agreed with a nod.

"While we're waiting for the paint to arrive," Ethan continued, "we'll need to prepare the walls. My brother's a builder, so I'm sure he can help with a sander. We'll start tomorrow."

"Okay. That sounds good. I'll take the week off from here and work from home while nutting out a plan," I said.

"Is there anything we can do now?" asked Ethan.

"There is actually." They followed me into my new office. "That furniture needs tossing out." I pointed at the desk. "There's a large industrial bin outside."

Clint asked, "You're tossing these out?" He ran his hands over the old desk.

Ethan smiled. "Clint's got a thing for dilapidated furniture."

"Oh, are you a sculptor?" I asked.

"Of sorts. I mainly restore. That's how I make a living between sales."

"How interesting." I tilted my head and studied the '60s furniture and, with fresh eyes, imagined their potential.

"They're yours," I said.

"Fabulous. I can give you first option on them once I fix them."

"Sure. Why not?" I smiled. I liked them. And it was nice to have a team around me.

The pair carried the furniture off and stored it in the basement.

By midday, my new office, although empty, looked clean and almost workable.

As there wasn't much to do until their equipment arrived, I suggested they come back in the morning.

After that, I called Florian.

"Hey, Miranda, how's it going?"

"Good. Um ... could we meet? There are a few things I need to discuss with you."

"Oh ... that might be difficult today."

"Then tomorrow?" I asked.

"Sure. Let's talk in the morning and set aside time for coffee. Okay?" He paused. "Did Ethan and his buddy turnup?"

"They did. We need some paint," I said.

"Let's talk tomorrow."

His rushed, tense voice tightened the existing knot in my tummy.

36

LACHLAN

I paddled out to the break, which was a fair distance from the shore. Massaged by the sun's warmth, my naked flesh sighed with bliss. All my anxiety melted away. I'd forgotten how nice it felt surfing without a wet suit. It reminded me of the surfing films I'd seen from the sixties, when guys in floral shorts rode on super-large boards. Back then, they were considered society's dropouts. Now everybody surfed.

Pushing off my board, I rode my final wave back to shore.

I showered on the beach and washed down the board before returning to my room.

After grabbing a beer, I flipped open my laptop. I'd arranged to Skype Miranda to find out about the Pollocks. I'd texted her earlier to make a time and to ask if she was okay with that. It felt really weird tiptoeing. But I respected her need for space, so I waited until she initiated contact.

Miranda arrived on my screen. Her thick red hair framed a smooth milky complexion, and she wore a low-cut blouse that instantly registered to my dick.

"Hey, beautiful," I said.

"Hey." She smiled back. "You look tanned."

"I had a long surf. The waves were perfect."

"I can see you look rested and healthy. I wish I could say the same for me."

I frowned. "Oh? What's been happening in your world?"

"I'm now setting up an art space that's geared toward new art, which will take risk, hard work, and financial sacrifice."

"But isn't that the path of all art?"

She shrugged. "I guess I was dazzled by the prospect of working with the big guns. Major acquisitions, like the Pollocks and..." Her grimace dragged me back down to the tetchy subject of money.

I sat forward. "Can you set up a sale of the de Koonings? Arrange it so you retain the commission."

"I can." She paused. "But only if your insurance is up to date."

"I'll get you to arrange that, too, if you don't mind."

"Anything to help you, Lachlan. You know that," she said with a gentle smile. "The traditional Sotheby's route would expedite the sale. Their commission's pretty high. But it's a safe bet."

"Then I'll leave it up to you. I just need some cash. ASAP."

"Are the authorities coming down hard on you?"

"Nothing I can't handle." I smiled, putting on my brave man act. "I'll be back tomorrow, and if he's still pussy-footing about, I'll confront Florian myself."

"You're not going to resort to violence, I hope."

I kept to myself my sudden urge to punch the art dealer in the face. "Don't worry. Go ahead and do what you can with the de Koonings." I fell into her beautiful dark eyes. "You're not wearing your glasses."

"You sound disappointed," she said.

"I like you with your glasses. But seeing you without is pretty hot too. You've got exquisite eyes. They take me places."

"Where do they take you?" she asked.

"Do you want the short answer or the long one?"

She smirked. "The long one."

"They make me long for you and they make him"—I cocked my head toward my dick—"long for you."

"Right. Long as in big." She giggled.

I shifted in my seat. "Tell me, what is it about me that's giving you doubts? Apart from that Linda situation."

"It's not doubts as such. I..."—she looked down at her hands—"I just don't know much about you. Other than you're highly sexed." She bit her lip, which made my mouth water for a taste of that sensuous rosy pout.

"There's not much to know. I'm a pretty basic sort of guy. Dull. Prosaic." I opened my hands.

"Prosaic?" Miranda giggled. "You're not that nor are you basic. You're a very talented musician. And you're working hard to right the wrongs of your father. That makes you a responsible, good person…"

"But?" I asked.

"All those women who pursue you. Especially as that sexy charm-oozing rock star."

"Charm-oozing?" I laughed. "And what about that normal guy-next-door version of me?"

"Have you got one of those?" she asked.

"You bet. He's me. That normal guy who fucks up. Like not updating the insurance of valuable art."

"Don't worry. I'll make sure he closes the deal. And the de Koonings are worth half a billion, I'm sure."

I released a tight breath. "That will almost do it."

"That's good, then, isn't it?" she asked.

"Sure. I wouldn't mind extra so that I can set up a legitimate company."

"Isn't that Peace Holdings?" she asked.

"It's still under my father's wing."

"Oh. I see," she said, leaning forward. I would have given anything to see her unbutton her blouse, but out of respect, I held back. "If you like we can join a book club together."

She shook her head and laughed. "A book club?"

"Why not? We can discuss books and all those worthwhile subjects that make people interesting."

She shook her head and laughed. "Oh my God, Lachlan. Are you for real?"

"I'd just like you to know that I'm receptive to doing other things than just ravaging you. We can go to the cinema. What's your favorite movie?"

"There are so many. I like the classics, especially movies with Audrey Hepburn."

"Let me guess, *Breakfast at Tiffany's*?" I asked, lounging back.

Her face lit up. "Yeah... how did you guess? And I'm amazed you even know that film."

"Are you kidding? My mother always took me to the cinema when I was growing up. She was crazy about classic movies, as am I."

"Have you got a favorite?" she asked.

"I loved the Rat Pack films with Frank Sinatra and crew. I loved *Bullitt*. There was a great Mustang car chase." I grinned. "Cowboys, war movies. You know, all the boy films."

She chuckled. "That figures."

I opened my hands. "But I can do a chick flick if you like. I don't mind as long as you're there."

"We don't have to do chick flicks or join book clubs, Lachlan," she said. "I can get all the book talk I need and more from my parents."

"I don't know anything about your folks. You know more about mine," I said, stretching my arms.

"My mother talks a lot, and my dad listens."

"Okay. So she wears the pants, I suppose," I said.

She nodded. "She does."

"Well, I don't mind that idea. I like strong women."

"She's extremely opinionated."

"At least she knows her own mind," I said.

"She certainly does."

"It's nice seeing you," I said.

"I like seeing you too." She tilted her head adoringly.

I smiled. "Then can we catch up when I get back tomorrow?"

"I'd like that," she said.

That put a smile on my face. "Great. Can't wait. I mean to see you, my best buddy."

She shook her head with a giggle. "I think we're more than that. But hey, I'm looking forward to seeing you too."

"Thanks for the catch-up."

"Bye then." She blew me a kiss.

I pursed my lips and kissed her back and closed my laptop.

***

Taking delight from the ever-changing sunset, I lowered myself onto a seat and devoured a burger and fries, followed by a chocolate bar.

As that great artist, Mother Nature, put on a show, I snapped some photos of the priceless work of art before me. A fiery sunset danced on top of the sparkling ocean, creating ripples of ever-changing color.

I chose my favorite and sent it to Miranda with the comment, *"I wish you were here to see this. With me holding you close."*

I'd never actually sent pictures of sunsets to girls I'd dated.

I couldn't even recall being with a woman longer than a month. What did that make me? An ADHD sufferer?

Given that I could spend hours practicing off-beats to a metronome, that seemed unlikely. However, girls... maybe. But none of those girls were Miranda.

My phone pinged. Miranda replied, *"I wish I were there too."*

The heart emoji was a nice touch, making me smile as I rose to return to my room.

I decided to drop in on Britney and tell her of my intention to leave in the morning.

Standing at her door, I heard music blaring. After I'd knocked loudly for a while, I entered.

I was about to call out when I discovered on the sofa, with his legs splayed, Rick with his eyes closed and his mouth wide open, groaning.

Moving her mouth up and down, Britney was on her knees, sucking the biggest cock I'd ever seen. Not that I'd seen that many.

Luckily, the room was dimly lit, and knowing Britney, she'd probably had a drink or five, therefore was less alert.

I snuck out as quickly as I could and headed back to my room, wondering how the hell that huge cock fit in her mouth.

37

MIRANDA

"Harry, stop pacing around. You're making me nervous," I said.

"I'll tell you what's making me nervous—Ava banging her feet day and fucking night."

I had to laugh at my niece's new found obsession with flamenco. "She looks cute doing it. And she's a natural," I defended.

"And now she's begging me for the shoes. Hell, the neighbors are going to have me tossed out."

"I'm sure it's not as bad as that. Just have her practice in the park or something," I suggested.

"And have all those perfect mothers find something else to laugh at?"

"This isn't really about your daughter's obsession with flamenco. It's about Ollie, isn't it?"

She picked at her nails. "Hmm... I guess."

"Harry, it was never going to be anything. He's a child."

"He's a fucking man. And the chemistry crackled between us."

"I noticed it too. But he's really young, and you saw the girls."

"Yeah." She knitted her fingers. "You're right. I'm old and ugly."

I rolled my eyes. "You're nuts, Harry. Guys fall all over you. You're stunning. And hell, you're only twenty-six. You better get your retirement home booked now."

Harriet laughed as Ava scampered through the door, wearing a rose in her wavy long hair.

She ran to her mother and hugged her.

"Who dropped her off?" I asked.

"Jane, the hippy mom. She's lovely. We do a swap. Tomorrow, it's my turn."

Ava kissed me on the cheek. "Hey, sweetie. You look lovely with that flower in your hair."

She threw her arms up in a perfect Spanish pose.

I looked at Harriet and shook my head. "You have to admit she's a natural."

"Yeah." Her sour face softened into that of a proud mother's smile. "Isn't she?"

Harriet and I watched as Ava demonstrated her new moves. "You're so good. Are you going to ballet too?"

She nodded. "But I like flamenco the best."

I rose. "I've got to go and look at this new apartment."

"Why don't you stay at Lachlan's fancy penthouse?"

"It doesn't feel right," I said.

"But he's not there all of the time. Offer him rent. It seems like a good arrangement."

"He wouldn't take it. And remember, we're in 'go slow' mode."

"And you need your head examined. In any case, you're talking. He's calling you."

I couldn't help but smile. "He is."

She pointed at me. "See. It's written all over your face. You're crazy about him."

"I never said I wasn't, Harry."

She shook her head. "You've always been stubborn. You take after Mom in that department."

"I don't. I'm more like Dad," I defended.

Harriet was right. In many ways, I tended to overthink, something my mother was famous for. As much as I loved my mother, the last thing I wished was to become a nagging perfectionist.

"Anyway, I think you're nuts," she said. "If I were in your position, I would've moved in by now."

"You're more adventurous than me. And you've had more experience with guys. You're better at heart break."

She rolled her eyes. "Oh God, Andie. What's life if you don't take the odd risk here and there?"

"Easier," I returned.

"And dull." Harriet stretched into the warrior pose.

She was right. It was boring. My resolve to take things slowly hadn't helped at all. If anything, my Lachlan obsession had escalated. "Maybe you're right. Let's see what happens. Anyway, must run." I gave her a wave and raced off.

As I headed to my car, I thought of Harriet's suggestion to move into Lachlan's apartment. It just felt weird. Especially now that we were fucking.

Was that all it would ever be? Just fucking? Nice as it was.

Lachlan often asked about my day and would share his thoughts and aspirations with me. He was also a respectful listener.

He was due back any time. And I missed him madly. I'd never been so distracted as this before, and I needed my focus. Especially now that I was to set up a business.

My phone buzzed just as I was about to drive off. Late for my appointment with the realtor, I went to ignore it, but when Lachlan's handsome head popped up, I couldn't resist.

"Miranda." His smoky voice slithered down to my pussy, and as always, my brain shut down.

"It's nice to hear your voice," I said.

"I'm back, and it's great to be home." He sounded chirpy.

"Oh…"

"Where are you?" he asked.

"I'm just heading out to see about an apartment to rent."

"Really? But you can stay here."

"I'd like to have my stuff around me," I said, looking for anything other than the truth. Whatever that may have been.

My heart hung out in two camps: A. Move in and set up home. B. Maintain a healthy distance. Be independent. Keep it real.

The latter, more rational option had the winning edge, even though my heart stood on the sidelines, booing.

"I don't mind that," he said. "You could have it repainted. Redecorated. Fill the place up with stuffed toys. Or I could buy you a puppy."

"A puppy? Stuffed toys?" I laughed. "I'm a grown-up, Lachlan."

"That you are. A puppy would be nice though."

It took me a moment to respond. "I don't need a puppy to feel at home in your apartment."

"I guess not. But hey, it's empty most of the time."

"What about those big nights out with your pals?"

"I've grown out of those, and if I did have the odd relapse, I could arrive unannounced and ravage you. Now where would the harm be in that?"

I giggled. "No harm, I guess." My lower regions fired up suddenly at the thought of his hungry mouth all over me. "I would just prefer to have my own space."

"Of course. And sorry, that was inappropriate of me. Seeing we are supposed to be taking things slow. So does that mean we can't meet up? Like now? I need to see your pretty face. Badly."

My face hurt from the sunny smile. "I'm good with seeing you now, Lachlan. I want to."

"I'm here at the apartment. I only came here to see you."

"That's nice," I said, bouncing on a dreamy cloud. Lachlan had drugged me again.

***

As soon as I'd stepped out of the elevator, Lachlan kissed me on the cheek and lingered. All it took was a whiff of him, and I melted into his arms.

Our lips met, and it was tentative and fragile. But then his tongue claimed me. The kiss felt like our first.

He virtually ripped my clothes off, ran his hands over my tingling skin, and groaned in my mouth while fondling my breasts.

Without uttering a word, he undid my fly and helped me wiggle out of my jeans. He then bent down, ripped my panties off with his mouth, and licked my clit in quick, rapid lashings that had me clinging to the wall to avoid falling to the floor in an agony of bliss.

He lifted me with his strong arms and pinned me against the wall. Lachlan hooked his arm under my knee and entered me in one sharp, deliciously deep thrust.

That was followed by slow, achingly pleasurable lovemaking, leaving my throat parched and my sanity clinging to the wall.

Raw and ravenous, he fucked me so intensely that my fingernails dug into his flexed muscles, and as a blabbering mess, I ended up in Kingdom Cum.

Two hours later, after emptying himself into me three times, Lachlan suggested we dine on something other than each other, which made me laugh and my stomach jump up and down with enthusiasm.

We ended up at the beach, sitting on the sand with a pizza balancing on our laps.

It was a serene, pleasant evening and the vermillion sun had just dipped into the shimmering ocean.

"My life's a real fucking mess right now." Lachlan turned and stared me deeply in the eyes. "I want you in it, Miranda." There was a hint of vulnerability in his gaze, which flitted from my eyes to his fingers and back. "Should anything come out in the next few weeks, you have to know I'm innocent."

"Is this about your father's investment scheme?"

His hesitant nod did make me wonder if there was more drama unfolding.

"The only thing that came from this trip was the builder that Britney hooked up with."

His lips twitched into a grin.

Instead of chuckling at his double entendre, I remained wide-eyed and expectant. I was more interested in knowing that Britney had sprayed her female scent all over someone other than Lachlan.

"You don't look too pleased," I said.

"I couldn't give a shit about who she hooks up with. Rick's the sidekick to Hector, who right now as we speak, is building a resort for us."

"Bird of Paradise, you mean? Is that going ahead?" I thought of the deleted files, which, although I had little time to study, I knew enough about that project.

"It is. But only some of the way. Just enough to show that it has stalled due to cash flow reasons." He scratched his chin.

"Won't they know it's just been built?"

"That's a good point." He nodded. "I made sure they sourced weathered material."

"Then it's going to be okay?"

"When I left earlier today, they had just delivered the supplies. And hopefully now they'll start... only..."—He sighed—"I've run out of capital. I can't even get the damn frame up."

"I called my old professor, who has contacts in the art scene. When I mentioned you had de Koonings for sale, he agreed that Sotheby's would be the quickest route."

"Good. Let's roll with that then." He rose and wiped the sand off his jeans. "I have to head back to the estate and deal with some business tomorrow."

Tossing a half-eaten crust to a seagull, I nodded.

I gazed up at him and drowned in those sparkling blue eyes. In the twilight, he looked gorgeous with those sensual lips accentuated by his stubbled jaw. His hair had grown and was brushed back and collar length. Long enough to get tangled in my fingers.

Persistent insecurity stalked me, however. I kept wondering whether Lachlan, who could silence a room of chatty girls with one stride, would continue desiring me after that honeymoon period of lust had subsided.

As though reading my insecurity, Lachlan stared into my eyes and said, "You're more beautiful like this."

"In what way?" I asked.

"No makeup. Hair loose. Rosy cheeks." He stroked my face and kissed me. "I love your flavor. I love you coming in my mouth."

"I love coming in your mouth. I've yet to return the favor," I said.

He drew me close and kissed my neck. "All in good time."

"Are you always this sexual?" I asked. What I really wanted to ask was if he was always this dirty. My body didn't seem to mind.

"Only with you." He pulled away to study my face. "We are exclusive. Aren't we? Despite us taking things slowly." He raised a brow at that suggestion, which I just knew would be impossible to fulfil, since we hadn't taken our hands off each other all afternoon. My heart was throwing one hell of a party.

"I'm not interested in anyone else, if that's what you mean. And you?"

His brows met sharply. "You're all the woman I need and want. I'm monogamous."

"Are you?" I asked.

He held my hand and looked into my eyes. "Miranda, I know my past isn't that great. And seeing Linda carrying on like that wouldn't have helped either, but I can say this to you…" He paused. "I'm besotted."

His eyes glistened with sincerity. I had to believe him. He couldn't have been that great an actor.

"So am I, Lachlan."

His momentary smile faded. "Then, that's all that matters. I was your first. That's mind-blowingly powerful. I didn't realize how much until I was away. And when you asked to slow things down, I experienced separation anxiety."

Taking a deep breath, I scrutinized his face. "It was insecurity and a need to focus. But I was more scattered when I didn't hear from you." I looked down at my fingers, hating how weak that made me seem. "It's difficult to process. While you were away, I thought a lot about it and realized that I was plain scared. I still am."

"I'm not going anywhere." He stroked my hair. "I couldn't stop thinking about you and…"

"And?" I asked.

"It's hard to put into words. I guess what I'm trying to say is…" He played with my fingers and then trapped me with his eyes again. "I love you."

"Huh?" My eyebrows squeezed together.

He smiled. "You should see yourself. I might as well have said I'm actually a brain-cannibalizing zombie."

I had to laugh.

His face lengthened. "Do you think it's too soon?"

"No … I mean maybe…" My heart raced. "Isn't it just lust? We fuck all the time."

His eyes hooded. "That's because I can't get enough of you." He ran his thumb over his swollen lower lip that I'd devoured earlier. "It's more than that, though. You're good. You're smart. Smarter than me. I like that. And you're a real woman."

"Good is boring, isn't it?"

"Oh God no. It's seriously not. You're a pure spirit. I need that. I'm over those types of wild women who only think about themselves and what I can do for them."

"So let me get this straight. You like me because I'm a good person and also good to fuck?"

He considered this for a moment. His brow creased. "I'm not great with words. But sure. That's about the gist of it. What else is there? It's simple, but it's complex at the same time. Meeting someone who I can trust and who I can talk to is just as important as desire. Although…" He ran his hand along my waist. "The fact that you're gorgeous and have a body that keeps me hard all night helps." He grinned. "I might not get much sleep. But I know you have my back, and I sure as hell have your back. I'd fucking kill for you."

My eyes widened at that heart-swelling, albeit gruesome admission.

"Come on, let's go back and…" He gazed at me with that cheek-dimpling half smile. "Make love."

My eyelids became heavy as his finger slid seductively along my hip and under my loose blouse, provocatively close to my breasts.

"Tell me, do you like dancing?"

"Huh?" That, I wasn't expecting. "I do. Do you want to go out dancing?"

He laughed. "No. I'm thinking of something a little more private."

"Oh." My face heated. "You want me to dance for you?"

"Yeah. A nice, slow, bendy dance. Let's go back. Before I get arrested for ravaging you in public."

"Bendy? I'm not that flexible."

"Oh you're very flexible, Miranda." He grinned.

Hand in hand, we glided along the boulevard. Everyone seemed to blend into the buildings. It was just us in our own little romantic bubble.

"You will be my girl, won't you?" he asked, turning to look at me.

I searched for a playful smirk, but under the evening light, his eyes shone with intensity.

It took me a moment to speak. My heart pumped madly as though I'd run for miles in pursuit of something vital. In this case, love.

"I'd like nothing more than to be your girl." The words trembled out of my mouth.

He took me into his arms, and his lips touched mine. Tender and sweet, as though it was our first time.

Fortunately, he held me close to his strong body because I might have floated up to the sky. Heartfelt and deep, his kiss, as though sealing our union, made my eyes pool with tears.

"Give her a good fuck for me," a guy shouted, stumbling past and breaking our spell.

We separated and laughed. I quickly brushed away a tear.

Lachlan saw it because he kissed my cheek, and his eyes shone with that deep understanding that two people have for one another. I'd seen it on my father's face in response to my mother's more fragile moments.

I let out a slow breath, wondering if someone had slipped LSD into the water. Because the past two months spent with

Lachlan had felt like a trip, replete with swirling color, levitation, toe-curling pleasure, and the type of madness that made one laugh or cry uncontrollably.

Lachlan reverted to his former playfulness and, taking me by the hand, swung my arm along as though we were kids. Only, we were inflamed adults about to surrender to lustful yearnings or, as Lachlan had sweetly put it, make love.

My heart skipped along. A happily for now would do me.

BOOK TWO

DEVOURED BY PEACE

1

MIRANDA

Lachlan and I spent our first weekend together at his sprawling estate. With Tamara in Miami and Manuel at his grandmother's, we had the house to ourselves. I read, sunbathed, and ate and drank to excess, while Lachlan either surfed, practiced drums, or fucked me nearly to the point of insanity.

Lazing on the couch, I flicked through the latest Sotheby's catalogue, drooling over some of the gorgeous collectibles on offer. As it was Sunday, I had to return to the penthouse downtown that evening for an early start in the morning.

Wearing nothing but a towel around his waist, Lachlan sauntered into the living room. I took a deep breath and pinched myself yet again. Was that man with the body of an action hero truly my boyfriend?

"Do you feel like grabbing some tacos?" he asked.

"Great idea. I love Mexican."

He joined me on the couch. "I've loved having you here. You suit this house."

"I've loved being here."

He hugged me, and I breathed his scent in deeply, as I would a forest after the rain. Though trees didn't set me on fire the way

Lachlan did.

Lachlan released me and slapped my butt, making me giggle. We were like two randy teenagers. I seemed to have a permanent tingling sensation between my legs.

I rose and gathered my belongings.

An hour later, dressed in jeans and a linen shirt that flapped in the evening breeze, Lachlan carried my duffle bag as we headed for his car.

I peered up at the sky, something I often did when in Malibu. At that moment, a star shot across the heavens, making me gasp. "Oh!" I pointed. "A shooting star."

Lachlan looked up. "Did you make a wish?"

"I forgot."

"You can still make one."

I filled my lungs with fresh, salty air and exhaled, thinking of a deep desire. Of course, Lachlan and his twinkling blue eyes entered my thoughts too.

"Are you going to tell me?" he asked, tilting his handsome head.

I smiled and shook my head.

As we neared the Mustang, I asked, "Are you driving?"

"Yep. I'm a free man. Got my license restored two days ago."

He opened the door for me then ran over to his side.

"I've missed this car," I said, stroking the leather.

He settled into his seat. "So have I." He smiled sweetly and turned on the engine then pushed down on the gas and made the engine roar. "Listen to that."

I laughed.

"What?"

"You're such a boy."

"And you're such a sexy girl." He slid his hand under my skirt and up to my panties.

I hissed.

"Are you sore?" he asked.

"A little. But it's nice pain."

"I'll have to go for the gentle approach."

"Mmm... I don't mind it the other way."

He gave me a slow smile. "Which way's that, Miranda?"

"When you go all feral on me."

"Feral?" He laughed. "You do bring the animal out in me."

And you me.

The invigorating evening breeze ran its fingers through my hair as we sped along the highway with the top down.

Twenty minutes later, we arrived at the Mexican restaurant and were seated at a table by the window.

Being at the beach always gave me a huge appetite, and when our meals arrived, my stomach rumbled.

Spicy, saucy, and deliciously cheesy, my beef enchilada exploded with flavor. I wiped my mouth. It was the best Mexican food I'd ever tasted, especially washed down with a tangy margarita.

Although the mariachi band was a tad annoying. Their novelty wore off after the third explosive tune. The deafening din wasn't helped by the people at the table next to us, who grew louder with each tequila shot.

"I'll arrange the insurance and for the de Koonings' sale in the coming days. Last week was pretty distracting," I said, almost yelling. "Did Florian get back to you?"

Lachlan beckoned the waiter. "Check, please." Then he returned to my question. "Yep."

"Oh..." I met his gaze with a question.

I'd had a big week at the warehouse. Every time I'd called my new boss regarding paint for the walls, I'd gotten nothing but voicemail.

After paying for our dinner, Lachlan jumped up from his chair. "I'm going there now."

"To Florian's office?" I almost sprinted after him.

"Yep. I'm going to pay him a visit."

"Right. Um... He may not be there. It's Sunday and after eight."

"He said he'd be there."

Given Florian's caginess, Lachlan's frustration was understandable. But seeing his sour face was still jarring.

"Do you mind if I... tag along?" I asked.

"It's up to you. I might actually punch the guy." He stopped walking and turned to me, his face softening. "I can drop you off at the apartment first."

"No, I want to come. Are you going to threaten him?"

"I already have. I'm sick of his fucking bullshit."

My shoulders tensed as I hurried along. No matter how often Lachlan reassured me to the contrary, I just couldn't shake off the guilt of having introduced them. And Florian had let me down too.

Ten minutes later, we arrived at the imposing tower.

As Lachlan held the car door open for me, I asked, "Is this going to get violent?"

He opened his hands. "Let's put it this way: I don't like being screwed around. Maybe you should wait here."

"No." I jumped out. "I've got questions too. He owes me my money."

He stopped walking. "Who the fuck is this guy?"

I bit my lip. "I should never have gone to him. But he has a huge reputation. I could never have thought..." I gulped back a lump in my throat.

Lachlan stopped walking and took my hand. "You're not to blame. Perhaps I'm just assuming the worst."

A few weeks had passed, and with the Jackson Pollocks holed up in Florian's vaults, Lachlan had good reason to be worried.

2

LACHLAN

Miranda didn't know I'd threatened to send in the heavies. I felt as though I were on a bad trip since I'd never had to resort to such gutter tactics. But I'd had enough of being messed around.

I wasn't surprised to learn that Tony Varela was a leading Mafia figure.

After I'd mentioned to him that someone owed me a lot of money and was giving me the run around, he laid his hand on mine and, with a raspy, paternal tone, told me he could fix it for me.

I couldn't believe this was the same man that had threatened to bury me under a condo development.

I paid him some of what was owed, and suddenly we'd become buddies it seemed.

He'd asked to see me face-to-face to discuss my debt and suggested we meet at a dark, seedy bar where girls gyrated around poles-slash-make-believe-metal-penises. It felt like I was in an episode of *The Sopranos*.

We discussed Florian in vague terms. I didn't mention the eight hundred million dollars owed to me.

While topping up his scotch, Varela explained that for the small sum of a million dollars in cash, one of his men could knock out Florian's teeth one by one.

I left that joint feeling sick to my stomach. Nevertheless, I called Florian, telling him that if he valued his pearly fangs, he'd better return my call right away.

In a flash, he called back. Speaking in that smooth Brit accent, he reassured me that his client was about to pay. I insisted on seeing him that night or else, and he agreed. At least I didn't need to resort to hiring one of Varela's thugs.

That I would stoop to something so radical made me wonder if I'd lost my mind.

But I had to clean up my dying father's mess as quietly as possible. I should have just let him fall on his sword, but I couldn't live with myself if I had. And it would have been a media bloodbath, leaving the Peace name forever tarnished.

For the sake of my late grandfather—whose honest, hard work had built the family empire—and for my future offspring, I had to ensure that the Peace name remained synonymous with decency.

Standing in front of the half-lit office tower, I turned to Miranda. "This shouldn't take long. Why don't you wait here?"

"I want to come."

Perhaps she could get more out of Florian with that art language they shared. I shrugged. "Okay, then."

I buzzed the intercom. A few seconds later, the door opened, and we walked into the dimly lit lobby.

Our steps echoed loudly as we made our way to the elevator.

As we rode up to the fifth floor, I took Miranda's hand. "Are you okay?"

She nodded.

As soon as we left the elevator, we saw Florian on the phone through a glass wall.

He gestured for us to enter then hung up quickly.

"Miranda," he said with a bright smile. "I was about to call you."

"You got my message about my pay?"

"It should go in tomorrow. Sorry about the delay. We're having a few cash flow issues at the moment. A big deal stalled." He smiled apologetically. "How's it going at the warehouse? They're sanding the floor, I hear."

"Ethan and Clint are great. Like me, they're driven. We all want to see the gallery up and running ASAP."

"Who are they?" I asked.

Florian interjected, "They're a couple of keen artists who I've procured for Miranda's new project. Ethan is particularly talented. I hold high hopes for him. He's also very photogenic. Good for the media." He grinned, looking between Miranda and me.

"What's the news from your Russian buyer?" I asked.

"I've decided to head in another direction." He held up a bottle of scotch. "Can I offer you something?"

"I'll have a drop," I said.

Miranda nodded.

He poured our drinks then passed them to us.

After a gulp of liquor, I said, "I'm taking the art back. I'm going through Sotheby's."

"Oh, you'll lose a few million that way," he replied.

"Small change."

"I've got a French buyer. She's booked a flight and should be here in a day. I'll drop my commission to seven percent." Florian raised his eyebrows.

"The office is bare. What have you done with the paintings and furniture?" Miranda asked.

"I'm having the room repainted," he said.

"Where are the works stored?" she asked. "You haven't been very easy to track down. You haven't returned any of my calls."

I nodded. "I had to resort to threats, which…" I pointed into his face. "Are real. I just need to make a call. My father had some pretty nasty contacts."

Miranda turned quickly toward me and frowned. I squeezed her hand gently to reassure her.

"I'll call my client now," Florian said, rubbing his nose. "She can talk to you." He picked up his phone and spoke to someone in French. Then he handed the phone over to me, and I gestured for Miranda to take it instead.

"She could be anyone," I said.

"She isn't just anyone." His eyes brightened under his black-rimmed specs.

"Do you mind talking to her?" I asked Miranda.

While she took the call, I led Florian to the other side of the office and said, "I need proof. I don't trust you. You've had us on the hop for nearly three weeks."

"Do I need to remind you I have my reputation to uphold?"

"That's why I dealt with you in the first place. I just don't like the fact that you've been giving me the run around."

He rubbed his bald head. "Please accept my apologies. I've been dealing with a few personal issues."

Miranda ended the call and said, "I know of that family's collection. She's a Rothschild."

"And?" I shrugged.

"Madeline Rothschild boasts one of the biggest modern art collections in Europe."

"Okay. So is she to be trusted?"

Florian chuckled. "Hey. She's got an even bigger reputation to uphold than I do."

"How do I know she's not a fake?" I asked. "Take me to the paintings."

He asked us to follow him, and we entered a dark room, and a dim light came on.

Florian opened a vault. "Here."

Lying flat, the canvases were individually covered in cloth. I couldn't believe I was staring down at eight hundred million dollars.

"I'm taking them back now," I said. "You've got until the end of this week to finalize the sale."

Florian shrugged. For some reason, I'd expected him to work harder at convincing me to leave them there.

"If that's what you want." He turned to Miranda.

I lifted a finger. "Can you give us a minute?"

Florian nodded and moved away.

"What should I do?" I asked.

"I would take them," she replied.

"Tonight? Now?"

She bit her lip and nodded. "I would."

"You weren't convinced by the buyer on the phone?"

"I'm not sure. If the insurance was up to date, I wouldn't be so concerned."

I took a deep breath. *Yet another reminder of my frustrating blunder.*

"We'll just have to be careful not to fold them." She bent down and lifted the protective sheeting from the painting on top, squinting at the work of art.

I stared down at the canvases. I could have carried them myself in one go, but taking heed of Miranda's advice, I agreed to handle them with care.

By eleven, we'd carted the paintings back to the apartment one by one. Each was covered with a sheet, just as Miranda had instructed.

"I'm sorry, sweetheart," I said, turning to her. She was slumped on the couch.

"Don't be. I was the one meant to deliver this sale."

"Hey, don't beat yourself up. If anyone's to blame, it's me." I headed to the fridge for a beer. "What can I get you?"

"I'll have whatever you're having," she said.

"Beer?"

"Sure." She smiled tightly.

We sat on the sofa and drank in silence.

"I'll talk to Sotheby's and Christie's tomorrow, if you like," she said.

"We'll wait and see what happens with the French collector. If nothing shows up in a day or so, then let's take that path."

I took her into my arms. "Let's go to bed."

Although I was tired, as soon as her soft, naked body rubbed against mine, blood rushed to my groin.

I rolled Miranda on top of me and trailed kisses all the way from her warm lips to her breasts.

Gripping her hips, I guided my engorged dick into her wet slit. I glided in and out, working up to a frenzy and falling into Miranda's hooded eyes.

Her muscles sucked in my cock to the point of no return, tipping me over the edge. She dug her nails into my arms and sighed loudly as her snug walls shuddered and drenched my dick, and all my earlier tension flooded out of me.

We fell into each other's arms, panting, and when my breath returned, I nestled into her warm neck.

Miranda's softness melded into my tired body, and all the stress I'd been carrying dissolved.

My heavy body surrendered to bliss.

3

MIRANDA

Lachlan's erection rubbing against my ass woke me. He tickled my belly then let his fingers travel up to my breasts.

"So, who's this good-looking artist you're working with?" he asked.

I knitted my brows. *Is Lachlan jealous?* "Um... he's not my type. In any case, I'm not looking."

"You're not looking for what?" he asked, teasing my inner thigh with his finger.

"For anyone. We're together. Aren't we?" I asked, my skin prickling.

"You're very sexy, Miranda." His breath left a warmth on my neck.

Lachlan turned me around and rubbed his big dick against my pussy, then he parted my legs and slid into me. The stretch made my eyelids flutter, and with each deep thrust, my sighs deepened.

"We *are* together. And you feel seriously hot," he said hoarsely.

He bit my neck gently and rocked his hips, angling his dick expertly. The friction made me burn.

As his thrusts grew in urgency and intensity, I wondered if he was stating his ownership.

I liked being his. I was helplessly in love. *Or is it lust?*

An orgasm rippled through me, and as I released, warmth cascaded over me. A contented moan left my lips as I collapsed into his arms.

He could have me—all of me.

His growl echoed in my ear as his cock spasmed, and I felt his seed entering me deeply.

We lay there holding each other, his chest rising and falling against mine.

"You've become a part of me, Miranda." He sealed his heart-swelling comment with a tender, lingering kiss.

Snuggling into his strong, comfortable body made me want to drift off to sleep. But then my phone buzzed. I had too much going on, and since it was a workday, I took the call.

"Ethan," I said, rising from the bed.

"We've finished sanding. The space is dust free and therefore safe to enter." He chuckled.

"That sounds good. You haven't wasted any time."

"We're keen. Only… I can't seem to find Florian. When the paint arrived, I had to pay with my credit card."

Although that didn't surprise me, I had an uneasy feeling my credit card was about to get a good workout again. "Okay. I'll be there in an hour. We'll discuss a plan."

I ended the call. Lachlan was walking around in his boxer briefs and making me hot and bothered again. With that tanned, tall, and manly physique, he was so devastatingly handsome that I couldn't believe I was even there.

"So, when are you going to introduce us?" A playful twinkle danced in his eyes.

"Whenever you like. Pop in. I'll text you the address. It's a big empty space with a ton of potential. Only if Florian comes to the party."

"Oh… him again." He shook his head.

"Hmm…" I thought about the paintings in the other room, which we'd carefully laid flat in the dark. "I'll arrange to update the insurance today."

"Thanks. The files are back at the estate. I'll email them."

Ethan and Clint wore big justifiable smiles and paint-splashed overalls. Their progress in just one week was staggering.

"This doesn't even look like the same room," I said, staring at the formerly stained, cracked walls, which were smooth and white.

"The hanging rails are next," Ethan said.

My spirit soared. The room was no longer shabby and run down but a space with potential.

"Has Florian been here?" I asked.

Ethan shook his head. "We haven't seen or heard from him. My brother and my cousin, who are builders, supplied the paint. They're also donating the timber for the picture rails."

"How generous."

"My brother wants to see me get ahead," he replied.

They followed me into the office, and when I opened the door, my jaw dropped.

"Hell, you even painted this room. And it's such a great color choice." The yellow walls gave the room a sunny appeal.

"Jack had some left over from a house he'd been painting."

"What a great guy." I looked around and discovered the furniture had been restored. Shaking my head, I turned to Clint. "You did this?"

He nodded.

"We're driven, Miranda," Ethan said. "We want to make this space to work. Whether Florian's here or not."

"And the rent?" I asked.

"We could host a few events. I'm thinking of a dance party. Maybe a few performance nights too."

"Oh?" I felt out of my depth.

He shrugged. "Why not? Rent parties are all the rage in the art scene."

"That makes sense. I need to get with it," I admitted, leaning against my desk. I loved my new office and started to imagine art splashed all over the walls. "I just can't believe you've done this in just one week."

"We had a few helpers." Clint smiled. "My new boy and his pals turned up. We had fun. Didn't we?"

Ethan nodded before turning to me. "So, Miranda, do you have a plan?"

"I'm thinking of an exhibition within the month." I had a sudden light bulb moment. "But first, I want to host an auction."

The idea was bold and perhaps even crazy, but hosting an auction of sought-after contemporary art was the best way to draw attention to our new establishment.

"Leave it to me for now. But arrange that rent party. I just hope it won't attract the cops."

Clint giggled. "That sounds kind of butch and yummy. I love a man in a uniform. Who doesn't?"

Ethan rolled his eyes. "Me." He laughed.

"Coffees?" Clint asked.

"Sure. Is there a takeout close?"

"No, but come with me," he replied.

I followed along the formerly dingy hallway.

"More of your brother's leftover paint?" I asked, pointing at the salmon-pink wall.

"Uh-huh. It's all the rage. His rich clients are going nuts over brightly colored walls."

"It's great," I said. "I'm a big fan of color."

They led me into the kitchen, which was freshly painted in red.

"Oh my. I don't remember seeing this room. I haven't even seen the bathroom, for that matter."

"We'll show you that in a minute," Clint said. I sensed he was the designer.

"It will have to be instant for now. But that espresso machine will happen." Ethan nodded with confidence.

As Clint switched on the kettle, I asked, "Do we know who the landlord is?"

Ethan shook his head. "No idea. Florian just plucked us out of college and gave it to us."

"Plucked you?"

"He met us at our graduation exhibition, and we got to talking. Florian mentioned how he'd procured a space and was looking for some young artists to run it. We jumped at the opportunity." Ethan passed me a cup of coffee. "We don't have milk."

"That's okay." I took the cup. "Thanks."

"How do you figure in all of this? Since you're technically our boss." Ethan studied me.

"Good question." I leaned against the wall. "Florian wants me to scout new artists to exhibit."

"Cool. And this auction idea?" Clint asked.

"I've been put in charge of selling six de Koonings among other twentieth-century pieces."

"Holy shit. You don't say. Wow, that's shooting high," Ethan said.

"It is. I have to plan this properly. We can't invite that kind of money here without at least something to offer."

"Hello, de Koonings," Ethan said.

I smiled. "Sure. But art buyers with that kind of money expect top-shelf champagne at least."

"Yes, but this is contemporary art, Miranda. I think it's time it came back to its roots. Don't you?" Ethan asked. "An old warehouse in an old industrial alleyway is a fitting home for de Kooning's works."

Clint nodded.

"That's an excellent point. But still, expensive champagne means they don't mind bidding higher. Rich collectors can be a competitive group. It's all part of the game of selling," I said.

Excitement sparked through me. All of a sudden, everything seemed possible.

4

LACHLAN

I thought of Miranda's pretty face as I dashed down to the beach with my surfboard tucked under my arm. At least love-making, surfing, and music, my three favorite pastimes, took my mind off the craziness going down in my life.

Even when the SEC breathed down my neck, and Varela threatened to bury me in concrete, I still wore a smile because of Miranda.

As I stepped onto the beach, Orlando Thornhill was laughing with Miles Chalmer, a neighbor, and another keen surfer.

"Hey there," I called.

"Here you are at last," Ollie said. "Long time no see. The surf's been pumping all week. And you didn't make it to the Thursday night jam. Dad was looking forward to having you twiddle those sticks."

"Twiddle my sticks?" I laughed.

The sea looked angry. "It's a bit rough," I said. "No one's in."

"That's what I'm thinking," Miles replied.

"Nuh-uh. It will be fun," Ollie argued. He was known for being adventurous.

His daredevil response egged me on. I hated to be thought of as a pussy. My father had bludgeoned recklessness into me, saying things like "Why be alive?"

He'd chucked me into the deep end of the pool when I was five, insisting it was the only way to learn to swim, while my mother screamed at him and jumped in to rescue me.

If ever I showed the slightest hint of fear, his fists would find their way into my gut. He avoided my face because he was smart enough to know questions would arise.

At least I'd had the sea, growing up. It consoled me whenever things turned ugly at home, especially when my father drank. I ran down and set up camp on the beach. On hot summer nights, I slept under the stars. My tears dried, and I stared up in wonder, knowing that somewhere out there in the heavens, my grandfather was watching and protecting me.

Once I'd developed a taste for girls, the beach became the setting for sexual discovery. Fucking under the stars and moonlight added something magical.

That was why that estate had to remain mine. My beach had always been there for me.

After we strapped ourselves to our boards, we ran out onto the shore and paddled out. The waves splashed up at us, pushing us around. I'd surfed a lot to know what we were doing wasn't a good idea. Despite that, being a strong swimmer and reveling in adrenaline, I persevered.

I paddled like mad as large waves thumped against me, threatening to swallow me whole.

When we were only knees deep, Miles said, "I'm going back in." Despite being younger, he'd always been the sensible one.

"I wouldn't miss it for the world!" Ollie yelled over the roar.

Although battered around, we kept paddling as the wild swell intensified.

A wave came barreling our way, and I paddled quickly to catch it. My choices were either ride or be wiped out.

I jumped up, but the surf was way too choppy. I only stayed up for a few seconds, then I tumbled into the turbulence. Spinning around as though I were in a washing machine, I battled to find the surface.

We'd made a crazy call. Adrenaline was one thing, but insanity was another.

When I eventually surfaced, my board narrowly missed my head. I jumped on the next smaller wave and paddled back to shore.

Nobody else was out there because doing so was plain suicide.

I turned to Miles. "It's fucking rough out there. Where's Ollie?"

"He got tossed by the same wave."

When he didn't surface, I ran back in.

The next few minutes felt like an hour. Huge defiant waves tossed me around. I got sucked back out into the deep, only to be picked up by a wave and dumped back to shore. I lost count of how many times.

I'd learned to deal with undertows, and taking a deep breath I waited for a friendly current. As another big wave headed my way, I dived under, praying to God. I wasn't ready to drown. I'd only just met my soulmate.

I managed to tread water long enough to see Ollie's board, which had ended up back onshore. I finally spotted Ollie floating on his back.

Adrenaline charged through me. I swam fast and furiously, fighting with the undertow and refusing to surrender.

As the current tried to suck me under, I envisioned Miranda smiling at me, instilling me with superhuman force. I dived under a huge wall of water, and when I came up, I reached Ollie.

He was out cold, so I clutched his waist, and after being pushed around again, I lucked upon a friendly wave that pushed us back to shore.

I laid Ollie on the sand and fell onto my knees, heaving.

Miles undid Ollie's strap, and although winded, I pushed down on his chest continuously.

When water spurted out of his mouth, I released a trapped breath, and Miles gasped with relief.

"Are you okay?" I asked.

At first, he stared at me, dazed, but then his eyes sparked with alarm.

"I can't move my fucking legs!"

I kept calm because Miles's face had turned pale. He was Ollie's best friend.

I turned to Miles. "You stay here, and I'll run and get some help, okay?"

He nodded and was about to help Ollie sit up when I stopped him.

"Don't move him."

I bent down to Ollie and said, "Just hang in there, buddy. Stay still until the ambulance arrives, okay?"

He nodded, looking lost.

I ran all the way up to Aidan's house, which was connected to a neighboring bay.

Clarissa opened the door. "Hello, stranger," she said cheerfully.

Her sweet smile soon faded when I didn't smile back.

I explained what had happened, and she covered her mouth and was about to run for the beach, but I stopped her, explaining that Miles was there.

Then I followed her back into the house and called for an ambulance.

After I finished the call, I said, "They're on their way." Tears ran down her cheeks, and I took her hand. "I'm sorry. I should have done more to stop him."

If I hadn't been such a fool and entered that turbulent surf, Ollie might not have charged ahead.

"Aidan warned him before he left. He went in for his morning swim, and it was so rough that when Ollie showed up with his board, I tried to talk him out of it. Oh God." She sighed. "But you know Ollie. He's so stubborn."

"Don't worry. It's probably just temporary nerve damage."

"I hope so." Clarissa bit her lip. More tears pooled in her eyes.

I held her hand. "He's a strong guy."

"I'll grab some water for him and a towel," Clarissa said, moving from one spot to another, looking confused.

"I'll do that. You just take a deep breath. Miles is looking after him. Ollie was talking fine when I left them. Try not to worry."

Two hours later, a nauseating antiseptic smell surrounded me as I sat in a hospital waiting room.

Aidan came running in with Allegra, Ollie's older sister.

When he saw me, he came over and hugged me. "Thanks for saving him."

"We were lucky to get the current. I just helped him along."

"Miles told me everything. You saved him." Aidan stared square into my face. "We'll never forget this."

He headed over to Clarissa and held her.

Her eyes were puffy and red. My heart went out to her, as I recalled my mother howling following Brent's accident. We, too, had been in the hospital, pacing about. Only the news was bleaker. My brother never regained consciousness.

As the doctors wheeled Ollie away to be examined, I froze at his wide-eyed fear as he held his mother's hand. He repeated that he couldn't move his legs.

It was gut-wrenching to watch.

Since there was little more I could do, I left to call Miranda. Exhausted by the emotion of it, I had to convince myself that Ollie would be all right.

Miranda's bright, cheery voice lifted my mood.

"Hey," I said.

"You sound flat."

"I'm just leaving the hospital."

"Visiting your father?"

"Nope. Ollie had a surfing accident."

"Oh God. Is it bad?"

"Well, at this stage, he can't move his legs."

"Hell."

"Yeah. What are you up to?" I asked, looking for some cheer.

"I'm at Harry's. I have to pick up Ava from your mom's class in an hour."

"You're back to childcare?"

"Harry's taken an extra shift. She needs the money, and now that I'm back here…"

"Why are you? I wish you'd take up my offer of the apartment," I said.

"I know, and it's so generous, but it's better this way. It will give us time to get to know each other properly. And I don't like free things."

"It's refreshing to meet someone who's not after something. That's why I like you."

"Is that the only reason?"

I smiled at her disappointed tone. "Nope. There are quite a few other reasons."

"Care to elaborate?"

I laughed. "Not here in this clinical place. Somewhere private and preferably without you wearing panties."

Her giggle helped me forget the drama unfolding around Ollie for a moment.

"I'd like to drop in and say hi to my mom, so how about I meet you at the dance class in an hour?"

"That would be nice."

"I'd better go. This is not looking good. Fuck."

"I'm sure he'll be okay. He's young."

"Mm. Got to go. Bye, beautiful."

I took a deep breath and rejoined the Thornhills.

"Any news?"

"They still need to do tests," Aidan said with his arm around his wife.

I touched Clarissa's hand. "I'm sure Ollie will be okay. He's strong."

She bit her lip and nodded as tears poured down her cheeks. My heart ached for her.

I thought of my mother and the pain that Brent had caused her. I'd always been the sensible one, despite the odd crazy decision, which I put down to teenage hormones. Maybe we'd been wired for fighting wars, only in our comfortable billionaire lives, it spelled mindless bravado with the potential to kill.

After leaving the hospital, I slid into my car, and for the first time in three months, I didn't feel the need to look around for cops. The one piece of good news to arrive that week—my license had been restored.

My foot hovered over the accelerator, about to push down hard, but I paused. My addiction to speed had to end. It was a miracle I hadn't had an accident, considering the crazy risks I'd taken on the road.

The biggest adrenaline junkie I'd ever met, Brent hadn't made it to his twenty-eighth birthday. And Ollie, although alive, had lost the use of his legs. It had to be temporary, I kept telling myself. How would he cope otherwise? With that restless energy, Ollie, by his own admission, planned to carve his initials on the moon.

I thought of Sam Chalmer and Aidan Thornhill. We often met on a dusty track at the back of Aidan's house, where we'd burn rubber and indulge in the grunt of our Mustangs. I could get my speed addiction out that way, I thought, sitting on the speed limit for once.

5

MIRANDA

Ava was a natural. She pirouetted and flung her arms up, stopped right on the beat, and clapped to the rhythm, as Lachlan's mom instructed. Her eyes were glued on Ava.

We'd plainly lost my niece to that fiery art form.

A little boy with big dark, friendly eyes stared up at me.

"Hello. Who do you belong to?" I asked.

Lachlan joined him, towering over the child. "He's with me."

Before I had a chance to respond, Lachlan kissed me and stroked my cheek affectionately. His blazing blue eyes held me spellbound, as they often did, and I remained transfixed on his handsome face.

The little boy, meanwhile, raced off into the center of the class and stomped his feet. Flamenco seemed to be an appealing art form for children, and he looked the part with his dark curls and big chocolate eyes.

While Lachlan laughed at the child's impromptu dance performance, my heart froze.

What isn't he telling me?

Everything went crazy from that point on. While the question remained stuck in my mouth, Belen, after seeing the arrival of the boy, shook her head at Lachlan and held her arms wide. She appeared just as puzzled as I was.

"*Un momento,*" she said to the guitarist.

After she acknowledged me with a greeting, her attention returned to Lachlan then to the boy, who'd scampered over to join us again.

Belen looked as though she was about to burst into tears. "He is exactly like Brent." She stared at Lachlan. "Is this his boy?

Tell me."

"No. Of course not."

I felt like an intruder, considering how personal the situation had become.

Is this Lachlan's weird way of introducing me to his child? And why only tell his mother now?

"The babysitter's sick, and as always, his never-there, couldn't-give-a-shit mother is in Miami. Manuel's my half brother," Lachlan said to me.

A sense of relief flushed through me, even though I had no right to feel that way. And I already knew about Manuel. For some reason, I'd totally forgotten—like many things, since Lachlan had entered my life.

"He's your father's son?" Belen's brow wrinkled. "But he doesn't look anything like him or that bitch."

"Mom, please. Not now." Lachlan cast me an apologetic smile.

Belen kept studying the child, who'd gone over to join Ava again. "*Dios mio.* He's exactly like Brent. I thought I was having a vision."

Manuel ran up to her and smiled sweetly. As much as her resentment toward the boy's parents was obvious, she melted at the sight of the beautiful boy.

She tousled his dark waves, and he giggled. And the longer they were together, the more I could see a resemblance between Belen and the boy. Their eyes were identical.

I also noticed that Lachlan's face hadn't relaxed the whole time.

"*Venga,*" she said, taking the boy's hand. "Go in there and dance." Holding up her finger, she became stern. "Only what I show you. All right?"

He flew over to the dance floor and stood by Ava.

Ava and Manuel looked so cute together that I couldn't stop smiling.

They were both naturals. Manuel took to the steps like a double-jointed person to yoga. Belen looked at her guitarist every now and then and shook her head in wonder.

When the class ended, I said, "That was pretty intense with your mother earlier."

"Yeah. You're not kidding. I had little choice but to bring him. When I returned from the hospital, Sherry, his full-time nanny, was unwell." He rubbed his shadowed jaw. "What a day."

Manuel ran over and wrapped his little arms around Lachlan's leg. I sensed the boy was lonely for a father, and Lachlan turned to me with a sad smile.

Although I loved his perfect body and aquamarine eyes, not to mention all the sheet-gripping pleasure, moments like that when Lachlan demonstrated heart-melting kindness were what affected me deeply.

Ava ran over and hugged me.

"That was fantastic, darling," I said.

Lachlan smiled brightly at her. "Hello, angel."

Belen joined us, while the children, who seemed to relate well, ran onto the dancefloor and practiced steps.

"I want that boy in this class," she said.

Lachlan shrugged. "It's not my decision, Mom. He's Tamara's son."

"He's not your father's," she said.

"He'd agree with you there," Lachlan replied dryly. "He doesn't even acknowledge him."

"He was always a cruel man. But I believe he's not the father. Manuel is the spitting image of your brother."

Lachlan's brow furrowed. "Look, I have to go. I've had a hell of a day. I came here to meet my girl." He put his arm around me.

"This is Miranda, by the way. My girlfriend."

"We've met. She brings her lovely niece here." Lachlan's mom leaned in and kissed me on both cheeks. "It's nice to meet you officially." She smiled. "Ava is a very talented dancer. I hope she continues."

"Oh, she will. She practices all the time," I responded.

"Good. The sign of a dancer," Belen said.

Manuel ran up to join us. "And you, cheeky boy, are going to dance too. Would you like that?" she asked.

He nodded, biting his lip.

Lachlan kissed his mother. "We have to go. We'll speak soon."

"We need to talk more about this." She cocked her head subtly toward Manuel.

After we said our goodbyes, the four of us left Belen behind.

As we drove, Lachlan remained lost in thought, while the children giggled in the back seat.

"You don't mind dropping Ava off at my mother's?" I asked.

"She can stay with us if you like. She gets on well with Manuel, and he could use a buddy."

I turned to study Lachlan as he merged onto the freeway. "Are you okay?"

"I've been better. I need to call Aidan when we get back."

His cool response made me ask, "Would you prefer to be alone?"

"No. I want you there. We can drop Ava off in the morning."

"It will have to be early," I said. "I have an appointment with the insurance valuers for the Pollocks. After that, I'll get them appointed to Sotheby's. Or…"

"Or what?"

"I could arrange an auction at the warehouse. For a tiny commission. Just enough to pay rent and cover costs."

"You'll get the market rate. You've got to survive, and it will put you on the map, won't it?"

The sparkling blue sea came to view as we drove onto the coastal highway.

"It would help," I said.

"Any news from your boss?"

"Florian's nowhere to be found. The landlord arrived yesterday. Luckily, we've managed to set up a group show to cover the rent for the month."

The group show, which was a great way to bring people into the space, felt more like a party. In many ways, it was to be a celebration of the new space. We'd decided to charge the artists rent rather than commission, and within a week, we'd signed up ample quality artists. It had almost been too easy.

"I'll cover the costs of running the business until you're able to make ends meet."

"You would do that?"

"You betcha." He smiled, bringing sunshine with him.

We arrived at the large estate and drove up the winding road past a line of poplars. The opulent honey-bricked mansion seemed to glow in the late-afternoon sun.

When Lachlan parked the car in the garage, the kids jumped out. Ava had a look of wonderment as if she'd stepped into one of her fairy tales. Manuel grabbed her hand as they ran to the pillared entrance of the enchanting two-story house.

Lachlan and I followed along the cobbled path. He smiled at me and took my hand.

Redolent of earth, salt, and flowers, the air kissed my cheeks.

Entering the house, I stepped onto a Persian rug in the hallway, clutching my arms.

"What's the matter?" Lachlan asked.

"I'm expecting Britney to charge at me, making demands."

Lachlan took me into his arms. "Don't worry, sweetheart." His lips brushed my cheek. "She's not here. We're alone. And you were here the other day."

"I know. But we hung out in the back. The last time I entered through the front was when I worked here."

"That's the only good thing Britney has done: find you."

"I don't think she'd agree with that. She hates me," I said.

"Don't let her get to you," he said.

The children came rushing in, and Manuel asked, "Can we watch television and have some ice cream?"

Lachlan smiled. He had a sweet way around the children. "Come with me."

I was about to protest that they hadn't eaten dinner yet but held back. Everything about that day was different.

The kitchen, with its marble benchtops and dark wooden

cupboards, was as large as the home I shared with Harriet.

Lachlan brought out two ice cream cones from a box in the stainless-steel double-doored fridge and passed them to the children.

"They'll be needing dinner," I said.

"That's true." He took a deep breath. "We could do take out."

"No. I'll whip something up for all of us. I make a very edible omelet."

"An omelet would be just great." Lachlan smiled brightly and kissed me.

He went off to make a call, leaving me to arrange dinner.

When I'd called Harriet earlier to explain that Ava was staying the night, I wanted to tell her about Ollie but thought it best I told her in person.

After we'd had dinner and the children had been put to bed, Lachlan brought out a photo album. I liked looking at the photos of him as a teenager and his school photos.

"You were gorgeous."

"Were?" He tilted his head.

"You're still pretty okay." I giggled.

He passed me a photo of a little boy.

"That's Manuel," I said.

"Nope. It's Brent." He handed me another photo. "That's my dad."

I stared at the fair-headed man with blue eyes, who looked like Lachlan but not Manuel or Brent.

"Brent obviously got his looks from your mom," I said.

Lachlan paced about, lost in his own world.

"What about Manuel's mother?" I asked.

Lachlan left the room and returned with a framed image of a blond woman in a wedding dress. "That's his mother."

Manuel didn't look anything like her either.

He ran his thumb over his lower lip. "My father insists the boy's not his."

When his phone buzzed, he stared at the screen. "I've got to take this."

I walked around the large living room and studied the Impressionist art on the blue walls, lingering at a small gilt-framed Degas.

A few minutes later, Lachlan returned, looking pale. He set his phone down. "That was Ollie's dad."

"How is he?"

"He's paralyzed." He slumped into the chair and buried his head in his hands. "Fuck."

I went over and knelt his side, taking his hand. "I'm sorry."

He nodded slowly then rose. "I need a hard drink. Can I get you one?"

"No. I'm still drinking my wine."

He returned and fell into his chair, shaking his head. "Fuck. I should've stopped him."

"But he would've done it, anyway. Ollie strikes me as a very confident, determined individual."

"Yeah. You've got that right." He exhaled.

I thought of Harriet. Although she and Ollie had only connected for one night, Ollie had gotten under her skin in such a profound way that I hadn't noticed with all her other guys.

"Look, it could be temporary. With the right rehab..."

Lachlan stared blankly at me. "Brent was the fucking father."

The sudden change in subject was jarring. "Huh?" I frowned. "Did your brother get with your stepmother?"

"It wouldn't fucking surprise me."

"Maybe it's just coincidence."

He shook his head. "No way. It makes sense. Brent was a man whore, and Tamara... Well, let's just say she likes young, buff males."

"Who doesn't?" I asked.

He stared at me for a moment, lost to his thoughts, then a little smile grew.

Patting his big thighs, he said, "Come here and sit on my lap. Enough of everyone's fucking dramas. I need to feel you."

6

LACHLAN

Miranda had this magic way of helping me escape in the healthiest of ways. Instead of alcohol or bad sex with a stranger—guilty escapes I'd once resorted to—she gave me pure unadulterated pleasure and something more. That *something more* was what surprised me the most.

I held her close as she slept. Her soft body melded perfectly to mine, and her warm breath tickled my chest.

The early morning had come, and I could hear the children running around.

I sat up, and Miranda stirred, opening her eyes.

"Sorry for waking you," I said.

"What time is it?"

"It's seven."

"Oh… you haven't slept?" she asked, sitting up along.

My morning wood rose with her. "No, I did. I only just woke up." Smiling at her, I put my arm around her. "A quick shower?"

"Sure."

Just the feeling of her curves undulating against my fingers sent blood charging through me.

The children ran into the room just as we were getting out of bed. I tossed a T-shirt to Miranda and wrapped a towel around myself.

"Hey. What are you up to?"

"Can we have chocolate ice cream?" Manuel asked.

Miranda shook her head, scrunching her face. "No. Just give me a minute, and I'll come and make bacon and eggs. Would you like that?"

The children nodded.

"Off you go."

They scampered off.

"I'll go and sort out their breakfast," she said.

I took her into my arms. "A quick fuck in the shower is out of the question, I suppose?"

She giggled. "It's rarely a quick fuck."

"No, you minx." My mood had bounced back. It felt nice having that domestic scene around me.

I held her close, clutched her perfect ass, and kissed her. "You feel hot in the mornings."

Miranda stroked my dick. "So do you."

"Mm… nice."

She pulled away. "I need to tend to the children."

"Put on my robe," I said, slapping her butt.

"Ouch."

"Sorry. You've got a very spankable ass."

"I'll take that as a compliment, shall I?" She smiled sweetly.

"Oh you should. It's a very shapely, sexy butt, and if we keep talking about it, you're going to have to come back here and bend over for me."

She tilted her pretty head, and went off to the kitchen.

A few hours later, I'd dropped Miranda and Ava off, and Sherry had returned to care for Manuel, so I made my way to the hospital to visit my dad.

It took a few minutes before he opened his eyes, and as he attempted to sit up, I held his frail body and placed a pillow behind his shoulders.

"How's that?" I asked.

"Okay. How long have you been there?" he croaked.

"Not long."

"Why didn't you wake me? I hate people watching me sleep."

"You looked very peaceful."

"Mm…" He adjusted his body and grimaced.

"Are you in pain?"

"Yeah. Where's that nurse?" He pushed a button.

Within a minute, a young nurse walked in. "And how are we

today?" She wore a bright smile.

His face warmed a little. Even in that condition, my dad still had a weakness for young, pretty blondes. "I need another dose."

She looked at her chart then at me and said, "Okay. You've had a fair bit already, I see."

"I don't give a fuck. I'm in pain."

She looked at me, as though seeking my approval, and I shrugged, unsure what to say. The situation was just sad.

The nurse left us for a moment then returned.

After the medicine had been administered, his face relaxed.

"Is that better?" I asked.

He nodded.

"Mom met Manuel," I said.

"The bitch met the bastard."

"Hey. They're family. And that's my mother. So get over it."

"Oh… you've grown balls at last."

"And fuck you too." I shifted in my seat. The comment about my mother reminded me of what an asshole he was. As much as I tried, I couldn't think of any redeeming feature that I could look up to. My mother, on the other hand, made me seriously proud, given her unshifting commitment to dance and drive to nurture talent.

"So, why did you go and do that?" he asked.

"The nanny was sick. And I needed to babysit my nephew." I studied his face for a reaction.

He stared at me blankly.

After a long, tense pause, he adjusted his position. "Your baby brother, you mean."

"Nope. All it took was one glance from Mom, and it all came out. Manuel is Brent's kid."

His face contorted. "What the fuck are you talking about?"

I removed two photos from my satchel. "Here. Who's this?" I handed him a recent photo of Manuel.

The shake in his hand made me regret my tone. But the truth needed to be known.

"That's Brent," he said.

I started to take the photo, but he wouldn't let me. "My life crashed with him that day. That's when everything went to shit. He was my boy." A tear fell down his withered cheek.

Even though his favor for my brother came as no surprise, resentment clung to me like a blood-sucking leech.

"That's Manuel, not Brent." I handed him another photo. "Here's your beloved Brent. So you see, Manuel is my nephew *and* your grandchild."

"That's bullshit. You've always been jealous of your brother. And he can't fucking defend himself. How dare you?"

I'd had enough. He could rot in hell.

I rose abruptly, fury pumping through me. "How dare you turn the Peace name to filth and leave me to clean up after your illegal fucking get-rich-schemes? I suppose you sold crack to homeless kids too." At that moment, I saw him only as the charlatan sharp-talker he'd always been and not a frail man. "You're a pedophile, a fraud, and a fucking cheat. And Brent was fucking Tamara. You were exactly alike. That's why you loved him."

His mouth opened, then he collapsed onto his pillow.

I squeezed my eyes shut. Instead of clearing the air, I'd dirtied it.

Did I kill him? I leaned forward and touched his neck, holding my breath until the vein pulsed faintly on my fingertip.

After I explained to the nurse that he'd fainted, I ran away, taking with me his cold, empty stare.

How the fuck could a man be that way? Especially close to death. Shouldn't he seek redemption? As a lapsed Catholic, I felt the sudden urge to see a priest, if only to help me deal with my gut-wrenching guilt from hating my father. *And why am I helping him? I should have walked away and let him rot in hell.*

My phone buzzed, and when I saw it was Miranda, my spirit warmed. "Hey, good-looking," I said, faking a cheery vibe.

"Lachlan, I'm at your apartment."

"Wearing little, I hope."

"I've got the insurance adjuster here. Can you get here now?"
"Sure. I'm only down the road. What's wrong?"
"Just get here."

She ended the call.

The cold, shivery sensation that had followed me out of the hospital turned glacial.

7

MIRANDA

I started my day with a spring in my step as I arrived at our freshly painted warehouse, which we'd named the Artefactory. Everything had started to fall into place, and I'd also made two new friends who happened to be driven and talented. I just had to figure out how to handle Ethan's lingering stares.

I entered my office, which I loved, even with its view of the barren parking lot, where trash blew about like tumbleweeds and discarded junk and broken bottles spoke of urban angst.

Sitting at my desk, I turned on my laptop to study the eclectic collection for our first show. The daring work radiated that fresh, honest mark of youth and also included Ethan's abstracts of twisted forms in clashing colors. But Clint's furniture—chests with crooked drawers and painted melty faces resembling wood grain—stole my heart.

Clint entered and set a cup of coffee on my desk.

"These look amazing," I said.

"It's a great collection, isn't it? I can't wait. It's going to be so much fun."

His contagious excitement put a smile on my face. "I love your pieces. They'll sell for sure."

"Thanks." He ran his hand along my table, which he'd sanded and painted.

"When I can afford it, I'll have to commission a set."

"I'll make you one. Don't worry about the money. I'm never comfortable taking it."

I studied his soft, feminine face. Clint was so beautiful that he defied gender. "But one has to survive, sweetie," I replied just as Ethan entered. "I was just saying to Clint how awesome the collection for the show is. And your pieces are very unique too."

He sat on the edge of my desk. "It's a great collection. I'm not sure about my work, though."

"Hey, it's fantastic," Clint said.

I nodded. "They're very commercial. And have a stamp of Bacon."

"You can see that?" Ethan asked, his face lighting up.

"I can. His somber colors. And the lines. They're unique."

"They can't be that unique if they remind you of Francis Bacon."

"Well…" I chose my words carefully. Like most artists, Ethan struck me as sensitive. "No one's ever totally unique. It's all been done before, hasn't it? An artist curates. They take or steal, as Picasso once admitted." I chuckled.

Ethan's smile grew as he stared deeply into my eyes. "You should put together a newsletter about the Artefactory's mission."

"Oh… like a manifesto, you mean?"

"Yeah," Clint replied enthusiastically. "Just like the Futurists and the Dadaists." He rubbed his hands together. "Let's do it."

His zest proved contagious. "Let's. We just need a mailing list."

"Print them out and we can leave them around colleges and cafes. It will promote the Artefactory," Ethan suggested.

"All right. Leave it to me. I'll make some notes and run it past you," I said, rising from my desk.

After a very constructive morning, I zipped over to Lachlan's apartment for an appointment with the insurance adjuster, who waited for me at the entrance of the state-of-the-art building.

He followed me up to Lachlan's penthouse in the private elevator, and after he declined my offer of a coffee, I led him into the darkened room where the paintings were and turned on the light.

I hadn't visited that room since depositing the works of art, which lay exactly as we'd left them, covered in canvas sheets.

I bent down and peeled off the protective sheeting. When I looked closer, my heart sank to my feet.

The adjuster, being an art expert, looked down at me as if to ask, "Is this some kind of joke?" "This a fake," he said in a cool, calm tone.

"Hell," I spat.

I crouched and peeled off the top canvas, only to discover that the rest were also fakes. I couldn't believe the forger had opted for such cheap acrylic paint. But given it dried quickly, I imagined it was the expedient choice.

When I got to the painting at the bottom of the pile, I discovered that Florian had left one original, which he'd cunningly laid on the top.

"That looks legitimate," the adjuster said.

I could barely talk. "Can you please value that one? Excuse me one moment."

I headed into the bathroom. My knees smacked onto the cold, hard tiles, and I vomited into the toilet.

After I gargled some water and cleaned myself up, I went back out.

"Are you okay?" he asked, studying me closely through his spectacles.

"It's come as a shock."

"I bet it has. This is a potential crime scene. Were you expecting to get away with this?"

My brow contracted so tightly that I felt a headache coming on. "Of course not. A crime's been committed but not by me or Lachlan Peace. Florian Storm's the person behind this."

"He's a respected dealer." He looked down at his pad. "Market value for the original?"

"Yes." I could barely speak.

"Eighty or a hundred million, I'd estimate. Although considering you have fakes here... I'm not sure whether the company will risk it."

"I need to call the police," I said, my head spinning. That he'd refused to underwrite a policy barely registered.

"Anyway, leave this to me." He snapped his notepad shut. "I'll be in touch. We can probably do something but with a substantial excess."

I nodded slowly.

After I walked him to the elevator, I slumped onto the sofa, biting my nails, and waited for Lachlan to arrive.

Ten minutes later, Lachlan waltzed in, looking gorgeous in a breezy green shirt hanging over jeans that hugged his athletic body so teasingly that I wished I could forget that past hour and have him turn me roughly to the wall, teeth on my neck, and fuck me hard.

"Hey, gorgeous," he said.

I let him hold me, and my spirit relaxed enough to break the heart-shattering news.

After I broke away, he studied me, and a line formed between his eyebrows. "What's the matter? You don't look well."

"Sit down for a moment."

He went over to the crystal decanter and lifted it. "It sounds like I need a drink. Do you want one?"

I nodded.

He made the drinks and passed me a glass. "Okay. Let me have it."

After I explained what had happened, Lachlan looked as though an asteroid were about to hit LA.

"What the fuck?"

He rushed into the room with the paintings, and I followed.

"Why did we not see this?" he asked. Lachlan's accusatory stare pained me.

The world fell on my shoulders. I'd created the mess.

Considering we carried each painting one by one, I should have noticed the fakes. But they'd been covered in thick cloth.

Lachlan bent down and lifted one after another, tossing each aside like trash, while I watched, clutching my arms.

He couldn't look at me.

"Lachlan, I..."

He raised his palms to me. "Please. Don't."

When he arrived at the original, he laughed coldly. "How nice of him to leave one behind."

The breaking point was when he left the room without acknowledging me. I took a deep breath and joined him in the living room, where he was pouring himself a full glass of liquor.

"I should've checked. The lighting was subdued in the vault—"

"I need to be alone," he said while staring down at his phone.

After uttering a hundred apologies and Lachlan ignoring me, rage raced through my veins. "Well, fuck you too," I snapped while stabbing the elevator button.

I waited with my back turned to him, hoping he would at least reassure me.

His silence screamed volumes. He blamed me.

A knife drove into my gut, and everything turned gray. I couldn't even wait for the elevator. Instead, I ran down forty flights of stairs, frustration and despair pushing me along.

By the time I reached the sidewalk, I hated Lachlan Peace for dragging me into his complicated life.

Why didn't I check the art before removing it from Florian's vault?

People rushed past me in blurs as I stood in the middle of the sidewalk, my leaden body gripped by indecision.

I eventually headed to a café, ordered a coffee, and sat there staring blankly out the window. I felt as if I were having an out-of-body experience. *Maybe this is what a bad trip feels like.* People's faces distorted before me like a Munch painting.

By the time I finished my coffee, my mind had finally settled, leaving behind a dull ache.

I couldn't get over how Lachlan's eyes had turned into daggers, stabbing with accusation. They were the same spellbinding eyes that shifted from tender turquoise to liquid fire when he fucked me raw.

He hated me, and I hated him—profoundly.

I scrolled through my contacts and called Gavin, one of my former lecturers.

"Hi, this is Miranda Flowers."

"Ah! Miranda, how nice to hear from you. I've heard about the Artefactory. If anyone can make that work, it's you."

Although the acknowledgment should have made me sit up and smile, I gulped back a sob instead. Taking a deep breath, I mustered the strength of Hercules to ward off tears.

"Um… Something has happened. It's serious. Can we meet?"

"I've got a free hour now if you can make your way up to the campus."

"Sure. I'm not far. I'll see you soon."

8

LACHLAN

After spending two hours with the fraud squad, I walked out of the police station. I couldn't decide what pained me more: being taken for a ride by Florian or how I'd treated Miranda.

If anyone was to blame, I was, for not getting my insurance in order.

I stopped walking when I realized the paintings were insured but not revalued.

I grabbed my cell and called Britney.

"I've been trying to call you all morning," she said.

"Yeah… well… it's been a fucking trying day."

"I've got good news," she said.

"Oh?" I let out a tired sigh.

"You could try to sound a little more upbeat."

"The Pollocks, bar one, have been stolen, and a close friend has just become fucking paralyzed. I'm not exactly in the mood to party."

"Holy shit. The Jackson Pollocks are gone?"

A compassionate person would have asked about the friend but not Britney. "Yep."

"I knew she couldn't be fucking trusted," she said.

"It's not Miranda's fault."

"That's your dick talking."

"Stop being crass. Dig out the insurance on the Pollocks for me. I'm coming now."

"How are you going to pay the investors?"

"We'll figure something out. I've still got half a collection of contemporary art, and there's always the apartment."

"You can't sell the penthouse."

"I don't know what that's got to do with you," I said.

"Well… it's a sought-after penthouse."

"I couldn't give a shit. I'll be there soon. I just have to drop into the hospital."

"Clarke's not doing too well," she warned me.

"I'm not visiting him."

"You sound angry. He's pretty upset about how you spoke to him."

"I don't give a fuck."

"He's your dad."

"I've got to go," I said and hung up.

Half an hour later, I walked into the hospital to visit Ollie, where I found him in bed, staring out the window.

"Hey," I said.

"It's weird, but I've never noticed that building before," he said, pointing at a silver skyscraper. "It's so pointy. Like it's stabbing the sky. Fuck. Imagine sky diving and landing on that. It would fucking impale you."

He turned to me for the first time. His mouth barely moved. Ollie didn't even look like the boy I'd known since he was a baby. His remote eyes had lost their youthful glow.

"I bought you a copy of *Mojo*." I set the music magazine down on the side table. "And some chocolates."

Awkward silence followed. I shifted my weight a few times, and taking a deep breath, I asked, "What's the news?"

"Not great. I'll probably never walk again."

"That's bullshit. You get yourself the best doctor, and before you know it, you'll be up and about."

"Hm. At least I've got my arms." He smiled sadly.

"And those very capable fingers. You're an amazing guitarist."

"Little good that's going to do me now." He looked away again.

"It's my fault." I exhaled. "I should have…"

"No." He turned sharply. "I fucked up. All that bravado crap."

"I should've known better. I mean, fuck, I went in, too, you know. Like an idiot."

"Don't beat up on yourself, man." He paused. "Hell. You fucking saved me."

I caught a glimpse of *Les Miserables* by Victor Hugo on his table. "You're reading that?"

His mouth twitched at my surprised tone. "Grandad is. He should be here soon. I protested at first, but it's grown on me. It's an interesting story. I hated the musical."

I laughed for the first time that day.

"I was dragged along to that musical as a kid. I haven't read it, though. Is Grant reading it?"

"No. Mom's dad, Julian. He's the brains in the family. Along with Mom." He smiled faintly.

"He brought in a whole lot of books. But when I told him I could barely think, let alone read, he started reading it to me. And before I knew it, I was actually hooked. It's a great story. I don't know why the fuck they had to sing through it."

I laughed. We shared similar musical tastes.

"Audiobooks are great. I enjoyed Keith Richards's biography, read by Johnny Depp. I'll drop it by. It's seriously cool."

He nodded slowly then returned to staring out the window. "Thanks for coming. I'm just tired. Mom will be here soon, fussing, and Dad too. I just wish everyone would leave me alone."

"I guess they're all... we're all wanting to support you."

"I don't want that. I just want to fucking die."

"Look, Ollie. Give it time. You've got—"

"No. Lachie. Please. Everyone's saying the same things. Please go. Thanks for the magazine."

He didn't even look at me. I had a feeling he was crying.

With a heavy heart, I stood and touched his arm. "I'm here for you. Remember that."

I left, and just when I thought the day couldn't get worse, it did.

When I arrived at my car, Varela stepped up to my side, making me start.

"A bit jumpy," he said.

"Where the fuck did you come from?"

"So... where's the rest?" he asked.

As I peered down at the tubby man, I wondered whether every Mafia dude in America had to do some kind of apprenticeship watching reruns of *The Godfather* before hitting the strip.

"Your pretty girlfriend's little warehouse happens to belong to a pal of mine. He's a chain-smoker, you know. It wouldn't take much for him to leave a cigarette burning while she's there working her pretty butt off. The insurance alone would be worth it."

Rage stormed through me. "Don't you fucking go near her." I stood close enough for his sickly-sweet cologne to waft up my nose.

"He's already casing the joint. He met your girl for the rent, and when he suggested she pay him off with her womanly gifts, she yelled abuse at him, threatening to call the cops." He lifted an eyebrow. "She's got more balls than you." He chuckled. "He's a businessman first and left her alone. But one word from me..."

"Now, listen to me. If anyone goes near Miranda, there will be fucking hell to pay." I stood so close that I peered down his head. "You got that?"

"Then stop breaking my balls. I want my money."

"You'll get the rest of your money. You're the first on the list. The art's going to auction. I've been fucked around by a deal that fell through."

"Because you're shitting me, it's gone up. Twelve big ones. *Capisce?*"

"That's two million more!"

"So? At least you've still got that pretty face. And let's not forget your sexy girl."

"If anyone goes fucking near her..."

An evil grin formed on his face. "Ah... ain't love grand."

I watched his short, stubby frame move off, wondering how

someone that small could be so fearless.

His threats toward Miranda put ice in my veins. I had to get him off my back—immediately.

I drove to the estate, and when I entered the office, Britney peered up from her screen. "Twenty million."

I stopped walking. "For what?"

"That's how much the Pollocks were insured for."

There is a God. That would pay Varela. "Good. Put in a claim right away."

"Sure thing." She gave me an army salute. "Have you reported it?"

I nodded.

"So, Golden Girl fucked up." A wicked smile touched her plumped lips.

"You're enjoying this, aren't you?"

She smirked.

"It wasn't Miranda's fault. It was mine. In any case, he was a reputable dealer."

"The project looks good." Britney's change of subject was welcomed. "I've got photos, and I'm compiling a report for the SEC. In it, I speak about how you're raising the capital to pay off the investors."

She looked pleased with herself. Though I'd grown to dislike Britney, she'd proved indispensable.

"I should be able to raise around half a billion from my remaining collection," I said. "That will cover everything."

"You'll have to get a move on. The bank's making noises."

"If need be, I've always got the apartment for a down payment."

"You'll be sharing this lovely house with Stepmommy, then. Oh, and speak of the devil, she's returned."

"Fucking great." I sighed. "I'll go and stay at the apartment, then."

"If you sell, you can always come and stay at mine." She moved closer to me.

"That's not going to happen, Britney."

"I'm the only one that can get you out of the shit if Tammy decides to press charges."

I studied her for a minute. I'd forgotten all about that encounter in the shower with my drunken stepmother.

"Just say the word. Or words. Ask me to marry you, and all this will go away."

I looked out the window over the expansive garden, where trees thrashed about in the roaring wind.

"We can keep the estate," she continued. "I've got dirt on her too. I know about Brent."

I turned sharply. "What do you mean?"

"I caught them together in the pool one night. They were drunk and didn't see me. I photographed it."

"And you were going to tell me this when?"

She shrugged. "Another trump card, I guess. I figured it might help Clarke when he was ready to leave her."

Her cold smile made me squirm. "Tell me something. Why didn't you marry him?"

"Clarke?"

I nodded.

"Because I wanted to marry you. The next in line. It's not just the money." Her face softened. "In any case, there'll soon be plenty of that. I can make us filthy rich." She moved closer again. "It's just that I've always wanted you."

I pulled my arm from her creeping fingers.

"What's she got?" she asked.

"Miranda was innocent before I came onto the scene. She's a pure soul. She's not in it for what she can get." I missed her like mad and hated myself for the way I'd spoken to her. Since then, she hadn't taken my calls. I couldn't blame her. I'd acted like a jerk.

"So she was a fucking virgin. What is it with you men and virgins?"

"That's not what attracted me."

"A tight cunt, you mean?" She tilted her head.

Refusing to dignify her crassness with a response, I left her standing there.

9

MIRANDA

"Ava!" Harriet snapped.

My niece stopped banging her feet and turned to me, placing a hand over her mouth.

I shook my head and smiled at her expressive little face. "Don't be like that, Harry. Ava's driven. There's nothing wrong with that, is there?"

Harriet tossed things about, which was her version of cleaning. She was like an alcoholic without a drink, only her grumpiness related to lacking a male in her life.

Thanks to my parlous financial state, I had to ask my sister whether I could stay with her again. My finding an apartment had stalled, and I'd hit rock bottom.

Although Lachlan had called two hours after I'd stormed off, I couldn't bring myself to speak to him.

Our romantic bubble had burst. My idealizing him had blinded me.

But his flaws weren't what prickled. He was fallible, like all humans, especially by not updating his insurance. The cold look in his eyes, which still made me shiver thinking about it, was what hurt the most.

Gavin, my former tutor, had turned pale at the mention of Florian. News traveled fast. Everyone in the industry knew of his disappearance. And rumor had it that Florian, having succumbed to a raging coke habit, had Interpol chasing him. Gavin apologized profusely for recommending the art dealer to me, but I just shrugged it off and muttered something about bad timing.

The easygoing—albeit rational—response came from my

public persona. Internally, regret seeped through my bones. I rued my decision to major in art history instead of opting for a law degree or teaching, as my mother had begged.

But I wouldn't have met Lachlan, a little tremulous voice whispered.

Are two months of endless orgasms worth this crushing pain?

"Harry, sit down for a minute. I have something to tell you."

Once I'd told my story, she asked, "So, does this mean you're moving back in?"

"I never really left." A lump formed in my throat.

She sat down and smiled sympathetically. "You should just talk to him."

"I don't know. He was awful to me."

"In the heat of the moment, people say things they don't mean. I'd want to be left alone if I'd been ripped off that badly."

"But don't you see? Lachlan had a point. I fucked up."

"Bullshit. You weren't to know that guy would run off. And Lachlan fucked up, too, by not getting his insurance together. He keeps calling you. At least talk about it."

I bit into the last nail I had to decimate. "Look, Harry… I've got something else to tell you." I hadn't seen my sister since I heard of Orlando's accident.

"What is it?" She wrapped her arm around Ava, who'd joined her on the sofa.

"It's about Orlando," I said.

She sat up and removed her arm from her daughter. "Go and practice."

"But, Mommy, you said…"

"I don't care. Just leave us for a minute."

I waited for Ava to leave the room and said, "He had a surfing accident." I paused for a breath. "He's paralyzed."

"What?" Her brow creased. "Where is he?"

"He's in the hospital."

"Well, obviously. Which one?"

"I don't know."

"I'll have to call Lachlan," she said. "Can I have his number?"

I rose and paced about. My heart raced again. "What good will visiting him do?"

She seemed far away and hadn't even heard my question. "Holy shit. You're fucking kidding. Just his legs? Or all over?"

"I think it's his legs. To be honest, I didn't get that much detail. All this other crap blew up at the same time."

"Give me Lachlan's number." She held her hand out.

A breath trembled out of me. The thought of Harriet speaking to Lachlan freaked me out. It would crush me if he didn't ask about me.

I scrolled down to his name and picture in my contacts. He wore a playful little smile—a reminder of our happier times.

Apart from missing him as much as I would an arm, I worried about him. Then there was Britney. A chill ran over me as I thought of her scheming to snag him into a relationship.

Leaving Harriet to talk to Lachlan, I entered my tiny bedroom, where strewn clothes and other messes reflected my sudden chaotic state.

I sat on the edge of the bed and buried my head in my hands. Harriet's murmurings came through the doorway. He'd picked up. Lachlan rarely took calls unless absolutely essential, so that made me sit up.

After I heard her say, "Bye," I raced out.

She passed me my phone. "He picked up right away and said your name as though he'd been dying to hear from you."

Warmth shot through me. "Seriously? You're not just saying that?"

She shook her head. "When I told him who it was, he sounded a little disappointed." She shrugged. "Maybe more surprised. He told me what I needed to know. I'm going to apply for a job at that hospital. Today." She moved around quickly.

"Why?"

"Because I am."

"Did he say anything else?"

"Not really. He did ask how you were, though."

"He did? What did you say?"

"I told him you hadn't stopped crying."

I frowned. "You're fucking joking."

She shook her head. "It's the truth, and I told him he was a jerk for blaming you."

"How did he respond?"

"He didn't say anything after that." She grabbed her bag. "Can you take Ava to dance class?"

Since it was Saturday morning, I needed to be at the Artefactory to help hang paintings for our opening, but I said, "Sure."

"Thanks, sis. And hey… he misses you."

"Did he say that?"

She shook her head. "I can just tell. Catch you later."

"We've got a big opening next week. And you're coming."

"Maybe. I'm not a fan of that arty-farty scene. But we'll see."

"You'd better. I'll need you there."

"You can count on me." Harriet kissed me on the cheek.

10

LACHLAN

My surviving art collection sold within a week. I had enough to pay off the investors, therefore satisfying the SEC and Varela in one smooth transaction.

The value of nostalgia proved higher, however, making for a hollow victory. That collection had been my grandfather's passion.

Despite the big turnover of cash, for the first time in my life, I was broke. I didn't even have enough money to make money. But I'd had my eye on an affordable-housing development that ticked all the boxes, fulfilling my desire to help those in need while bolstering Peace Holding's finances. I couldn't wait for the insurance money because the theft of the Pollocks was still under investigation.

The thought of selling the apartment turned me upside down. It held special memories. I'd fallen in love with Miranda there, and I'd been her first. I hadn't even washed the sheets since she left. Her sweet perfume was the last thing I smelled every night before falling asleep. I'd been spending most of my time there to avoid Tamara, who was hanging around the estate like a bad smell.

My phone buzzed with a text. *Gig tonight. $300. Interested? R&B covers.*

I answered, *Count me in.*

He replied, *There's plenty more for a hot drummer like you. Ready to work seven nights?*

Three hundred bucks used to be my breakfast bill.

I answered, *Sure thing. Thanks, buddy.*

The offer had come more quickly than expected. I'd contacted a few college pals I used to jam with, asking about gigs. A few hundred dollars here and there would at least stall the sale of my apartment, even though it wouldn't go far enough to cover Tamara's massive credit card bills. The sale of the remaining Pollock would solve my money issues, but it needed to be authenticated. I didn't know what the holdup was, and I couldn't wait for that as the bills mounted.

I headed back to the estate to get some practice on the bigger drumkit. Playing softly on pads in the penthouse may have worked for jazz but not for rock.

Britney met me at the entrance just as I was turning the doorknob.

"We're out of the shit. That sale fixed everything."

"For now." I exhaled. "What about Tammy's fucking bills? And why the hell are we paying off her credit cards?"

"Hello... she's married to your father. I've already confronted Tammy about her excessive spending."

"I can imagine her fucking response." I shook my head. The shower debacle had only happened a few weeks ago, but it felt like years.

I regretted not going to the authorities, but the media would have turned it into a soap opera. And Tamara, with her B-grade acting skills, would have told the world I'd tried to rape her.

"I visited Clarke earlier," Britney said. "He wants to see you. I don't think he's going to last."

I kept walking.

"You need to see him." Britney followed me.

I nodded. Of course, I would go and see him.

From the living room, I heard Tamara yelling at Sherry in the kitchen. In the middle of her tirade, she turned, and seeing me there, she asked, "How dare you ask Sherry to take my son to that fucking witch's class?"

Heat flushed through my body. "That's my mother you're talking about. She's got more class in one atom of her DNA than your entire common family put together. So shut the fuck up."

Her plumped lips twitched into a smile. "Mm... Is that testosterone I smell?"

I rolled my eyes at Sherry. "Can you give us a moment?"

After the nanny left, I said, "Mannie's the happiest I've seen him. You're rarely here. So why would you give a shit?"

"Because as his mother, I make the rules."

"Then you should show some interest in him."

She gulped down her vodka. "I didn't ask to be a mother. I hate what that kid did to my body."

"You're fucking sick." I started to move away.

"Speaking of which, my lawyers have gone over the prenup. I want it torn up. This house is mine."

"Over my fucking dead body."

"It might be over your jailed body." She laughed.

"It's your word against mine," I said.

"The hospital has a record of my injuries."

"You're not getting this house." I thumped the bench then charged off before I punched a hole in the wall.

Britney came up behind me.

I turned sharply. "What do you want?"

She touched my arm. "Marry me, and it will all go away."

I held my arms wide. "Why would you want to marry someone who's completely uninterested?"

"I'll take what I can get. I'll do threesomes. Anything kinky. And we'll be fabulously rich."

My stomach churned. "I'm not that guy anymore."

"You can fuck Miranda too. I'll turn a blind eye."

I shook my head.

"Just one night a week with you would be enough for me." Her eyes softened, and in a rare moment, they shone with a hint of vulnerability.

My body and soul craved only one girl, and she was too good for me. I had nothing to give her but trouble, especially if Tamara kept her game up. I imagined the police inquiries, and just the implication of me screwing my stepmother was enough to bury me in shit.

"I've got to go and practice," I said, turning my back to Britney.

I entered my music room, removed the dust cover from my drumkit, and sat down. Instead of warming up slowly and properly, I smashed the skins as though exorcising a demon.

Manuel came running in and watched with his mouth wide open, as though seeing something rare.

"Hey," I said, putting down my drumsticks. "I hear you're quite the little dancer."

He bit his lip and shrugged.

"Do you want a go?" I asked.

"Yeah," he said, brightening and reminding me of Brent again.

I stepped away from the kit and adjusted the seat.

Manuel jumped on and banged the drum, creating nothing but noise.

"Here, let me show you something." I leaned over him and held his little hands while balancing the sticks in mine. I played a simple pattern, hitting one drum only.

"Let me do that," he said.

I positioned the sticks properly in his hands, and instead of going nuts, as kids were known to on drumkits, he stuck to what I'd shown him, proving he was a natural.

"You've got groove," I said, smiling for the first time that day.

We messed around for a while, then noticing the time, I said, "How about if I give you a little pad to practice on? Would you like that?"

He looked disappointed. Manuel rarely had someone to connect with. I suspected that was why he enjoyed my mom's classes. My heart cried for the little fellow.

"Do you want to come down to the beach? I've got a boogie board here somewhere."

"Oh yeah!" His face lit up.

An hour later, as I waited for Manuel, Tamara tottered in. Her eyes wandered over my naked chest.

"Mm... you're being a pussy teaser." She chuckled.

I couldn't tell what pissed me off the most, that she was eye-fucking me around her son or that she completely ignored the poor kid, who'd come running in clutching a boogie board.

"Are you ready, little man?" I asked.

He nodded.

Tamara rolled her eyes and staggered off.

I hoped her lack of interest in her son wouldn't affect him.

As I clasped his little hand, an overwhelming need to shield him from harm made my heart swell.

11

MIRANDA

I stepped back to study Ethan's impressive nudes, which were abstracted by smudged paint.

"What do you think?" he asked.

"I love them. They're very sellable."

"Commercial, you mean?"

"Hm. Yes, but that doesn't diminish their artistic worth." I smiled reassuringly.

"I think this is a very well-curated collection," he said, pointing at the art on the walls.

A sense of pride and achievement flushed through me. I loved the collection, which I'd worked tirelessly to collate.

If it weren't for a horrific encounter with the sleazy landlord and my missing Lachlan like crazy, I would have bounced along.

That frightful meeting with my landlord made me realize two things: One, if I wanted to succeed at running my own business, I would have to learn to stand up to bullies. Two, Lachlan was in trouble. The landlord, in his mangled rasp, had mentioned something about Lachlan being buried in concrete if he didn't pay up. That terrified me more than the threat of having the Artefactory torched.

Just as I answered Ethan's lingering gaze with an awkward smile, my phone vibrated, making me jump.

Lachlan's face smiled up at me, and my heart skipped a beat.

"Your boyfriend?" Ethan asked.

Am I being that obvious? "Um... I don't have one."

"It's just that you've gone red."

"No, I haven't."

I decided against taking the call, just to prove a point, though maybe more to myself. Though I craved Lachlan as one did water in the desert, I needed to focus on my career. While we were together, I lost myself to him.

All week, I'd tried to avoid those ugly memories of our last meeting by focusing on my work. Every now and then, caught off guard, I slipped back into thinking about Lachlan, and the tears, with a will of their own, poured out again.

Why didn't he try to call and apologize sooner? If that's even what that call is about.

Although I could understand his frustration, it was low of him to sink the boot in just when I already felt terrible. I kept beating up on myself with the same thought on loop—I should have done more to stop Lachlan from leaving the paintings with Florian.

Unable to eat, I hated Lachlan for possessing my body and soul. Every moment was filled with him. He even had a starring role in my dreams.

"Where should I put this?" Clint asked, carrying a chair with a mask aimed at the sitter's face.

I pointed at a corner. "I think there, so that the mask creates a silhouette on the wall."

My phone rang again. "Excuse me."

Though I'd hoped it was Lachlan again, Harriet was calling.

"Hey."

"I need you to take Ava to dance class. I've got an interview."

"Oh… sure. What's the job?"

"It's a role at the rehab trauma unit."

"Oh? Let me guess—the same hospital Orlando's in?"

"Yep."

"I hope you know what you're doing."

"Oh, I know what I'm doing, all right. I'm going to heal him if it takes everything I've got."

I took a deep breath. Harriet's drive was new and sudden. "Got to go."

When I hung up, I noticed another missed call from Lachlan.

My heart sang.

I stole a glance at Ethan. He was skinnier than Lachlan and lacked that same animal allure. But Lachlan Peace was a one-off. No man would ever compare.

In any case, I wasn't in the right state to think about potential boyfriends. Hating how consumed I'd become, I craved the old me—that driven art lover.

My phone vibrated again. Seeing Lachlan's seductive face on the screen made me smile. I hovered my finger over the screen. Then a voice within told me to make him work harder.

After that, the day flew. I made sure everything for the opening was set to go, including stocking the fridge with snacks and cheap champagne.

After struggling through the late-afternoon traffic, we finally arrived at the dance school, where we found Lachlan's mom sharing a laugh with her guitarist.

She smiled at us. "Ah... Miranda and Avita."

Ava giggled at her Spanish name and ran over to the box of shoes. It broke my heart to see her rummage for them.

"Thanks for letting Ava borrow shoes."

Belen held up a finger. "Ah. Look what I've got." She reached into a bag and pulled out a small pair of red shoes.

Ava's eyes bulged with delight at the gorgeous Cuban-heeled shoes, while I, too, was having my own *The Red Shoes* moment.

Before I could respond, Ava was on the ground, tying them up.

"They're so beautiful," I said.

"They were mine. They're hers now," Belen said.

"But that's so kind. You don't want to keep them for a..."

"A grandchild, you mean? I've had my children." She smiled. "Maybe one day, Lachlan—"

Her sudden pause made me wonder if Lachlan had told her about our breakup.

"I have a trunk of shoes," she concluded. "And they're all very nice."

Ava sprang up and did a perfect turn.

"She's a beautiful girl. I want her in a concert with Manolito. He should be here." She looked worried.

Just as she spoke, Manuel ran in and straight into her arms, in what was a touching scene.

I turned, and Lachlan stood before me.

My legs barely held me up. "Oh."

"And hi to you too," he said with a gleaming smile, though it was only surface deep. As I held his gaze, his tiredness became apparent.

Belen hugged Lachlan and then, narrowing her eyes, studied him closely before turning to me.

"You two are acting like strangers. The other day you couldn't take your hands off her."

"We've both had a lot going on lately." His labored breathing betrayed his struggles.

"Don't let that crazy family get in the way," she said with a subtle wink directed at me. "I'm sure Miranda can take it. Can't you?"

I managed a small nod.

"You're embarrassing her, Mom." Lachlan grinned at me.

"I've got to start class. Come back later and watch these two." She pointed at Manuel and Ava. "I have them dancing a *Sevillana,* and I want to eat them, they're so cute."

I chuckled along with her.

Belen left us, clapping to gain her students' attention.

"I'll have to come back in an hour," I said, shifting from leg to leg.

"I've asked Sherry to pick up Mannie. Otherwise, I would've loved to watch the kids dancing," he said, following me out.

Lachlan stared down at his feet then looked up slowly, and again his eyes trapped mine.

"I've got to go and do a sound check. I should be there now," he said.

"Oh. You've got a gig?" I visualized a cluster of clawing groupies and Lachlan sitting at his drumkit, all sweaty and sexy.

"For the first time ever, I've had to resort to cheap gigs." He scratched his stubbled jaw.

I nodded, lost for words. The speech-governing part of my brain had shut down.

With his cologne drifting toward me, sparking all kinds of feelings, I was lost in him.

"I've tried calling you over and over."

"I've been busy getting the gallery up and running."

As I fell into his eyes, I saw pain and struggle. Lachlan looked different, as though he'd aged. But instead of making him uglier, it made him seem a little untamed in a sexy, inflaming way.

"I hope you can accept my apology for the way I behaved."

After taking a deep, steadying breath, I said, "You were awful to me."

"I know. I acted like an ass and should never have laid that guilt trip on you. Will you ever forgive me?"

"It's been difficult. And after what happened…"

"I know I have to do more than just apologize." He combed his fingers through his hair. "Whatever it takes, Miranda. I need you in my life. It's been hell without you."

I studied his face, trying to read him. "I guess we fucked a lot."

"It's not just the sex." His lips curled at one end. "I mean, of course I can't stop wanting to devour you. And that I was your first has affected me more profoundly than I could've imagined." He paused, waiting for me to say something. "But it's more than sex. I like being around you." He took a step closer and brushed my cheek. "I love you."

My lips trembled, making it impossible for me to talk without bursting into tears. "And I love you. That's why it hurt."

He took my hand and played with my fingers. "I'm sorry. If I could rewind, I would. Honestly."

I nodded slowly and smiled.

"How are the gallery preparations?" he asked.

"Yeah... things look promising." I appreciated the sudden shift in subject. It gave me a chance to breathe again. "I'm enjoying it. And I'm my own boss, which is like a dream come true."

"That's the best news I've heard all week. I'm pleased for you. And you'll kick ass. I'm sure of it."

"Thanks. There's an issue with cash flow. I'm going to have to moonlight as a waitress in the meantime."

He shook his head. "I won't let that happen. I'll make sure you're taken care of until everything sorts itself out. That is, if you let me..."

"You don't owe me anything, Lachlan."

His warm hand remained in mine. "I wish I didn't have to run. Can we meet later?" His eyes softened.

I couldn't remain angry when he looked like that. Even in his loose, worn T-shirt, knee-length shorts, and flip-flops, Lachlan could still entice a room full of swooning women to donate their kidneys on a platter just for a taste of his lips.

"But aren't you working?"

"I am." He sounded frustrated. "What about tomorrow? Early. Given that I have a gig again. Every fucking night." He rubbed his neck.

"You don't sound keen."

He shrugged. "I love playing. But every night's a bit too much." He paused for a breath. "Tomorrow? Late afternoon at the apartment?"

"The gallery is having its opening tomorrow. Early evening. I'm going to have to be there all day, preparing."

"I'll come along, then. That is if I'm invited." He took my other hand and stared deeply into my eyes.

I had to tense my muscles to avoid falling into his arms. "Of course. The more, the merrier."

Have I forgiven him?

"You bet!" my heart bellowed.

He took one step closer, and the electricity between us almost sparked.

As painful as it was, I had to remove my hands from his. "I'd best be going, then. I'll send you an invite." Before his hypnotic turquoise eyes made me forget my name, I turned and left.

After a few steps, I realized I was actually parked in the opposite direction, so I turned and nearly ran into him. He hadn't moved.

"My car's over…"

I started to point, then he grabbed a hold of me. He lowered his eyelids, and a whiff of him was all it took. I fell into his strong arms, and his mouth claimed mine. His velvety tongue caressed then parted my lips, making me lose all sense of space and time.

He pushed his hard body against mine. His desire throbbed against me, and my heart pumped wildly in response.

His savage kiss teased and devoured me at the same time.

"God, how I've missed you, Miranda."

His eyes softened, and I nearly melted on the pavement.

His forehead touched mine. As we soaked in each other's gazes, it felt like the sun on naked skin.

Lachlan stepped back. "I should let you go.

"Sure." I smiled. My aching need to be with him made me wish I possessed the confidence to unzip his pants and take his dick in my mouth there and then. His kiss had whetted my appetite, and the rest of me craved every sexy inch.

He smiled tenderly and brushed my cheek. "Tomorrow, then. I'll drop in before my gig, then later, we can catch up." He tilted his head so adorably that I would have agreed to walk a tightrope over a pit of snapping alligators to be with him.

"Just remember to wear those red panties."

A deep, swelling ache throbbed through me at the way his eyes turned from soft and affectionate to that delicious bedroom shade of erotic.

He pressed himself against me again as a reminder of just how hard I'd made him.

We shared another deep, passionate kiss, then I floated off.

12

LACHLAN

Miranda had done a stellar job with the Artefactory.

A colorful crowd milled about, chatting and pointing at the eclectic art, which was bold and brash. If I hadn't been so short of cash, I would have loved to purchase a piece or two.

Miranda sparkled in a green dress that hugged her curves, just as my body craved to do. Her long, wavy hair bounced teasingly over her breasts as she glided about. Sipping on champagne, I observed her moving from one group to another, chatting while moving her hands expressively.

I knew then that she would do well.

Harriet came up to me. "Hey. Good to see you back."

"I couldn't stay away."

"I so hope you're not going to break Andie's heart again. She's been pretty low this past week."

I studied her. The sisters were like day and night when it came to socializing.

"My life's complicated," I said. "I'm here, though." I returned my attention to Miranda and noticed her business partner sticking close by. I cocked my head toward them. "He's a bit too fucking friendly."

"Ethan. He's got the hots for her," she said.

"I'd better go and claim her, then," I said, playing the possessive boyfriend role for the first time.

"Before you go, have you seen Orlando lately?"

I scratched my prickly jaw. "No. He doesn't wish to see anyone."

Her face pinched. "That's such tragic news."

"Did you visit him?" I asked.

"No. One better. I'm working there."

I studied her. "So have you seen him?"

"Not yet. But I'm on his ward. I'm going to make sure he walks again. He's going to be my project."

"He's young. There's hope."

"That's what I think. He's just got to get this to work for him." She tapped her head. "The power of belief is everything."

"True." I thought of Ollie's depression and dark moods. I'd never seen that side of him before.

"It's nice that you've taken a deep interest." I smiled tightly. "I'm just not sure if he's ready for a girlfriend."

"I'm not doing it for that," she replied defensively. "I'm too old for him, anyway." She looked away. "I'm off to get a drink. Nice to see you."

I wanted to say, "Nonsense," but I had no idea what Ollie thought of Harriet.

Noticing Ethan's shoulder rubbing against Miranda's, I headed over to see her.

"Miranda's the brains behind all of this," he said, pointing at an artfully arranged display of eye-catching figurines and sculptures.

Miranda's unassuming smile made me proud. I loved her humility.

She turned and saw me for the first time. "Lachlan, you made it."

I stepped in and hugged her, giving her a lingering kiss on her cheek. "This is sensational. I'm so proud of you. You're also very sexy in that dress."

She giggled. I could tell she was tipsy, which made me hate that I had a gig to go to, especially with Ethan acting all chummy.

"Come outside for a minute," I said.

Miranda looked at Ethan, whose smile had quickly faded.

"This is Lachlan." She gestured. "And this is Ethan."

"I'm the business partner." He sounded so cocky that I disliked him immediately.

"I'm the boyfriend," I said.

Miranda looked at me then Ethan and back and squeezed her lips as though trying to avoid giggling.

I led her out into the alleyway, where a large, noisy crowd smoked and loitered about.

"This is a great turnout. You must be pleased," I said.

"I am." She studied me with a frown. "Are you truly my boyfriend?"

"To him, I am."

"And to me?" she asked, tilting her head.

"I'm all yours, Miranda." I held my arms wide.

She stopped walking and scrutinized me with a questioning frown.

"Are we good?" I asked.

Miranda nodded slowly, as though trying to make up her mind.

I tucked a strand of hair behind her ear and ran my fingers over the curve of her neck. "I want to be with you, Miranda,"

"Is it because you just want to have sex with me?"

"It's more than just fucking." Taking a deep breath, I searched for the right words. "I've been with a lot of women, Miranda. And none of them have made me feel the way you do. I like being with you. The simple things, like you lying about, reading barefoot on the couch. Or us playing Scrabble and chess, even when you beat the pants off me. You're real and beautiful and smart." I pointed at the chipped brick wall stenciled with street art. "And I love what you've done with the Artefactory."

She stared up at me wide-eyed and ran her tongue over her lips, drawing my attention to them.

I traced my finger around her lips, kissed her softly, then waltzed her away from the flickering lantern to a shadowy corner.

"You look good enough to eat," I said, running my finger from between her breasts down to below her stomach.

Arousal grew between my legs as I rubbed myself against her, almost dry-humping her.

Her dress had a front opening, designed just for me, an impatient and horny lover. I hooked my finger inside her panties. "Oh God, you feel nice."

I brushed her breasts as my mouth ate at hers. My tongue whipped around hers as though it were my cock inside her.

Someone walked past and whistled. I stopped, realizing we were putting on a show.

"Come to my gig," I said.

"I can't. I have to lock up."

"Can't Lover Boy do that?"

She chuckled. "You don't like Ethan, do you?"

"He wants to fuck you, and he strikes me as cocky."

"Takes one to know one," she sang.

"I'm not cocky."

Miranda laughed. "No. I guess not. But you do come across as confident." She smoothed her dress, which had flapped open, revealing her shapely thighs.

"Hey. I was enjoying that." I ran my hand up her leg. "I'm not as confident as you think. I'm just good at pretending." I reached her pussy and sighed. "Holy shit. You've got those little red panties on." I hooked my finger around them and felt her wet heat dripping.

"Come with me to my gig. Please."

"I guess I could get the guys to lock up," she said breathily. "I've been here all day. And I got here hours before they did. So they kind of owe me."

I took her by the hand. "Good. I'll wait here."

13

MIRANDA

Squeezing through the crowd, I looked for Clint, choosing to avoid Ethan. The drunker he got, the flirtier he became.

"It's such a great night," Clint said in his cheery, high-pitched voice. "This is Shane."

Clint's lovers rotated through a swinging door. I'd met a few that week when they came in every day to help. He had the type of head-turning beauty with his wide, friendly blue eyes and long, blond, pink-streaked hair.

"I'm going," I said.

He looked disappointed. "But the DJ hasn't started yet. We sent Malcolm, who you met earlier, to buy supplies." An eyebrow lifted. "We're going to sell booze."

"Really?" I asked.

"Why not?" Although soft and fluffy, Clint had a fine instinct for making money.

"We don't have a liquor license."

He shrugged. "There's no one around. The place is deserted, except for us. This is where the action is." He bounced a little. "It's such a great vibe."

Clint's contagious exuberance helped allay my concern.

"Then try to remind everyone to keep it under wraps. We don't want to get fined or arrested," I said.

"We won't." He grabbed my hand. "Stay."

I sighed. "I've got my boyfriend—"

"Ooh, he's your boyfriend now," he sang. "The other day, he was the enemy."

"Yeah, well." I held my arms wide, wearing a guilty grin.

"He's so sexy. And gorgeous. Oh my." He fluttered his hand

over his face. "Those big shoulders. I bet he's got tattoos."

I nodded, feeling the contagion of his heat flush through me.

"He's got a gig," I said.

"Oh, he's a musician. Yum."

"That's why I want to go. The girls are like vultures."

"I bet. Oh well… you'd best be off. By now, I would've chained him up and had my way with him." He giggled.

"You're wicked. Even if that's not a bad idea." I kissed him on the cheek. "Can you let Ethan know?"

"He'll be gutted to hear you're back with your man. He had hopes."

I nodded. "I kinda sensed that. We need to keep this platonic if it's going to work."

"I guess so." He fluttered his wrist. "Off you go to that Adonis. I want all the juicy details on Monday."

I smiled and walked off. Noticing Harriet chatting with a guy, I felt a sense of relief. Her sudden obsession with Orlando had made me uneasy. All my fickle sister needed was a new guy, I told myself, and I left without saying a word to anyone else.

Lachlan was leaning against the wall, tapping his muscular thighs with earbuds in, obviously practicing for his gig. My breath hitched. *How could such an insanely hot man be interested in me?*

Considering the crushing pain I'd endured from our short separation, I was gripped with trepidation. I should have taken little steps back to him. But as he turned to me and ran his tongue over his erotic lips, I virtually leaped into his arms.

He took my hand as we walked to his car. "Lover Boy was heartbroken?"

"No. I told Clint. They've got a big bash organized for the night. A DJ is about to come on. He was disappointed."

"You made quite a sacrifice to come with me. I'm glad, though." He stopped walking and gazed into my eyes.

Making light of his sudden intensity, I said, "I can't have all those girls jumping all over you. And you were pretty horny earlier." I raised an eyebrow.

He laughed. "As much as I'm dying to fuck you, I do possess some control."

He wrapped his arm around my waist and drew me tight to his big body, and we moved as one.

Lachlan parked the car at the back of his gig's venue.

He opened my door, and taking my arm, he helped me out.

"I am capable of doing this myself," I said, releasing his arm gently.

"Are you offended?" He frowned.

"No. I like it. It's just strange. That's all."

"Good. I like doing it," he said, smiling.

I waited for him to collect a bag from the trunk, then we walked toward the venue hand in hand.

Noticing a huge line waiting at the door, I said, "This is popular."

"It's Saturday night. And there's no door charge." He smiled tightly. "It's also a bit trashy. Not like the Red House. And there are often fights."

"Oh. The men brawl?"

"And the women." He chuckled. "Don't worry. I'll make sure you're looked after. I'll place one of the guards close. In that dress, you're sure to get propositioned." He stroked my arm. "I know I'd proposition you if I didn't know you. You're beautiful."

"You can still proposition me," I said with a smirk.

"Ah, role playing. Sure. If that's what you want. I'll do anything to get into those red panties." He drew me close, and my nose settled on his hard chest, where a whiff of him made me swoon.

"You don't have to do much." I sighed.

He kissed me on the lips, and as he withdrew, he said, "Oh, I plan to do all kinds of things to you."

Desire burned through me as I fell into his devouring gaze.

We entered through the back alley, and after the security

guards let us in, we walked down a dark hallway and entered the band room, where a motley bunch of musicians sat about, drinking, smoking weed, and laughing raucously.

"Ah... Ginger Baker's in the house," one of the men said.

"Ginger Baker?" I asked.

Lachlan saluted him and said quietly, "He's a legendary drummer."

There was so much I didn't know about the rock scene. My father had been into folk music, and my mother lived in the dark ages, listening only to opera and musicals, the type of music no one in our neighborhood listened to. Harriet used to plead with her to turn it down. But on special occasions, if my mom exceeded her sherry limit, she ramped up the volume and sang along, much to our horror.

Lachlan grabbed his drumsticks and a drum pedal from his backpack. "I'm going out there to set up the kit. Do you want to come and watch?" He touched my cheek affectionately.

"Sure." I didn't feel like breathing smoke. And I was already feeling lightheaded.

A guy started to pass Lachlan a joint, but he declined.

Lachlan held my hand. "Let me buy you a drink."

After Lachlan delivered my drink, I settled in a quiet corner.

He then whispered something to a burly security guard, and the big man nodded sternly.

"He'll make sure nobody hits on you." Lachlan grinned. "I've got a tab at the bar, so knock yourself out. Not too much, though." He leaned into my ear. "I want to make you come until you draw blood."

I grimaced. "Draw blood?"

"Those fingernails of yours are rather sharp." His eyebrows rose, and he leaned in close again, making my heart race. "And what's more, I fucking love it."

"Oh. I thought you meant you would fuck me so hard that I would bleed." The thought of that made me burn, for some twisted reason.

"I want to fuck you hard, all right, but not to that extent. Just have you coming on my cock all night."

My pussy throbbed. Lachlan's dirty talk was turning me upside down. He planted a soft, warm kiss on my lips.

I indulged in his sexy, purposeful stride, which was emphasized by his jeans, which showed off his long, lean legs and very pinchable ass.

Thumping, wild, and stirring, the music started. Lachlan drove the pelvic-thrusting rhythm. He played like he fucked—hard and skillful. Just like at the Red House, I was mesmerized. Although seated, I moved my body, hypnotized by the beat.

By the gig's end, women swarmed around Lachlan, even while he packed up. I couldn't believe how forward they were. He glanced over at me with an apologetic smile. But always the gentleman, he nodded politely, excused himself, then joined me.

"Let's get out of here. It's a feeding frenzy," he said.

Some of the women had followed him, anyway.

I laughed. "You're not wrong. With those big, sexy arms exposed, you're radiating animal attraction."

"My arms?" He grinned. "I would've hoped it was my musical talent."

"That too. But..." I placed my hand in his back pocket and squeezed his firm ass. "You're sex on legs, Lachlan."

"And so are you." He stroked my cheek tenderly. "In a natural, sensual way. My type of woman."

"That's nice to know." I narrowed my eyes. "How often are you working here, again?"

"Not for too long, if I can help it."

"You don't enjoy it?" I followed him to the band room.

"As much as I like R and B, as any drummer might, jazz is my passion."

"This is definitely more of a pounding, primitive style. I loved the complex and colorful rhythms at the other gig you played. But it's all great."

"Thanks for noticing my brushwork. I spent years cultivating that technique." He drew me close, crushing his hard body against mine. "You're making me fucking hot. Your nipples never seem to go down." He licked his pillowy lips so suggestively that steam issued from my damp panties.

14

LACHLAN

Miranda stared at the discoloration on the wall where the Pollocks had once hung.

"I'll have to buy some new art. Only…" I rubbed my neck. "That's if I don't sell."

"Oh. You're going to sell this apartment?" she asked, knitting her brow.

"I might have to." I shrugged. "Unless I can find a spare few million soon."

She shook her head. "I don't even know what that much money looks like."

I removed some crumpled notes from my pockets and set them on the coffee table. "This is the first time I've received cash for a gig."

"Did you sell the one genuine Pollock?"

"Not yet. It's going through a process of authentication."

"But you have a certificate of provenance."

"After what happened with the others, they need to go through the proper channels to ensure it's genuine."

"I suppose that makes sense," she said thoughtfully. "It shouldn't take long, though. And it's worth eighty million or so."

I nodded. "I was meant to pursue it. Hurry them along. But I've had my head in a fog. What with you not talking to me and the bullshit back at the estate with Tammy."

"Tammy?" Miranda asked.

I gulped down my drink. "She's just hanging around more often and giving me the shits."

"Then you'll need to keep this apartment."

I sat on the sofa and patted it. "No more money talk. I need you naked."

She smiled apologetically. "I shouldn't have brought it up."

"No. I needed reminding." I brushed her rosy cheek affectionately then took her soft hand and played with her fingers. "My life's complicated. My father hasn't behaved well. So in the coming weeks, if anything happens to me, remember this…"

Her eyebrows knitted.

I stared into her eyes. "You're the best thing that's happened to me in a long while. I've grown up at last, and now I'm seeing what matters the most."

"And that is?"

"This. Us. Connecting with someone on a deep level. And not just for the sex, even though that's pretty amazing. You're so different from all the others."

"All the others?" Her dark eyes shone with curiosity. Miranda wasn't going to let that comment pass.

"I haven't been a saint." I bit my cheek. "Oh, fuck." I took her into my arms. "Enough talking. I need you naked. Now."

Our mouths touched, and things heated up from there. Before I could think straight, I was on top of her, ripping off her panties.

I lifted Miranda off the couch and carried her to the bedroom.

She laughed. "I'm too heavy."

"Bullshit. You're as light as a feather."

She touched my arm. "You're just strong."

"And you're very fucking sexy." I placed her on the bed, untied her dress, and virtually ripped it off.

Her full tits spilled out of a tiny lace bra, and I ogled her before taking her in my arms.

When I unclasped her bra, her breasts fell into my palms, and blood raced down to my dick.

She unzipped my pants, and I tried holding on to her while taking them off, stumbling about.

Miranda giggled, which made me smile.

I sat on the edge of the bed, and instead of joining me,

Miranda went down on her knees and placed my dick in her mouth. Her warm, soft lips licked the head, sending a bolt of electricity through me.

My head fell back as she took me in deeply, sucking and licking my dick as if it were a delicious treat. The gentle scrape of her teeth sent an excruciatingly pleasurable burn through me.

"I'm going to come if you keep doing that."

Miranda remained on her knees. She tightened her fleshy lips around my dick and moved up and down, taking it in deeply. My balls tightened as she played with them while sucking my dick to the point of no return. Unable to hold back, I shot my seed to the back of her throat.

I waited until my mind stilled from the fireworks and lifted her off the ground. "Holy fuck. That wasn't meant to happen."

She wiped her lips and smiled. "You didn't like it?"

"I more than liked it," I said, stroking her face.

Miranda looked beautiful with her witchy eyes and her thick hair messy and wild.

"Come here and sit on my face." I tapped the bed.

Her jaw dropped. "What?"

"Pop yourself on top."

"But I'll squash you," she protested.

"No, you won't. I insist."

She held onto the padded bedhead and lowered herself onto me as I held onto her ass. Then I nibbled her clit as I would a treat. Her musky slickness thickened the more I licked. Miranda groaned. Her bud throbbed on my tongue, and I went on the attack, swallowing and licking her juices until she trembled in my hands. Determined to take her past that magic threshold, I continued even though she asked me to stop.

"Aah!" she cried.

I kept going until her screams filled the air.

She fell onto her back and let out a contented sigh.

Turning onto my side, I gazed at her. I loved the way she looked after coming. Her cheeks were rosy and her pupils dilated.

"Are you back?" I asked.

She rolled into my arms. "That was something else."

"I'm glad you enjoyed it. I did." I held spun her around so that she was on top of me. "I need to be inside you."

I gripped her round, firm ass, guiding her over my dick, and released a slow groan as I filled her. A tormented murmur left her parted lips.

"Are you okay?" I asked.

"Yes."

"Oh God, I've missed this. And you're so deliciously wet."

She sat up, and I sucked on her nipples as she bounced up and down on my dick. It was hot, deep, and erotic.

"I need you to come," I said as though struggling for air.

Her climax built, and as her pussy contracted around my cock, she flooded me. A cataclysmic explosion swept me away. I came so hard that I felt the earth move.

Then she fell into my arms, and our hearts pounded together.

After Miranda performed her newfound talent for feasting on my dick and I devoured her sweet pussy for breakfast, we finally left the apartment wearing matching smiles. Endless orgasms did that to a person, and our night had been one of endless fucking and whispering sweet nothings—well, sweet somethings. I told Miranda I loved her. She was the only girl I'd ever said that to. It felt so natural, as though my soul were doing the talking.

After checking my app, I discovered the conditions were just right for a much-needed surf.

"I don't have a swimsuit," Miranda said as we drove along the coastal highway.

"Better still, you can go in the nude."

"But aren't people around?"

"Probably. We'll find something. A T-shirt, even."

"A T-shirt with my boobs?" she asked.

"Mm... nice. A wet dream come true."

She shook her head. "You're a sex maniac."

I laughed. "Maybe. Blame it on your sexy curves, beautiful face, and clever mouth."

"How would my clever mouth make you hot?"

"Hearing you talk passionately about art turns me on."

She turned sharply to face me. "Does it?"

I laughed at her surprised expression. "Hell yeah. Gomez wanted to ravage Morticia when she spoke French, and I want to ravage you when you talk about the virtues of Bacon's frenetic lines."

She giggled. "That was Egon Schiele. But hey, I didn't even think you were listening."

"Oh, I listen. I just don't comment, because it's not my area of expertise."

"I'm the same when you talk about five-four rhythms and downbeats. I don't have the foggiest idea what that means. But hell, it sounds sexy."

I laughed. "*Mission Impossible.* The original sixties version."

Miranda knitted her brow. "Huh?"

"That's five-four timing."

I tapped the rhythm on my steering wheel and sang the tune for her.

Her face lit up. "Hey, that's so cool."

"Yeah. Five-four rhythms are super cool. 'Take Five' by Brubeck, another famous tune." I hummed it for her.

Miranda shook her head.

"What?"

"You remind me of a boy."

"I'll take that as a compliment."

"You should."

"Does that mean we can only hold hands and kiss with our mouths shut?" I asked.

She laughed. "No way. I need that tongue in deep, swishing around."

"Swishing around? Lapping up your juices, your mean."

Her hand landed on my thigh, close to my growing dick.

"Careful, Miranda. I'm driving."

As we drove back to the house, the sea glistened in the late-morning sun. Life felt complete. I had no debts, and I could almost be myself. If only that dark cloud related to my father along with Ollie's recent accident would drift away. Then there was Tamara. But my endorphin-drunk heart had the winning edge, especially with Miranda there by my side.

We decided to put some music on during the drive.

"What do you feel like listening to?"

"Anything. I'm not picky," she said.

"Jazz?" I asked.

She nodded. "I like it."

"Great. We'll get on well," I said, pressing on my console.

She turned to stare at me with curiosity etched in her eyes. "You judge compatibility by music tastes?"

"No. I'm not a jazz Nazi or anything." I smiled at how ridiculous that sounded. "We're compatible, though. Aren't we?"

"I suppose if my clawing into your flesh while having multiple orgasms and you're ripping my panties off with your teeth is a sign of compatibility, then sure."

I laughed. "We also talk about things. I love talking to you. Remember our first date? You in that horrible brown dress."

"How could I forget?" She smirked. "Britney acted like a super bitch, and I had to jump to her every command."

"You were magnificent. No bullshit. Unlike all the other girls with their mindless gossip. I've never been with a girl I can talk to about music, art, and the bigger things in life."

"The bigger things being?"

I shrugged. "The environment, politics, and whether you're wearing your red panties."

She giggled, which made me laugh. "You're just as shallow as those girls you just put down."

"I know. At times, I'm a disappointment to myself. But how can I be with someone with a body like yours and not think dirty thoughts?"

She shrugged. "I have dirty thoughts about you too."

"Do you?"

Biting her lip, she looked so innocent, as though she'd admitted to something wicked.

"Well? Are you going to reveal?"

"You know, um... I think about how you feel."

"When I enter you?"

"Yeah."

Her shy smile made my cock jerk. "Keep looking like that, and I'm going to have to stop the car."

"Are you always this frisky?"

"It's hard not to be. You're not wearing a bra, and your delectable nipples are very perky."

Miranda ran her soft hand up my thigh and stroked my dick, which had thickened again. "You feel nice too."

"Miranda, I'll have an accident if you're not careful."

She removed her hand and smiled.

I tapped on my steering wheel in time with the music. "This is my favorite drummer."

"Who is he?"

"Billy Cobham."

"You're just as good," she said.

"If you keep flattering me, I'm going to have to devour you."

"Mm... is that a promise?"

"More than a promise."

"Only if you let me suck your dick."

I smiled at her. She blushed when she talked dirty.

"Then it will give me great pleasure to indulge you." I crept my finger through the opening of her dress and felt her thigh. "I love this dress."

"I thought of you when I bought it. Knowing how impatient you can get."

"Only with you, Miranda." My smile faded. "I want us to be together. Just you and me. No one else. Not Ethan."

"And not Britney?" she asked.

I turned sharply. "What gives you the impression I want to be with her?"

"What gives you the impression I want to be with Ethan?"

"I asked first," I said.

"Something you said in your sleep."

We drove up the driveway.

"I forgot how palatial your house is," she said.

I was still wondering about her last comment. "What did I say in my sleep?"

15

MIRANDA

Lachlan pulled into the driveway and turned to me with a questioning frown.

"You called out Britney's name. Most of the time, it sounds like you're having a nightmare."

"That makes sense. Britney *is* giving me nightmares, which would explain her creeping into my subconscious."

"Have I crept into your subconscious?" I asked.

"Oh yeah. Especially after I saw you in that ripped T-shirt, the night I stumbled into the apartment drunk."

I smacked his big bicep. "Then I've snuck into your dick."

He smiled. "Mm… And how." He took me into his arms. "I'm crazy about you, Miranda. That's all you need to know."

I took a deep breath and nodded with a smile that matched the bright sunshine.

He jumped out of the car and, as always, ran over to my door to open it for me.

"That cute little gesture goes with the car," I said, stepping out.

"How so?" His eyes sparkled in the sunlight.

"It's from the same era," I said, tapping the car's hood.

"This car is from the late sixties. That was the burn-your-bra era. I can't imagine too many young women approving," he said as we sauntered along the cobbled path to the house.

"They would've appreciated it," I said. "They just wouldn't have admitted it." I chuckled. "It's nice having a strong man do the heavy lifting."

He stopped walking. "And it's nice to have a pretty little woman at home, cooking the evening roast."

The slowly forming curl of his lips made the tirade that I was about to hit him with stall. "I'm a shit cook."

"That's why chefs were invented." He tilted his head so adorably that I wanted to slap him for being so gorgeous.

His smile faded. "I've got your back, Miranda. Remember that."

I wrapped my arms around him and kissed him. "And I've got yours too."

We walked hand in hand through to the pool area.

"I've never seen this part of the house before. The garden is exquisite." I bent down to smell a carnation in a terra-cotta pot.

Butterflies and insects buzzed about, and the fertile sprawling grounds boasted a celebration of color and textures.

"I love this place," he said with a wistful half smile. "That's why I sold my grandfather's collection."

Just as I was about to respond, Britney appeared.

Lachlan's face darkened. "What are you doing here? It's Saturday."

"I had some work to do. And my apartment's being painted, so I thought I might crash here for the weekend."

He rubbed his jaw, something he often did when challenged. "That's what we were planning." He took my hand.

She cast me one of her blood-freezing stares. "It's a big house. I'll stay away. I'll be out for the night, anyway." She was about to move off when she added, "You do realize Tammy's here."

Lachlan rolled his eyes at me. "We can stay upstairs. We've got everything we need. A juice or coffee?"

"I'll have whatever you're having?"

"Coffee, then. We have a new espresso machine." He looked at Britney.

"I can make it," she said.

I jumped in. "No need. I can do it."

After one more lingering icy stare, she sauntered off. Dressed in shorts and a tight T-shirt, she had the slim physique I'd always wished for, which pissed me off.

While I stood in front of the coffee machine, Lachlan stepped behind me and squeezed my butt. "I can make it if you like."

"No. Let me. I like doing it," I said, turning the knob.

"And I like your curvy ass." He breathed down my neck, and the steam coming off me matched that from the espresso machine.

Lachlan brought out the milk and passed me the sugar. After I managed to whip up a couple of very passable lattes, I felt pleased with myself.

"Thanks." He took a sip. "Mm. Perfect. Let's go upstairs."

Clutching my mug, I climbed the grand old winding staircase, which was flanked by scrolled ironwork. I slid my hand along the polished wooden banister, careful not to spill my coffee on the carpet.

Lachlan's room was the first of many along the long second-floor landing. There was so much to see that I felt dazzled by his opulent home.

I walked around his massive bedroom, which could have housed a small family, checking out cute photographs of famous cities and a collection of old surfing posters from the sixties. Then I stepped through the stained-glass doors onto the balcony and stared out to sea.

After taking a deep breath of salty air, I said, "This is gorgeous."

Lachlan stood behind me, wrapping his arms around me and resting his chin on my shoulder. "I love my home," he said "My father's room's even bigger."

I recalled his stepmother being there. "Is that far from this room?"

"We have a room separating us." Crushing me with his strong body, he kissed me. "You can squeal that sexy head off all you like."

I pulled away and laughed. "I don't squeal."

"You do." He grinned. "I love it. Especially when your fingernails dig in."

He lifted his T-shirt and turned around, showing me his scratched back.

"Shit. I've drawn blood," I said.

"I like it. Marks of passion."

"That's a great name for a Harlequin romance."

"If I leave my day job, I'll consider writing one."

I laughed. "Your day job? Writing?"

"I *am* literate. I didn't completely blow those fourteen-odd years of education."

"You don't have to justify yourself, Lachlan. You're very talented. And you have a mercurial mind."

"Is that the same as having a dirty mind?" He untied my dress and let it pool on the ground.

I quickly stepped back inside, just in case a gardener saw us.

His hands roamed all over my goose-pimpled skin, making me forget our conversation.

"No underwear is fucking sexy as hell too," he said, bending down and sucking on my nipple while fondling my breasts.

"I thought you were going surfing," I said, struggling to speak.

"Oh, there's time for that. And the surf's gone a little flat. Not like you. You curvy minx."

He waltzed me to his bed. "On your hands and knees," he commanded.

I didn't normally like a bossy tone, but where sex was concerned, it proved to be one big clit-burning turn-on.

He parted my thighs and placed his tongue on my throbbing bud, making me tremble.

After he'd drained an orgasm out of me, he asked me to lie on the bed and open my legs wide.

"I need to see your wet pussy."

Come trickled down my inner thigh. Lachlan's dick was red-hot and hitting his navel. His eyes were heavy with lust, and his lips glistened from feasting on me.

He held his big dick and drove it in, making my eyes roll to the back of my head.

"Fuck, you feel hot," he said, sounding tormented.

He thrust in deeply then moved in and out, building up

speed and intensity as we held on to each other.

I released my gripping muscles and took off. A wave of engulfing heat grew just like his deep, ferocious thrusts.

Lachlan's breathing was ragged as his mouth landed on mine. His sweaty body pressed against mine, and his scent of cologne, sex, and the sea seeped into me.

The harder and faster he plowed into me, the louder his groans grew.

He growled like a beast as he shot deeply into me.

Then we fell onto our backs and lay waiting for our senses to return.

Lachlan turned and smiled at me. He stroked my cheek affectionately then kissed me sweetly. "You feel amazing."

"And so do you."

"I wasn't too rough?" he asked, resting his ear on his palm.

"A little. But it's very primal."

He ran his hand over my body and kneaded my butt. "I love this ass against my balls."

"I'm not into ass fucking," I said.

"I should hope not." He smirked.

"I mean not having it done to me, silly."

"I'm not into anal. I like pussies."

"Pussies?"

"I mean *your* pussy." His fingers crept up my thigh, and I winced as he touched my clit. "Too sensitive?"

I nodded. "I only just had three orgasms."

"You get this dreamy look in your eyes when you come." He smiled.

"And you sound like you're being mauled by a tiger."

"More like mauled by a pussy."

We both laughed.

Then he turned serious. "Look, Britney's in thick with my dad. While he's alive, I can't exactly get rid of her."

I sat up. "Does that mean she'll leave your side one day?"

"You bet. I only had her here because of my father. Now that I've paid off the investors, she'll soon no longer be needed." He combed back his hair. "That day can't come quickly enough."

He rose, headed to the bar in the corner, and opened the fridge. "Can I offer you juice or water?"

"Water, thanks. So will you continue developing condos?"

He unscrewed the top and passed me the bottle. "I'd like to go down the sustainable-housing path."

"What about just playing music for a career?" I asked, thinking of all the girls that came with that chosen field.

"The past two nights have told me two things. I don't want to gig for money, and I only want to play music I love."

"But you're good at rock. A natural," I argued.

"Thanks. But it exhausted the crap out of me, and it's not my scene."

"The Red House is classier, I suppose," I said. "The music's more cerebral."

He nodded slowly. "Mm. That's why I like it. It challenges me. It has depth too. It's not entirely here." He tapped his head.

"No. But one can't really dance to it."

"I don't know. I've been known to." He chuckled. "After a few drinks and while I'm alone in my room."

"I'd love to see you dance."

"You already have. Remember, we danced together at the gala auction."

"How can I forget?" I tilted my head.

"It's been an interesting few months, hasn't it?" He smiled faintly, then his mood dropped again. "I'd better visit my dad today. I'd invite you... "

"It's fine, Lachlan. I don't expect it."

"I just don't like the man. As much as I've tried." He looked down at his hands glumly.

"Your mom's nice."

"She likes you. You're also the first of my girlfriends she's ever met." He sat by my side on the bed, placed his arm around my waist, and drew me close. "Which means everything to me."

His blue eyes darkened, not in that smoldering way but soulfully.

"You've gone all serious," I said.

His gaze penetrated deeply to my core. "You're mine. All mine."

My mouth parted to speak, but I remained silent.

Yes, I was all his.

As our eyes remained trapped in mutual contemplation, as though we were exploring each other's inner world, a lump formed in my throat.

I'd never cried so much in my life.

He snapped out of it and rose. "Come on. Let's go to the beach."

"What am I going to swim in?" I asked.

"I just thought of something. Come with me."

He crooked his finger, and I followed along.

16

LACHLAN

I rarely entered Brent's old room, which was more like a museum.

When I was a teenager, Brent had a drawer of women's underwear and bikinis, which he'd once proudly showed me, as one would a cabinet of trophies.

There were quite a few pairs to choose from, and feeding my fantasy of seeing Miranda in a tiny bikini, I opted for the smallest one I could find.

Miranda scowled at the tiny bits of fabric dangling from my fingers.

"You can't expect me to wear that. It wouldn't even cover my nose."

I laughed at that ridiculous image. "You've got a very pretty nose. It would be a shame to cover it."

She rolled her eyes. "Don't obfuscate."

"Huh?"

"My mom always said that whenever I directed a conversation away from the point."

I nodded, impressed. "She sounds bright."

"She's a word Nazi."

"Wow. That's both intense and fascinating. I'm intrigued." I frowned. "She's not sadistic, is she?"

Miranda giggled. "Bad grammar makes her cranky."

"Let me guess—a schoolteacher?"

She nodded. "She's a great mom. But I was a disappointment to her for not becoming a teacher."

"Tell me about it. My father hated that I wasn't like Brent." I dangled the bikini.

"Was that one of his?"

I burst out laughing at that ridiculous notion.

"He collected them from all the girls that visited him in here. He didn't wear them himself. He was very straitlaced in that way."

Miranda walked over to the balcony. "Does your father appreciate you now?"

I sank into an armchair. "I doubt it."

"He sounds difficult."

I sniffed. "That's a nice way of putting it. Let's just say Brent was more like my father than I could ever be. Their morals were pretty aligned."

"Off-center, you mean?" she asked.

I nodded. "Oh yeah. Totally crooked. Like the Leaning Tower of Pisa. Only closer to the gutter."

Miranda's face brightened. "What a great analogy. Even my mom would like that one."

I rose. "Why, thank you." I bowed, and she giggled. "So, this bikini, too small? I was looking forward to seeing you jiggling around."

"You've seen me jiggling around all morning since I'm not wearing a bra."

I went over to her, placed my hands around her small waist, and drew her close. "I've been hot all morning."

"I've noticed," she said with a smirk.

"Why don't you rummage through the collection?"

"They've probably been worn," she said, pulling a face.

"We can wash them. They'll dry within a minute."

Miranda walked around the room. "This is such a boy's room. Is it always going to stay this way?"

"Not if I can help it. This is out of respect for my dad. It stays this way while he lives."

"You didn't have a room like this?" She pointed at the posters of football stars, cars, and busty blondes.

"Nope. I had pictures of famous drummers and cartoon characters. It drove my dad crazy." I pictured my father's disgust when he saw Homer Simpson on the wall and not Pamela Anderson.

Choosing a blue bikini, Miranda smiled. "This should fit."

One hour later, we walked onto the beach hand in hand. The water sparkled, and the sun's warmth puckered my skin. Life felt great, especially with beautiful Miranda by my side in her skimpy bikini, which heightened what had become an almost permanent state of arousal.

We plonked the surfboards onto the sand.

Miranda shook her head. "You're seriously determined to watch me making a dumbass of myself."

I laughed. "I just want you to experience the buzz."

"Surfing strikes me as difficult."

"Not when you get the hang of it. It's all about placing your weight properly on the board."

We applied sunscreen and then headed for the shoreline.

I laid the board on the sand. "Let me show you how to spring up."

"Spring up?" Miranda laughed. "I'll be struggling just to stay on it."

"Just try it." I pointed at the board. "Lie on your tummy."

Down she went on the board. "You just want to ogle my big ass."

"Yep. You got that right."

"Hey," she protested. "You're not meant to agree."

"Oh… but I do want to check your sexy ass, which is not big. Just firm and chunky."

"Chunky? Shoot a girl down, why don't you."

I chuckled and slapped her sexy butt.

"It's cold down here," she said.

"Now I want you to push off with your arms and land on your knees in one nice fluid movement."

"Ouch," she complained, having pulled off the move well.

I laughed. "Be sure to take your weight on your arms. Like this." I demonstrated the maneuver.

"You've got big muscles."

"You're only taking your own body weight," I argued.

After a few goes, Miranda had mastered it enough to take the board out.

"You're doing splendidly," I said.

We paddled in the shallows.

"It's a small swell. Ideal for practicing that move onto your knees," I said as a wave formed and came toward us.

"Oh God, I can barely stay on it," she said.

"You're doing well. And the view's pretty nice."

"The sky, you mean?"

"Mm… that too." I grinned.

I jumped up and rode the tiny wave.

"Show-off!" she yelled.

"Come on. Next one," I said, lying back down on my board.

Noticing the swell was at its peak, I yelled, "Now!"

Miranda managed to push off perfectly, but as she landed on her knees, she fell off the board.

I paddled over to make sure she was okay.

She laughed. "I feel so clumsy."

"No. That was a perfect mount. You just needed to get your balance. It takes a fair bit of practice. You're doing well."

Miranda smiled. "Thanks. It's kind of fun."

"Isn't it?"

We remained out there for a while longer. And Miranda actually managed to ride a wave for a few seconds on her knees before falling off, which was a triumph of sorts.

After that, we took our boards back to shore and returned to the water to play around.

I took her into my arms. "This is so nice, being here with you."

"It is. Thank you."

Our salty lips fused, and we kissed passionately with the sun warming our faces. One of the great advantages of having a private beach was being able to remove Miranda's bikini and suck on her nipples. She wrapped her thighs around me, and I entered her in one deep, hard thrust. My eyes watered at how she tightened her muscles around my dick.

17

MIRANDA

It had been a beautiful day. Lachlan had taken great care when teaching me to surf. And although I knew I would never make a good surfer, it was still fun.

But things got a little weird after that.

We were sitting at the island in the kitchen, snacking on dips, chips, and all kinds of delicious treats, when a woman joined us, teetering in the highest heels I'd ever seen.

Resembling a sheet of silk, her blond hair sat motionless on her shoulders. Her skintight dress barely covered her butt, which, like her breasts, resembled two distended balls.

I noticed Lachlan's face tense when she entered, which made me wonder if they'd had sex. And she devoured him with her eyes. But as soon as her heavily made-up eyes met mine, she went stony.

"Oh, you're here," she said in a prickly tone.

"I do live here," Lachlan said. "This is my girlfriend, Miranda." He turned to me. "This is my stepmother."

She scanned up and down my body. "Tamara's the name."

Then Manuel ran in and stiffened when he saw his mother, but he went to Lachlan and hugged him in a touching moment. Tamara's face soured. My heart went out to the boy. She was so inconceivably cold to her beautiful son my heart broke.

"How dare you take him to dance classes with that witch."

I was about to rise when Lachlan took my hand.

The nanny walked in, also appearing a little fidgety. "Um… there's a concert tomorrow."

"What kind of concert?" Tamara asked, pouring a glass of wine.

The nanny looked at Lachlan before answering. She was older than I was and very plain in a down-to-earth way, which I appreciated.

Another glamour-puss sauntering about would have been unbearable.

Tamara and Britney owned that title. They even smelled alike, as though they'd been dipped in a lake of cosmetics.

"This is Sherry." Lachlan gestured to the nanny. "And this is Miranda, my girlfriend."

He smiled sweetly at me, and my spirit soared. I could never tire of hearing myself described as his girlfriend.

Tamara's face, however, remained blank, and returning her attention to Lachlan, she said, "I don't want him dancing. I don't want him becoming a fag."

Manuel's big dark eyes shone with emotion.

"Do you like going there?" Lachlan asked Manuel.

He stood against Lachlan's thigh, and with his little finger on his lip, he nodded. The way he looked up to Lachlan for protection and support was so touching that I nearly cried.

"Are you going to deny him that?" Lachlan asked Tamara. "You're hardly ever here, anyway."

As Sherry snuck off, Tamara said, "I haven't finished with you."

The poor girl returned and plonked down in a chair.

Lachlan had his arm around Manuel. "So you're performing tomorrow?"

Manuel nodded, looking down at his feet, as if avoiding his mother's glowering attention.

"A word," Tamara said to Sherry, who meekly nodded and followed her mistress out of the room.

Lachlan rolled his eyes at me.

"What's a fag?" Manuel asked.

After giving me a sad smile, Lachlan returning his attention to Manuel. "It's a silly grown-up word that means making a fool of yourself. Which you are not. Remember that. You like dancing. Your grandma thinks you're great, and that's all that counts."

"Is Belen my grandma?" he asked.

Lachlan squeezed my hand. He was out of his depth. "She's like a grandmother to you. Think of her like that."

Sherry returned, looking a little shaken. At the same time, Tamara came back in and poured another glass of wine. Since it was four in the afternoon, I assumed she was a heavy drinker.

"A word," she said to Lachlan.

He touched my hand. "Back in a minute."

Tamara left the room, and Lachlan said to Sherry, "Don't let her get to you. Did she threaten you?"

"She told me that Manuel's not to attend the dance classes. I don't know what to do. He'll be gutted." Her eyes had a watery film.

"He's going, all right. I'll see to it. You're important to Manuel. And I want you here."

A line formed between her eyebrows. "I just don't know what to do about her."

"Don't worry. Leave it up to me," he said.

Lachlan's heart seemed to shine. When called for, he could balance the weight of the world on his very big, manly shoulders.

He left the room, and after preparing Manuel a sandwich, Sherry also departed with the young boy following at her heels, since she'd promised to let him watch cartoons.

I remained in the kitchen, snacking, and I heard Lachlan in the adjacent room say, "You've got no fucking proof."

"That's where you're wrong. I have your T-shirt with my blood all over it."

"Do your worst."

"You know what you need to do," she said and clip-clopped away.

Lachlan stepped back into the kitchen, raking his hair roughly. He took a deep breath. "I need to go visit my father. While we were out, I got a call. He's not doing too well."

I nodded. "Sure. I can go home." I was dying to ask him about the T-shirt and what Tamara meant by it but decided not to. Lachlan's mood had darkened, and he appeared distracted.

"Don't worry about Tamara. We can stay at the apartment if you like," he said as we made our way to the car. He turned to me and asked, "Will you come with me?"

"To the hospital?"

Lachlan took my hand. "I just want your company. For the drive. Do you want to come?"

It took me a moment to gather my thoughts. "Yeah. Sure. I thought I might get in the way. I mean, don't you need to talk to him about Tamara?"

"You heard?" He opened the door for me.

"It was hard not to hear. You were both talking loudly."

I got in the car, then Lachlan slid behind the wheel and turned to me.

"Yelling, you mean." He huffed. "She's a fucking piece of work. Tamara wants me to convince my dad to rescind the prenup. She wants the house."

"Can't you buy her out?" I asked.

"Well, technically, I'm set to inherit a fortune. But even that comes with a caveat. And she wants much more than the house."

He reversed the car then swung it around, and we headed down the steep hill onto the highway.

"Let's not talk about her anymore today," he said, giving me a tight smile.

"Caveat" rang in my head, as did the word "blood." Although curiosity had taken a grip of my senses, I let it go for the moment. The last thing Lachlan needed was an inquisition.

When we arrived at the hospital, he said, "I've got that gig tonight, which will be my last. I wish I could cancel, but I'd be letting the guys down. I promised."

"I don't have to hang around," I said, though I hoped he would drag me along if only to keep him away from all the girls.

"No. I want you with me this weekend. Is that okay?" He stared into my eyes, and I asked myself how I'd ended up with someone so handsome. Lachlan must have been the only person I knew who looked sexier when angsty.

"You can stay at the penthouse if you like. Or you can come along. I just want to sleep with you in my arms."

"I'd like that." I returned his tender smile.

He kissed me on the cheek. "It shouldn't take too long. He doesn't have a lot of energy for conversation, I'm afraid."

I settled down in a chair in the waiting area. "I'm fine. I need to call my mom and Harriet, anyway."

I watched him stride off and wiped my brow. Being with him was definitely an emotional roller coaster ride.

18

LACHLAN

I'd been sitting in the hospital chair for ten minutes or so before my father opened his eyes.

"Lachlan," he said.

"Dad." I leaned over and kissed his withered cheek.

His lips twitched into a slight curve.

"How are you?"

"I'm nearly dead," he said soberly.

"You need to keeping fighting."

"I'm in too much fucking pain."

"Do you need some morphine?"

He shook his head slightly. "You know about the bullion. Britney has the details. There's a clause."

"What kind of clause?" I asked.

"You're to marry her, then the money's yours."

"*What?*"

"She set it up that way."

"But didn't you say it was sixty-forty or something like that?"

"I thought it was, but on her last visit, she corrected me." He paused. "She'll be good for you. She's an expert at making money. She's got a good head on her shoulders. That killer instinct."

"Right. Like the 'Bird of Paradise' deal that has had me selling all of your father's collection to avoid having my head blown off from some Mafia dude named Varela."

I might as well have told him I'd lost at cards. He looked blankly at me. "That was my doing. I needed some quick cash. Britney tried to warn me against it. I should've listened to her.

She's level-headed and would make a good wife."

"I'll go without, then."

"I put two billion aside just in case you got stubborn. Britney doesn't know. But you still have to go to Geneva. Hank's got the details. You have the estate."

"About that…" I took a deep breath.

His forehead creased. "Oh, I forgot. It's mortgaged."

"Not anymore. I sorted that." I took another breath. "Tammy's got this thing over me that could see me jailed."

"That bitch," he growled. For a dying man, he still had some pep in him. "Hank can deal with her."

"She wants you to rescind the prenup."

"I bet she does. The whore. She fucked my son. How sick is that?"

"Why the fuck did you marry her?"

He stared into space, as though trying to solve a puzzle. "For the conversation." His eyes slid back to mine, and a smirk touched his mouth. Then within a blink, his face darkened. "She's not getting anything. Knock the bitch off."

"You don't know me, do you?" I couldn't believe what I'd just heard.

"What the fuck has she got on you? You didn't try to fuck her, did you?"

I jerked my head back. "Are you crazy? I can't stand her."

After I explained what had happened in the shower, he looked perplexed. "Why didn't you lock the door?"

I gave short laugh. "In my own home? It would never have crossed my mind."

He looked out in the distance for a moment. "Go to Hank. He's always got good ideas. He'll help you nail the bitch."

"She wants this expedited now and is threatening to go to the cops."

"Go to Hank. He'll know what to do." He touched my arm. His fingers were like ice, just like my heart. "Goddamn it, Lachlan, marry fucking Britney. You'll be wealthy as all hell, then you can fuck whoever you like. She's liberal-minded, that girl. I should have married her."

"How did she come to have all that gold?"

"A Columbian cartel and cans of chili." He chuckled.

I frowned. "It's fucking drug money?"

"So what? If we hadn't pocketed it, some other fucker would've."

"Then I don't want that fucking bullion. I'll do it the honest way."

"There's no honest way. You might as well believe in Snow White and the seven fucking dwarfs if you believe that."

"I'm going."

He grabbed my hand. "I have always loved you. Remember that. You disappointed me, sure. And Brent broke my heart when he died. But you're my one and only. Make the Peace name good again. Rich and powerful. Like we've been for a century." He began struggling to breathe, and his face scrunched with pain. "Call that nurse."

A tear ran down my cheek. Something told me we were having our last conversation. If only for my sanity, because my soul was polluted, I kissed my father.

I withdrew and said, "As a boy, I always looked up to you. I'm sorry if I let you down. Do you want me to wait here with you? Hold your hand?"

His eyes resembled shriveled peas. "No. Please go. Make the Peace name good again. Marry Britney. That's my dying wish to you."

After I called the nurse, I loitered about in the hallway, unsure of whether I should stay or go.

The nurse patted my arm and said, "I'll see to it that he's peaceful."

"Should I hang around?"

She shrugged. "He's still got a bit of time. We'll let you know when he's close."

I thought of Miranda and headed back to the waiting room, where I found her reading a magazine.

"He's not in a good shape. I—" My voice cracked. I was a tangle of nerves and emotion.

She rose, took my hand, and led me out of the hospital with her arm around me. Without words, she understood. And for that, I loved her. I couldn't have handled questions.

While driving off, I finally found my voice. "So there's Manuel's concert, and I'm sure your niece would be stoked to see you."

"Only if you feel like it. I'd like to go." She studied me for a moment with her hand on my arm. "Are you okay?"

I shrugged.

"If you want to talk, I'm here."

I turned to her and cracked a faint smile. "Thanks."

Half an hour later, we walked up the stairs to my mother's studio and found a crowd of people milling around in the foyer, drinking sangria and chomping on snacks. My mother floated about, chatting and kissing newcomers' cheeks.

She saw me, and her face lit up. "This is a first." She hugged me then, noticing Miranda by my side, kissed her. "It's so nice to see you too. Little Ava's a star. You just wait. Her mother's here somewhere."

"That's good," Miranda said. "Are you dancing too?"

My mother smiled at me. "Maybe a small piece. Just to show the families that the teacher knows what she's doing." She laughed.

"Something tells me they already know that, Mom,"

We entered the studio and took our seats, and Harriet joined us.

She hugged Miranda then turned to me. "Good to see you, Lachlan. Your little brother's gorgeous. He's made quite an impression on Ava. They're kind of inseparable. It's cute."

I returned a faint smile, which quickly faded. "I hear you're working at the hospital. Any news on Ollie? He won't see anyone."

"Tell me about it." Harriet sighed. "I've seen him. He refuses to recognize me, but I check on him and give him his meds. He won't let me wash him. The older nurse does that. It's strange.

I don't know whether he's blocking me out on purpose or he's plain forgotten who I am."

"That's sad." I shook my head. "Is there any hope? Can he get his legs moving again?"

"In quite a few cases, if its nerve damage, it can heal within six months. A lot of it depends on him. At first, he showed absolutely no interest in rehab. But I'm glad to report he's finally agreed to talk to the physio. That's something."

"Thanks for the update," I said.

Although unsure of how I felt about Harriet becoming Ollie's nurse, I could see she meant well.

The show started, and the children were sweet. My mom was right—Manuel was a natural, as was Ava.

Miranda turned to me and shook her head in amazement. It felt heartwarming to see young, spirited kids with a ton of talent, and Manuel had a dancer's instinct. It especially showed in his posture and the fire in his eyes when he danced.

19

MIRANDA

The audience was mesmerized by Belen's seemingly effortless intricate footwork. Her guitarist's passionate accompaniment synchronized perfectly as the pair built up to an exciting crescendo. She swayed her hips swayed sinuously and twirled her wrists artfully. A dramatic expression coated her dark eyes, giving her a formidable, almost dangerous air.

I cheered her on, swept along by a chorus of "olé." Her performance was so visceral that I became breathless, as though I'd been dancing. The children followed her, their tiny feet tapping in time to the guitar. I couldn't stop smiling.

When the performance ended everyone leapt up from their seats and cheered loudly.

Harriet whispered, "Oh my God, Ava's awesome. I didn't realize she was so damn good. And so's Manuel. They're going to be stars."

"See? I told you she was great."

"I always knew that, silly. But who would have thought she'd be great at Spanish dance?" She shook her head in wonder. "Say, Lachlan's mom's a great teacher, and hell, can she dance. It's like she's fucking possessed."

I nodded while ogling my boyfriend, who was chatting with the guitarist while Manuel stood close. My heart warmed to see the return of Lachlan's big smile, and I loved how he was around the children.

"Lachlan takes after his mom in the talent area. He's one hell of a drummer," I said.

"That he is." Harriet sighed.

"What's wrong, Harry?"

"Orlando." She smiled sadly. "It's breaking my heart to see him like that."

"Sweetie, I hope you're there for the right reasons."

"What do you think?" she snapped. "I don't expect to become his girlfriend or anything. I'm just determined to help him walk again."

I looked over her shoulder at Lachlan, who'd come to join us.

"Hey, that was sensational," I said. "Your mom's world-class."

He nodded, looking justifiably proud. "That, she is." He let out a deep breath. "Sherry's here to take Mannie back. Do you want to go to the apartment?"

"Sure. I'm happy going anywhere, as long as you're there." I surprised myself by admitting that.

After we left the studio, we headed back to the apartment so that Lachlan could relax before his gig. I couldn't help sensing a wall between us, but despite all the questions banking up, I remained quiet.

A few hours later, I stood in a crowded, noisy bar, watching four heavily tattooed men who looked more like bikers than musicians.

Wearing a Rolling Stones T-shirt and worn jeans, Lachlan looked good enough to eat as he pounded away on the drums, moving his head to the beat.

Although he'd suggested I stay home and enjoy a film instead of enduring loud, thunderous rock, I was glad I'd gone. After a few drinks, I loosened up and forgot all about Lachlan's mood shifts and the earlier disturbing exchange with his stepmother.

I'd called Harriet to join me, and when she turned up, we danced like mad.

We took a break so that Harriet could have a cigarette. Although I hated her smoking, I followed her out, mainly because my ears were ringing from the loud music.

"He's very sexy up there," Harriet said.

"I know." I frowned.

"Hey, I'm not interested. Don't worry. I know who I want."

"Harry, Orlando's got a long journey to make. The poor thing."

She shrugged. "He won't even look at me. He stares out the window, lost in his own world, or barks orders. He's actually quite nasty at times. But who can blame him? If it was me, I'd be pretty fucking shitty with the world too." She shook her head. "That hot boy. That hot body. It's fucking tragic."

"And he doesn't remember you?"

"Mm... I notice him stealing a glance here and there." She took a drag on her cigarette. "Anyway... it's a great job. I love it. Even without him being there."

"I've got an issue or two myself," I said.

I told her about the conversation I'd overheard at the estate.

"Shit, that sounds like a murder investigation."

"That's a tad dramatic, Harry," I said.

"Hello... Blood on a T-shirt. You have to talk to him. You seem very close. And he's into you, Andie."

"You think so?"

She nodded. "You bet. He can't take his eyes off you. Even when he's banging those drums and the chicks are circling."

"Tell me about it. That's why I'm here. It's his last gig."

"I hope I see Orlando playing again. He's so fucking talented."

"Does he have his guitar at the hospital?"

"His dad brought it in, but Ollie refused to look at it. He hardly said a word to his father. It was heartbreaking. God, his father's fucking gorgeous too. And you should see the mother, Clarissa. She's stunning. No wonder Ollie's hot." She stamped out her cigarette. "They're broken. It's so sad."

"I bet they are. Come on. Let's go back in."

After we'd danced to the point of exhaustion, Harriet struck up a conversation with a guy. I left them alone and headed to the bar, where a guy came up and started talking to me. Although he seemed nice enough, I declined his offer to buy me a drink, mainly because I didn't want to give him the wrong idea.

"I haven't seen you here before," he said.

"A friend of mine's in the band."

"Oh? Who's that?"

"The drummer."

His eyebrows shot up. "You know Lachlan Peace?"

"You look surprised," I said.

"He's not boyfriend material, you know."

"Why would you say that?" I studied him closely. His eyes darted about, as though he was looking for someone. "Let's just say he stole my wife."

"*What?*"

"Uh-huh. She went to one of his gigs. He fucked her, and after that, she left me."

"Oh, I'm sorry to hear that." My heart sank to my feet.

His expression had gone dark, and his voice had an edge to it. "The name's Mike." He held out his hand.

I took it, even though I didn't want to.

"Um… I guess I should be getting back," I said.

"You didn't give me your name." His creepy dark eyes had a sinister glow that I'd only just noticed.

"Miranda."

"Well, Miranda, let me say that you could do better than affiliating yourself with an asshole like him."

"Thanks for the advice. I need to get back to my sister. Have a good night." I walked away quickly.

My chest finally relaxed when the band finished. Mike had creeped me out so much that I wanted to leave. Lachlan was chatting with a bunch of girls, charming the pants off them with his twinkling smile, while they giggled and touched his muscly arms.

I spied Harriet in a corner, laughing with a guy, and joined them.

"Hey, Harry, can I have a word?"

She whispered something to the guy before joining me.

"He's cute," she said, half-drunk.

I explained what had happened and cocked my head subtly toward Mike, who remained pitched at the bar and waved back at me.

"Shit. He knows we're talking about him," I said.

"He looks like a loser. If I'd fucked someone like Lachlan, I would have left him too."

"Harry, that's a shit answer. Why are you like this?" I needed some sobering words.

"Hey. Chillax. It's all good. I mean, look at him. He's just pissed off. You can't get upset with Lachlan. You don't know the whole story. She could have thrown herself at him. There are always two sides to every story. And Lachlan's thirty." She opened her hand. "We're all a bit grungy at times. Just because you've decided to do things the old-fashioned way doesn't mean we're all picky about who we fuck."

Despite Harriet's crude logic, my stomach tightened as Mike's creepy stare clawed at my body. I left Harriet to talk to a much younger guy, who looked harmless enough, and positioned myself at the edge of the stage, where Lachlan was chatting with an annoyingly pretty woman.

That Lachlan didn't even notice me hurt. When he continued to ignore me, I left.

Just as I stepped outside, a hand landed on my shoulder, and a smile touched my lips. I expected it to be Lachlan.

But when I turned around, I bit into my lip, virtually drawing blood.

"If you were my girl, I wouldn't leave you alone," Mike said, wearing a sleazy smile.

He grabbed my arm roughly, and I screamed, wriggling like mad to free myself. He proved too strong and managed to drag me to a dark alleyway.

I kept screaming, so he muffled my mouth with one hand while the other clawed at my body.

"You're hot," he said with a heavy breath.

He tore my shirt open and smothered my breasts. Tears poured down my cheeks. Anger burst through me, and I crunched his balls with my knee.

He jumped back, but when I tried to run away, he grabbed me again.

"Let me go!"

As he ran his hands up my legs, someone came from behind me and pulled Mike off me with such force that I nearly toppled over.

I turned, and Lachlan knocked my assailant to the ground with such a powerful punch that a sickening crack sounded.

Harriet ran toward me. "What the fuck?" Her eyes were wide with shock. "Did he try to hit on you?"

"He tried to fucking rape me." My voice trembled as sobs constricted my throat.

Lachlan continued to pummel the cowering man, who lay scrunched up on the ground.

I finally snapped out of my daze and yelled, "Stop! It's not worth it. You might kill him."

Lachlan panted heavily. "Did he touch you?"

I nodded.

He started hitting and kicking Mike again. Mike held his gut, whimpering.

"Stop it! Just call the cops."

Lachlan picked up Mike as though he were a child, pushed him against a wall to hold him still, and wiped his forehead.

I bent down and gathered the things that had spilled from my bag. "I'm leaving."

He turned to me. "Don't go. I'll call the police. I would have killed the fucker if you hadn't stopped me." Lachlan's eyes darkened with alarming intensity.

I didn't recognize him, the way he was acting. All of a sudden, I wanted to be alone, to wash the anxiety and the rapist's stench from my skin.

Lachlan pulled out his cell. "Here, I'm calling them now." He placed his weight against Mike's writhing body and dialed.

20

LACHLAN

Miranda sat on the sofa, staring out into space. After what had been a long night, we'd finally left the police station and returned to the apartment.

She turned to me. "He's Linda's husband. He said that you fucked her, and because of that, their relationship ended."

"She told me he beat her and that she'd left him."

"That's easy enough to believe. He's a pig. No wonder she was so unhinged. At the time, I looked down on her. Now I feel sorry for her."

I held my arms out. "Why did you go outside with him?"

"I didn't," she said. "I left to go home."

After gulping down a shot of bourbon, I asked, "Why?"

"You were ignoring me. I waited for you. And you just kept laughing and chatting with a bunch of admirers."

I moved to sit by her side and placed my hand on hers. "I'm sorry. Gigs are like that. People come at you. And I didn't want to appear rude. One of the women was the lead singer's sister, and she went on and on."

"She was very pretty," Miranda said, staring down at her hands.

"Not like you." I smiled faintly before souring again. "Where did he touch you? You wouldn't tell me at the station."

"He squeezed my breasts, but he didn't go much further. You arrived just in time."

"I'm so sorry. He's a fucking danger to women. I'm glad you pressed charges."

"I'm also sensing something else is eating at you. Is there an issue with your stepmother?" She studied me closely.

The time wasn't right to tell her about Tamara's threats, especially since my father had refused to rescind the prenup.

"I'm good. What about you? Are you going to be okay?"

She took a deep breath. "Sure. I feel a little better now. And you did save me. I probably could've been a little more gracious in that department. I was just pissed off with you."

Stroking her arm, I said, "You're everything to me, Miranda." I held out my hand. "Let's go to bed. We can sleep in."

Miranda studied my knuckles. "They're bruised. They must be sore."

"I'll live."

It frightened me how far I might have gone. I'd wanted to kill him.

"Where did you learn to fight like that?" she asked.

"At school. On the streets. In bars." I sniffed. "I've had my share of black eyes."

She frowned. "Why?"

I shrugged. "Booze. Girls. The regular shit. Hormones make us act like dicks. We want to come across as heroes, I suppose."

"But you're a musician. You need those hands to play."

I leaned in and kissed her. Her lips were soft and transported me to that heavenly place where I could find the good in myself. Miranda didn't need to know how my father had pitted me against Brent for his entertainment, like those twisted scumbags who extracted entertainment from watching animals killing each other.

"I won't be playing for a while." I rubbed my sore knuckles.

"Maybe you should ice them again."

I walked her to the bedroom. "Nope. Bed. Sleep." I untied her robe and slid my fingers along the indent of her waist.

She winced.

"Too much?"

Miranda smiled sweetly. "No. I'm ticklish."

I laughed. That was the easiest we'd been together for hours. And I needed some of that. I tickled her a little more just to hear her laugh.

We ended up on the bed, and my mouth found hers. I devoured her lips as though it were our first kiss.

While watching Miranda dress, an unsettling thought swept through me: *how will she handle the shitstorm about to hit?*

I should leave her so that she could enjoy an easy life. Miranda deserved a good man from a wholesome family—if such people even existed. At the least, she should be with someone with less drama going on.

But how could I do that?

I'd never felt so crazy about a girl before. Miranda might come across as sweet, but the girl could kick ass when needed. My respect and desire for her only grew stronger in knowing that.

As we drove back to Miranda's place, I managed to talk her into spending the day with me. It was a picture-perfect Sunday, and I was dying to go surfing.

She seemed a bit uncertain, but after she'd collected what she needed from her place, we headed off to Malibu.

"Why don't you move into my place downtown?" I asked as I drove up to the house.

She shrugged. "I'd like to see how things go. There's so much happening at the moment."

I pulled up next to Tamara's BMW, and my heart sank. "She's here. Damn."

"At least it's a big house."

I jumped out, and after opening the door for Miranda, I ran up the stairs to the front entrance, which boasted a great view of the surf.

"Great. There's a swell," I said as Miranda joined me.

I needed to go surfing badly, even though my hands ached.

"Maybe I'll just sit and read," she replied with a gentle smile.

I took her by the hand. "I'm glad you're here."

The sun highlighted the hints of red in her hair. I couldn't stop looking at her.

"What?" she asked.

"You grow more beautiful." I lifted a strand. "I love your hair. Is it naturally that color?"

"It sure is. My granny was a redhead. I take after her."

I tapped her pretty nose. "You've got the cute freckles."

She giggled. "Stop it. You're making me feel exposed."

I laughed and took her by the hand, and we walked up the garden path to the pool area at the back of the house.

When we entered the house, Manuel was alone, watching television.

"Hey, little man," I said, rubbing his head.

He bounced up. "Hey."

Miranda kissed him on the cheek, and he looked shyly up to her.

I turned to Miranda. "Why don't you invite Ava and Harriet to spend the day here? We can all go to the beach, and Mannie can play with Ava."

I turned to Manuel. "Would you like that?"

"Yeah. I'd love to go to the beach."

"Where's Sherry?" I asked.

"She's not here."

"And your mother?"

"She's here with Trent."

I frowned. "Where are they?"

"In bed."

"Have you eaten?"

"I had some chips," he said.

I placed my arm around his shoulders. "Come on, let's have eggs and bacon. And then we'll go to the beach."

His little face lit up as though it were Christmas. Miranda wore a sad smile as she looked between Manny and me.

She helped me prepare the breakfast, and Manuel followed us around,

happy to help in any way.

We ate silently and hungrily. Manuel wiped up the remains of his food with a piece of bread.

"Did you eat dinner last night?" I asked.

He bit his lip and gave an unconvincing nod.

"Was Sherry here?"

He shook his head.

"You were here alone?" I asked, my voice rising slightly.

"No. Tammy and Trent were here too."

"And they didn't feed you?" I asked.

"I had some chips, chocolate, and ice cream."

I stared at his little hands. He looked skinnier than before.

"Where's Sherry?" I asked.

"Tammy sent her home." He stared at me, his dark eyes glistening. "She cried."

Miranda had left to call her sister, and she returned. "They would love to come over and should be here within the hour." She turned to Manuel. "Ava's excited. You can both go to the beach and play."

His little face lit up, and my heart went out to him.

Living in such big houses separated by high walls meant that children didn't get together unless arranged. At least I'd had Brent as a playmate when I was Manuel's age.

"I'll be back in a minute," I said to Miranda, who was being led by the hand by Manuel. She was wonderful around him, and her face lit up at a drawing Manuel showed her. My spirit warmed to see her with him.

As I ascended the stairs, I could hear Tamara's squealy giggles. I sprinted to her bedroom door—the room she'd shared with my father and where my mother had once slept.

Her endless cackling snuck through the cracks as I banged on the door.

"Go away!" she yelled.

"I need a word. Now!"

She opened the door an inch or so and peered through the crack. "What do you want?"

"Where's Sherry?" I asked.

"I sent her home. She's a flirt."

"Oh, and you would know," I said. "Listen, your son was here alone. That's gross fucking negligence."

"You're here. He's your little brother." She wore a towel and let it slip so I could see her tits, which did nothing for me.

"I'm calling Sherry. Now. We'll look after Mannie today. But tonight, he needs someone here. To cook for him."

"You're here."

"You're still married to my father, who's dying in a hospital while you're fucking another man in his room."

"It's none of your business," she said.

"Oh, it's my fucking business, all right. I live here. He's my dad."

She narrowed her eyes. "You forget. The hospital has reports of my cracked skull. Just watch yourself. If I decide to press charges, you'll be fucked up the ass literally." She chuckled.

"I'm calling Sherry. And she's staying."

"Go away." She shut the door.

I leaned against the wall for a moment to steady the fury rushing through me.

Pushing aside her threats of having me convicted, I headed into my room to grab my swimming gear.

Losing Miranda frightened me much more than the idea of being in prison. I also had Manuel to think about. My mother would adopt him in a flash, as would I if I weren't rotting in prison.

I regretted not reporting the shower incident. But it would have been Tamara's word against mine. And when it came to bullshitting, she was the queen. My stepmother could have gotten a starring role in a soap opera.

The media had made a meal of Brent's antics, and it had me by the balls, forcing me to make stupid decisions for the sake of the family name.

Manuel would end up a wreck if he stayed with Tamara. Something told me he could grow up doing great things. He reminded me of my mother, in that they shared the fire in their eyes.

I called Sherry and asked her to return that same night, instructing her to reach out if Tammy caused problems.

Harriet and Ava arrived just as I descended the stairs.

I joined Miranda and whispered, "Have you changed into that sexy bikini?"

She rolled her eyes and giggled. "Not around the kids."

"Bikinis are all the rage," I appealed.

"I grabbed my tame one-piece."

She tilted her pretty head, and I kissed her sweet lips.

Ava skipped over to Miranda and gave me a big smile. I knelt and kissed her rosy little cheek. She was so cute, and with Manuel there by her side, the kids melted my heart.

"Thanks for inviting us," Harriet said. She lowered her voice. "How are your knuckles?"

"I'll live. It's not my normal behavior. I hope you realize. Your sister…"

"Thanks for protecting her. What a prick. I hope they throw away the fucking key."

I nodded. "How's Ollie?"

"I worked a shift yesterday. He didn't talk. He's angry."

"Will he walk again?"

"Depends. If it's inflammation around the spinal cord, then once that goes down, he will. I helped give him an ice bath. He wasn't very cooperative."

"I'm glad someone connected is looking out for him," I said.

Miranda came and joined us. "What are you two whispering about?"

"Orlando. What else?" Harriet grinned.

I grabbed my surfboard, and the girls carried the boogie boards. When we landed on the beach, a dog came up to me, panting.

"Hendrix," I said, patting the friendly cattle dog, which I'd grown up with. He was as much my pet as the Thornhills' since my father had refused to let me have a dog.

As our beach adjoined the Thornhills', it was no surprise to see Aidan and Clarissa there with their daughter, Allegra.

"Hey." I headed over to my neighbors, kissed the women, and hugged Aidan.

"It's a great day," he said.

When I introduced everyone, Clarissa and Aidan seemed surprised to see Harriet.

"You're Orlando's nurse," Clarissa said.

"I am."

"Harriet's Miranda's sister," I said.

"What a small world," Aidan said. He returned his attention to Harriet. "Did he eat after we left?"

"He did. When I wasn't looking," Harriet replied with a tight smile. "I think he's improving. And we managed to get him into that ice bath."

"Oh, really?" Clarissa's face lit up.

My heart went out to them. The strain was written all over their faces.

Aidan asked, "Do you think it's only inflammation?"

"I'm not sure. But the ice baths are a good idea. And if we can convince him to go to rehab and have an attitude change, he could be okay within six months. That's normally how long it takes for this kind of trauma."

"So he may not be like that for life?" Clarissa asked, her face shining with hope.

"He's young and healthy. We just have to convince him, I suppose."

"He's not keen on seeing us," Aidan admitted. He shifted his attention over to me. "Have you seen him?"

"I went in a few days ago, but he didn't want to see me either. I hope he doesn't blame me."

Clarissa touched my arm reassuringly. "You saved him, Lachie."

It didn't feel that way to me. *But who am I to jump down from the hero's podium?*

"He should be here for his birthday. I thought we might have a small gathering," Clarissa said, looking at her husband.

He nodded and took her hand.

"That sounds like a great idea," I said, uncertain whether Ollie, in his current state, would want that.

"We'd love you to come," Clarissa said to Miranda. "And you're more than welcome. Harriet. Thanks for caring for him. We've noticed he's a little more responsive."

"It normally takes a while," Harriet replied. "And thanks for the invite. That would be lovely. It's beautiful here. You live in a paradise."

"That, we do," Aidan said.

They waved at us and headed off.

21

MIRANDA

On Monday afternoon, I dropped by Lachlan's apartment to retrieve my phone.

When the police called Lachlan, his body tensed. But as the conversation progressed, color returned to his face, which helped me breathe again. I'd developed a bad habit of taking my emotional cues from the ever-changing landscape of Lachlan's moods.

He ended the call, a perplexed expression on his face.

"What's happened?" I asked.

"I've got to go in now. The Pollocks have been located."

My jaw dropped.

He nodded. "The insurance company sent their investigators after I put in a claim. Although measly compared to the entire collection, it was still twenty million."

"They found Florian?" I asked. "That sounds too easy."

"Either that, or Interpol didn't try." He raised his eyebrows. "I have to go there now. To the station."

"And I have to return to the warehouse. I'm setting up a new exhibition. But I can't wait to hear about it."

"Me too. I'll keep you posted." He kissed me and rubbed my butt. "What are you wearing? Granny panties?"

"Yes, I've gone all Bridget Jones." I giggled.

"I have no idea what you mean by that. But they're kind of sexy."

"That's what Hugh Grant said."

He shook his head and pulled a face. "I'm not into girly films."

"I've noticed." He'd had me watch one Thor movie too many.

The only thing I liked about those films was how similar Chris Hemsworth was to Lachlan. They shared twinkling blue eyes and sexy buff physiques.

We rode the elevator down and his hands hooked inside my pants again. "What happened to the little panties?"

"You ripped mine off this morning, remember? And these were the quickest I could find on the way to work. I couldn't exactly turn up without, could I?" I cast him a teasing smile.

"Not with Mr. Lover Boy sniffing about."

"Sniffing about?" I laughed.

"Men smell sex. And you smell of sex."

"Ick." I frowned. "But I shower."

"That's not what I meant." He burrowed his finger between my folds then removed it, placed it in his mouth, and sucked on it. "Mm… I love the smell of your pussy. The dirtier, the better."

My pussy burned, even though his comment was on the filthy side of sick.

His hands crept under my blouse and rubbed my nipples. I felt his erection against my thigh.

"You make me hot, Miranda."

I laughed. "We had sex only this morning. In the shower. Remember?"

Our morning antics had come after a night of fucking in a variety of positions that would have put yoga freaks to shame.

"You bet. You sexy thing." He kissed me again.

The elevator arrived, and when the door opened, he was groping me. A couple looked at us in horror, and in return, Lachlan, wearing a cheeky smirk, saluted them.

When we hit the sidewalk, he said, "Dinner. Tonight. Somewhere special. We'll have to celebrate."

His contagious sunny smile radiated so much inspiration and hope that I wondered how one could bottle it. "Can't wait," I said.

Lachlan walked in the opposite direction with an athletic stride befitting a sports star or even a superhero.

When I arrived at the Artefactory, I found Ethan sharing a

joint with an artist about to exhibit with us.

Sylvester Cavallo looked more like a soldier than an artist. His work was extraordinary and so sellable that I regretted not arranging commission rather than a hire fee.

Ethan started to pass me the joint, but I shook my head.

Three of Sylvester's abstract canvases lay on the floor on their stretchers. How he worked color was what made the magic happen.

When Sylvester headed out to buy a six pack, I said, "This is turning into party central."

"Hey, it's business."

I reminded myself that we were dealing with artists, who were known to be lushes. *As long as great work is produced, who am I to judge?*

I pointed at the art. "These are amazing. He's set to become a name."

"He already is. He's got thousands of Instagram followers. And he's already sold these."

"You're kidding."

"Nope. I watched. He posted them online, and within a minute, they were sold."

My mouth watered at that kind of effortless efficiency. "How much?"

"Ten thousand each." Ethan shook his head. "I'm fucking jealous."

"Your work's great," I said. "You just need to get a little more productive."

He sighed. "Speaking of which, that's exactly what I'm going to do today. Get to work."

"Good. Your latest series shows lots of promise." I couldn't stop thinking about Sylvester Stallion's popularity. "We need to start charging commission."

"I agree."

"We're covering rent and costs, but there's little left, and I need to make a living somehow. Why's he hanging here, anyway? I mean, he could be killing it in New York."

"He's an LA boy. We went to college together. We're buddies."

"We should offer him the whole space for a solo show."

Sylvester returned a few minutes later, and I smiled. He was wearing an outlandish, paint-splattered jumpsuit with a horse's head printed on the back. He set the beer down on a table. His black curly hair was wild, and with his big, dark eyes, he reminded me of a pirate.

Then he ripped a bottle from the six-pack, handed one to Ethan, and offered me one.

With a business deal to discuss, I accepted.

"I have a proposition," I said then removed the beer top and took a swig.

His lips curled up at one end. "I'm happily married. But thanks."

I chuckled. "These are beautiful." I pointed down at his canvases. "And Ethan says they've been sold. Congrats."

"Thanks. I've got a ton of them. I'd like to hang them still, with a red dot to indicate that the art's been sold." He smiled boyishly.

"Of course," I said. "I've been thinking—what if I could get you triple that amount?"

He stared at me then turned to Ethan, who nodded.

"I'm not going to New York," he said. "I'm hanging here. I hate flying."

That glimmer of vulnerability endeared him to me. "No need. They can come to you."

"Why not. Sasha wants a new house. We're expecting."

Ethan hugged him. "Shit, man. That's great."

"Thanks," he said and returned his focus to me.

"It will be commission-based, but you'll end up with more in your pocket. And the more exposure, the higher your prices." I lifted an eyebrow.

Ethan said, "He's already got impressive online exposure."

"Sure. But the clients I'm thinking of are avid collectors with deep pockets, who I'm sure don't do Instagram."

Sylvester rubbed his hands. "Let's do it."

"How many paintings have you advertised on Instagram?" I asked.

"Only these three. I prefer the buzz of people seeing my art live than making a sale. The old-fashioned way."

"Sure." I turned to Ethan. "Melody Green dropped out, didn't she? That means the entire room is free for a month."

Ethan nodded. "I was hoping to run an exhibition." He sighed. "But I'm lacking juice." He looked a little downcast.

"You'll get it back, man. You just need to get laid," Sylvester said.

Ethan gazed at me before returning his attention to his buddy. "I've been laid plenty of times. I'm searching for my muse."

"Oh. They're not so easy to find. But look at you. You're a fucking good-looking dude. Hell, if I was gay, I'd marry you." He laughed. Sylvester returned his attention to me. "Okay, then. You curate, nominate the price, and take your commission. I get that you guys need to survive. And I can just concentrate on painting and ninja training." He emptied his beer in two gulps. "Let's kill it."

I stifled a giggle, thinking of him flying through the air with that big, bulky body of his. But those types of individual eccentricities were what made the art scene both fascinating and entertaining.

22

LACHLAN

Sam Chalmer patted me on the back. "Hey, it's been a while. I looked for you at the Red House."

"I've had a few issues to deal with."

"You're the hero of the moment. I heard how you saved Ollie." He shook his head. "It's sad, though, isn't it? I'm relieved Miles didn't go in."

We were in the Thornhills' lush gardens, and Miranda joined us.

I introduced the two of them and added, "Sam's one of our neighbors. He runs a local brewery."

He leaned in and kissed her cheek. "Pleased to meet you. I think this is a first." His smiling eyes shifted over to me again.

"A first?" Miranda asked.

"You're the first girl Lachlan's invited to one of our little get-togethers."

Miranda smiled, a hint of a blush touching her cheeks. "That's nice."

I squeezed her hand gently.

"So, where's Juni?" I asked.

"She's with Clarissa somewhere. Probably talking clothes, as usual." He chuckled.

"Sam's wife, Juniper, is an amazing designer. Remember that shirt with the dinosaurs that you liked?" I asked.

Miranda nodded. "Sure do. Did she make that?"

"Her partner prints the fabric, and Juni designs. She's got a local shop. I'll introduce you."

"I'd love that."

Aidan was standing with Ollie, holding a beer and chatting

with Miles Chalmer.

I touched Sam's arm. "I'm just going over to see Ollie."

Miranda walked by my side, her hand in mine. "Harriet's amazed that they asked her to become his private nurse," she said.

"So was I. At least he's almost himself again."

We walked over to the terrace, but when I spotted Juni and Clarissa, I changed direction. "I'll introduce you."

Clarissa wore a white dress with red roses and had her hair up in a bun, a red rose that matched her dress clipped to it. As always, she looked striking. She was smiling brightly.

"Hey, Lachlan." Clarissa turned to Miranda. "So nice to see you here. Welcome."

Miranda smiled. "It's lovely being here. The gardens are exquisite."

I turned to Juni. "This is Miranda. She's a great admirer of my dinosaur shirt."

Looking as colorful as ever, Juni wore a crimson dress with sewn-on blue-and-yellow flowers. With her long, golden hair hanging in braids, she reminded me of a sixties flower-child.

Clarissa and Juni were two very creative and earthy individuals, which was a refreshing change in our normally overdressed, designer-obsessed neighborhood. And Miranda matched them in individuality and earthiness.

Juni kissed Miranda on the cheek. "Lovely to meet you."

"I'd love to see your designs," Miranda said.

"I have a store up the road. Drop by. I'll give you a card."

Leaving Miranda to chat with the girls, I headed over to Ollie, who was talking to Harriet.

Harriet smiled up at me. "Hey, future brother-in-law."

Maybe I should have told her to slow down, but the idea of marrying Miranda didn't seem to freak me out. It actually had a nice ring to it.

"So you got the gig," I said.

"I did."

When I heard that the Thornhills had hired her to be Ollie's house nurse, I thought I should tell Aidan that Harriet and his son had shared a short history. But Miranda stopped me, saying that it would only complicate matters.

Ollie appeared the happiest I'd seen him since the accident, and perhaps having Harriet there was a good thing after all.

After Ollie had wheeled over to the table for a snack, Harriet continued. "I don't know why he asked for me. He was rude and impossible at the hospital. But I got a call from his mom, asking if I'd look after him at home. The pay's amazing. And to be honest..." She placed a hand at the side of her mouth and whispered, "It's dead easy. The food's out of this world, and I've even managed to convince him to play his guitar again."

"Now, that's great news," I said.

Ollie joined us again, and I patted him on the arm. "Hey, rock star. Harriet tells me you've been playing again."

He took a swig of his beer, and his eyes had an unmistakable shine. Seeing him smile again made my heart sing, and if beer was responsible, then it was as medicinal as some claimed.

"I've stopped feeling sorry for myself. Although I have my moments."

"Tell me about it. The mornings are the worst." Harriet rolled her eyes.

He smiled, and they shared lingering gazes, which made me wonder about their relationship.

Aidan joined us. "When are we going to see you at the Red House?"

"This week," I said. "I've had so much going on. Remember I told you about that art dealer?"

"Sure do. It was a fucking horror story. Clarissa freaked when I told her. She knew that fucker in college."

"She'll be interested to learn that he's hiding in Berlin."

"How did they find him?" Aidan asked.

"The insurance company sent in the investigators."

"Where's the art?"

"Apparently, it was sitting in a vault, about to pass hands. Great timing."

"That's a stroke of luck."

"I guess. It's been pretty fucking stressful."

"What are you going to do with them?" he asked.

"I'm going to keep them. I've paid all my dad's debts, but I'm a bit low in cash, so I might have to sell one to get a few projects off the ground."

"Well, I can help. If ever you need a loan…"

"Thanks, buddy, but I'll manage." I patted him on the arm. "Say, Ollie's looking good."

"Yeah. He's better. Tell me, what do you know about Harriet?"

"She's outspoken. A little out there," I said, unsure how to put it, out of respect for Miranda.

"By 'out there,' you mean she fucks around?" Aidan raised an eyebrow.

"Maybe. I mean, look, Miranda's very different. She's serious and is happier with a book and looking at art rather than hanging out at clubs."

"You got a good woman. Like I did with Clarissa. Twenty-two years married, and I love her now as much as I did then. If not more."

"I can see. You guys are inspiring. My dad wasn't exactly a great role model." I sniffed. "But seeing you and Clarissa and Sam and Juni… You're all so suited. It's always a pleasure visiting. None of that tension that one feels around unhappily married couples."

"Yeah, I didn't have much of a role model either. It hit me by surprise. But I knew right away, from the moment we got together, that she was the one."

I glanced over at Miranda, who was chatting with Clarissa. They had a lot in common, and I imagined they were discussing art. Like Aidan with Clarissa, my soul told me that Miranda was the one.

"I'm a little concerned about Harriet," Aidan said.

"Why's that?"

"She's older. She's kind of wild, and Ollie looks at her that way."

"Why did you hire her?"

"He demanded it." Aidan wore a tight smile.

"He needs caring for, I imagine."

Ollie took a drink and laughed with Harriet, who was also drinking.

"Is it her day off?" I asked.

"Nope. But Ollie insisted she drink with him." He shrugged.

A loud squeal rang through the air. Grant, Aidan's father, had arrived with his much younger wife, Tabitha.

"How's your dad's health?" I asked.

"He's okay. He had that throat cancer scare. Had it cut out, and he's doing well. He's given up the smokes, and is now eating weed."

Tabitha moved to stand by Ollie and cracked a joke, which made him laugh.

"Speaking of marriages, I never expected those two to last. They were both sex addicts. But she's stuck around. Tabitha was great when Grant was going through chemo. She looked after him really well," Aidan said.

"People change," I said. "Hey, don't worry about Harry. I'm pretty sure she's going to do her darnedest to help Ollie walk again."

Anguish seemed to leach from Aidan's eyes, as though I'd revealed something vital. "Thanks. That helps. Clarissa's not concerned. It's just me. I don't know. In my old age, I've grown conservative. I'm too aware of Orlando's wild ways. The girls, I mean." He smiled. "The apple doesn't fall far from the tree."

"I bet you broke a few hearts," I said.

He sniffed. "I fucked my brains out. It's not something I'm proud of. But it was an escape. And for a while there, I had a thing for older women."

"Then maybe turn a blind eye. Boys will be boys."

Aidan nodded pensively. "Come on, let's get another drink. And talk about Mustangs and Weather Report."

"You're going to talk about the weather?" Miranda asked,

joining us with Juni.

Sam came over, and he and Aidan laughed raucously.

"It's only one of the best seventies jazz fusion bands," Sam said.

"Oh. You're also into that style of music?"

Juni jumped in. "He's obsessed. They all are. Mustangs, jazz, and beer. The three amigos, right here."

I smiled proudly. It felt good being among those older, wiser friends.

23

MIRANDA

"You said that?" I asked, chomping on a muffin.

"Yep. 'Future brother-in-law.' Lachlan didn't even blink. He just smiled, as though it sounded normal."

Lachlan had been the most relaxed I'd seen him in a while. We'd had a great night the previous night. When we made love, he was so tender and loving that it brought tears to my eyes.

"The party was great," I said. "And it was nice to see Ollie playing the guitar. I thought Clarissa was going to cry. And Aidan too."

Wearing a sad smile, Harriet nodded.

We were at a ritzy café in Malibu and planned to visit Juniper's shop. An idea had come to me at the party—to host an exhibition of original worn art. When I suggested it to Juni, her face lit up.

"So do you stay over?"

Harriet took a sip of coffee. "Maybe. There's talk of me moving into a cottage within the estate. I guess they want to see what happens."

"What about Ava?" I asked.

"She'll come, too, of course." Harriet seemed bright and healthy, despite having had a few too many drinks at the party. "I'm here for a month. After that, who knows. Orlando might pitch one of his hissy fits and tell me to fuck off."

"The last time we spoke, he was being uncooperative. And now suddenly you're here."

"It's nuts. When Clarissa called the hospital and requested that I become their private nurse, I nearly fell over."

"Who suggested it?" I asked.

"Orlando did. He asked for me. Or so Clarissa said."

"Have you spoken to them about the time he stayed at our place?" I asked.

She shook her head. "He acts as though I'm his nurse. But…" She grinned. "He checks me out. Especially when I bend down toward him. He looks at my tits."

"Can he get an erection?"

Harriet nodded, and her smirk grew into a wicked smile.

"You're fucking kidding me. You haven't, have you?"

"Nope. The pay's too good for me to fuck it up. But when I wash him, his dick goes hard, and it's challenging for me to remain unaffected, as I normally would be. Being a nurse, I've seen it all." She raised an eyebrow.

"I bet you have. I don't know how you do it. All that vomit and shit."

"You're putting me off my breakfast, sis." Harriet picked up her muffin.

"Sorry. But you two were pretty thick yesterday. I mean, you were by his side for the entire time. And I noticed he watched your every move when you chatted with Miles Chalmer, who's good-looking, too. Hell, what do they feed these people around here?"

"Did he?" Her face lit up.

"Harry, you have to keep this professional. You could lose your registration. Imagine if his parents found out. They're genuinely nice people."

"Relax. Anyhow, this morning, he was awful to me. Didn't even look at me. Only barked orders. He can be a total asshole when he wants to."

"He's probably distressed. The poor guy."

She nodded. "That's why I tolerate it. It's common. God, if it were me, I'd bite people's heads off."

"You can walk, and you still bite people's heads off at times."

She laughed.

Harriet paid our bill since she'd just scored a very well-paid position, then we headed over to Juniper's shop.

"Beautiful but Strange. Hm... good name for a shop," I said, admiring a display of baby clothes with images taken from *Alice in Wonderland*. "I love that." I pointed at a toddler's T-shirt with the Mad Hatter's face. "I'd wear that if they had adult sizes."

We stepped into the shop, which smelled of roses. The pastel colors everywhere reminded me of a field of flowers.

Juniper came out and welcomed us with a bright smile. "Hey, you two. Welcome."

"I love it already," I said, looking through a rack of women's wraparound dresses. "These are so pretty. I love the one you wore yesterday."

"I've got this thing for applique. It's an old-fashioned technique of sewing on shapes. I'm now creating my own shapes too."

I pulled out a green dress with stitched-on purple and mauve flowers. "This is nice."

"It will look gorgeous with your long red hair. Hey, take it. It's a great way to advertise my clothes."

My jaw dropped. "What? But..."

Harriet pulled out a T-shirt with an image of a huge bone hanging from a dog's mouth. "This is hilarious."

"My partner, Jess, prints those. That's a fresh batch. We were laughing about my wedding ceremony. Jess's husband's into building dinosaurs."

Harriet's eyes widened. "Really?"

She nodded. "At our wedding, my dog turned up with a bone in his mouth. He'd stolen earlier. A t-rex bone that Jess's husband had searched a lifetime for. It caused a huge ruckus. Anyway, she made that as an anniversary gift for Sam. He's been wearing it around, and everyone wants one."

"That's such a great story," I said, laughing. "I love the fairytale theme. The Mad Hatter is great."

"I'm rather partial to them myself," Juni said. "Check this out." She showed us a shift with the Queen of Hearts printed on the front.

"That's awesome," I said.

"I'm rather proud of it. Jess is a great printer. I come up with the designs. I like classic shapes. Nothing too busy, to allow the prints to do the talking."

"So, about the parade we discussed yesterday, I'd love to host it on a Saturday night. Just to bring in a new crowd. Are you still interested?" I asked.

"You bet. I'm crap at promotion. Most of my sales come from the locals and street trade. There's enough to keep me happy. And with Sam and the brewery, which is popular, we're pretty blessed."

"Lachlan set up a date for us to have dinner at the brewery with Aidan and Clarissa. We'll have to let you know and make it a night. I like beer," I said.

Juniper smiled before switching her attention to Harriet. "Do you think Orlando will walk again?"

"I have a feeling he will." Holding the dinosaur-bone T-shirt, Harriet said, "I might buy this for Ollie."

"Take it," Juni insisted.

"But you need to make a living," Harriet protested.

"If it puts a smile on Orlando's face, then it's all good."

"Your son's a keen astronomer, I hear."

"He is that. If only I can get him to stop chasing the neighbor's older daughter."

I had sensed Miles had a thing for Allegra Thornhill.

"She's older?" I asked.

"Only by five years. Miles is nineteen going on forty." She giggled. "It's not that. It's just that she's got boys going after her from every direction. Have you seen her?"

"She's stunning. She looks like her dad with her blue eyes and long, fair hair," I said. I didn't have the heart to tell Juniper that I'd spied Allegra flirting with Miles too. "Miles is pretty gorgeous too. Not that I'm interested." I smiled shyly.

She tilted her head. "Lachie looks so happy. You look great together. He's had a shit time. His father's unwell. And that Tammy... ick." She pulled a face.

"Yeah. Tell me about it." I sighed. "And there's Britney too."

"Britney's not to be trusted around men, married or not. Be careful around her."

"What do you know?" I asked.

"Not much. Only that she's never gotten over Lachlan. But he's crazy about you. I can see it. We all can. He's so much more grounded."

I should have been buoyed by Juni's encouraging comments, but instead my head exploded with thoughts of Britney and Lachlan. She'd made no secret of her designs on him. But it still plagued me that Lachlan hadn't mentioned he'd actually slept with her.

After a while, we left the store, carrying our shopping bags. Instead of feeling high from scoring a gorgeous new dress to wear, I had a knot in my gut.

"Listen, Andie, don't go all glum. If Lachlan were going to marry Britney, he would've by now," Harriet said, reading my mind. "And he's crazy about you."

My sister knocked some sense into me, and instead of allowing Lachlan's sexual history to eat away at me, I took her by the arm and sprang along. "I can't wait to wear my new dress."

24

LACHLAN

I ended the call. Miranda was lounging on the sofa, her lustrous hair hanging over the edge.

"They've managed to salvage three pieces."

Miranda set her book down. "That's something."

"Florian's being extradited as we speak." I sighed.

"You don't seem happy about that."

I shrugged. "It's just having to deal with the cops and press charges and the mess that comes with that."

"Doesn't that mean you'll now be debt-free and in the clear?"

"I've been debt-free for a while. The de Koonings saw to that. And a suspiciously acquired Degas helped set up the Grenadine development."

"What happened to that project?"

"Britney plans to finish it when she can find the money."

"By marrying you?"

It felt as if she'd dunked my head in a bucket of water. "What?"

"She's made no secret of it. She told me straight out and even suggested you needed her."

"That's bullshit." I headed over to the fridge and grabbed a beer. "Do you want one?" I held the bottle up.

Miranda shook her head and adjusted on the sofa, allowing me to cop an eyeful of her pussy and lose my train of thought. She pulled down my dinosaur print T-shirt and rose.

"Hey. I was enjoying that," I said.

Miranda smiled and stood before the scrawled art I'd bought at the charity auction. "Are you sure you want me to have this?"

"You bet. It's significant, from our first-ever date."

"Fake date, you mean." She grinned.

"It might have been fake, but it's still significant for me."

"And me," she replied with a dreamy smile. "I'll hang it in my office. That is if I can afford to insure it first."

"I'll pay for it to be insured. Along with the Condor."

She turned sharply. "The Condor? You haven't had that insured yet?"

Sucking in a breath, I shook my head. "It must seem as though I don't have a clue. But it's been a hell of a few months."

Miranda's dark eyes shone with sympathy. "I can help."

"I'll arrange it when speaking with the insurers about the Pollocks."

"Are you going to keep the Pollocks?"

"Maybe. Tammy's credit card bills are huge."

She shook her head. "The opulent lifestyle's expensive, I guess."

"If it were just me, money wouldn't be an issue." I went up to her and took her into my arms. "All I need is a sexy redhead with a deliciously curvy body and a smart mouth." I ran my thumb over her pouty lips. "And I could live anywhere." I stroked her hair. "I'm proud of what you've achieved."

"I'm not there yet. But thanks for saying that." She paused. You're hard again. Does it ever go down?"

"Not around you."

I waltzed her to the bed and pushed her gently onto it. My hands smothered her warm, soft curves. "I love this naked-under-a-T-shirt look."

"I like wearing it. It smells like you."

I placed my face on her soft, milky thighs, ran my tongue up to her engorged clit, and licked her as I would a delicious ice cream cone, building up to soft and rapid lashings. Her musky flavor dripped down my throat.

Moaning, Miranda arched her back and pushed her pelvis into my face. Her clit grew hard on my tongue, and she cried out.

Sliding my fingers into her, I groaned. Her tight little slit made my dick throb.

I turned Miranda on her tummy and entered her in one sharp thrust.

"I can't get enough of you," I said, running my tongue along the nape of her neck. "I need to fuck you hard."

"Yes." Her soft voice turned my cock into steel.

Then I positioned her on all fours.

"You're beautiful," I said, taking her hair into my hand and twisting it. I pulled on it gently, and her head fell back as I mounted her.

I slammed into her as though I hadn't fucked for ages.

"Come for me," I said and bit her ear gently.

Her ass pushed against my pelvis, inviting my cock in deep.

We danced well together, matching rhythms.

A fierce release shot through me just as she cried out. Her muscles clenched tightly around my dick, and we hit that magical peak together.

After we'd returned to the land of the living, I rolled onto my side, took Miranda into my arms, and kissed her tenderly.

After a walk along the beach, Miranda and I settled down for a meal with Manuel and Sherry.

My phone buzzed, and since it was Sunday, I ignored it. But when the person kept calling, I checked and noticed it was the hospital.

Not having visited my father for two days, I couldn't bring myself to go there. He hadn't shown any remorse whatsoever, and after he'd suggested that I have Tamara knocked off, I couldn't take it anymore.

"I'm sorry. I have to take this," I said to Miranda, who was admiring Manuel's coloring skills.

The nurse's somber tone pretty much said it all, so when I ended the call, I headed straight for the hospital. Miranda offered to come, but I wished to be alone with my father.

I got there quickly and parked in front. Then I slipped inside and headed straight to his ward, where a doctor hovered close to his door.

He recognized me. "Any minute now, I'm afraid." He wore a sympathetic frown.

I entered the room, and the closer I stepped toward the bed, the more audible my father's struggling breathing became.

I took his lifeless hand. "Dad. It's me."

He continued to look up to the ceiling. "Is there a God?"

That threw me. "Um… I don't know."

We were lapsed Catholics. My Scottish grandparents had been churchgoers but it stopped there.

"Do you want a priest?" I asked.

"He's been."

"He heard your confessions?"

"Nothing to confess." He struggled to speak.

I took a deep breath. "I love you, Dad" left my lips, and a lump formed in my throat.

He squeezed my hand. "Get rid of Tammy. Marry Britney."

"I'm marrying Miranda. The Peace name will shine again from good deeds and hard work."

He gestured for me to come closer.

"Geneva only happens if you marry Britney," he whispered.

I kissed his cheek but didn't answer.

"I will see Brent soon. My boy." He touched my hand, then he fell back and died.

I covered my eyes, and tears of frustration soaked my palms. He'd been so tied up in himself that he couldn't whisper a final testimony of love for me, his remaining son.

The funeral, a week after my father's passing, was held at the same gothic church that my grandparents frequented and where, as boys, Brent and I had taken our communion.

The guests had congregated outside, and I was staggered by how many people had turned up. All the investors that had harangued me for their money, including Varela, were there.

The Mafia don came up to me and kissed me on both cheeks.

"My commiserations." His resonant accent hit me in the ribcage.

I wanted to laugh as I stared into his dark, sympathetic eyes. *Is this the same man that threatened to bury me in concrete?*

Miranda stood by my side. I kept holding her hand. Even when she started to remove it, I took it back.

"Are you okay?" she asked. Her dark-red hair was pinned up in a bun, revealing her long, milky neck, which I wanted to nuzzle into. Dressed in a black knee-length dress with a modest neckline and roses around the hem, she epitomized the type of individuality and style that money couldn't buy.

"I'm good." I adjusted my cuffs.

"This may seem inappropriate, considering the occasion, but you look divinely handsome in that tux."

"And you look exquisite," I said, kissing her cheek.

"Hm. Aren't we all loved up."

I turned to see Bevan Jones, wearing the same smarmy expression as always.

"You've scrubbed up well," he said to Miranda. "That brown dress hid all your considerable assets, I see."

I clenched my fists. I was dying to punch his smug, Botox-filled face. But I held back. A funeral was hardly the place to brawl.

"So you got the boss," he continued.

Miranda returned his smirk. "No, the boss got me."

Pride filled me at her quick return.

He turned his back to her and said, "Britney's broken. She was your father's favorite. A great girl." He was clearly trying to get at Miranda.

"Hm," I responded just as I caught sight of Tamara, who was inappropriately dressed in a short, tight skirt.

"She's out for everything, that one. Court case, here we come," Bevan sang.

"Sorry to disappoint, but there won't be a court case. She'll get what she wants."

His brow creased. "Clarke wouldn't have agreed to that. He

hated her guts."

"He married her." I pushed past him, clutching Miranda's hand, and we walked into the church.

"I don't like that man," she whispered.

"Makes two of us."

I'd been asked to present a eulogy but declined. Despite using my dislike for public speaking as an excuse, I actually had nothing good to say about my father.

During the service, Britney spoke, dressed modestly in black but teetering in her spindly heels, her blond hair swept up into a bun.

Tears were in her eyes, and it wasn't an act. Britney had loved my father. Despite my disgust about their relationship, something about Britney's unwavering devotion to my dad moved me. Perhaps I felt a sense of relief, within that innate familial tie that bound one to a parent, that someone had genuinely loved him.

She rattled off a list of his benevolent causes. All were tax write-offs, of course.

After some hymns and the priest's long sermon, we made our way out.

Hank, my father's lawyer, had arranged a gathering at his palatial home in Beverly Hills, which suited me. Everyone knew my father's marriage to Tamara was a sham. It would have been too tasteless, even for my father's morally challenged cohort, to have ended up at the estate with Tamara hosting.

I caught Tamara's eye as we were leaving, and she swayed over, ignoring Miranda. "We have to talk. Tomorrow."

I didn't say a word, knowing deep down that drama was about to unfold.

25

MIRANDA

Harriet had dropped Ava off for the weekend, and Ava jumped into the pool, joining Manuel. They squealed with laughter and splashed about, while I lounged back with a juice that Sherry had kindly whipped up.

A week had passed since the funeral. Lachlan had reverted to his old self and started working on a retirement home for black musicians in New Orleans.

He joined me on the patio, wearing nothing but a pair of knee-length shorts, and handed me a sheet of paper. "Check this out."

I studied the architectural drawing of condominiums complete with gardens and balconies.

"They're very symmetrical, and it's a welcoming design," I said.

Lachlan smiled brightly.

His father's passing had brought up some emotions, but after two days of retreating, Lachlan had headed back into his office, where Britney hung around like a bad smell.

I'd taken the week off from the Artefactory to spend time drafting a one-year plan. Following the success of Sylvester Stallion's exhibition, which had delivered a decent wage, I was inspired to look for burgeoning young talent. I just needed to strategize and focus.

When Lachlan had suggested I hang out at the estate, I jumped at the chance. I loved being there, especially taking long walks on the beach. Only I could have done without Britney turning up daily. Lachlan had admitted he needed her to clean up loose ends and to help him draft a budget for the running of Peace Holdings. I suggested he find himself an accountant, preferably one that didn't want to see him naked.

The way she lingered, stealing glances pissed me off. Lachlan explained that Britney had served the business for fourteen years and that in many ways she was part of the family.

"I'm not sure if there's room for both of us," I said. "She hates me and is rude."

His lack of a response bugged me. I sensed that she had something over him. But considering he'd only just lost his father, I held back on bickering about her. Also, he'd been nothing but supportive of our relationship. I just wanted her gone.

In the early evening, after eating burgers, the kids watched TV while I lounged in my favorite room, a former ballroom with a high curved ceiling and teal walls. Reclining on a chesterfield sofa, I was reading *Rebecca*, which happened to be my favorite Hitchcock movie.

Lachlan joined me and said, "Let's go upstairs. The kids are settled. And Sherry's here."

He walked his fingers up my legs, and I melted into his sexy gaze. I rose, mesmerized at the thought of his ravishing tongue and his dick turning me into an oozing mess.

"Good night," he called to the kids.

"Don't stay up late," I added. "School tomorrow."

"Night-night," Ava said.

I poked my head in the TV room. My angelic niece and Manuel were sitting with Sherry.

"Thanks, Sherry," I said.

The nanny smiled sweetly, and I returned to my horny boyfriend.

The following morning, we ate pancakes that Lachlan had masterfully whipped up.

The children had gone to school, and I sat at the island, drinking coffee and ogling Lachlan's naked, rippling chest as he walked about, wearing nothing but shorts.

"Are you sure you don't want to come down to the beach?" he asked, clearly itching for his morning surf.

"No. I'd better get to work. I'm arranging a new exhibition."

He leaned in to kiss me, then Britney appeared. Whether I liked it or not, she was there to stay for a while. I had to accept that Lachlan didn't have a handle on his father's affairs. I just hated her turning up in the private quarters, as though she lived there.

"Um... the police are here," she said to Lachlan.

His brow creased. "What do they want?"

She was about to answer when two officers entered.

"Lachlan Peace," one of them said.

He crossed his arms and nodded.

"I am arresting you on the sexual assault and attempted murder of Tamara Peace. You have the right to remain silent. Anything you say may be used against you in a court of law."

The next few minutes played out like a scene in a TV police drama. I almost wondered if I'd eaten moldy bread, because it felt like I was tripping.

Lachlan shook his head. "I'm innocent."

Before my next breath, Britney, whose eyes I wanted to scratch out, had returned with a T-shirt for him. *Where the hell did she find that?*

Lachlan pleaded with me as they cuffed him, "I'm innocent."

"I'll call Hank. We'll get this sorted," Britney said.

"Wait," I said. "At least let him get dressed."

The police agreed and followed him up to his room. I wanted to join them, but the policeman shook his head.

Britney grabbed my arm. "Let them do what they have to do."

I yanked my arm away and turned my back to her.

A few minutes later, they came back down the stairs.

Lachlan had changed into a shirt and jeans. "This is bullshit," he said. "I'm innocent, Miranda."

My heart broke when I saw the anguish in his eyes.

He turned to Britney. "Get this sorted."

She nodded decisively. Her posture had straightened, as though she were about to take over a company or something. She'd suddenly become relevant.

My heart shriveled into a pea. Tears blinded me. *What am I supposed to do? Wait? Go to him? Profess undying love?*

I took a deep breath and heard the cold stern voices of the officers in the background. One of the policemen clutched the arm of the man I'd given everything of myself to. I'd stroked and kissed that same strong arm.

The unbearable sight of terror etched in Lachlan's eyes made me cry.

Britney, meanwhile, chattered endlessly, while walking by his side. I couldn't make out what she was saying, but she was out to save him. And for that, I hated her.

Why can't I fucking save him?

Lachlan left with the officers, and I remained standing there like a zombie.

Britney gave me a sly smirk. "He needs me now," she said before sauntering off in her immaculate pencil skirt, looking very much like the head of a corporation.

I stared down at my clothes, the remnants of a lusty weekend. Lachlan had a thing for ripping my clothes. I didn't mind. He could do almost anything to me. *But this?*

He'd described Tamara as a scheming bitch and said that he would fight like mad to keep the estate. I thought of how he was with the children. That was always a good sign of a person's character. I needed anything to help convince me of Lachlan's innocence.

I gulped down a glass of water. My throat stung as the liquid passed through. Then I went into the bedroom and grabbed my belongings and, like a ghost, drifted out of the house, leaving a part of myself behind.

As I passed my old office, where it had all started, I glanced in and saw Britney on the phone with her feet up on the table, smiling, as though she owned the world.

She was enjoying Lachlan's nightmare.

26

LACHLAN

With his undereye bags and ill-fitting suit, Hank should have been lounging back with a pipe and a book rather than advising the son of a shady billionaire. Nevertheless, he'd been an expedient choice, and he felt like family.

I shifted on the hard seat in the gray, windowless room, holding a cup of cold coffee in my trembling hand. Rage and frustration had made me edgy. I'd never been locked up before. It terrified me. I could fight my way out of a bar brawl but not a prison full of desperados.

"She's bullshitting. I was in the shower when she appeared out of nowhere. Before I knew what was happening, she was on her knees with my dick in her hand. I pushed her away. *Gently.* Then she slipped."

"You should have reported it," he said.

I took a deep breath. *I should have done a lot of things. Like divorce that family.*

"It would have been my word against hers."

He nodded. "Britney's going to testify against Tamara. I'll let her explain." He rose. "You'll make bail."

"Will you get me out today?"

He touched my hand. "Britney's there right now, arranging it. We'll have to apply for a hearing. But it can be sped along. You've got a winnable case. That she waited until now to report you will certainly work in your favor. From anyone's perspective, we have a disgruntled widow who's out to blackmail."

I held my head. "Can you get me something to read?"

He nodded. "Sure. Don't worry, buddy. We're on it. You'll be out any minute now."

But I wasn't released until the next day. Britney was there to hold my hand. I would have preferred Miranda's, but something told me she'd written me off.

As I stepped onto the pavement, the first thing I discovered while squinting from the sun's glare was that freedom smelled like exquisite perfume.

I headed to my favorite café, where I ordered eggs and bacon for breakfast. I hadn't eaten for twenty-four hours, after I nearly retched at the mushy excuse for food offered to me in my smelly cell.

Britney sat opposite me, sipping on coffee. I didn't think I'd ever seen her eat.

"It will take a long time to go to trial," she said. "But there *is* a way for this to go away. Now." She raised a well-plucked eyebrow. Her blond hair looked white against the sun's rays, making her seem older.

"What do you have?" I asked, refilling my cup. A cup of coffee had never tasted so delicious.

"I'll testify to witnessing her entering your room and that she'd been drinking. And I'll come up with something nice and salacious about when I asked her what she was doing." Britney grinned. "I'll describe how she staggered about, naked, and when I tried to stop her, she pushed me away and entered your bathroom."

I narrowed my eyes, sensing the punchline.

"I'll testify on one proviso." Her cool blue eyes bored into me.

"Marriage?" My weary response reflected that of a man about to be crucified.

She grinned. "Uh-huh. Then this will go away."

"Tammy did you a service that day." I narrowed my eyes. "Or did you put her up to this? Is this some kind of twisted scheme you both devised?"

Her brow lowered. "Are you fucking kidding me? I hate her guts. As if... I mean... That's nuts."

"Why not? The secrets. She fucked Brent. You fucked my father. For all I know, you could be fucking Tammy. I wouldn't put it past any of you. You're all fucking trash. My father included."

"Hey. Don't disrespect him." Fire lit her eyes. "In any case, I'm not a fucking lesbian. Never been there. It's fucking sick. I like real dicks. Big ones. Like yours."

I rolled my eyes. She was beyond repair. "You're willing to perjure yourself?"

Without warning, Miranda and her beautiful, soft dark eyes entered my thoughts. I needed to see her and explain why Britney had me by the balls.

"I'll do anything to be with you. And there's Geneva. Six billion dollars."

"I thought it was four." I paused to think. "I don't give a fuck about the money."

"You wouldn't be a free man without it." Britney tapped her long, pointy nails on the table.

My heart had become a lump of lead. I needed my mother. She would know what to do.

"I have to make my statement soon," she said. "I've set up an appointment with the attorney."

"I get it." I took a deep breath. "Give me until the morning.

After leaving Britney, I headed straight to my mother's studio.

When I arrived, I found her sweeping the studio. "Don't you have a cleaner for that?" I asked.

"She's sick." She dropped the broom and hugged me.

My mother hadn't heard about my arrest, which unsurprisingly was all over the media. The shock on her face filled me with self-loathing. Although I shouldn't have blamed myself, I did.

Having listened to my dilemma, she said, "She's a *puta*. A scheming witch."

"Who? Britney or Tammy?"

"Both. Why don't you wait and see if they can find something on Tamara? She's been married three times. I bet there's something there. She's only twenty-eight."

I nodded. "The trouble is that I've got to give Britney an answer tomorrow."

"Then agree. Explain it to Miranda. She'll understand. And when all this is settled, divorce the bitch."

I gritted my teeth. The last thing I wanted was the stain of divorce.

After I left my mother's studio, I headed to the Artefactory, which was only a few blocks up. Even if I had to knock down the door, I was determined to see Miranda.

I walked down the alleyway, which I barely recognized. The once-lifeless strip had become a cultural statement, with murals fighting for space.

I pushed open the door and walked straight into the gallery, where an exhibition of abstracts graced the walls.

Clint sashayed over. "Hey." He gave me a big, welcoming hug, which helped ease my nerves.

I wasn't sure if Miranda was close enough with her colleagues to reveal our issues, and from the way he looked at me, I sensed he didn't know about my legal predicament. Either that, or he was just great at hiding it.

"It's looking great in here," I said, noticing the funky furniture that he was working on. "They're great pieces."

"I've found my niche at last." He smiled. "Sculpture is so difficult to sell. Functional pieces are far more accessible."

"They're wonderful." I examined a chest of drawers with faces painted on it. But then another one caught my eye. It had the curve of a female's torso and hips. I ran my fingers over it. "I want this. Can I buy it?"

His face lit up. "Of course. It's yours."

"Consider it sold."

"You don't want to know the price?" he asked.

"I'm sure it's worth it."

He looked over my shoulder at Ethan, who'd just walked out of Miranda's office.

I clenched my fists. He was a talented, handsome dude who wasn't about to be falsely imprisoned for allegedly assaulting some bimbo parading as a stepmother.

Ethan wore a faint crooked smile, which quickly faded.

I nodded at him. "Hey."

"She's in there," he said coldly and stalked off.

Though I fantasized about punching his perfect nose, I couldn't blame his cool reception. Had I been him, I would have reacted the same way.

When I entered her office, Miranda was sitting on top of her desk with her phone to her ear, staring out the window.

She turned, and her face changed instantly, as though she'd seen a ghost or something just as disturbing.

27

MIRANDA

Unshaven and with circles under his eyes, Lachlan rubbed his face and stared at me.

A million thoughts charged through my mind. I'd resolved to tell him to leave me alone so that I could live a sane life and focus on my goals.

But instead of telling him to leave, I set my phone down and pointed at the door. "You better close that."

My brain demanded that I stick to my resolve, but he looked so crushed. I couldn't kick him out. It would have been too cruel.

"When were you released?" I asked.

"Three hours ago."

His eyes hadn't left mine. He didn't even blink, and I had to look away to gather my senses.

The last couple of days had been the hardest I'd ever experienced. To avoid falling into a rabbit hole of despair, I threw myself into work. I found three promising artists and managed to sign a lease for a refurbished seventies condo within walking distance of the Artefactory.

Things were going well, except that I hadn't stopped crying.

I'd raced into life head-on, fearful of pausing. Night fell, and with it came pain and an endless stream of memories. I kept seeing Lachlan's warm presence, his eyes reflecting a belief in me. "He's a good guy," my heart kept insisting.

"Can we go somewhere to talk?" He spoke at last.

"We can talk here."

With each step he took toward me, my heart rate increased.

"Miranda, I love you."

I searched his unflinching gaze for traces of pretense but only found the soft, tender glint my soul recognized.

I loved him, too, despite hating him just as madly.

His hand landed on mine, sending a shock of energy through me.

"I didn't go near Tamara. She came to me."

"Why didn't you tell me?" I asked, snapping out of my Lachlan-besotted twilight zone and removing my hand.

He walked over to the window. "I don't know. It was so fucked up. It disgusted me to even think about it, let alone talk about it." He kept his back to me. "I was afraid you might not believe me and get the wrong idea."

Lachlan finally turned and looked at me. I remained silent, despite a barrage of questions banking up.

"Why didn't you report it?" I asked after he kept penetrating me with his impossibly blue eyes.

He huffed loudly. "I wish I had. If I could rewind the clock, I would."

"Britney..." I croaked. A sob had tightened my throat.

"What did she say?" He came closer, and I smelled his blood-heating scent, breathing him in as I would a rose.

"She told me what happened in the shower and that you'd tried to hit on Tamara on a few occasions."

His brow furrowed. "That's fucking bullshit. I can't stand that woman. I have never liked her. And as far as being attracted..." He rubbed his neck. "You've got to be fucking kidding me. You can't believe that, surely."

My wall of resistance broke, and tears fell to my cheeks.

Lachlan wrapped his arms around me and pressed his body against mine. His heart pounded against my cheek as he rocked me gently. *Or is that me rocking him?*

When his lips trembled on mine, I had to believe him.

Painfully tender, the kiss was almost chaste. But then his hard dick throbbed against me, and our lips crushed together.

He pushed me against the wall and lifted my leg, hooking it under his arm.

His kiss grew hungrier, his tongue lashing mine. It felt so wrong, but I couldn't help myself.

Then he ripped my panties off and placed the head of his wet cock between my drenched folds. In one sharp, painfully pleasurable thrust, he entered me. The stretch was so intense that I bit into his mouth.

The ferocity of his need was matched by my desperation to feel him again, as though it would be our last time.

He ground his pelvis against mine, entering me so deeply that my breath hitched. His mouth stuck to mine as his dick slid in and out, igniting a blaze of sparks before my eyes.

It felt as though we were fucking after a lifetime apart. I didn't even care if anyone heard us.

My eyelids fluttered as spasms rocked me. My muscles released and sent me soaring. I opened my mouth and let out a deep, fulfilled sigh.

Lachlan groaned into my neck, pumping furiously to his climax.

We remained locked in our embrace, waiting to catch our breath.

"I don't know why I let you do that," I said, stepping away.

Angry with myself for being so weak, I handed Lachlan tissues then wiped myself down.

After he wiped his still semi-erect penis, he stroked my cheek tenderly. "I love you, Miranda. I need you in my life. I want to marry you."

I frowned. "But you're about to go to prison."

"I know I'm not a good catch." He stared deeply into my eyes. "I'm innocent. Please say you believe me."

"I know that Britney wants you for herself, and that she'd say anything to break us up."

He released my hand. "She's got me over a barrel."

"How?"

He explained how Britney had offered to testify in return for his hand in marriage

"She's determined," I said with a heavy heart.

"She sure is." He sighed.

My mind buzzed. "Lachlan, you can't go to prison. You're innocent. I believe you."

He took me into his arms again. "That's all that matters. It's all I needed to hear."

Moisture coated his eyes.

As I burrowed deep into his blue gaze, I read fear.

I bit a fingernail. "You can't go to prison. That will break you."

"I'm stronger than you think."

"Can you get yourself a good lawyer who can argue your case? I mean, Tamara seems to get around, so there's probably a lot of evidence of crap she's done."

"You're not wrong. She's a whore." His lips curled up at one end. "Sorry."

"No. She is. I agree. I've seen what she's like." I recalled her swaying around drunk, wearing very little. "I'll help you fight this."

Lachlan's face brightened. He pulled me into his hard chest and held me tight. "I can tolerate anything, knowing you're there supporting me. Thanks." He gazed into my eyes. "I adore you."

28

LACHLAN

Seeing Miranda in the office she'd made her own filled me with pride. Her star was rising, the thought of which put a smile on my face—my first in days.

I pointed at the scribbled work of art I'd gifted her. "I see you've hung it."

Miranda gave a faint smile.

"It's a reminder of me falling hard for you," I admitted.

Her eyebrows narrowed. "You liked me then?"

I nodded. "It started when I walked into that room and caught you staring at art. Even with you wearing that ugly dress, I felt a tweak."

She laughed. "A tweak?"

I sat on her desk and smiled.

"I like having that piece up there. It suits this place. I have a sentimental connection to it too." She studied me. "The Condor was a bit generous, though."

"I wanted you to have both. You propped me up when the wolves circled and the vixens were in their shadows."

"That's so poetic, Lachlan."

I chuckled. "I'll have plenty of time to write poems when I'm imprisoned." I took a deep breath. "I also have to go to Geneva with Britney to collect my inheritance." I laughed at how ludicrous that sounded. "My father's doing. There are two billion dollars for me. But she has to be there."

"Your father wanted her in the family, I guess."

"He sure did. How fucking twisted is that?" I sniffed. "I have to go. I'm going to meet with my attorney and see what we can do."

"But you can't go to Geneva now, can you?"

"True. I can't leave the country. Apparently, I'm a criminal." I shook my head over my nightmare.

I held her and buried my nose in her soft hair, which smelled like a field of flowers. Then I gazed into her deep, dark eyes and touched my lips to hers. As I held Miranda in my arms, I extracted nourishment and courage from her warmth.

"Please don't push me away," I said.

She sighed. "I can't push you away, even if I wanted to. I'm in love with you."

"And I'm in love with you, Miranda Flowers. Madly." Our eyes locked. Tears fell from her eyes, and I leaned in and kissed her damp cheek. "I'm sorry for making you sad."

"I'd be sadder without you," she admitted.

"You're so beautiful." I smiled. "Can we meet later on?"

"I have to arrange keys for my new place."

"I wish you'd move into my apartment."

She smiled. "It's good like this for now."

I twisted a strand of her silky hair around my finger. "I meant it, Miranda. I want to marry you."

She gave me one of her searching stares. "Let's just see," she replied. "I should be free tonight after seven."

"I'll call you." I kissed her again, and she followed me out into the gallery.

"This is great art." I pointed up at the hanging canvases.

"It's been an outstanding success. I'm finally earning a wage."

"I'm so proud of you."

Ethan entered, and when Miranda returned his smile, my chest tightened.

She walked me out, and as we stepped into the alleyway, I said, "He wants you."

"I want *you*. Your life's complicated as hell, but I can't stop myself from wanting you." She wore a sad smile.

Her eyes misted over as our eyes locked.

I'd never felt such strong love for anyone before. "I'm going to do everything to make this work, Miranda."

Her face relaxed. "I don't like Ethan, by the way. Not in that way."

"Well, then, maybe you should introduce him to someone he can redirect those puppy-dog eyes to."

Miranda laughed. "Puppy-dog eyes?"

"He's got those eyes that girls, I'm told, go for."

"Not me. I go more for blue-eyed muscly guys who like to surf and play music. And can lift me with one hand."

I laughed. "If you're referring to my training with your scrumptious body instead of weights, then I'm ready for another session. Naked, of course."

"Like the Greek athletes?" she asked, tilting her pretty face.

"Not me. You. Naked. Those clothes will only add precious weight."

"I think it's extraordinary that you can do that with me. I'm not exactly slim."

"You're fucking perfect." I traced her waist with my finger.

"Later, then."

"I can't wait." I brushed my lips against hers and lingered, savoring her sweetness.

As I walked away, my phone vibrated, so I pulled it out of my pocket. Satan's sister was calling.

"Tamara."

"I can make all this go away," she said.

"You're not getting the estate. Two hundred million's a fair offer. Wouldn't you say?"

"I want more."

I took a deep breath. The two billion dollars in Geneva came to mind. I could move on and enjoy a peaceful life with Miranda.

"Meet me in an hour." Because of my bail conditions, I wasn't meant to go anywhere near her. But that was my home.

"I'm at the house now," she said.

"Okay. I'm on my way," I said.

I jumped into my car, which I'd parked at the penthouse, and headed back to the estate.

Driving as though possessed, I saw a police car nearing, so I eased off the gas. Much to my relief, a speeding Ferrari had drawn their attention. My speeding habit, which had become second nature, needed breaking.

I pulled into the driveway and parked next to Tammy's black BMW. I felt like running my key along it—or drawing a dick and balls. As juvenile as that was, it would have helped me blow off some steam.

When I entered the house, I headed straight to my office, where I ran into Britney carrying a cup of coffee.

She asked, "Have you thought about my offer?"

"I'm just about to go and negotiate with Tammy now. So, if all goes well, I won't need it."

"Do you realize you're breaking the law by being here?"

I shrugged. "So what? I'm about to get her to withdraw her charge."

"You'll need me for Geneva, especially if you're going to pay her what she's asking for. I'm about to book a ticket."

With nothing to add, I walked away.

I found Tamara lounging by the pool with a cocktail.

"You'd better get a drink, I suppose," she said. "And be careful. If this doesn't go my way, I'll report you for breaching your bail."

I stuck my finger up at her and headed inside to grab a strong drink, where I found Manuel watching cartoons. He ran up to me and wrapped his little arms around my thighs. I bent down, picked him up, and gave him a big hug.

It broke my heart to see him there alone with his evil mother. I loved that kid. He was Brent phase two, minus the smartass attitude.

"So what have you been up to?" I asked.

"Just school."

"Dancing?"

He looked down at his feet and shook his head.

"Why not?" I asked.

"Mommy won't let me."

"We'll see about that. Don't worry. You'll get back to it."

"Are you moving?" he asked.

"No way. This is my home. And yours."

That put a smile on his handsome little face.

As soon as I cleaned up my mess, I planned to arrange for Manuel to remain with me. Whatever it took, he was staying.

Tamara was on her phone, barking orders, when I returned with a drink. I sat down and sipped it while I waited.

She set her phone down and scowled at me. "You'd better make this good."

I shook my head. "Have you always been a money-grubbing con artist?"

Tamara rose, sauntered over to a bottle of vodka, poured herself a drink, and drained a third of the glass. Then she lowered herself down, tipped her head slightly, and regarded me with narrowed eyes.

"You've had a silver spoon up your ass all your life, so I can't expect you to understand what it's like living on scraps and going without food for a day."

I started to speak, but she held up her finger.

"One learns pretty fucking quickly that it's all about survival and nothing else. It's hurt or be hurt, especially where I come from. The trailer park was full of people like me. Only God saw fit to give me a nice set of tits, a pretty face, a hungry pussy, and a cold heart." She sniffed. "Being nice was never going to feed me. I dropped out of college because I was too hungry to concentrate. My mother drank too much to care, and I didn't know my father. I soon discovered that I could survive using this"—she tapped her pussy—"and this." She touched her head. "So you can call me whatever the fuck you like. But I play this game to win. And I won. And that's all there is to know. Don't jump on your fucking high horse with me. You probably would have hocked that sexy ass of yours if all you had were your fucking wits to survive."

"You can't say that. There's such a thing as honest hard work," I said.

"Honest hard work doesn't buy one this." She stretched out her arm. "Honest work buys one a bad fucking back, a shit marriage, children that suck the life out of you, and a husband that thinks being married entitles him to bash you around when life sucks."

An icy wind blew my way. I remained silent. Tamara had never shared so much about her former life. She painted a grim picture of reality. And I wasn't so naïve as to believe that such desperation didn't exist.

She sauntered over to the bottle again and refilled the glass.

It was barely five in the afternoon.

"One billion," I said at last. "I'll give you a billion for all of this and you to go away. I also want to adopt Manuel."

Her plump lips rose at one end. "You've always had a thing for your brother's son."

Anger burned in my gut. "Hey. Don't you fucking dare go there."

"Go where?" She smirked. "That's your garbage head thinking."

"One billion," I said, dying to see the back of her. My soul had been polluted. And while she'd tweaked a sympathetic muscle when showing me what life growing up with nothing looked like, I still hated the woman she'd become.

After staring at me with a blank expression, she said, "I'll get my lawyer to draft an agreement, then." She was about to walk off but paused and added, "You're free for now. But you've got a month to raise the cash."

As I watched her sway off, the breath that had been trapped in my lungs finally left my mouth, and my chest untangled.

Although her deceitful game had left a bitter taste, at least I wouldn't sit on a bug-infested bed or endure the stench of a foul prison cell again. I would go to Geneva, get the gold owed to me, and pay her off. And I would put that dirty money to good, honest use to atone for its origin.

29

MIRANDA

Harriet paced about while Ava busted some jaw-dropping dance moves that were difficult enough for an adult, let alone a child. I switched from watching my restless sister to my dazzling niece. With Lachlan's earlier visit still heating my body, I couldn't sit still either.

"Ava, sweetie, go into your room and play. We'll get pizza, okay?" Harriet said.

"You weren't watching."

"I was, darling. You're so talented. It makes Mommy really proud. And I'll work on your costume this weekend. Promise."

Ava scuttled off.

Harriet said quietly, "So much is happening. I'm going nuts."

Rising from the sofa, I said, "Come and talk to me while I pack some boxes."

She huffed. "I wish you wouldn't move."

"We're crammed in here, and I'm not far away."

"Why didn't you just move into Lachlan's penthouse?"

I shrugged. "It's complicated."

"Things are always complicated. It would be dull otherwise," she said with a sigh.

"Okay. So what's happening with Ollie?" I knew her well enough to recognize boy troubles.

"He's flirting with me big time. And when I say big time, I mean like *that*." She lifted her eyebrows.

"Oh. Like that? Have you?"

"No. But he keeps touching me. It started playfully on the arm, then he pinched my ass. And yesterday, when I was leaning over to sponge him, he touched my breast." Her voice cracked.

"Oh." I frowned. "You don't like it?"

"I'm crazy about him. I mean, he's still bossy and can be a real asshole. But he's also sweet and funny. And fucking sexy. Even like that."

I nodded slowly. "But you're in his home. What if his parents see this happening?"

"He's got his own space. A cute cottage. It's been fitted out for a wheelchair. There aren't any stairs, and it has easy access to the house."

"So I take it you're left alone together."

"Uh-huh. We play video games. He plays the guitar." Harriet shook her head. "He's so talented. I could listen to him all day. I keep encouraging him to play."

"How's rehab going?"

"Good. We have the physio coming every couple of days now. And I'm working with him in between. He's actually making progress. That is when he's in the mood. But then he takes my arm, and I look into those big dark eyes and…" She released a breath. "Shit. What should I do?"

I removed clothes from my wardrobe and placed them in a large plastic bag. "You're being well paid. Do you want to stay?"

"You bet. But I'm developing feelings."

"It sounds like he's attracted too."

"I think I'm a distraction. A reminder of when he was free and wild."

I opened my drawers and poured the contents into a bag. "Just be careful, I suppose. I'm not sure whether his parents would be happy knowing you're playing doctor with their young son."

"More like nurse and horny patient." She picked up a hair clip from the floor and passed it to me. "He's asked me to wear a nurse's uniform." A grin touched her lips.

"I take it's not for professional reasons."

"Nope. He wants to play out some fucking fantasy. And you

know, I would love to do it. I've got the right outfit. That short one I wore to a sex party once."

"A sex party? I don't remember you telling me about that." My sister and her seedy little escapades shouldn't have shocked me at that stage.

"I didn't tell you because you would've freaked. Now that you're sexually liberated, I can talk to you about these things. Thank God. You're my bestie." She put her arm around my shoulders.

"What happened to your nurse pals?"

"Oh, we still hang out. Go out for our wild nights. We went to see a male strip show last week for Bonnie's birthday. That was a hoot."

I studied Harriet, as I'd done on numerous occasions. We were so different that it was hard to believe we were sisters. "That sounds like wholesome cheap entertainment."

She laughed at my irony.

I tied up the bags I'd filled and threw them on the floor next to the boxes. I was almost done.

I gazed up at the Condor. "Lachlan's out on bail."

"Have you seen him?"

I nodded and smirked. "He came to the warehouse. Had a pissing contest with Ethan. They don't like each other."

"Woo-hoo. My little sis has a couple of sexy hunks fighting over her."

I shook my head. "That's crazy. I'm not enjoying it at all." I exhaled loudly. "I'm confused about Lachlan, though I've taken him back. I can't stay away from him."

"So you believe he didn't try to hit on his stepmom?"

"Yep. She's very skanky, in the skankiest way known to skank-kind."

Harriet laughed. "Ollie says that Lachlan would never do that." She turned serious again. "What should I do?"

"Keep the job. Act professionally. And hope he'll walk again. You'll win kudos for doing a fabulous job, and life will smile on you."

"I'm going to miss you, sis." She hugged me again.

"I'll probably see you every other day. I'll still take Ava to dance classes and help where I can."

"You're the best. Come on. Let's order pizza. I'm starved."

My phone buzzed, and seeing that Lachlan was calling, I picked up. "Hey."

"Hey, beautiful. What are you up to?" he asked, sounding brighter than earlier.

"Packing."

"I'm off to the Red House for a jam, and I'm taking Ollie. Do you want to come? He asked me to ask Harriet."

"Oh. There's Ava."

"Bring her. She can stay here at the house. It's the weekend. The kids can play, and Sherry can drop them off at dance class in the morning."

"That's so nice of you and her. Ava loves visiting."

"Then it's all arranged."

"Ollie wants to perform?" I asked.

"He does. When I visited him earlier, he looked so much better. And he's moving his legs, thanks to your sister's good work. She's a star in that household."

Harriet watched me keenly, trying to guess the conversation. I stuck my tongue out at her and made her smile.

"Okay. I can drop Ava off. It's still only six. As long as Sherry doesn't mind."

"She'll be fine."

"You sound happy. Has something happened?"

"You bet. I'm free, and I'm in love with the sexiest and smartest girl in town."

"Oh? Anyone I know?" My huge smile almost hurt.

"You know her better than most, I believe."

"I'll drop Ava off now, then. And I'm sure Harry will be keen to go."

"Great. Catch you soon." He kissed into the phone.

"Back at you," I said.

I ended the call and wondered what had happened, because

he sounded like a different person from the one I'd encountered earlier.

When I told Harriet of the plans and asked if she wanted to come, she replied, "You bet. Did he really ask for me?" Her face brightened, and she gave a huge smile.

"He did."

"He needs me to be there to help him and to cheer him on," she said, racing out of my bedroom, I assumed to look for a suitable outfit.

I headed into Ava's room, and when I told her she was off to Malibu, she jumped up and down. For Ava, that house was like a fairy palace. I felt the same. That place had magic woven into its walls—wicked witches and all. But as long as Lachlan remained my knight in shining armor, protecting me from fire-breathing dragons like Tamara and Britney, that sprawling estate would continue to charm.

30

LACHLAN

Aidan lent me his SUV, which had been modified to transport Ollie. He and Clarissa had decided on a quiet dinner and passed on joining us for a jam.

It had been a while since I performed with the jazz outfit, and I couldn't wait to hit those skins.

I lifted Ollie out of the car and placed him on his chair.

When Miranda offered to help, I shook my head. "I lift heavier weights."

"Now you're bragging," Ollie said.

"I've got this." Harriet took the handles of his chair and pushed him along.

"I'm getting a motorized one on Monday. That should be fun."

"You won't be needing it for long," she replied.

In response to my questioning frown, Harriet added, "Ollie's moving his legs. He couldn't do that until a few days ago."

Ollie kicked his legs out to prove the point.

Miranda shook her head in wonder. "That's fantastic. Well done, you."

"Thanks." Ollie lifted his chin toward Harriet. "I couldn't have done it without Harry."

She smiled sweetly, and they shared lingering gazes. Miranda raised an eyebrow at me. All that mattered to me was that Ollie was happy.

When we entered the band room, the musicians from Round Midnight patted us on the back. Excited to see us both, they treated Orlando as they would have before his accident, which I was sure he appreciated.

"Hey," Eddie said. "The band hasn't been the same without you two."

I smiled. "Thanks, man. It's good to be here."

Miranda wore a pair of jeans that hugged her curves like a second skin. Her hair was down, and a hint of mascara accentuated her gorgeous eyes. She'd blossomed since setting up her gallery. A strong, driven woman had come forth, and I loved her for it.

Ollie had his usual admirers, cheering him on when he rolled onto the stage. He couldn't stop smiling, and neither could I.

The tune began with a walking bass line, and I jumped in, syncopating my heart out. The bass player held the beat, allowing me to drum like a demon, taking out my recent drama on the skins.

Ollie played like someone possessed. His lead breaks blew the roof off, sending the audience into a frenzy as they cheered him on.

After we finished the set, I patted Ollie on the arm. "Hey, dude. That was incredible. Jeff Beck, eat your heart out."

"I've been practicing a bit lately," he replied.

"I see your rock-star allure is still as strong as ever." I cocked my head toward a crowd of girls gathering around.

He laughed. "Surprising but nice. Although…" He looked over at Harriet. "I've kind of fallen for my nurse."

I started wheeling him to the band room. "I've noticed."

"Is it that obvious?"

"For me, it is."

"Don't tell my parents. They'll freak. I mean, they love Harry. And they should. She's been amazing. I was such an asshole. Especially in the hospital."

"Hey, you're going to come good. I know you are."

"Thanks, Lachie." He reached into his pocket for a cigarette.

"I'd better go and grab the girls before they're hit on," I said.

"Good idea. Harry's gorgeous, don't you think?"

"Sure. I mean, I'm more taken with Miranda. But Harry's pretty."

Before I could go get them, Harriet and Miranda came and joined us.

"Coming?" Orlando asked Harriet, offering her a cigarette.

"You bet."

As we watched her push Ollie's chair, Miranda said, "That was an amazing show. I can't believe how talented you all are. And you, Mr. Hot Drummer"—she wiped her brow—"you made me hot and bothered."

I laughed. "Good. Nice and wet, I hope." I took her into my arms and held her close.

She felt good. *Life* felt good. That one night in jail had helped me reflect on what truly mattered. I'd always expected everything to go my way in life, not due to some inflated sense of entitlement but because I'd always been an optimist. While staring over the edge, I suddenly realized just how fine the line was between misery and happiness. But not until I'd admitted to myself that Miranda was my soulmate did hope take center stage.

Life suddenly began to move at a whirlwind pace. Two days after the Red House gig, I landed in Europe.

Despite the sunshine, the crisp air felt like cold water to a sleepy face, reviving me after the long flight.

Britney clutched her arms shivering. "It's brisk."

The flight had been comfortable enough, apart from Britney drinking to excess, becoming frisky, and offering to suck my dick. One of the advantages or disadvantages of traveling first-class was that one could easily join the mile-high club. I was a member. But not with Britney. I'd pushed her away, reminding her that I was in love with Miranda, and turned up my earphones.

I pulled out my cell and texted Miranda. "Arrived safely. Love you."

My phone pinged almost immediately. "Love you too."

I smiled and put my phone away.

Instead of going for a tour around Geneva, as Britney had

suggested, I headed straight to my hotel room and crashed. I'd never been good at sleeping on planes.

The following day, we went to an office with antique furnishings and dark wooden shelves filled with leather-bound books. The full-length windows boasted unhindered views of mountains that resembled giants watching over the shimmering blue lake. Mesmerized, I welcomed that feeling of warmth one got when seeing something rare and beautiful. It also inspired me to book a European trip for Miranda and me when life returned to normal, which I hoped would happen soon, after sorting out my inheritance.

A spectacled bald man directed us to sit on leather armchairs. A few moments later, his PA delivered a tray with cups of coffee along with cognac in crystal glasses and chocolate cake.

I'd discovered that an early-morning hit was the norm in Europe. And with my gut a little tight from anticipation, the spirit was timely.

Because of Tamara's demands, the smell of money had me in its thrall. I'd never had such a desperate need for cash before, and I hated how it made me feel.

After we'd gotten over the small talk, the solicitor said, "You receive six billion dollars but only on the proviso that you marry Britney Gane."

I shot up like a rocket and turned to Britney. "That wasn't the arrangement. My father said he put two billion aside if I chose not to marry Britney."

He passed me a document. "It's all there."

I took the folder from the man and, without waiting for Britney, charged out of the office.

Britney raced after me. "Hey, you need to sign."

Our voices echoed in the marble lobby. I wanted to yell so desperately that it became painful to whisper. "Who fucking set this up? And what about the promised two billion dollars that came with no fucking strings attached?"

She studied me. A hint of triumph shone from her cool stare.

"We both set it up. He agreed to my terms."

"Your terms?" *My father must have lied about the two million.* "Then it was you."

"Clarke wanted me in the family. He felt I'd be a good influence."

"Cut the crap. What did you have over him?"

Her lips curled up at one end. "He owed me. Didn't he?"

I studied her. "For sleeping with you?"

She nodded. "I was only fifteen. I have proof, and he knew it. And I could've had him charged, but I didn't. Because I loved your father." She took my hand. "And I love you."

"Strange kind of love. Blackmailing someone who can't stand you into marriage."

"It didn't feel like that at Aspen. You fucked me all weekend. Don't you remember?"

"I don't. That was drunken, wild me. I left him behind."

"Well, I want him back. And this gold will buy him back."

I sat down in an armchair by the elevator and placed my head in my hands. *What am I going to do?* Our flights were booked for the following day.

"We need to sign now so they can arrange the transfer. Or I get it all." She paused. "If you want to remain a free man, you need this."

"I'm trying to decide which is worse: trapped in jail or trapped into marrying you."

"Gee, thanks," she said with an ugly smile.

Seething with rage, I ached to punch a wall and or break something.

"How long?" I asked.

"Two years. Then you get half. Three billion."

"Then I go to jail, don't I? Because Tamara wants her cash now."

"She'll get her money as soon as it comes through."

"So you're hoping within two years I'll fall in love and become a doting husband?"

She shrugged. "I can make you happy."

I scoffed at that impossibility.

If I went to jail, what would happen to Manuel? What would happen to my relationship? But then, if I married Britney, Miranda would run.

Indecision had me by the throat. I was damned if I did and damned if I didn't. I had to think about Manuel's future, and I would have a record, tarnishing my future.

Even if I sold the estate, the penthouse, and the two remaining Pollocks, I would still fall short of paying Tamara, by about half a billion.

Could a brilliant lawyer get me off these trumped-up charges?

A protracted court case would become a blood sport for the media, and the Peace name would be forever affiliated with the ugly chapter.

Time was against me. If it weren't for that bloodied T-shirt, the case, according to Hank, probably wouldn't stand up in court. *And how did Tamara find that Goddamn T-shirt in the first place?*

When questioned, I'd argued the T-shirt was to clean up the blood. But she'd alleged that I'd tossed my T-shirt out, which meant I was hiding something. If only I'd been the one to call the ambulance and not Britney.

I'm fucked.

My father's trickery had landed the biggest blow. He'd dangled a two-billion-dollar carrot in front of me. With the benefit of hindsight, the stipulation that I fly to Geneva with Britney to claim my inheritance should have alerted me to the ruse. But I would have gone to jail without the money.

31

MIRANDA

Ethan stepped into my office with a bottle of vodka, for what was to be a celebration drink. We'd just signed up a popular new artist, and with the last show being a sell-out and quality artists lining up to be part of our scene, the Artefactory was making a nice profit.

Buyers seeking original art had arrived in droves. We'd filled a gap that Florian had left. I'd earned it, after the deception he'd pulled. On the flip side, he'd at least procured the space, which made me wonder if Florian had been handing over the reins to the lucrative art scene as a gesture of atonement.

Ethan handed me a shot, and I tossed it back, grimacing as it burned all the way down.

So much had happened in the past fortnight, and Ethan had been there for me.

From the airport, Lachlan came straight to Harriet's, where I'd dropped in to finish packing.

I was exercising, which was something I'd only taken up since Harriet brought home an exercise bike.

Sweat poured from my armpits when I answered the door to Lachlan, who was looking worse for wear. His blue eyes seemed so bright against his dark rings. I sensed something major had happened, but his need to crush me with affection swept me off to our romantic bubble.

He ran his tongue around his full lips and ate at mine as though we'd only just met or we'd been apart for ages. Then he ripped off my panties and ravaged me within an inch of insanity before fucking me so savagely that I came all over the sofa.

We had something to eat and tried to watch a movie, but he

couldn't take his hands off me.

Lachlan made slow, passionate love to me that made my eyes water. By morning, I was so raw that I ached in the most delicious way.

A call came for Lachlan as we were sipping coffee on the balcony, catching the morning sun.

When he ended the call, he turned to face me. His penetrating stare wore that same dark edginess as when he'd been arrested.

"I love you, Miranda. And if I had it my way, I'd ask you to marry me now." Puffing out a deep breath, he ran his fingers through his hair. "I want you to have my children."

My heart clung to his words about love and family. But then "If I had my way" sank in.

"What's happened, Lachlan?"

He fidgeted, looking down at his hands. "I'm married."

I was lucky the sofa was close, because without it, I would have crashed to the floor.

My mouth opened, but nothing came out.

He explained everything. He'd had to marry Britney in Geneva so that he could arrive home a free man.

"It's a fucked-up situation. I won't touch her. I won't go near her," he said savagely.

"Why didn't you tell me last night?"

"Because one look at you, and my body went into overdrive. You do things to me, Miranda. I can't get enough of you. And I love being around you. I'm proud of who you are. You're gracious, smart, and steady. Apart from my mother, I've been surrounded by selfish people all my life. Brent was like that. My father..." He raked a hand through his hair almost violently. "He's thrown me into this shit show."

The hatred in his voice sent a shiver through me.

"Why did Britney have that much power over him?"

My stomach twisted into a knot as he described how Britney had threatened to report his dad for statutory rape.

"She's paying Tamara as we speak. I'm free." He chuckled sardonically. "Not free to be with the only woman I've ever loved, though."

His big hand took mine. I wanted to remove it, but I couldn't. Our eyes locked. Mine filled with tears, making his handsome face blur.

"I'm going to divorce her as soon as I can. The trouble is she now owns half of the house too." He knitted his fingers with mine.

"Can't you buy her out?" I asked, barely able to speak.

"Britney would never sell. She knows how much that house means to me. I have to stay married to her until I can find a way out of this fucking mess."

I took a deep breath. My heart had almost stopped beating.

"What about us? I'm not sleeping with her. I never will."

"I don't know what to do, Lachlan." I removed my hand.

"We can still see each other secretly."

I frowned. "Secretly?"

He rose and paced about. "I know you deserve better. Much fucking better. I hate hearing myself suggest that. But I wouldn't be cheating, technically. I hate that woman. I'm never going to go near her."

"But you have once already, haven't you?"

"That was a mistake. I was drunk, and she took advantage of me. That's Britney for you, a scheming bitch."

I let him hold me then followed him to the door and told him I needed time.

As I closed the door, through the closing gap, I caught sight of his pleading blue eyes. He looked as broken as I felt.

I cried my heart out then threw myself into work, where Ethan stood on the sidelines, waiting for me.

As we shared a few shots and I began to thaw, I said, "Ethan, I'm not ready to be with anyone. I'm still in love with Lachlan."

He shrugged. "I've started seeing someone, though I'm not into it. I want you. You know that."

I smiled. "She seems nice."

"Hm. She's not you."

"Ethan, don't." I let out a sigh of frustration, more with myself than him, because I could do worse. If Lachlan hadn't stolen my heart, I would have dated Ethan for certain. "I hope this won't affect our working relationship."

"No way. I love this place." He took another shot of vodka. "My life's changed. I've got direction now."

He poured two more shots, and we clinked glasses. *That's what matters,* I reminded my pained spirit. *Direction.* My ambition had been realized much sooner than I could have dreamed of, only one year after college. Not many in my chosen field, an industry crowded with unemployed graduates, could claim that brag-worthy achievement. Lachlan or not, my life was on the right trajectory.

I smiled at Ethan, then my phone buzzed. I took a peek, and there was Lachlan's sexy bedroom gaze. I inhaled deeply and read the text.

I need to see you. I'm missing you, he wrote.

Just like all the countless other messages he'd already sent that week, I ignored it.

I'd never been so strong in my short life, because walking away from Lachlan felt worse than losing an arm.

Harriet, unsurprisingly, screamed at me to keep being his lover and to stop the Stepford wife act. "Passionate love is never tidy. But it's all that matters," she argued.

But I could never be anyone's mistress, not even Lachlan's.

32

LACHLAN

I walked along the cobbled pathway toward Orlando's cottage at the back of his parents' stately mansion.

He opened the door, wearing the biggest smile I'd seen since his accident. He'd returned to his former upbeat self.

After declining my offer to push his chair, he rolled himself down the hallway.

"My arms are getting bigger," he said.

"They were already pretty big, you gym junkie." I grimaced. "Sorry. I probably shouldn't remind you of that."

"Hey. It's all good. I'm good."

"I can see that, and it's fucking awesome."

He paused at a handrail by the wall. "Hey, check this out." He lifted himself off his chair.

I went to help, but he shook his head.

His legs trembled, which broke my heart as I recalled how vibrant and athletic he'd once been. After getting over that initial shock, I nodded and cheered him on, since it was a major milestone for any paraplegic to do that.

He looked pleased with himself as he held on to the rail for balance.

I was ecstatic for him. "That's fantastic."

"That's Harry's doing. Every day, she pushes me. Even when I'm feeling like shit and I say all the wrong things." He sat back down in his chair. "I'm not proud of those moments. It's like this monster takes over. I have no fucking control. I never used to be like that."

I knew exactly what he meant. "It happens. You'll soon learn to take a breath and wait for the rage to pass. You've been through a major upheaval. If anyone would understand, Harriet would. She worked at a drug rehab clinic, Miranda told me. I'm sure she's seen it all."

I followed him into the living room. "You just stood up. That's impressive. You're on your way."

"Mom cried," he said, offering me some M&Ms. "I've become a chocolate addict."

I reached in and grabbed a handful.

"My parents love Harry."

"Do they know that you're fucking?"

"We haven't. I'd like to. But she's trying to keep it professional. Or so she says. Maybe she's not into me anymore."

"I don't think that's the case. You had girls throwing themselves at you the other night," I said, crunching away.

"Hey, let's have a beer," he said as though it was something we shouldn't do.

"Sure. I can get it."

"No. I'm good." His tattooed arms flexed as he moved nimbly along. "I've got a motorized chair for the grounds. It's a bit of a hoot, rolling down the hilly path."

His boyish excitement at the type of adrenaline hit we males craved made me smile, despite Orlando being the sad proof of an adventure gone wrong.

He passed me a beer then unscrewed the top to his bottle and took a swig. "How's your relationship with Miranda? You seem all loved up."

I wiped my lips. "Not so fucking good."

He studied me. "You've broken up?"

"I'm married to Britney."

His jaw dropped. "What? How?"

I told him about the Tamara incident, pouring my heart out as I poured beer down my throat.

"Holy crap," Orlando said. "Your father did that? Forcing you to marry Britney for your inheritance? Why?"

I took a deep breath and told him how Britney had blackmailed him.

"That's fucking low." He stared at me as though what I'd just revealed had affected him just as profoundly.

"What is it?" I asked.

Without answering me, he wheeled out of the living room. "I think we need something a little stronger."

Curiosity had me following him into the kitchen, where he reached into the cupboard and pulled out a bottle of bourbon. I offered to help, but he seemed lost in his own world.

He passed me a half-filled glass.

"Thanks." I took a sip. "So, are you going to tell me what's going on?"

I followed him back to the living room and sat down.

"Remember Mom's fortieth?" he asked.

"Yep. It was a great bash."

"It was. And you snuck drinks to me even though I was only fifteen. I knew you'd make a good buddy after that."

I returned his smile.

"Anyway, Britney…"

"Britney what? Did she hit on you?"

He nodded slowly. "She sure did."

I sat forward. "All the way?"

He nodded with a guilty grin. "And I was only fifteen."

"Did she force herself on you?"

I thought about how she'd burst into my room in Aspen and before I could say, "Leave," she had my dick in her mouth.

"Well… I didn't take much convincing." He chuckled.

"Did you feel violated?"

"I felt guilty, with it being Mom's party and all. It happened in here."

"Had you been with a girl before?"

He shook his head slowly. "Nope. I was a virgin."

I raked a hand through my hair. "So, no one knows about this?"

"Nope."

A thought struck me. and hope surged through my veins. "Do you realize this could save me?"

"I do. That's why I told you. Use it, if you like."

"You'd be prepared for the potential shit show?" I asked. "After everything you've been through lately?"

He took a sip. "You've been like an older brother to me, Lachie. You risked your life to save me. I won't forget that. I'll call her if you like."

"No need. I'll talk to her." I couldn't remove the grin from my face. "Holy shit. Talk about twisted karma. She did to you what my dad did to her."

He shrugged. "But hey, I'm glad I can get you out of this tangle. And Miranda's a great girl. You suit each other."

"I can't disagree there. I just hope it's not too late."

"Nah. She's crazy about you."

"Thanks, pal." My heart felt light for the first time in weeks. "So... what have you been listening to lately?"

"Stevie Ray Vaughan. That dude's got soul, man."

"He had soul. He's no longer here, sadly. But yeah, he's amazing."

"Do you feel like listening to him?" he asked, heading for his turntable.

"Sure. I've always got time for Stevie."

Two hours later, I sprinted all the way back to the house. With the wind at my back and driven by an inner force, I felt like I was flying. For once, I hoped Britney would be there.

I entered through the back door and headed straight to the living room, where the TV was blaring.

Britney clutched a glass of wine and had her bare feet on the table. "Manuel's got to go," she said.

"The only person going will be you," I said, turning the TV down.

"Hey, I was watching that." Her heavy eyelids suggested she'd taken a Xanax.

"We need to talk. Just wait a minute."

I stepped into the hallway, set my phone to record, popped it into my pocket, then returned to Britney.

"Manuel's not staying," she said.

Tamara had left her son behind so that she could concentrate, I speculated, on nabbing her next victim—some rich sucker.

I loved my nephew, and with Sherry on board, that was one arrangement working in my favor, and I planned to continue it.

"I've just had an interesting conversation with Orlando Thornhill."

She lifted her slouched form from the couch and poured herself a glass of wine. "And?"

"He told me all about how you pounced on him at his mother's fortieth and how you fucked him in the cottage."

"Well, he fucked me."

"Ollie was only fifteen, and from what he revealed, you virtually pushed him into a dark corner, undid his fly, and blew him."

She grinned. "Did that turn you on?"

"It made me fucking sick."

"You didn't seem to mind shoving your cock into my mouth that time."

"I don't want to discuss that. This is about you taking advantage of a minor."

"I heard no complaints from him."

"He was a fifteen-year-old boy. You knew that."

"So what? I was a fifteen-year-old when your father fucked me senselessly."

Bile reached my throat. "So that makes what you did right? Is that how you justify it?"

She rolled her eyes. "Fuck you, Lachlan. What is this?"

"I'll tell you what this is. It's either we have this sham marriage annulled, and you leave this house forever, or I go to the cops and have you charged with having sex with a minor. You'll be known as a pedophile. Am I that worth it?"

Britney turned off the television. "That's ridiculous. He looked so much older."

"The authorities won't buy that. You should know that since

you were going to sting my father with the same charge."

She paced about. "You're a nasty cunt teaser."

Her voice cracked, and tears welled in her eyes. I felt sorry for her. After all, my father had started the rot.

"Britney," I said, keeping my tone calm and understanding. "I know that without your help, underhanded though it was, I would've ended up locked up for my dad's malpractices. But you can't force me into this bullshit marriage. When I marry, it will be for love."

She rolled her eyes again. "Oh God, that fucking fairy-tale shit."

"You're a very attractive woman and filthy fucking rich. You can have whoever you want."

"I can't. I want you." Her mouth trembled, and a sob escaped. She turned away from me. Her tough façade had crumbled.

"You can't have me," I said. "I don't want to go to the cops. But if I have to, I will."

"You can fuck Miranda. I don't care." She stared at me, wide-eyed. "I regret the day I hired her."

"I don't. But even without Miranda, I still wouldn't stay married to you. Don't you see, Britney? I'm not in love with you."

"But that weekend in Aspen." She sounded like a young girl. "You fucked me all weekend. You were fucking hot. Greedy."

I rubbed my jaw. "Well, I'm not proud of that. That was me then. I'm not him anymore."

"Pity. You rocked." Her sad smile melted away. "If it weren't for me, we wouldn't be billionaires now. You do realize that."

"Yeah. Drug money."

"You took it," she said.

"I'm going to use it to develop low-cost housing for victims of drugs."

"Aren't you good." She shook her head.

I glanced at my watch. "I need to be somewhere. Tomorrow, we'll discuss an annulment. Yes?"

"Whatever." She turned away from me.

After I left Britney, I headed to a little bar downtown. By

midnight, after downing a few more drinks and with Miranda blocking my calls, I decided to pay her a visit.

I called Harriet and got Miranda's new address and where her apartment was in the building. Determined to see her at any cost, even if I had to scale the building.

When I arrived, disappointed to discover the entrance locked, I buzzed the intercom.

"Yes" came a sleepy voice.

"It's Lachlan."

"Go away. I don't want to see you."

"Please."

"No."

"Just hear me out."

"I don't want to see you, Lachlan. Go away."

I buzzed again and again, but she didn't pick up.

Leaning against the wall, I took a deep breath.

I stood under her balcony, calling her name repeatedly until finally, she appeared on her balcony.

"Go away," she said in a loud whisper.

I'd climbed a ton of trees during my misspent youth. Only then I'd had the earth to fall on, not concrete. Overlooking that small detail, I managed to grip a ledge and hook my foot onto the first-floor balcony.

Just my luck, a dog barked, and an elderly woman drew open the drapes and glared at me.

I returned an apologetic smile.

"If you don't get off my balcony now, I will call the police," she said.

"Sorry, ma'am. I've locked myself out. I'm up there on the third floor."

She studied me for a moment. "You don't look too harmful, I suppose. Come on, then."

"This is so nice of you," I said, following her. I reached into my wallet and found a one-hundred-dollar bill. "Here. For your trouble."

She looked at it then at me. "This is a bit too much. How can you afford this, young man?"

"Please take it. You may have saved me from falling to my death."

She shrugged. "Why not. I'm a bit short this week." She opened the door. "There you go."

I saluted her and sprinted up two flights. When I found the right number, I knocked on the door.

Miranda opened it.

"Let me in, please." I pushed past her.

I stepped into the living room, only to discover she wasn't alone. Ethan had his arm stretched out along the top of the sofa, as though he were part of the furniture.

"Oh, you've got company," I said, feeling like a dumbass.

Miranda looked shaken. Her eyes darted from me to Ethan and back.

A beautiful woman like Miranda wouldn't stay single for long, and Ethan shouldn't have come as a surprise, since he'd been circling for a while.

"Oh," I said. "Are you together?"

Miranda pushed me toward the door. "That's none of your business."

"But it's only been a few weeks," I protested.

Ethan came over and stood between Miranda and me.

I clenched my fists. "Get out of my face," I snarled.

"Lachlan, don't start a scene," Miranda said. "Just go."

I stared into her angry eyes.

Before I could speak, Ethan pushed me out the door. I grabbed him by the shirt, my nose virtually clashing with his.

I shoved him off. "Don't fucking touch me."

"Leave him alone!" Miranda yelled. "Get out of here." Her eyes were wide and angry. "I don't want to see you."

I released Ethan then turned and stared at Miranda. She turned away quickly and slammed the door in my face.

I lingered there, unsure whether to bang on the door. All I could see were Miranda's icy, hostile eyes.

I released a tight breath. Whatever it took, I would win her back. I hated the idea of someone else being with the only woman I had ever loved. That she'd given herself to someone so quickly made my heart shrivel into a pea.

I shuffled off with eyes on my feet.

Once on the first floor, I heard someone ask, "You're going out again?"

I looked up, and it was the lady who'd let me in earlier.

"Um… yeah. I left something in the car."

"This time, I hope you've got your keys."

"Mm… Sure."

I took a deep breath. I was too torn up to feel bad about fibbing to the snoopy neighbor.

33

MIRANDA

"He's keen," Ethan said. "Can't say I blame him."

I paced about, something I'd become good at since meeting Lachlan.

He'd changed me—made me act deranged.

"This was probably not a great idea. I'm not over him," I said at last.

Ethan tapped the cushion by his side. "Just sit down. I'm not going to hit on you."

I joined him on the sofa. "The other night…"

"Don't worry. It was nice, anyway."

"We didn't do much," I said.

We'd just hosted an art show, and Ethan and I had had a bit to drink. We ended up smooching in a corner. His hands crept under my tank top, and it got steamy, though perhaps more for him. I felt numb, as though I'd desecrated something with Lachlan.

"He's married," an inner voice screamed, so I allowed Ethan's hungry groping to continue in the hope of releasing Lachlan from my system. Instead, it increased my yearning for him.

Then like a scene from a movie, Lachlan climbed a wall to see me. *How ridiculously romantic, if not touching too.*

But I wasn't going to be his mistress, regardless of his obvious disdain for Britney.

Ethan rose. "Okay. I'll go." He looked disappointed.

"Sorry." I grimaced.

I walked him to the door and hugged him. "It's probably better this way. We have to work together."

"Sure." He pecked my cheek and left.

A week had passed since Lachlan burst through my door, and in order to forget him, I threw myself into work.

With the fashion parade and exhibition of screen prints opening that night, Juniper and Jessie, her fabric designer, were arranging the clothes on racks and hanging their prints on the walls.

"This looks great," I said, admiring the stock of limited-release T-shirts bearing surreal designs as well as Juni's range of three-quarter-length unisex pants printed with graffitied scrawl.

Sam, Juni's husband, brought in crates of his craft beer that Ethan and Clint helped carry into the kitchen, which was now fully equipped with two large fridges. A table had been set up for the beer, with Clint's younger brother and sister there to serve drinks.

Everyone's chipping in was what made the Artefactory special, giving it a great family atmosphere. And because of that, we'd hosted some fabulously inspiring shows. Trendy and well-attended, the Artefactory had steadily become a brand. Ethan had even designed a fun logo depicting an animated machine pumping out blobs of color.

I directed the six models Juni had hired for the fashion parade into my office. "It's not much of a dressing room." I pointed at a full-length mirror. "It's pretty makeshift."

"It's great. I love this place," Juni said. She was wearing floral flares and psychedelic wedges with a flower on top.

She hung the clothes to be paraded on a clothes rack.

"Can I help in any way?" I asked.

"No. It's all good. Six outfits each. Shouldn't be too difficult." She turned to one of the beautiful girls and asked, "Allegra, have you met Miranda?"

We acknowledged each other and smiled.

"Yes, you're Clarissa's daughter. I met you at your house," I said, struck again by how stunning she was with her big blue twinkling eyes and golden waist-length hair. And she was sweet. Even though men's eyes had been all over her, she maintained a gentle and unassuming air.

Juni held up a dress against Allegra and moved her head from side to side. "That should work on you." She chuckled. "You could wear a potato sack and make it look good."

Allegra smiled as she held up the turquoise dress which had an empire waist and butterflies stitched on, as though they'd just landed on her chest. The front of the garment went to above the knees, while the back cascaded to the ground.

"Is your family coming?" I asked.

Allegra nodded. "Even Ollie."

"Great." I hoped he and Harriet wouldn't flirt openly.

Thoughts of Lachlan filtered through again, as they'd continued to do. I hadn't spoken to him since that midnight visit, and that he probably assumed Ethan and I were dating made it hard to eat.

We put the finishing touches to the catwalk, and the models were good to go.

Two hours later, everything was in full swing. The gallery was packed with newcomers.

Hearing the cash register ringing and seeing red dots on Ethan's paintings put a smile on my face. Clint's unique chest of drawers proved incredibly popular too.

Guests laughed and chatted while sampling Sam's brew.

Sam insisted I try his beer. He was such an amusing man, and he loved beer—not in that drunken, disorderly way but as a passionate connoisseur.

As I giggled at one of his silly jokes about how many Irish men it took to cross the road with a chicken, Lachlan appeared behind him, and I forgot to breathe. He was so beautiful with his swoony turquoise eyes.

Lachlan strode over to me in an easy-going manner, as though we were buddies, not former addicted lovers, and kissed my cheek.

"This looks fabulous," he said, leaving behind his teasing scent, which flooded me with burning memories of him ravaging me.

"Thanks." I acted as though we'd never even touched. "Are you here alone?" I wasn't in the mood for Britney. The only positive thing to come from our breakup was not having to endure her dirty looks.

"Sure am." He pointed. "Ah. I see Sam's set up a table of his beer. Just what I feel like."

And off he went, just like that.

It felt as though we'd never been together. I wanted to run into a room and stand in the dark crying. Instead, I had to paint on a smile.

When the parade started, Harriet came and joined me.

"The clothes are so outrageously colorful, and isn't Allegra a natural model?" she asked.

I nodded, doing my utmost to keep my eyes on the models and not Lachlan. He was hanging with Aidan and Sam, clinking beer bottles, chatting, laughing, and charming every eligible woman and man in the room without even trying. A few of the young models kept giving him the eye. My nails came close to drawing blood from my palms.

"Have you spoken to Lachlan yet?" Harriet asked.

I let out a deep, audible breath. "Uh-huh. It's fucking killing me, having him here."

"He's no longer married, you know."

I turned so sharply that my neck cracked. "What? How do you know?"

"Ollie told me earlier. It's just happened, apparently. He's getting a divorce, and she's left the house. Lachlan's living there alone with Manuel and Sherry."

I gazed at Lachlan, whose eyes landed on mine and remained there. The smile he wore from joking with his buddies melted away, and his expression turned intimate.

"Look, he's eye-fucking you," Harriet said. "You're crazy. I would have stayed with him, married or not. She forced his hand."

"Oh, Harriet, don't go on about it." That they'd separated

meant everything. I just needed Lachlan to tell me himself.

Why hasn't he? Why was he acting so fucking cool? I'd blocked him. And he thought I was with Ethan. *Hell.*

As the night progressed, the merchandise sold out, and Juni became swamped with orders.

When Clint's DJ boyfriend cranked up the music, things heated up, and the room exploded into an impromptu dance party.

Ethan cozied up with a model, and it warmed my heart to see him smiling. Lachlan kept his distance, which annoyed me. I wanted him to come over and win me back. He should fight for me. *Can't he see Ethan and I aren't hanging together?*

Harriet grabbed my hand. "Come on. Let's dance."

I followed my sister onto the dance floor, and swinging my arms in the air, I tripped off into my own little tipsy universe. It felt nice. The space was loved, and everyone was having a ball.

As I swayed, I felt the presence of someone behind me. I turned, and Lachlan was smiling and dancing close to me. Just as my heart skipped along and a smile touched my lips, a gorgeous brunette, one of the models, joined him. Talk about falling from a great height. My heart sank, and I left Harriet to dance alone.

I stepped out into the alleyway, found a quiet little corner away from the smokers, and looked up at the stars. Tears made everything appear blurry. I ached for Lachlan. The pain was unbearable, especially seeing that pretty girl dancing so close to him. And just to punish myself even further, I imagined him ravaging her.

Just as I was about to go to my car and cry my eyes out, I heard, "Where are you going?"

The man who had stolen my everything stood there.

"Oh. Um..." My brain had melted at his sight.

He took my hand.

"Why aren't you in there with that girl, dancing?" I asked.

He tilted his head. "Are you jealous?"

I looked down at the ground. "Stop turning this into a game.

I'm not as shallow as you. I can't just act like nothing happened between us."

"I'm not shallow. I'm just good at hiding my feelings."

I gazed up at him. His eyes had gone dark and as I burrowed deep, I could see his recent struggles.

"I know you're not shallow. I wouldn't like you if you were."

"Oh, you still like me." His grin dimpled his cheeks.

I wanted to slap his handsome face. "Stop playing games, Lachlan. You know I do."

"No, I don't." He'd turned serious again. "Last time I saw you, you were with Ethan. That fucking hurt. Let me tell you." His stare penetrated to my core, making me gulp.

"I was never with him. We didn't do anything. I mean, he kissed me."

He stepped closer. "That pisses me off." He ran his thumb over my lips. "These are my lips. I want those lips for me only."

I had to smile at how preposterous that sounded, but it was nice too. "How do you think I felt, knowing you were probably sleeping with Britney? I know how forceful she can be." I raised an eyebrow.

"She didn't come near me. The marriage has been annulled because she'd followed in my father's footsteps. They deserved each other." He let out a tense breath. "It's been an eventful month. And fucking lonely without you. I've missed you."

Tears burned my eyes. "I need a tissue. I have to go inside," I said, though I wavered because I didn't want to kill the moment.

Our eyes locked again, and I remained stuck there on the spot.

He ripped his T-shirt and handed it to me. "Here."

"You've just ruined your shirt." I took it anyhow and wiped my nose.

Lachlan shrugged. "I don't care. I only care about you. I want to stare into your beautiful eyes and see that fragile look you get when I'm deep inside of you. Making me want to smother you. Love you. Hold you."

My knees gave way, and I fell into his strong arms.

34

LACHLAN

Miranda stared at me. "You're abducting me?"

Her shocked disbelief made me chuckle. "That, I am."

"Why?"

"Because I'm greedy. I want you all to myself."

"Where are we going?"

"It's a surprise," I said, turning to indulge in her pretty face.

"But this is the desert. It's kind of creepy out here in that *No Country for Old Men* way," she said. "What if we break down? Or run out of gas?"

I laughed. "You've always had an overactive imagination. That's why we're using the SUV. The tank's full." She kept staring at me as though I was a weirdo. "Are you scared I'll stop the car and take advantage of you?"

She laughed. "You've already done that once tonight."

"You struck me as a willing participant." I raised my eyebrows. "Going on how wet and screechy you got."

"Screechy?"

I laughed. It had been an interesting evening. And it was eleven o'clock at night, and we were an hour away from Las Vegas.

I'd carried Miranda to my car as she giggled and hit me at the same time, telling me to put her down. By the time we fell into the back seat of my car, my lips and every other part of me had touched every part of her.

"You're not cold, are you?"

"No. But I'm bit breezy down there," she said, tilting her head downward. She crossed her legs and clutched her arms.

"I'm sorry. Those panties were just in the way."

A diner's bright lights shone from up ahead. "Let's stop. I could use a coffee and a bite to eat. Is that okay?"

"Oh God yeah. I'm starving. Only I'm not wearing any panties."

"Now why did you have to say that?" I pulled up in front of the weathered old diner, which seemed to be wearing its original coat of paint, then I leaned in and kissed her warm, soft lips.

"I guess we should go in and eat," she said, unravelling from my arms.

I jumped out of the car and ran to her side to open the door. "Madam, after you."

She laughed at my silly British accent.

"Are we going to Las Vegas?" she asked as though it had finally dawned on her.

"We are." I wrapped my arm around her waist and drew her close.

"Then why didn't you just tell me? We could have stopped at my place for some clothes and underwear."

"Because I'm impatient to get there." I also had other motives, but I kept them to myself.

"But Las Vegas?"

I laughed at her shocked expression. "Why not? It's as far away from our lives as I can think of without having to fly."

She touched her dress. "I'm not dressed for that place."

"You look perfect. All kinds of people go to Vegas. There's no specific dress code." I played with her hand. "In any case, we can go shopping and buy you clothes, underwear, whatever your sweet heart desires. As long as you're with me. And when we're alone, we won't need clothes, will we?"

Miranda smiled.

"I could murder a burger," I said as we entered the diner.

The bright lights and gaudy colors made my eyes hurt. But then the unmistakable aroma of grease made my tummy plead for an assault of artery-clogging food.

We slid into a wooden booth with faded, torn padding and

ordered burgers, fries, and coffee.

When the food arrived, we ate as though it were our first meal in days.

"Are you going to tell me what happened to your marriage with Britney? It seems implausible that she just allowed the annulment to go ahead."

"Let's just say that the dirty game she'd played to win back-fired."

Miranda placed a fry in her mouth and cast me a questioning frown.

"She fucked Orlando when he was underage."

Her eyebrows shot up. "Shit. And he didn't want it?"

"She cajoled him with that big mouth of hers."

Rolling her eyes, Miranda shook her head. "Are all men and boys beholden to their dicks?"

I shrugged. "Young men can be a horny bunch." I kept it short and sweet and hoped she wouldn't ask about my, at times, regrettable history of excess.

At exactly midnight, we arrived in Vegas. It wasn't hard to find a place to stay, and within half an hour, we were in bed, naked, and Miranda was tucked in my arms.

The last thing I remembered before falling asleep was whispering, "I love you," and feeling at peace with the world at last.

The next day, we ended up having a hell of a fun time. We played the machines and I entered a poker game and actually won, but then I lost it all at blackjack.

Miranda looked beautiful in a red velvet dress that she'd bought. I was more excited by what lay beneath that pretty outfit. We'd visited a sexy lingerie store.

In many ways, the trip was like a honeymoon, despite that we weren't married. But I did have a plan.

After dinner and a few drinks, I said, "I want to take you somewhere special. It's the main reason why I brought you here."

Her brow creased. "So you did have an ulterior motive?"

"Ulterior? My God, Miranda, you've got a suspicious mind. Is it just me?"

"I'm like that with everyone," she said. "I get it from my mom."

"Why haven't I met your parents yet?"

She shrugged. "I don't know. We've been together for nearly six months. Let's wait and see."

"Wait and see?" I asked. "You don't have faith in us?"

"Well, after everything that's happened…" She twirled a strand of hair, drawing my attention to her milky cleavage.

"I never stopped thinking about you or wanting you." I held her hand. "And now I need you to come with me."

"Where are we going?"

"A surprise," I said.

"Am I dressed for this place?" she asked, pointing at her new dress.

"You look classy. And the ankle boots and lace stockings are a nice addition."

"I'm more Brooklyn than Las Vegas."

I laughed. "That's why I love you."

Miranda looked as though she was trying to understand me.

"You don't believe me?" I asked.

"I… do. I think."

I held her in my arms. "Seeing Ethan at your place that night broke me. I'd never felt that kind of jealousy before."

A soft glint touched her eyes. "We didn't do anything."

"That's a relief. Even though I would have understood." I stopped walking. "I haven't been with anyone since you. I want you to know that."

She bit her lip. "I'm glad."

With our arms linked, we arrived at a chapel, and Miranda stopped suddenly. "What are we doing here?"

"We're going to church to pray."

"I didn't realize you were religious," she said with a frown.

We stepped through the door. The small chapel had an almost cartoonish vibe, like all of Las Vegas. Even the candles were fake.

I stopped and turned. "Miranda, I dragged you here for one reason."

Her eyes darted from my face to our surroundings and back. "That being?"

I got down on one knee. "Will you marry me? Now? Here?"

Her jaw dropped. "Here? We don't have rings. And my parents… My dad… I mean…"

"Hey, it's more of a fun thing. We can do it properly later. I just wanted to show you that I'm in this forever."

Her smooth brow creased. "Forever?"

"Do you need some time to think about it?"

"Um… Wow. So that's why you brought me here in such a hurry?"

"Uh-huh."

The celebrant I'd hired while Miranda shopped arrived.

Miranda turned to acknowledge him, and her eyes nearly popped out. She turned sharply toward me. Wearing a shocked smile, she said, "You hired an Andy Warhol impersonator?"

Feeling pleased with myself, I nodded. "It was either a dwarf, Elvis, or Andy."

She laughed. "This kind of makes a mockery of marriage."

"Well… it's a bit of fun." I played with her fingers. "I'm serious about it, though." I paused for her response. "That's if you want to."

Miranda nodded slowly, as though it was all starting to dawn on her. Then she turned and greeted Andy.

"Good evening, madam," he said in that wimpish, otherworldly tone associated with the famous artist.

"Hello," Miranda giggled. To me, she whispered, "He sounds exactly like him."

"Yeah. He's great." I pulled a box from my pocket. "So, what do you think?" I opened it, and a large ruby-encrusted diamond ring sparkled under the lights.

"Oh… is that real?" she asked.

"It sure is," I replied. "I bought it in Switzerland, at an antique jewelry store."

35

MIRANDA

I felt like I'd fallen into a parallel universe. The chapel's faux gothic vibe and the Andy Warhol impersonator added to the eccentricity of the moment.

The ring sat in my palm. It felt cold but quickly warmed on my skin. Enchanted by its beauty, I slid the ring onto my finger, and it fit.

"Oh my God. It's perfect."

"It sure is," Lachlan said. "And it suits that dress."

"Doesn't it? And you weren't there to help me choose the color."

"There. You see? We're in sync. A sure sign." His eyes twinkled with warmth and belief in us.

I choked up. As we held each other's gazes, I fell into his magic blue orbs like Alice through the looking glass. Only instead of a mad cast, I was met with the promise of sharing my life with Lachlan. Although something told me that we were about to embark on an adventure. As long as he was there, I was prepared for anything, even drugged-out mice or men with a predilection for crazy hats.

"Ask me again," I said.

He got down on his knee and placed his hand on his heart. I laughed at how clichéd that was, but it was really sweet.

"Will you be my wife?" he asked.

"Yes."

Music came on, and we both broke into laughter.

Lou Reed started singing about it being such a perfect day.

"Oh, I love this song," I said.

"I chose it from the list that came with Andy Warhol." Lach-

Ian's cute, boyish smile made me want to pinch his cheek.

"They got that connection so right. Lou Reed set up the Velvet underground. They were part of Warhol's Factory," I said with excitement. "I did my thesis on the sixties New York art scene. How did you guess?"

He held his arms wide. "It wasn't much of a stretch. Contemporary art's your thing."

I fell into his arms. "Thank you."

"Thank *you*. For accepting me."

I kept it to myself, but I'd decided to say yes within a second. *How could I not?*

"There's something that I haven't told you yet, though." He paused as we headed to the altar.

My breath hitched. *More surprises?* I'd had enough to last a lifetime.

"Manuel's with me. He's going to be part of my family."

Compassion and love shone from his face, and my heart grew. "I'm totally cool with that. He's a great boy."

"Then we're good?" he asked.

I took his hand. "We sure are. Let's go and hang out with Andy."

While we struggled to hear the mock priest, who mumbled and mangled words from his script, someone turned up and asked if we wanted it filmed.

Thrilled at the prospect of having a memento of the eccentric and momentous occasion, I nodded enthusiastically.

The "I do" quivered from my lips, and a tear ran down my cheek as we kissed. The heat from his lips surged through my body and into my soul.

We gazed into each other's eyes, and instead of Lachlan's typical cheeky twinkle, I recognized tender sincerity. He looked different—older and sexier. And he was my husband.

I hugged Andy, who, remaining in character, returned a timid grin, just as I imagined the real Andy would have responded.

The person filming took some photos of us standing with

Andy, then we glided out.

A moon glowed over the pretend Venetian canal. It almost looked real and was strangely beautiful. I'd misjudged Las Vegas. I'd had the time of my life.

The next day, we drove back through the desert to our lush paradise.

My spirit was so high and filled with possibilities and promise that I felt like singing. I didn't, but Lachlan did. He had a great voice and sang along to a Frank Sinatra song.

He turned me. "How do you feel?"

"Great."

We smiled at each other.

My heart sang at the prospect of being devoured by Lachlan Peace for happily ever after.

THE END

It Started in Venice (Malibu Series 3) explores Orlando and Harriet's journey from their points of view. In that book, Lachlan and Miranda have their official wedding ceremony with family and friends present, and we get a glimpse into their life together as a happily married couple.

Printed in Great Britain
by Amazon